I0764496

THE Education of Annie

By
Angie Cameron

This novel is a work of fiction. Names, characters, businesses, and incidents either are the product of the author's imagination or are used fictitiously. Any resemblance to actual events or persons, living or dead, is entirely coincidental.

Library of Congress Cataloging-in-Publication Data

Cameron, Angie.
The Education of Annie / by Angie Cameron – 1st ed.
p. cm.

ISBN 0-9717610-0-0
1. Young Woman/Struggles/Life/College – Fiction
2. Mississippi – Fiction. I. Title.
PS3603.A4475E48 2002 813'.6
QBI33-218

PRINTED IN THE UNITED STATES OF AMERICA

First Edition

1 3 5 7 9 10 8 6 4 2

Book & Cover Design
The Adam Group, Franklin, Tennessee

THE Education of Annie

Dedicated

to

Ken & McKenzie

Acknowledgements

I am especially grateful to my editor, Carole Taylor Betts. Without her hard work and integrity, my story would have stayed muddled inside of an enormous manuscript. Thank you, Carole, for your wisdom and encouragement.

Thanks to Rebecca Bailey and Sharon Goad for helping me have enough time to work on this book.

I would like to thank Jeralyn Johnson and the Adam Group for the book cover design.

1963-1985

CHAPTER ONE

A day didn't go by that I didn't want to leave home. A day didn't go by that Mama and Daddy didn't gripe. Rarely did I see them happy. Never did I see them show affection. Mama hated sex, yet bore five girls and miscarried many more than that. Daddy lusted, most of the time for other women.

I was born Annie Rochelle Lee on a hot August morning, nineteen sixty-three, in the town of Soso, Mississippi. The second daughter of Burl and Penny Lee. We didn't have any money — I grew up thinking that was just luck of the draw. And moving from house to house seemed a normal existence.

When I was two, we left Soso on a Greyhound bus for Nashville, to stay with Aunt Edna and Uncle Victor, who made us as welcome as leprosy. I was a scared little soul when Mama was sick in the hospital with her heart and miscarriages. We were mistreated, my older sister Gloria and me. No hugs when we cried. Not a kind word or a question answered. I wet the bed in the middle of the night once, and my crying woke up Gloria, and then my eyes opened to find my aunt and uncle standing over us with grim faces. Their children, who were older, were taken to dance classes and on shopping trips, while we were told to go outside and stay away.

Edna and Victor hated Daddy, had warned Mama not to marry him. I didn't know Daddy was on the run from the law, behind on the child support he owed for his first family in Alabama. Had I known then what I know now, I wouldn't have just hidden in the closet whenever the whispered conversations about us turned to malicious regret for letting us stay.

When Mama got out of the hospital, we moved in with Aunt Mooney. Times were happy, and I could hold on tight to Mama. Mooney was young, nineteen, and newly married to Uncle Melvin. She loved Gloria and me. She spent time with us, teased our hair, painted our fingernails. We slept on an old wrought iron bed next to a gas heater. We ate grits, eggs, and biscuits for breakfast. For lunch and dinner, it was peas and cornbread and fried chicken.

The rent house across the street became available when the tenants left, and we moved over there. Mama would let us cross the street to see Aunt Mooney, who'd be unlocking the screen door and laughing at our antics. But Daddy was running around again. There was no money. For food and warmth, we again had to stay with Aunt Mooney. Mama would cry and curse, Daddy would come home for a little while and things would settle down, then start all over again.

Mama complained that we were killing her, that she would leave if it weren't for us. Gloria would ask her why she had us, and she'd say, "I couldn't take the pill," as if we knew what the pill was. We were made to feel like burdens. I didn't want to be a log that weighed Mama down. But then she stopped holding me and had another baby, and then another.

Daddy took a job with Harper's Moving Company when I was five. For a steady paycheck, he was out of the house, driving all over the country. We were living at 2520 Third Avenue, my home for the next fourteen years. Mama picked up his paycheck on Fridays, took us to the grocery store, paid the fifty-five-dollar house payment every month and the utilities.

Gloria and I were enrolled in the first grade together, because she had been held back a year. We were the only freckled-faced redheads in class. Gloria was a fighter, so she wasn't teased. I would cry. With my buckteeth and raggedy dresses, grades one through six weren't a picnic. Whenever Gloria wasn't around to protect me, my name was "fire ant" or "redheaded woodpecker." I hated school and was counting down to the end of twelfth grade, when I'd be out on my own.

When I was in the fourth grade, Daddy stopped going on the road. Nerve spells, Mama said. We came home to a filthy house, with Daddy parked in front of a blasting television. No chance for *Sesame Street.*

Daddy had ideas. He was going to work for himself. Do carpenter work. Buy the supplies, mark them up, charge for labor, make a good profit. But there were no steady paychecks. Weather hampered his jobs. Winter months were worse than summer. He didn't keep up with receipts. Undercharged to get jobs. Wrote hot checks. We had no health insurance. When we were sick with the flu, Mama spent hours at the charity hospital with us where we had to lie on the grimy floor, because it was so crowded. She wrung her hands when the utility companies came by on a Friday morning, threatening to cut off the power, water and gas that afternoon.

To make her feel better, I cooked, washed clothes, and picked up the yard. I waited to hear Mama brag to my aunts and the neighbors how Annie was the only one who helped her, and how she didn't know what she'd do without me.

Our house was the ugliest on Third Avenue. Daddy didn't paint it or mend the ripped-out screens. Instead, he brought home toilets, bathtubs, and junk, and left them all lying in our yard.

I forgave Aunt Edna and Uncle Victor's stinginess and looked forward to seeing them when they came down from Nashville to visit every December. Mama and I would clean for days to get ready. They'd bring a couple of garbage bags full of gifts from the dollar stores for my sisters and me. The clothes never fit, but I didn't care. I was happy to get anything — a hairbrush, a bottle of watered-down perfume, a box of powder I'd keep on my dresser for months. Aunt Edna took over the housecleaning and washing. Uncle Victor would work with Daddy, and that meant Daddy would go to work. They'd buy cold cuts, bread, and sweets. Aunt Edna and Mama would cook good meals. Edna made up pans of biscuits for the freezer. In return, Mama would cart her around to Bill's Dollar Store and the Super Five-and-Ten.

Then their visits stopped. Aunt Edna's heart had acted up, and she could no longer travel.

I hit puberty at age twelve, with budding breasts and a broadening behind. I wanted to be as beautiful as Gloria. I wanted pretty clothes. I wanted to buy Barry Manilow records. I needed money for a science class. Mama screamed, "I ain't got any money!" Daddy wasn't working enough for a regular paycheck. Some weeks he didn't work at all. He had an ulcer, was eating antacids, watching the television, gobbling what food we had, reading the Bible, and bitching. I prayed he'd get a job out of state. I prayed he'd work on the Alaskan pipeline. I prayed he'd work anywhere. I prayed Mama would leave him. Then, I prayed he'd just die.

At some point, all the love, the worrying about Mama's heart trouble and that she might die and leave me, disappeared. I hated her. I talked back. I begged her to leave Daddy. "I ain't got nowhere to go," she'd grumble. I told her I was going to travel, become an actress. She and Daddy ridiculed me. They told me I was being selfish. I had to suffer, too.

My life changed in the seventh grade when I met Kirby Hamilton. She was a quiet girl with shoulder-length brown hair and blue eyes. She sat in the last chair on my row in history class. Kirby had an innate goodness in her. She shared her allowance, her TV, her mom, and laughter.

I stopped asking Mama for money and settled on being penniless 'til God knew when. It was hard to wait until Fridays, when Kirby's mom would buy me a Big Mac, Coke, and fries.

Kirby stayed at my house occasionally, but it was crowded. We had one bathroom for the six of us. There was no privacy. So I spent every night I could at Kirby's.

Her mom worked at night as a nurse's aide, and slept all day. Her dad, a successful plumber, worked long hours, not coming home until ten at night. Her older sister was married and out of the house, so we were alone most of the time. We danced around in our nightgowns to KC and the Sunshine Band and the Bee Gees. I got to go with her to visit aunts and uncles. I even went to her family reunions, and her mom took us for pizza, swimming, and movies. I spent weekends in her bedroom watching cable TV and stuffing myself with potato chips and dip, Nutter Butter cookies, and pizza. While Kirby stayed slim, my weight ballooned.

Mama didn't like Kirby. Kirby had a problem, she warned. Boy-crazy. She shouldn't be wearing halter tops, with breasts that big. I listened to Mama's acid remarks about Kirby, but they didn't faze me. I still needed goodies to eat and someone to laugh with.

When we turned fourteen, Kirby got a boyfriend named Yancy Dean, a skinny kid with acne. Kirby was crazy over him, and after dating a short time, she wasn't spending weekends with me anymore. I was hurt, and worse, I knew why. She was sneaking Yancy in her bedroom window when her mom was asleep. She told me, Gloria, and all her friends the sordid details.

The night he broke up with Kirby, she tried to cut her wrists. Her mom called me, and soon I was back in her room, watching television and feasting on junk food.

Daddy was still working erratically, and Mama became extremely depressed. She took to her bed, and it was hell. I thought everything was my sisters' and my fault.

The summer before I turned fifteen, I got a job bussing tables at the Soso Country Club. This job gave me some power and control over my life. Even being ignored by the kids I went to school with didn't bother me. While they were dining on fine foods, swimming in the club pool, and taking tennis lessons, I had a real job.

By the end of the summer, the manager said she couldn't keep me. I had to be twenty-one to work around liquor, so I was back to no money and dependent on Mama and Daddy.

Mama was thirty-six when she gave birth to Wiley. We were proud to show her off to the neighborhood kids, who weren't as fortunate to have a newborn sister. But Mama had a rough delivery. The surgery to tie her tubes made her sick. By the time she came home with the baby, she was physically drained and irritated. We were blamed for messing up Wiley's schedule when we wanted to hold her. Then we were *made* to hold her when she cried, night after night, with colic. Kirby had a thing for babies and came by regularly to comfort her.

When I turned sixteen, I went job-hunting again. The North Soso Curb Store needed a part-time cashier, stocker, deli worker, and floor-mopper. I worked after school and on the weekends. North Soso was where prominent people lived, and I enjoyed talking to doctors, lawyers, judges, policemen, and the "popular" kids from my high school. I didn't get to go to football games or movies, but I didn't think I was missing out. I had my own car, was paying my own note and insurance, and had a little left for records and clothes. Mama and Daddy didn't mind telling me I was selfish for holding out on them.

I bought myself a small TV, paid the cable bill, and stayed in my room when I wasn't with Kirby or working. Ted Turner's station WTBS in Atlanta came to Soso, and I stayed up late every night to watch reruns. My room was my sanctuary, where I could dream of escaping. Where I could take my plate of food and eat in solitude. Where I was not "Scared Annie" from Soso.

Mama got so disgusted with Daddy not working that she took a job at the Handy Pantry, a curb store a block away from our house. We now had health insurance, but it took up most of her paycheck. We were back to very little or no money unless Daddy decided to do something.

For a while, Kirby came to visit me at my job. Then she found herself a new boyfriend. Ray was handsome and worked after school for a machinery company. Kirby took his virginity, and at sixteen she became pregnant. Two families were torn apart, feuding. His parents hated her, called her names. Her mom cried to me, and her dad took her to New Orleans for the abortion. I never told anyone.

Into my senior year of high school, I was working every evening and weekend at the curb store. I was too busy to date. Mama was still working to get the health insurance. Daddy was still unreliable.

My senior year was to be my last year of school forever, and I made it a goal to get good grades. I made honor roll and got the notice that I was going to be in Who's Who in High School. Gloria, however, got pregnant.

Two months before graduation, Mama told me that Gloria was dropping out of school. She didn't want any of the kids to know. Thought her stomach would show. I told her she was tall and thin, that she could get away with it, but she dropped out anyway. I was heartbroken.

I graduated with Kirby, who by now had Ray back in her life. She was going on to junior college. I was going on to bigger things.

The day after graduation, I went to work full-time at the Sunflower Grocery Store. It was across the plaza from the North Soso Curb Store. It paid a dollar more, and I had health insurance. I loved the job, planned to save my money. I brought food home. I still paid the cable bill, so I could watch my TV shows. Music videos became popular, and I stayed up until two in the morning watching videos of Cindy Lauper and Sting. I ordered subscriptions of magazines like Stage and the New Yorker. I bought books on self-improvement and studied each and every step on how to better my life. But Mama and Daddy were still grumbling on the other side of my door.

Hiding in my room didn't help my weight, and I was still chubby, but somehow that was going to work itself out, and I was going to do big things. I did sit-ups every night while Gloria's husband laughed and made cruel jokes about me. Mama said I looked fine and not to be doing any stupid dieting. That drove me to dream harder, to see how I wanted to look and talk and walk when I got away from them. I was going to move to Los Angeles, become an actress, make some money, then move to Colorado and the mountains.

I got the call at work that Gloria had given birth to a little girl at the charity hospital. She named her Holly. But the thug she was married to wasn't working and began abusing them both. Mama had him arrested, and Gloria divorced him. He didn't pay child support, moved away, and started another family. Mama and Daddy forked out for Holly. I brought home baby food for Holly to eat, and diapers. Gloria was hired at the curb store where I used to work, but she spent her money on herself, not on the baby. She ran around to bars and dated men who weren't as enthralled with her as she was with them.

At my job, I was the star cashier. I made more money at my cash register than anybody. The manager and assistant manager bragged about me. The other cashiers grew jealous. They taunted me for not going out to bars with them. *What are you afraid of, Annie?* I worked hard, while everyone else got paid the same and didn't try. Thirty-year old women who looked fifty. Divorcees making the same mistakes over and over, fighting over losers, bellyaching but rooted in, bitching and back-stabbing. This wasn't going to get me out of Mississippi.

Two events changed my life. Daddy filed bankruptcy, causing us to lose the house on Third Avenue, along with our cars. We had to move. But where? My childhood was in that house.

The second event was a new assistant manager named Buck Webster. He was handsome, twenty-six, and divorced. All the single, married and divorced cashiers liked him. But he liked me. I was nineteen and inexperienced. The first few months he worked at the store, he couldn't do enough, especially for me. He was courteous, getting me change whenever I ran out, and approving checks when the amount exceeded a hundred dollars. When he asked me out, I said no. I'd never had a date, and didn't want Buck to be my first. When I kept refusing, things turned ugly. When I asked for change, he'd make me wait. When it was my quitting time, he'd take his time before blocking my lane from more customers. In front of the other cashiers, he bellowed out, asking if I was a virgin. I begged him to leave me alone. He stopped speaking to me. Then, the other cashiers began giving me the cold shoulder. I didn't want to go to work. I was crying a lot. There was no one to talk to. No one to protect me. I took in my smocks on my day off and handed them to the manager. I told him I was burnt out and that I had family problems. I didn't give a two-week notice.

With a car note and insurance looming over my head, I took over Mama's weekend shift at the Handy Pantry. I felt sorry for her having to work ten hours on Saturday and ten more on Sunday. It was long, but business was steady. The money paid for my car, but I was so empty inside. We were living in a rent house on Amy Road and could be kicked out at a moment's notice.

Kirby dropped out of junior college to marry Ray. She got pregnant right away and had a little girl she named Lenny.

I wanted a career, to be successful at something extraordinary. I immersed my mind in reading self-help books and had quite a collection of stacks in the corners of my room and on my dresser. At the curb store, I read health magazines about the current craze over aerobic exercise. Losing weight seemed impossible. And I couldn't take much more of life at home, with no money and dead-end jobs. In desperation, I drove over to the First Baptist Church. The youth minister was a young mother of two, married to a police officer. She knew just what I should do. She told me about a free aerobics class at the church, and she suggested I go to college.

I drove to Ellisville and talked to the financial counselor at the junior college. Since I had earned less than eight thousand dollars at the grocery store, I was approved for financial aid at Jones County Junior College. I was elated, because college grants didn't have to be paid back. All I had to do was make good grades.

Kirby and I joined the aerobics class and went three times a week. I eventually lost down to one hundred twenty pounds.

I began junior college at age twenty. Each day, I ate my peanut butter sandwich under an old maple tree, amazed that I was there. College happened for other people, kids whose parents had money. Not kids whose parents were perpetually bankrupt.

My family was kicked out of the rental house and moved to a place off First Avenue, an old two-story with roaches and no yard, no driveway. A railroad track was across the street, with an industrial area beyond it.

Mama was promoted to helping with bookkeeping and Western Union at the Handy Pantry, but she didn't get a raise. Daddy worked whenever he wanted. He didn't want to, too much. Mama would get pissed, take Wiley and Holly, go stay at Aunt Mooney's a couple of days, leaving the rest of us with Daddy. He wouldn't speak to us, blamed us for her leaving, and would hang around Aunt Mooney's until Mama came back home.

By the time I was about to finish my two years at junior college, I still didn't have a major. The University of Eastern Mississippi was thirty miles away, and I phoned to get their catalog mailed to me. Looking through all the bachelor degrees was overwhelming. So many classes were needed, yet I had already taken the easy ones at the junior college. All I needed was a major. If I went with theatre, I'd actually have to perform. I'd never been in a play, never even tried out for one. I had been busy working. I needed something that would get me a job easily, anywhere. So much information to go through, and I was confused, afraid of making a wrong decision. Mama and Daddy couldn't help. I drove around town listening to my radio and worrying. But I wasn't going to die in Soso, Mississippi.

1986

Chapter Two

I was twenty-three when I moved away from home and into a dormitory at UEM. I lived in the central area of campus, Borden Hall, fifth floor. I got along well with my resident assistant, Suzy Wilcox. She was what Mama would call a "pretty girl." She was tiny, her eyes chestnut brown, and her short hair dark brown. Two doors down from Suzy was Denise Hayden. She had a slight Cajun accent and was from Biloxi, on the coast. Beautiful as a fine piece of artwork, she was willowy and tall with brown hair flowing down her back, stopping just above her behind. We quickly became friends, eating in the cafeteria and visiting one another in our rooms. Denise didn't cuss, so I was careful of what came out of my mouth. She brushed her teeth right after dinner, so I took up the habit. She adored her parents, couldn't wait to see them on the weekends. When she told me about going shopping with her mom, I'd tell her my mom and I went shopping. I didn't tell her it was to the Piggly Wiggly for Mama's cigarettes and Diet Cokes. Denise ate like a bird, never finished what was on her plate. I ate every crumb. My favorite part of college, so far, was the cafeteria.

The weather had changed overnight, and I awakened to a cold room. I felt homesick, although I had to be an utter moron for wanting to go home. The phone rang, and I threw back the covers in fury. I could think of only one person who would call at six in the morning. I stumbled across the floor and snatched up the phone.

"Hello, Pop."

"Annie? You up?"

"Mama! Yeah, I'm up. Is something wrong?"

"Did I wake your roommate?" Marge's bed was empty. It hadn't been slept in for two days.

"She's not here," I said. "What's wrong?"

"I'm sick. We're outta food," she sobbed.

I cleared the sleepiness out of my throat. "Is Daddy working?"

"Shit. You know, he's piddlin'. What else does he ever do!"

"You sound . . . Do you have the flu?"

"My kidneys are infected. I've been bleedin' from 'em."

"Mama! That's the third time. Go to the doctor. You have insurance." She wasn't listening.

"Me, Wiley, and Holly are starvin' to death. Gloria doesn't help out. You know how she is. She don't make much at that two-bit job she has. It's just like my job. Doesn't pay shit."

"Isn't Daddy worried?"

"Said he was gonna do some work for ole lady . . . I don't remember the bitch's name . . . the one he worked for last year." A flick of her lighter and a long inhalation. "You won't believe what he did yesterday. Me and the kids were starvin', hungry all day, and he comes in with a plate lunch and eats it in front of us! All I had was some grease, a little flour, and those canned tomatoes Mooney gave us. I was half-dead from work, but I made us a few biscuits and some tomato gravy. Then he starts in on our little bit of food. He ate half the biscuits."

"Why do you stay with him? He could care less about us."

"I didn't call to depress you. I just had to get it out. When are you comin' home again?"

I was in silent tears, with a bulging bladder. "Next weekend. I'm going to the football game tomorrow night with Denise. Are you in any pain?"

"Yeah. Yesterday I took Advil, I took Tylenol, I took aspirin." Here it comes. "Nothin' eased the pain until I took some BC's. My back's been killin' me."

"Why don't you go to the Westwood Clinic and see Dr. Thompson?"

I heard a puff of smoke blast out of her mouth like a cannon.

"I'd like to blow up those bastards at Westwood. They don't give you nothin' there. You could be dyin' in pain, and they still wouldn't give you anythin'." She meant drugs. "I'm not payin' thirty-five dollars to be told that I have to go to a damn kidney specialist. If I had the money, I'd go. I don't need them to tell me that."

"Make an appointment with the kidney doctor yourself. They'll probably file your insurance for you."

"No they won't. They make you pay up front."

"Who are 'they'?"

"You know—those stupid receptionists who do the insurance. Bitches."

"Call them. You won't know unless you do. You've met your deductible, with all the medicine you're taking."

"I'm not takin' that much."

"No. Just eight different pills a day."

"Well, I can't help it. That's what medicine's for."

"If only there was a pill for getting rid of a useless husband! But why have health insurance if you don't know how to use it?"

"I do know how to use it . . ." she said with her voice fading out as she swallowed some Diet Coke. "I gotta get off the phone. He'll shit if he sees the phone bill."

"Who cares, it's your phone, too. You're the one holding down a job."

"I'll cuss his ass out if he says anythin' to me. I'm fed up with him."

"Please go to the doctor."

"I need to."

"Just go. Daddy goes when he thinks he's sick. Hell, he's worn out the blood pressure machine at Tri-Mart."

"I need to get off the phone and clean this filth up. The dishes are piled to the ceilin'. Nobody helps me."

"Speaking of nobody helping, how's Gloria?"

"Fine. Her boss works the hell outta her like mine does me."

"I miss the kids."

"They're so pitiful. They're both sick with colds. I need to take 'em to the doctor."

"I guess I should go, Mama. I have a class at eight. I'll call y'all next week."

"Well." Her tone churned up guilt in my three-meals-a-day belly.

"Bye, Mama."

This was the only call from home this semester. *Another episode of "Psychotic Family," in Technicolor.* The walls seemed to close in. *What can I do? It's not my mess.* I gathered my towel and toiletries and dragged myself to the showers in a stupor. The hot water wasn't washing away the fear as the bar of soap slipped from my hold. I backed against the tiled wall with my hand clasped tightly over my mouth. The scream was silent. *You can't cry. What if someone hears you? Catch hold, Annie.* I dried my freckled legs and arms. *It's not normal to be spotted. I deserve to be in college.*

In the mirror, I was an image of nothingness, translucent without the mask. I began the ritual of putting on makeup, smearing and blending in, but why? Nothing could cloak the humiliation in my expression. I took in a deep breath to calm myself. *Can't let Denise see me this way. She'd know.*

Years of worrying had drained the life out of Mama. So had being married to Daddy. Talking to her was like talking to a stoned person. She was on anti-depressants, yet I had never heard her be positive over anything. Mommy the gloomy-doomer. "It's my fault none of you girls have any self-esteem." *What is self-esteem, anyway? It's just a word. I'm getting on with my life. Can't get off track.* I opened a notebook and began the list of goals, hoping that writing them down would solidify them. I stopped, and put away the notebook. I wanted food.

On the way to the cafeteria, a lump throbbed in my throat. Tears fell, and I rubbed them away with the back of my hand. I had to get through college, and soon. Mama and Daddy had always lived this way — always a new plight, a dire emergency. I picked up a tray and silverware, deciding that I would send her twenty dollars. That was all I could spare. My decision settled my head but not my stomach. I picked at the scrambled eggs that lay cold on my plate.

At noon, I walked back to my room to put my books away. Marge was in from class and had just gotten out of the shower.

"Can I use some of your perfume?"

"Sure, use all you want," I answered.

She squirted a tiny bit on her neck.

"It smells so good. Chanel Number-Five. Pricey!"

"My grandparents bought it for me. I don't use much, so a bottle lasts me a long time."

"Thanks a lot. It smells great."

She was going out, spending the weekend with her boyfriend, Ed. From my mirror, I watched her button up the same old blouse she wore every week to classes. We both had the bare necessities. She was clean, took care of her things. She didn't have a job but needed one. Her parents were farmers and sent her what little money they could, and she could make it last. My parents sent me nothing, and I was used to it. When I was in junior college, Mama would scrape up a couple of dollars once in a while if I ran short on gas, but I felt criminal taking it, especially if she gave me a five-dollar bill. "Take it," she'd say. In another breath, she'd complain, "I'm so tired of bein' broke all the time."

"Going to the game?" I asked Marge.

"Yeah. Ed got us tickets. You goin'?"

"Probably."

She left, and I sat on my bed. Marge. How happy she was. She had a boyfriend and no money. I picked up the phone, called Suzy, and told her that I had to go home. My mom was sick, and I had to run errands for her. She could pass the word on to Denise, I thought, as I threw clothes and books into my laundry basket. I bypassed the cafeteria and lunch.

CHAPTER THREE

As I drove up Highway 49, I couldn't figure what I had to look forward to. Maybe I'd see Aunt Mooney or one of my sisters. I loved my dog, Trudy. I had lost faith in Mama and Daddy. I had their blood running through my veins, but I was the stranger in my family. I would never settle for so little, the way they had. I looked out the car window and felt like I was in a small corner of the world. To my left I saw the Arby's sign. I spent the last of my cash on a turkey sandwich, fries, and iced tea. I needed my stomach full to face the empty cabinets, the refrigerator with butter several months old, and maybe a bowl or two of tired leftovers from days ago. I sat in my car and ate, and it felt divine.

I had been home less than five minutes, and it seemed like years. I stood next to my car, racking my brain and wondering how in the hell this family could turn a shack into an outhouse. A black shutter that was partially attached to the window the last time I was home was lying on the ground. I figured Daddy got a wild hair up his butt and decided to fix it but abandoned the task. The garbage bags plastered over the broken windowpanes had come loose and fluttered in the wind. A flat tire from Daddy's truck lay in the grass on the side of the house. On the termite-infested side porch, trash, cables, and tools garnished every space. An old dishwasher from one of his widow women's houses sat rusting on the porch. Not only had it been rained on numerous times, but the inside was filled with mud pies, some of Mama's better dishes, and the kids' toys. My folks had as much use for a dishwasher as they did a financial planner. The yard, front and back, might as well have been a garbage dump. I started picking up, while Trudy was watching me from below the collapsed steps.

The back door flew open. "Annie!"

"Hey, Wiley!"

She looked "throwed away," as Mama would say. Her blond hair needed brushing, and her face was wearing dirt and leftovers. She was eight, the youngest of us five girls.

"You need a bath, baby."

"Are you spendin' the night with us?"

"Yeah, I'll be here a couple of days."

"Yaaaaay!"

"Trudy, Trudy girl!"

She was a two-year-old mutt with short brown hair. I had her spayed by making payments to a veterinarian I knew from my grocery-checking days.

"Roll over, girl." I rubbed her stomach. *I love God's creatures . . . except for . . . .*

I picked up my basket and opened the back door.

"Shi-oot."

I didn't want to disconnect from Wiley, whose tiny hand was clasped to the hem of my sweater, so I went on in to face the music. My eyes wandered about as I eased the basket down at my feet. Sitting half off a burner was Mama's large black frying pan with grease floating on top of the gravy that remained in it. Margarine-laden hominy and a boiler with scorched rice were what was left of lunch. I took a spatula and scraped at the rice and let it drop. On the table were pots of old food and five dirty frying pans stacked on top of each other. *What if we had company? What if the pastor dropped by like he did in 1976? What if Senator Tucker's wife dropped in like she did the year Mama had her hysterectomy?* Lying in the middle of the room was a butter knife with mayonnaise smeared on it. I picked it up and dropped it in the sink of dingy dishwater to meet whatever else was hidden in the murkiness. Daddy had been cooking again. A stagnant smoky haze filled the air. In this house, one not only saw the air, one bumped into it.

Wherever I moved, I stepped on garbage. No use in avoiding it, I trampled over it. I carried my basket to the laundry room, vowing to leave this place. *I refuse to let the life be sucked out of me. UEM is a far cry from this hellhole.*

"Oh no," I groaned.

Jumbled heaps of dirty and clean clothes buried the floor, the washing machine, the dryer. I carefully picked up one of the kid's shirts and flung it down. It smelled like Daddy's underarms.

He's fumigated the entire house.

Underneath it all I found mildewing clothes. I lifted the lid of the washing machine and began loading, imploring myself to get through it. *Everyone thinks we're filthy. Dirty house means trashy people. I won't live like this when I break out. I'll have a brick house in the mountains where the air is clean.* I trudged from room to room accumulating armfuls of clothes and dishes until I couldn't see straight. After that, I went into the bathroom. The Tidybowl man would change his vocation if he saw the damage Daddy had done to the toilet. This is what overeating does to Daddy, makes him blow out.

He's supposed to be a carpenter. Why can't he fix up anything for his family?

I was trying not to cuss, but my family could make the Pope swear. Daddy had tried to fix the brown vinyl couch. It had several tears that he'd covered with silver duct tape, some of which was coming off. A long strip of black electrical tape hid the most recent tear. Red bricks substituted for the missing legs. Industrial-strength deodorizer couldn't shroud the smell of Daddy on the couch, which he'd used as his bed for years when he stopped being wanted in Mama's bed.

The love seat I named the gripe seat. There was Daddy's green recliner, which none of us ever got the chance to sit in. It no longer reclined. Under the cushions were dirt, paper, nails, and coins he had dropped out of his pockets. The middle couch cushion was smashed flatter than a pancake. Beneath the couch and gripe seat were more dirt and paper, toys, dirty socks, pens, pencils, and crayons.

Mama was proud of the school pictures of us girls and of her only grandchild, Holly, though not proud enough to frame them. Most were thrown in a crushed egg box stuck in a closet. There was one family picture enclosed in a brownish frame hanging sideways behind the couch. I was in high school when it was taken at the Baptist church we attended sporadically. Daddy never went with us, and getting him to go get a picture taken was comparable to convincing him to cut back on eating. That day he was pretty irate about having to miss a boxing match on television. My sisters and I received the worst of it. It was a loud showdown, with Mama using varied cuss words up until we went to the church. I was sweating when the photographer told her, "Tell your husband you love him, and smile."

Daddy could not live without his truck, his television, and the VCR that was given to him by one of his rare clients. Receiving the local stations wasn't suitable for him, so he frequently rented movies no one else in the house wanted to watch.

"Annie?"

"I'm in here, Mama."

The dishwater was thick and cold as my hand searched for the stopper. Mama stood bleary-eyed, inhaling nicotine and scratching her head. The red lipstick used to work wonders. It was a miracle she didn't have any gray hair in her brunette mess, considering the miserable creature she was. Her beauty had been wasted on Daddy. Her stomach muscles were broken from years of childbearing. Her feet were wide, which she blamed on wearing flip-flops in her twenties. Her brown eyes were small, and her skin olive. I had Mama's shape of face, the same high cheekbones, but there was no denying Daddy as my father. My hair was orange, my skin freckled, my eyes a blend of green and brown, my nose large with the same bump in the middle of it.

Mama's tone was soft. "I thought you was stayin' at school."

"I didn't want to."

"I didn't mean to make you come home."

Yes you did.

"I didn't feel like staying."

"I think I got a fever," she said as she touched her forehead with the back of her hand.

"Did you go to the doctor?"

"Went and saw Dr. Coleman. He said I had a urinary tract infection. Gave me a 'scription for some Keflex. It's so expensive."

I sighed.

"Why don't you rest, Annie."

"I will. Trudy's eaten up with fleas and ticks, Mama. We need to get her dipped."

"Well, just put her to sleep."

"No! All she needs is a bath. Dr. Neil's office only charges ten dollars for a flea dip."

"I ain't got any money to be gettin' the dog dipped. Hell, we hardly have scraps to give her."

"Maybe Daddy will help me pay for it. I need to go by Tri-Mart and get some of that O'Freddy's dog food. It's cheap, and she likes it."

"Huh, good luck gettin' any money out of him."

"Where is the Reverend?"

"He's workin' for Mr. George again. At least he'll pay him." Her weary gaze followed me as I moved dishes from the left sink to the right. "I'm half-dead from work. Ole lady Walker took off last week again, and I had to work her shift and mine. I'm still tired from all those extra hours. Been too tired to clean up. Burl half-ass cooks and feeds the kids. Gloria doesn't do anythin'. She stays depressed."

"You need to make them help. And Gloria has no reason to be depressed. She's useless."

"Huh! Tell me somethin' I don't know."

Wiley tugged at her. "Mama?"

"What, baby? Mama's tired."

"Where's my paper doll?"

"Oh, Lord, I don't know, Wiley. Probably in this mess somewhere."

"Baby, I'll find it later. Let me clean up first, all right?" I said.

"Okay, Annie."

She ran out the crumbling back door, letting it slam. By next weekend, the door would lie in the backyard with the rest of the debris.

Mama went back to bed to rest her legs, her ankles swollen from long hours and little sleep. A woman of forty-four, she was prone to these diseases, she said. It was her father's fault she had the high blood pressure and her sisters had heart trouble, so why shouldn't she blame it on them. I picked up an empty tuna can and stared at the mountain of trash between the refrigerator and stove. The garbage can was under it.

"Why can't Daddy empty the garbage? Lazy slob," I seethed.

Three hours scrubbing the kitchen, and it still smelled like a lard pit. But the dishes were put away, and the garbage can was wiped out and a new bag put in it. I did the bare minimum on the stove, a swift wipe-down just to get off the current food stains and grease. The burners were black as soot and the oven demolished, and I wasn't about to tear up my hands to scour what would soon be undone after Daddy cooked another meal. I lugged five bags of garbage down the driveway, flinging each bundle at the end of the ditch.

My five-year-old niece, Holly, had soaked the mattress she and Wiley slept on. I stripped the bed, disinfected the plastic lining with Pine Sol, and picked up the urine-soaked clothing. In this family, bed-wetting was a disease. Mama said Holly must have inherited it from me and Cousin Pee Wee, who she often called "a big ole tittie baby." I was a bed-wetter until the age of ten. Having my older sister Gloria as a bed partner meant I was in for malicious taunting, but it was Mama's brutal fussing I couldn't bear.

"You pissed again!"

My aunts' dooming voices spat out disciplinary advice:

"Penny's girl wets the bed!"

"Don't let her drink anythin' after seven."

"Switch her legs good!"

Daddy would join in, telling me I was too big to be wetting the bed, but I didn't see how it was imposing on him. To avoid the hassle, I washed my own sheets.

Now, as I loaded wet clothes in the dryer and crammed more dirty clothes into the washer, I felt like a robot on an assembly line. The slamming of the kitchen door and heavy footsteps told me who had arrived.

"Mama, where's Annie? Mama, where are you? You asleep?"

"I was," she groaned.

"You feelin' better?"

"No."

"Where's Annie?"

"She's cleanin'. She shouldn't have to come home from college and work this hard."

"I know, Mama."

Daddy was coming to hug me. Mama stumbled out of her bed-room behind him with a cigarette in her hand. I reluctantly set down the basket of clean clothes. He stunk of perspiration. Without even sweating, he stunk to high heavens. Deodorant didn't help his body. His potbelly mashed my ribs, and I knew why the shelves were empty.

"Hey, baby. How was your week?"

"It was busy. I made an A on my accounting test, though."

"Did you hear that, Mama? Our daughter made an A on her test. Yeah, it won't be long and you'll be a college graduate."

Mama cracked a grin, one side of her face and hair flattened from her drugged sleep. A constant patron in every convenience store in the county, Daddy beamed with a large paper cup of 7-Up in his hand. By mistake, I sat on the smashed cushion, but I was too pooped to get up, so I stayed put and folded.

"What have you been doing, Daddy?"

"Workin' for ole man George. I sure am tired. Did Mama tell you what we got yesterday?"

"No."

"We got a twenty-six-dollar refund check from the light company," he grinned.

"Oh. Only twenty-six dollars?"

"You don't know, Mama and I was so broke."

"Yes, I do know," I said.

"It sure come in handy, too. I was outta gas. Mama was outta her Diet Cokes and cigarettes. Shoot, you wouldn't believe how many refunds they had to give out. Sister Cooper got, I believe she got eighty-two dollars from 'em. Bunch of crooks. They've been beatin' and cheatin' people for years. I told Mama I think they been cheatin' us, 'cause our electric bill is never under a hundred and fifty dollars."

"Daddy, y'all run the power all the time," I said. "You keep the TV on all night. This house isn't insulated."

"Still it shouldn't be so high. People like us can't afford these high bills."

"Then turn off the lights."

"Ooh, mercy me." Rubbing his neck, he cut himself off, which he did on occasion when he was sick or having spells of reading the Bible and feeling holy. "I been so sick with my 'hiation hernia.' I ate some chicken tenders from that new curb store on Highway 28 the other day. They sure are good. I ate some and they put too much black pepper on 'em, and black pepper don't agree with my stomach, that reflux I have. You know I get that reflux, too much acid in my stomach. I was so sick."

It was impossible to have an intelligent conversation with him, but at least it was peaceful. Then he turned on the television and the peace was over.

"I'm gonna write that sorry station and tell 'em a thing or two. I'm sick of these nigger shows."

With hostility, he changed the channels.

"Blacks have just as much right to make TV shows as anyone else," I said.

Mama sat in the gripe seat, smoking and watching me. Her eyes told me to cool it.

"Well, you watch what you want, and I watch what I want."

"I would if you'd share the television," I said.

"That's what's wrong with this world, the niggers and lesb'ans. They're destroyin' this country."

Deadbeat dads come to mind.

"Well, maybe they'll come up with a show called the Lesbian Connection," I joked.

"They probably will, since they worship those bunch of fat ugly bags and freaks. They're so ugly, they can't get a man, so they run the roads picketin' everybody."

"Daddy. I don't want to hear it." *It'd be a riot if he knew my political science teacher is a lesbian.* "Now I won't come home anymore if you start." I abruptly got up.

Mama displayed signs of fury and closed the conversation.

My nerves were fried, and I felt like driving back to school. I stuffed the towels on the bathroom shelf. My head hung down as I clenched my fist. *Why am I doing this?* I caught hold of myself and walked back to the living room. Maybe Mama didn't want to bother to get anything from him, but I did.

"Daddy, I need you to help me get Trudy a bath."

He rubbed the back of his neck. "Baby, I can't bend over washin' that stinkin' dog. My back hurts."

"No. I need a few dollars to get her dipped at Dr. Neil's clinic. I have a little money to get her some dog food. I just need help getting her dipped."

"I think there's a bag of dog feed by the washin' machine," he said.

"No, the bag is empty. Maybe we can go by Tri-Mart tonight and get her one of those big bags that are always on sale."

"Well . . . we can," he stammered. "I need some Alka-Seltzers."

"I can ask Gloria to help me pay for it," I said.

"No! Don't get her started, please," Mama begged. "I can't stand listenin' to her bitch half the night."

"I . . . I think I can scrape up a little money," he said.

I looked at Mama. Mama was looking at Daddy. Daddy wasn't looking at either one of us.

"She's eaten up with fleas and ticks," I continued.

"I can't take her in my truck," he grumbled.

"I'll drop her off in my car."

Mama spoke up. "Did Mr. George pay you, Daddy?"

"Yeah. He gave me a check. I was gonna go by and get it cashed at Jitney Jungle tomorrow."

Holly burst through the back door and into my arms. "Aunt Annie!"

"Hey, baby."

"Damm it, there's mud all over the backyard! Where's Annie?" Gloria tossed her burlap bagged black purse on the kitchen table. "Hey. When did you get in?"

"One thirty," I answered.

"My job's killin' me. I'm sick of workin' with that bitch Glenna. I hate her."

"Didn't you get a raise?"

Mama cut in. "Did y'all get a burger?"

"Yeah, we did, Mama. Mr. Lowery gave me a fifty-cent raise. He works the hell outta me. I do all the stockin' and cleanin'. I think Glenna's screwin' him, 'cause she don't do shit."

"I know people like that," I said.

"That bitch rubs up and down on him. She's nothin' but an ugly old whore. Worn out, I'm tellin' ya."

Mama added, "That's the way it is. The wore-out ugly whores get more outta life, don't they?"

"That ole Glenna Saunders ain't nothin' but a road whore. Her and those fat-ended gals she runs around with have bad reputations," Daddy said, forgetting that he had broken every Commandment.

"What about your buddy Lynette?" I asked.

"She's just like the rest of 'em," said Mama.

"I like Lynette, Mama," said Gloria.

"I wish you'd find some nice friends instead of those fat ugly whores," said Daddy.

"Leave me alone," Gloria snapped. "Better than your ole cruddy brother friends."

"Don't start, Burl," Mama warned.

"I ain't sayin' another word to her."

"Do I look like I've gained any weight?" Gloria asked. "Mama said I look like a box."

"I said you looked like a box in that navy dress you bought. It wasn't flatterin' on you," Mama said.

Looking at Gloria, it was hard to believe she weighed one hundred seventy pounds, having been a slim teen. Excelling in gymnastics. Artistic. The beautiful and talented one got knocked up in high school by the thug down the street. Daddy ate all the food at home, so she almost starved like the rest of the family, except she hid from him the Beanee Weenees, ravioli, and soups in her bedroom closet. At her job, she ate deli food and anything else she could grab.

Daddy's mood picked up as he readied himself for a trip to town. I cringed as he closed the bathroom door. Five minutes later, he came out with wet hair combed to the side and the fragrance of stale cologne.

"Wanna run up to Buk-A-Day and rent some movies?"

"I guess," I answered.

"Mama, you want anythin' from Tri-Mart?"

"I ain't got any money," she answered.

"Well, I thought since today was Friday . . ."

"Burl, when do I ever have anythin' left after I pay for the health insurance, your gas, and all that other shit you charge. I wish you'd fix your truck and quit chargin' that motor oil on my tab. Hell, I gotta have some cash in my purse. All I got left is fifteen dollars. I had to stop by the drugstore to get my blood pressure medicine. We ain't got anythin' to eat."

Except cigarettes and Diet Cokes.

"I'll get my check cashed, and Annie and I'll pick out some pretty hens to fry."

"I ain't cookin' tonight, Burl," she raged. "I been on my feet all day."

Gloria sighed. "Sick of this shit."

"Don't worry, I ain't askin' you for a damn thing," Mama glared.

Gloria's bedroom door slammed, rattling the house. I grabbed my purse and opened the back door. "Come on, Daddy. I have to study when I get back."

At Tri-Mart, I had just picked up a bag of dog food for Trudy when Daddy was ready to go. I was broke, but I still wanted to look at the makeup, perhaps stare at the clothes. It was best I leave, I told myself. My time would come, when I could walk into any store and not think about money.

The next day was Saturday, and my mood should have been as bright as the sun that warmed my face through the windshield. But as always on the way to these excruciating visits with my benefactor, Henry Price, I was consumed with worry, trying to figure out what to say and how to act when he began his inquisition.

I knew Henry would help me when I drove over to his house last spring to tell him I wanted to expand my education to a four-year degree. I knew he'd know what to do. He optimistically offered the hundred-dollar deposit to hold my dorm room for the fall. Not having much connection with my own grandparents, who had chosen to be unloving and detached until they passed on, I was gratified to have someone who cared.

Actually, it was his loving wife's unconditional kindness that brought us to this stage. It was through her that Henry gained his reputation of helping those in need. Pearl Price would give every dime she had to anyone who needed it. She just loved to love. When Pearl laid eyes on my haggard-looking mother at the First Baptist Church, her heart melted. Mama, a young woman dragging her little angels to Sunday school. Little girls with impoverished faces. Pearl called on us many times, bringing over food and hand-me-downs from other church members. We were the charity cases, samples of poverty for them to study. Hauled along like mannequins by our Sunday school teachers to shop downtown at Efird's department store. The saleswomen huddled around us like hens, looking at us with pity as they whispered about how nice it was these ladies bought us dresses, slips, and patent-leather shoes. Mama thought it was grand, while Gloria and I wore our Easter dresses in shame, praying none of the other kids knew.

Perhaps it was a mistake that I sought Henry's advice that spring day. But seeking encouragement from my parents was a dead-end street. "College" was a not a concept in my family — it could've been a French cuss word, for all they knew. A "higher education" meant high school, at best. Bone survival was all you deserved.

"I thought you was done," Mama told me. "Those universities are expensive. I don't know how you think you can go unless you can get some more of those grants. We ain't got the money."

"Baby, we can't afford . . ." Daddy began.

"I don't expect you to pay for it," I said. "I've already been approved for financial aid like I got at junior college."

"Your car ain't gonna make it commutin' to Hattiesburg every day, and mine's had the hell ran out of it," Mama grumbled.

"I'm not after your car," I said. "I'm thinking about staying in the dorms."

She reacted as if she had been slapped. "How much is that gonna cost?"

"About eight hundred dollars a semester. I have to come up with a hundred deposit. . . ."

"I ain't got it!" she screeched.

"Whew, that's way too much money. I think it's a crime to charge the prices these colleges do. I tell ya, only rich crooks can afford to send their kids to college," Daddy fumed.

"I said I'm getting financial aid."

"Poor people like us, you know we can barely afford to pay our rent," he continued.

That was the extent of their interest.

I parked in the Prices' driveway but stayed in my car. Though I wasn't expected here this weekend, the side door was left open, just in case.

North Soso was where the upper crust lived, but the Prices' house was modest in comparison to the surrounding two-story brick homes. It was a one-story brick, painted white, with black shutters.

I peered into the glass door. They were in their usual positions: Pearl was on the couch, while Henry sat facing her in his recliner. She saw me and brushed Henry's knee with the *Reader's Digest* she pretended to be reading.

"Looky there," she grinned.

He turned and smiled. His fingered his hearing aid as he stood, then eagerly opened the door.

"We were praying you'd stop by. You look so beautiful today, dear," he purred.

He hugged me, giving a firm squeeze. Some type of drugstore cologne cooled his shaven face, and the heavy scent glued itself on me. I could smell Listerine mouthwash on his breath as he released me to Pearl for a hug.

"Hey, Pop. How are you? Mommy Junior, you look well today."

At the drop of a hat, she shed tears. "Oh dear. I wish I looked as beautiful as you do. Henry, isn't she just beautiful?"

His eyes hadn't left me. They handed me back and forth, and it was his turn again. With his hands planted on my shoulders, his eyes inspected my face.

"She sure is. Yes, she is." He scooted me to the couch. "Here, sit with Mom."

He removed his daily Bible lesson out of the recliner and sat across from us. With his socked foot he stroked my tennis shoe and chuckled. I didn't like the footsie-playing, but I held on. I glanced down at the age spots on Pearl's hand as it clung to mine. Her skin was thin and soft. She nudged me while making faces like a youngster. He launched his interrogation.

"How's school, honey? You okay with your professors?"

"Yes, they're all fine. I'm learning a lot."

"Oh, I'm so glad to hear that. You see, Mom, Annie's getting a good education. She needs to get that degree so she can get a good job. It's very important."

She nodded.

"I'm so happy," he said.

"Now this is high school?" Pearl asked.

"No, honey. Annie's going to college, remember? The University of Eastern Mississippi."

"That's right."

"I made an A on my accounting test this week, Pop."

"Did you hear that, Pearl! I knew you could do it." He leaned over and hugged me.

"I'm so proud of you." She choked up again. I pulled a tissue out of the Kleenex box on their coffee table. "Thanks, sweetheart."

"It was a hard test on depreciation. But . . . are you okay, Mommy Junior?"

"Yes," she sobbed with a silly laugh, waving the tissue in the air. "Go ahead."

"I studied and did the homework. It paid off."

"That's right. You do the work and it pays off big. Well, I know you can do anything," he said enthusiastically. "Talked to Sam Reynolds the other day. His daughter, Patty, uh, Patricia is majoring in liberal arts at a college, uh, let's see, I think the school's in New Orleans. She's an honor student."

The Prices were friends with every wealthy and prominent member of the church. That didn't bother me. The predictable church stories did.

"The Reynolds are good people . . . . What's this?" I held my breath as his frowned face came within an inch of mine. With his index finger, he rubbed my chin and I thought he might pick it off. "You have a blemish!"

Why are you smiling, because you enjoy doing this to me? One thing I did have was very good skin. But I had gotten careless. I didn't bury the pimple with makeup. Henry looked for the flaws, the bitten fingernails, the blackheads and whiteheads, and the weight gain.

"Want to go to Shoney's, sweetheart? Since our granddaughter's here," he beamed.

"That's fine," Pearl nodded.

"I need a break from cooking." His expression turned serious. "It never ends. I get up and cook Mom breakfast. Then a couple of hours later I have to start getting her lunch ready, then I clean that up. Then, it's time for supper. I cook all the time."

"That's fine, Pop. You deserve to eat out."

He smiled, then reached for Pearl's hand. "Honey, want to put on your red dress?"

"I guess so," she said as she slowly lifted off the couch.

"Annie, want to help Mom?" he asked.

In her bedroom, I found the red dress lying over her vanity chair. She had worn it out somewhere. Under the dress she was wearing, she had on a girdle and a pair of nude pantyhose. Her legs were twigs, the blue and purple veins endless roads to service her dying organs. The flesh on her stomach was folds of drooping skin from aging and weight loss. The smell of the elderly depressed me, and her room reeked of it.

"Should I put on a slip?"

"Do you want to wear one?" I asked.

"Nah," she said. "Shoot. Won't be gone that long."

I unzipped the dress, and she stepped in to it. I zipped her up. I found her red high heels and a red purse in the closet while she dug in her wooden jewelry box for some red beads.

"I need to powder my face," she said, as she sat in front of her mirror. The compact was silver, old, and the powder in it dug deep. She patted her face until it was beige. Her thin eyebrows she painted unevenly in black, then she smeared dark pink lipstick on her lips.

"I look awful. Shoot," she frowned.

"You look pretty," I replied.

"How do you get your makeup on so pretty?"

"Practice, I guess."

Henry grinned when we walked back to the living room. He stood and kissed Pearl's cheek. "Wait, honey," he told her as he took the purse from her hand. "That isn't the right shade of red."

I went back to my spot on the couch. Pearl shrugged her shoulders and sat next to me. He stayed in the bedroom several minutes, and I could hear him mumbling to himself.

"I saw it the other day. Now where is it?" He came in, satisfied. "Here it is, honey. See, that looks better."

He held it against her dress, then handed it to her. She set it in her lap. He sat down and looked at his watch.

"Well, we got about twenty minutes until they start serving lunch. Now I had to ask you something, Annie, and I can't remember what it was."

I didn't encourage him and kept my mouth shut. Pearl was confused and digging frantically in the purse. She paused to glare at us in bafflement.

"What's the matter?" Henry asked calmly.

"Can't find my billfold."

"Honey, remember? You don't need to carry one. We don't want you to lose it. I'm paying for lunch, okay?"

"Oh, okay." She wasn't convinced and stared at my purse. "Do you carry a billfold?"

"Honey, of course she does. She needs hers, but you're not driving. Remember what we talked about?"

"Oh, yeah," she nodded, not so sure she did remember.

"Mom gets a little confused from time to time."

"That's okay. I do, too," I said.

Pearl shrugged her shoulders and giggled like a precocious little girl.

A white Ford with a cover over it sat under the carport. Pearl's keys had been taken away for fear that she might drive away and not find her way home. Weeks earlier, I spent an hour with Henry, searching their house for her wedding ring. She had placed it under the lamp in her bedroom. Why she did that, she couldn't recall.

He backed his tan Impala out of their driveway. I sat between them. Unhurried, he drove up Fifth Avenue and turned right on Quinn Road to get to the highway. We passed by several churches and the cemetery, then he stopped at a red traffic light. As soon as the light turned green, she said, "Go, honey." He didn't hear her and turned left, puttering along Highway 17. I was watching convenience stores and banks go by, then a Dairy Queen and Western Sizzler.

"That's okay. Go on, if you're in a hurry," Henry waved. The motorist raced past him. So did numerous others.

Shoney's was two miles away, but it took ten minutes to get there. At a leisurely pace, he drifted into the parking lot and into a parking space, then backed out and pulled in again and again to straighten the car. A couple of cars waited for him to finish. He smiled, waving a hand to the people in their cars as they passed by impatiently.

As soon as the Prices walked into Shoney's, a big to-do was made over them. The waitresses gushed and treated them like royalty.

"How are you, Mr. Price? Mrs. Price, you sure look pretty today," the robust waitress said.

"Thank you, honey," she said.

Henry gripped the waitress's hand and arm and stared deeply into her eyes. "How are you, Ginger?"

"Just fine, Mr. Price."

"That's good. How's your circulation been?"

"Much better, thank you."

"I'm so glad to hear it. Remember," he said pointing to the heavens, "The Lord is watching."

"That's right, I believe that," she replied uncomfortably.

He smiled broadly and patted her arm. Reaching around without turning to Pearl, he said, "Come on, Mom."

We were seated in a booth.

"That one, uh, Ginger, oh, I forgot her last name. Law—, Law—, I can't remember." He seriously tapped his head with his fingers. I prayed he'd remember, because it would drive him and me crazy until he did.

"It doesn't matter," Pearl said, looking slightly agitated. "Ginger is her name."

He didn't hear her. "Lawson, yeah. She joined our church a couple of months ago. I've been talking to her when Mom and I come in here, and I could sense that she needed someone to take an interest. So I asked her if she attended church regularly, and she said no. I told her about the good people at First Baptist, and she's been going ever since."

"That's great," I said.

"Oh, yeah—that's what I wanted to ask you. Have you found a church in Hattiesburg?"

"Well, when I stay on campus for the weekend, my friend Denise and I go to the First Baptist on Hardy Street."

Once, and I only went because she was going and I didn't want to be left out.

He purred, "That's wonderful. I told Mom I was so happy you found a nice friend like, um, Denise, yeah, that's her name. Denise."

"That's right," I nodded.

He opened his menu. "Honey, get what you want. You can have dessert, some strawberry pie, if you want it, you hear?"

I wanted a junk food feast, but that would bring on more needling and leering than I could handle.

"Pearl, I'm going to order the baked chicken for you. Would you like a salad, too?"

She was looking at her menu but not reading it.

"Annie, what would you like?"

"I think I'll have the baked chicken, myself."

"Are you sure? You can have anything you want."

"Yes, sir, that's good."

"You see, honey, Annie watches her weight. She eats healthy." He openly looked at my body and asked, "How much do you weigh now?"

"One twenty."

"You look good." Picking up my left hand, he whined, "Please don't bite your fingernails. Do it for Pop."

"Okay," I answered to get my hand back.

"Now if we could do something about your hair. I don't like your bangs like that. It's too much in your face. It looks too unkempt." He smiled. "We can talk about it later." He paused before he got up. "Oh, I didn't tell you. Mom weighed one hundred thirty pounds this morning. She was one thirty-two on Thursday."

He overdid it with her diabetic diet. One hot Saturday afternoon while I was visiting, she begged for a vanilla wafer cookie. Grudgingly, he pulled one out of the box and offered her a glass of diet cola.

"I guess one cookie won't hurt Mom."

Pearl savored every crumb. Afterwards, she brushed off her lap, unfulfilled, but she didn't dare beg for another. A woman of eighty-three and she got there on her own, I thought.

"Mom, you stay here while Annie and I get our salads at the salad bar."

He pecked her lips and slid out of the booth. Like a princess, she smiled, lovingly. Not once had I ever seen Mama and Daddy kiss on the lips, and these two acted like honeymooners. As soon as Henry wasn't watching, Pearl stuffed some Sweet-N-Low and sugar packets into her purse. Holding a finger against her lips, she whispered, "Shhh."

After he took a salad to her, he enthusiastically fixed his, all the while telling me to get as much as I wanted. I was wary, for I knew the penalties for over-indulgence. A little lettuce, three slices of cucumber, and a few drops of lowfat dressing, and I went back to the booth before he did and waited with Pearl, who didn't touch a bit until he was seated. His plate was brimming with cottage cheese, peaches, raisins, and other goodies he missed out on at home, where he ate the same meager diet he fed to Pearl. He said a quick prayer, while people at the other booths and tables chewed in sin.

I was dizzy with hunger. I wished I had gotten more, but there wasn't a chance I was going back to the salad bar. I sliced everything into smaller pieces to make them last. Then Henry's grumbling put a stop to my craving for food.

"Annie, slow down."

"Huh?"

"You're eating too fast," he spoke, as if he were revolted. "Slow down. Mom always eats slowly. It's better for you."

I swallowed, not knowing how to eat. I took sips of iced tea between nibbles and watched their salads vanish off their plates. I left a few bits of cucumber on my plate. Henry swiped his mouth with a napkin and made happy faces at me. *You have to control everything.*

"Would you like pie today?"

"Yes, sir. Can I share a little with Mom?"

"I guess so. Mom, would you like some strawberry pie?" He asked as if it was his idea.

"I sure would."

"I guess it doesn't hurt to let Mom have a little dessert now and then. Dr. Wallace said her blood sugar's perfect and to keep it up with the diet."

"That's right, Pop. Mommy Junior deserves it," I smiled.

I didn't want the pie, my appetite dampened after his remark. I held the fork, cut a tiny piece and chewed slowly. Pearl's cheeks were chock-full, with a pink surplus of strawberry ooze seeping out the corners of her lips.

"Mmm, this is delicious, Mom," he said.

"It sure is," she garbled. "Annie knows how to pick out good desserts."

They grossed me out. The way they ate, I could see the inside of their mouths, the food between their teeth, and I had to avert my eyes to avoid gagging. His fork made a dreadful racket as he scraped the plate for the leftover whipped cream. While he was wiping his mouth, Pearl's eyes twitched. She wanted another piece, but she was a good child and didn't ask.

"Next time, we'll get the hot fudge cake. I bet it's delicious," he said.

I was ready to go, and I thought he was, too, but he pointed to his cup, and the waitress refilled it.

Great. I'm stuck. Even worse, this means he's going to talk. Pearl began sweeping up the table crumbs.

"You know Dr. McClure, don't you?"

"I know his wife from the grocery store. He's the dentist, right?" I answered.

"That's right. Danny has been a dentist the last ten years or so. Mom and I used Dr. Hillary until he retired in seventy-eight. Anyway, to make a long story short, I talked to Danny the other day at his office. I told him about your situation and about you going to college. How hard you work and that you have a job. Well, to get to the point, he's agreed to clean your teeth free of charge."

"All right," I answered.

"Danny McClure's a good boy, yes he is. His father owns a construction company. Whenever he needed employees, he'd call me. Yeah, they're good people. We've known them for thirty years. In the next few weeks, give his office a call and set up an appointment. His receptionists know all about you."

Give us a chance to pay this off. Annie's in college. She works hard. You'll get your money, you hear? Good ole Pop. He knows how to talk to people. Don't give them all your money at once, dribble it out to them. Don't let them think you're rolling in dough.

Mommy Junior had cleaned up every crumb. Using her wadded napkin, she wiped the table and began stacking the plates and silverware.

Henry turned cantankerous. "What are you doing?"

"Tidying up," she answered.

"Pearl, they'll clean it up. That's their job, you hear?"

"Oh, okay." She looked at me, shrugged her shoulders, and let her napkin fall onto a plate. I touched her hand.

"Thank you, Mr. Price. It's good seein' y'all again," the waitress said.

"Thank you, honey. I hope your little boy gets better," he said.

He adjusted his glasses as he studied the check.

"Henry, that waitress is a little on the heavy side," Pearl whispered.

"Yeah, she's a little large. She probably doesn't watch what she eats. There's a lot of big ones around here."

"These people need to push away from the table," she continued.

With purpose, he placed his wallet on the table. "You see, Annie, Mom doesn't like to see people overeat."

I thought she should see Daddy eat, then she would have reason to gripe. After he pulled the money out of his wallet, he laid two dollars on the table. Pearl abruptly grabbed it and shoved it in my hand.

"No, Mom. That's for the waitress. We'll give Annie some money at home, you hear?" He took it from her and placed it back down on the table.

"Okay."

Her eyes had the look of resentment as she slung her purse on her arm. She wanted me to have that money. Moving unsteadily from side to side on her heels, she whispered to me, "That waitress doesn't need it."

He drove us back home, weaving slowly in and out of the highway lanes.

"Ooh, watch it, honey," she warned.

"I see it, darlin'. Mom always watches out for me when I drive."

"That's good," I said.

"Honey, remember W. L. Simpson? He's buried right over there."

"Oh, yeah," she said. "Wasn't his wife . . . oh, fiddlesticks, Shirley was her name, wasn't it?"

He fumbled with his hearing aid. "Huh?"

"Shirley! He was married to Shirley!"

"That's right. Her name was Shirley. She was his second wife. His first wife died in seventy-two."

"She was younger than he was," Pearl whispered. "Stuck-up thing."

On the couch, I was uncomfortable, waterlogged from the iced tea and coffee. I tried to hold my belly in so he wouldn't make any mention of it. I just wanted to get home, let my gut hang out, and relax. Pearl wasn't on planet Earth, sitting beside me picking at her false teeth. I yawned and quickly covered my mouth. I couldn't stand being grilled by him anymore. As the day went by, he'd become more derogatory, because he needed a nap.

"You going back tomorrow?"

"Yes, sir."

"Are you coming home next weekend?"

"I'm not sure. If I don't have any tests, I will."

"Mom and I'd like to see you again."

"All right."

"I mean, we don't want to hog you from your family." He shrugged and leaned on the arm of his recliner. "Your mom doing okay?"

"Yes, sir. She's still working at the Handy Pantry."

"Where does she work now?" Pearl asked.

"Honey, you remember. Penny works at the HANDY PANTRY," he said slowly.

"Oh, that's right." She nodded her head and rubbed her dress. She was uncomfortable, too.

"What about Burl? He keeping busy?"

"A little. Some weeks he works hard. Some weeks he doesn't work at all."

"Well." His face showed absolute dissatisfaction. "I don't understand why a man wouldn't want to take care of his family. As long as I can remember Burl, he's been like that. Your Mama, oh, she's sweet as she can be."

"I'm glad I'm in college," I said.

"Sure. You'll have more choices. It scares me to think that you couldn't go to school. Thank the Lord, you're ambitious and want to learn."

"Penny is sweet as she can be," Pearl said.

"Yes she is, honey. You see, Mom remembers. I remember when we first met your mother. She was so worried, because they were having such a difficult time. Burl was in some kind of trouble. Mom went over there to your house on Third Avenue. She loved you girls so much."

"I remember," I said.

"And now, we're so proud that you've turned out to be such a lovely young woman, aren't we, Pearl?"

"We sure are."

She was slumping down on the couch. I used that as my cue to leave.

"Pop, I should probably go. Mommy Junior's tired, and I have homework to do."

"All right, honey. I know you have to get back. I just hate to see you leave," he said sadly. "Here, say goodbye to Mom."

I hugged her, and she staggered. "Bye, Mommy Junior. Thanks so much for lunch."

"Oh shoot, anytime, sweetheart."

Henry held me a long time. His stale perfume had faded away, leaving his natural musty odor that was about to choke me.

"Be careful now, going back, you hear?"

"I will, Pop. It was good seeing y'all. I love you, Mommy Junior."

"Love you," she said.

I wasn't home free. They were following me, and I didn't know if I should wait or not. I wasn't chancing another delay, so I got in my car, put my keys in the ignition.

"Wait, honey," Henry said. "Something's on your hood." *This is the price I have to pay for getting money from the Prices.*

I couldn't close the door because now they had to finish examining it for dirt and bird droppings. Pearl began picking leaves out of the windshield wipers.

When I finally backed out, they stood waving their arms like children until I was out of sight.

An evening at home was nothing to brag about, either. My family behaved as if we were thrown together from different orbits, the communication incoherent. Mama and Daddy should have gone their separate ways years ago. I had the feeling my sisters and I were all accidents. Our family life was one of uneasiness, constant selfishness, deprivation.

I was on the couch, my Accounting 301 book opened on my thighs. The birds were chirping, and the bugs conversing with one other — this was the joy of living in the country, where diverse sounds played night and day. But I was lost in my dreams. I was hearing the roars and cheers from the stadium. I saw Denise standing, clapping, wearing her bracelets, not wondering what happened to me. *Annie's missing out.*

Daddy was clicking the stations until I thought the television knob would fall off. He was sitting at the edge of the couch, his stomach fully overloaded with the biscuits and gravy Mama had made with canned corned beef for supper. She threw together what she could to cook a meal, because I was home, and he ate three-fourths of it. A daily custom, he stuck his rancid shoes in the corner, with dingy socks he'd wear again stuffed inside. Every time I saw him, I wanted to hose him down to get rid of the stench.

After being worked over by Henry, I was a zombie. I was suffocating emotionally. It might be a blessing if someone would place a pillow over my face while I was asleep and finish the job.

Coming from the Prices' house to my own was unbelievable. No wonder they felt sorry for me and wanted to help out. I hated being pitied—I wasn't a pitiful soul. Henry had seen every dump we had moved to. He made it a point to drive by and get a good look for himself. He knew we had moved around too many times, and he knew why. He knew Daddy wouldn't do anything to fix up any place we lived in. Henry felt sorry for Mama. Daddy was driving her into an early grave, and she was letting him. Daddy would live to be ninety.

Mama? Who knew. I wanted her to live a long, long time so she could see me be successful. I wanted to make loads of money so I could help her. But I'd be helping Daddy, really.

Daddy was fingering his neck in search of his pulse, a dreadful habit, he'd picked up years earlier when he was in center stage of nightly emergency room visits. Daddy said it was his heart. The doctor said something didn't agree with his stomach and that the heart and stomach were connected by the same nerve. I say it was a lack of peace, and gluttony.

A trail of exhaust streamed down Old Mill Road. From behind the thick haze appeared a brown LTD. It rumbled up our driveway at a snail's pace, idled, then backfired at the side of our house. Orange paint was smudged on the driver's side. A stubby, timid man stepped out and slammed the car door until it finally shut. His hair was reddish blond, and he looked younger than his thirty-nine years. He carried a Bible, King James Version. From her window, Gloria saw who it was and let it be known she wanted no company.

"Not that fuckin' idiot."

"Shut up, he can hear you," Mama warned.

Daddy stood up and slipped on his shoes. "I don't know why she has to act completely crazy."

"Not another night of listenin' to you two condemn everybody," she complained.

She stormed into the bathroom and slammed the door. The faucets squeaked as water filled the tub.

By now, the man stood at the front door. Daddy happily snatched it open.

"Come in, Brother Buddy."

I looked up from my accounting book and sensed by his small darting eyes that the brother was having anxiety attacks again.

"How are y'all?"

"Just fine," Mama answered in a soft voice.

She enjoyed Bible talk with him. She already had a glass of Diet Coke, a lit cigarette, and was seated. Unlike Daddy, Buddy had a better grasp on things and studied every day. Meaning, he knew more Bible verses. And unlike Daddy, he admitted openly to his sordid and sinful past. Daddy thought all of his sinning, past and present, didn't count. Buddy, like Daddy, was a self-ordained preacher. Meaning, the both of them had never studied in school. In truth, Brother Buddy usually wanted to use our telephone to call up his brother friends. Upon seeing me, he livened up.

"Hey, Annie. How's school?"

I set my book on the end table. "Fine. How are you, Buddy?"

He tensed up as he pushed one of the kids' naked dolls out of the way so he could sit down. "Doin' good, I guess."

I picked up Daddy's empty coffee cup because I wanted a reason to escape to the kitchen, and I didn't want to sit by him.

"Sit down, uh, don't take that cup," Daddy told me as he took it from my hand. "Brother Buddy, you wanna cup of coffee?"

"No, my ulcer's botherin' me again." He sat with an unsettled expression on his face.

I was in a vicious mood. Usually I didn't give a hang and wouldn't waste my time on these clowns. But this time, I moved to the gripe seat and waited for the show.

"Yeah, my ulcer and hernia have been buggin' me so much lately. I ate some fried okra the other day, and I sure paid for it," Daddy said proudly.

"Well, Daddy, the doctor told you not to eat greasy foods," I said.

"I can't help it. Jitney Jungle has some good food in their deli, almost as good as Mama's cookin'," he grinned.

"I can't touch fried foods. Earlie May broils everythin'," Buddy said. "Anythin' spicy or greasy sets me off and makes me so sick."

"Yeah, that ole spicy food tears me up," Daddy said.

"Annie loves that stuff," Mama said.

"Wait until she gets a bad stomach."

"I'm not looking for one, Daddy."

Mama added, "Annie has a spastic colon."

"It was the stomach flu," I said.

"Well, you do have one."

"I do, too. I have to take Librax to calm mine down," Buddy said.

"Mama, what was that medicine I was takin' that time, you know, the one Dr. Collins gave me?" Daddy asked.

"It was Librax."

"It was?"

"Yeah. You were havin' those spells when we lived at the house on Jersey Drive."

My God, they were boring. Gloria came out of the bathroom with a blue towel around her head, a scowl on her face, and her butt drooping out of cutoff shorts. She walked into the kitchen and fixed herself a glass of tea. She came back out to the living room and sat in a corner, daring Daddy and Buddy to look at her. They didn't.

"Brother Lee, I preached a three-day revival in Leakesville last week."

Daddy perked up. "You did?"

"Yeah, I did. Twelve people got saved."

"Is that right?"

He shook his head, yet showed no satisfaction at all. Yep, Brother Buddy was full of torment tonight. He rubbed his neck while his eyes bulged like those of a wild animal. I could sense that Mama wanted to nurture him. I wanted him to leave.

"Yeah, I, uh, still haven't heard from the Social Security yet," Daddy said.

"It took me two and a half years to get my disability."

"I don't understand it. A man works hard all his life . . ."

I rolled my eyes and looked at Mama.

"And he can't even get any help when he's down and out. . . ."

"A lot of people are down and out," I said.

"But no, you got these bums on welfare. The government needs to put these worthless good-for-nothin's to work. No, they're too busy givin' 'em all the money. This country's gonna crumble up and fall down. And then you got these battle-axes runnin' all over the country wantin' to get rid of our guns so we'll be at the mercy of a bunch of freaks. It's sad that law-abidin' citizens have no rights."

He must have forgotten the child support he didn't pay to his three kids from his first marriage.

"That's right, Brother Lee," said Buddy.

"I don't wanna hear this," Gloria whined.

Daddy continued. "And you see what's on TV? A bunch of punks playin' that rock music."

"There's nothin' wrong with rock music. Better than that shit you try to sing," she said.

"Don't cuss. Gospel music is sanct . . . sancti . . ."

"Sacred," I said.

"It's, uh, sacred. These pillheads that make that rock music are nothin' but a bunch of satanic worshippers. I wish these girls would quit listenin' to that junk. It's demonic."

"It'll destroy your soul," Buddy shuttered. "I can testify to that."

"I'm not listenin' to y'all's shit. This is my only night off," said Gloria.

"Don't start that ugly talkin'," Daddy said.

Mama cut in. "No one can enjoy relaxin', Burl, 'cause you're always harpin' on stuff that doesn't matter."

"I was only sayin' that these punks—"

"I heard you, Burl."

Buddy rubbed his neck and squirmed. "When I played in a rock n' roll band thirteen years ago, I did drugs. I slept with whores. . . ."

Gloria's face turned to stone.

"I was livin' a life of abomination. It took an electrocution to wake me up."

"What electrocution?" I asked.

I knew nothing of this story. Mama had heard it, I was sure, because her eyes came to life.

"One night we were playin' in a bar in Mobile. I was drunk, up to my knees in drugs. I didn't see the torn speaker wire until it was too late. When I stepped on it, the force threw me off the stage and onto a woman sittin' on a stool. I saw the angel of death before me, and I knew I was hell-bound unless I changed my life."

"Amen, Brother Buddy," Daddy laughed.

"Oh, brother," Gloria said.

"It blew my shoe apart, and two of my toes turned black."

Mama loved this part and gave him a look of empathy.

"And tell us what happened to your toes, Brother," Daddy said.

"I lost the toenails, but they grew back."

"Yeah, if you believe in the Lord, he'll heal anything, includin' your toes," Daddy affirmed.

"I haven't seen you this excited since the convenience stores started carrying fountain drinks," I said. Mama snickered as she flicked an ash into an ashtray. "Well," I said, "you have to help yourself and meet God halfway."

"That's right, sister," Buddy said.

"Yeah, uh, I was drivin' to the store the other day and this punk pulled out in front of me . . ."

"Please, Daddy," I moaned.

"I'm not listenin' to this," Gloria snapped. She got up and stomped to her bedroom and slammed the door.

"I wish she wouldn't act that way," Daddy said.

"I have homework to do," I said.

I took my accounting book and went into Gloria's room to hide out. After a few minutes of muddled sounds, the praying began.

Gloria fumed. "I can't believe he comes his ass over here this late at night to pray. Fuckin' bastard."

"I know. That's like coming to skid row for financial advice. God, I hope they hurry," I said. "I need to take a bath."

"Listenin' to Daddy pray makes me sick," she sneered.

"He needs to pray for himself more than Buddy."

Mama's voice was barely audible, but Daddy was letting loose, and I couldn't take much more. Brother Buddy was crying and beseeching forgiveness, healings, and blessings. With five kids and no job, I'd be praying hard myself. Between welfare, disability, and handouts, he hadn't fared too badly.

Chapter Four

Back in my dorm room, I organized my books and notes. It was good to be back, yet I felt homesick again, and I was ashamed about it. Other women were coming off the elevator laughing. They seemed so full of life, while I felt like a dull blade, too introverted for my own good, unable to express any emotion for fear it'd be the wrong emotion.

I finished my last class on Monday and walked to the commons for lunch. It was the main cafeteria, located in the center of the campus. Denise was standing near the entrance with her books resting on her hip. Her long hair was thrown over her shoulder, and I decided that day I was growing my hair at least to my shoulders. A guy blocked my view, and I knew he was inviting her to eat with him. She glowed like Venus, and it was hard not to envy her. But he walked in without her, and she was coming my way.

"About time, chick," she said.

"Didn't know you were waiting for me."

I opened the door, and we stood in line at the end of the stairs. The line moved quickly, and we walked to the main food line.

"Aren't you goin' to get the diet line?"

Do I look fat?

"Maybe," I answered. "I have to peek in here and see what they have. It looks like grilled cheese sandwiches. I have to have one."

At the table, I pinched a piece of sandwich, slipped it into my mouth, and chewed slowly and deliberately. My eyes moved to Denise, but she wasn't watching me. She had been moving the same three pieces of potato around in her soup for the last twenty minutes. Like a pouting child whose hand had been spanked, she cut her eyes down and up in my direction. Rolling them over toward the main food line, I eased my head around.

"Do you see?" she whispered.

"What?" I asked.

"Leslie Lang," she said.

"Oh, yeah. It's okay with me if she sits with us," I said.

"I don't care. I just get tired of hearin' her complain, that's all."

Leslie was at the milk machine. Her hair was cropped short, naturally blond and straight. She wore glasses. Instead of a purse, she carried a white cloth bag on her shoulder. She turned just in time to catch Denise, who barely cracked a smile. She rushed our way with a gigantic grin.

"Hey, Denise. Hi, Annie. Can I sit with y'all?"

Denise softened. "Sure, chick. Pull up a chair."

She was blushing as she placed the cloth bag at the end of the table. After a good long pause for her to settle into a chair, Denise asked, "How are classes goin'?"

She was rankled as she pulled down her tee shirt. "My professor in sociology won't let me make up an exam I missed."

"Why did you miss your exam?" I asked.

"I was so exhausted from bein' up with my sinuses. I have chronic postnasal drip, and I was worried I was goin' to get nauseous. If I get nauseous, I start throwin' up, and if that happens, I dehydrate." Then she looked to Denise for sympathy. "Denise, you know how easily I dehydrate. I couldn't take another night in the emergency room, so I stayed up most of the night worryin', and then I overslept."

"I'm sure he'll let you make it up by lettin' you do some extra work or somethin'," Denise calmly told her.

She cut through her lasagna and pushed her glasses off her nose. "I don't know what to do about it."

"Did you tell him you were sick?" I asked.

"He don't care. No one cares. Don't know why he has to be so hateful," she fussed as she shoved in the lasagna.

"It'll get better," Denise said. "Wonder where Suzy is."

Denise was the expert at changing the subject. She had no interest in negative conversations. *Don't talk. Don't touch. Don't have problems.* I wanted to blurt out to Denise how awful I felt inside, and that I hated getting up in the morning to face life. Would she tell me it'd be okay?

Leslie would tell anybody about her problems in a split second. I had gathered a lot from eating with her in the cafeteria. Notably, she was in college for the fifth year with no degree in sight. She was not allowed to receive college grants, because she used up the maximum limit. Student loans were her sole income. Her grades were below average. She lived in an apartment off campus.

"I don't know why they make the food so greasy," Leslie snapped. "I should've gotten the diet line. You and Denise are so skinny."

"I walk a lot," I said. "Around that big track near Borden Hall."

"I wish I could walk. I've had knee problems since I put on a hundred pounds. My lower back's been achin'. I think I twisted it."

Denise rolled her eyes and looked at me. Ignoring her, I had to hear this. "You gained a hundred pounds?"

Leslie chewed, paused, swallowed, and nodded. "You know what Fasty-Sweet is?"

"Yeah," I answered, as Denise's chest sank.

"They put it in soft drinks and powdered drinks," she said. "Anyway, it caused an allergic reaction in my fat cells, and I gained a hundred pounds in six months."

"I've never heard that before. Did you go to a doctor? That sounds very serious to me."

"The doctors don't know anything. I did my own research and figured out that it was the Fasty-Sweet. I used to be as skinny as you."

"Are you goin' to the football game next Saturday?" Denise interrupted.

"No," she said. "I couldn't get a ticket. I wanted to go with Jason, but he's goin' with some of the other students from our film class. They didn't even mention it to me. I'm really mad at that little booger for not gettin' me a ticket."

By Denise's expression, I could tell she regretted asking. "He was probably distracted and didn't mean to not include you."

"I'm really disappointed. Now, I have nothin' to do. What are you guys doin'?"

"Don't know," I answered.

Denise was still watching her but gave me the cue that she wanted to leave by tapping my foot with hers. After a few minutes, I said, "I have to get to work-study."

Chagrin appeared in Leslie's face as she was picking up her cloth bag. "Oh. Okay. I wish we could talk longer."

"I need to get goin', too," Denise said.

We dumped our trays into the tray return and walked outside. I left Denise with Leslie on the sidewalk and rushed over to the education and psychology building where I did work-study.

"Nell, tell Annie to come in here, please!"

"She's coming. Annie."

I stood, shifted some papers to the side, and walked into her office. "Do you need me, Dr. Dearman?"

She dug a sticky quarter from the bottom of her purse and handed it to me. "Go get me coffee with lots of cream."

I exited the main office, walked quickly down the hall and up the stairs to the lounge on the second floor. Dr. Doris Dearman was the toughest professor in the undergraduate teaching classes. Any student that was going to be a teacher didn't want to get her. She was fifty-nine, she told me, and wasn't one to hide her age. And she couldn't, not with the over-permed brown hair, crimped skin texture, and brusque personality. I was edgy as she took the coffee from my hands.

"Thank you, dear."

"You're very welcome. Do you need anything else, Dr. Dearman?"

"Not right now, but thanks for asking," she answered in her sweetest voice. Sweet voice or not, the lady was intimidating, and I was scared of her.

Nell Johnston had worked as secretary in the education department for fifteen years. Her hair was completely gray, but for having had four kids, she looked younger than her sixty years. She was legally blind, so she used a large magnifying glass to type memos and to read the mail. I was back at the small wooden table against the wall, stapling together thirty handouts Dr. Dearman needed in twenty minutes.

"Are you almost finished with that?" Nell asked with a tinge of panic.

"Just about."

"Good. Sorry you're being rushed. You know how it is. They give us things to do at the last minute."

She was struggling with the typewriter ribbon. It was a mess of ink and fabric as she pulled and tugged. A sweat had broken out on her forehead, and she talked in an annoyed tone while trying to be professional.

"Annie? Can you help me? I think it's jammed."

I frowned. Coming up behind her, I pulled the ribbon out and slipped a new one in before she tore up the machine. "Okay, Mrs. Johnston, it's ready to go."

"Thank you. I have to get this memo done today."

I stood and stapled in a hurry before she did something else, then she stood up from the typewriter, looking flustered.

"Will you proof this for me? Dr. Katz needs it done today."

Sentences were typed in the margin and off of the paper. The typos looked like some kind of code.

"Uh, Mrs. Johnston, there's a few—"

"Well." She was looking over my shoulder. "You'll have to retype it."

Put the monkey on my back, I thought. I loaded the orange typewriter with a sheet of the department letterhead and typed away while she shuffled papers on her desk. The phone started ringing, and she grabbed it so fast that it slipped through her knobby fingers. She caught it with her other hand.

"Education, this is Mrs. Johnston. Yes. How are you, Dr. Purvis? No, Dr. Katz won't be in until six o'clock. Yes, he has your manuscript. I'll be glad to give him the message." Traces of fruity perfume came from her direction as her silk blouse brushed my shoulder. She scribbled a large note on the message pad, missing the lines on the paper. "Very well, then. Goodbye, Dr. Purvis. Oh, Lord, Annie. I hope Dr. Katz has read that manuscript."

She hurried out the door and down the hall to his office. I heard her drop her keys and the sound of struggle as she tried to unlock his door. She used the wrong key again.

At five, I headed back to the cafeteria for dinner. I sat at the first empty table I saw and placed my purse and books on the chair next to me. On my plate was tuna casserole made with green peas, pimento, noodles, and cream sauce, things we could never experiment with when cooking at home, because of Daddy's stomach. I was used to Mama's version. Two cans of tuna packed in oil, two cans of cream of chicken soup, and a large bag of potato chips crushed at the bottom. Fattening, yet tasty. I bit into a noodle. Thirty seconds later, I was chewing voraciously and reaching for the salt and pepper shakers. Then I sensed someone looking at me, and my eyes glanced upward.

"May I join you?"

I put the pepper down and swallowed the food.

"I'm Peter McBride."

I didn't say anything.

"Suzy's friend," he said.

"Hi," I nodded.

He slid his tray across the table with a smile and sat confidently beside me. "How are your classes? Suzy told me you're majoring in accounting."

"Yeah, uh, the classes are fine. Hard," I said.

"So are mine. How long have you known her?"

"Who?" I asked.

"Suzy."

"Just this semester."

"What year are you in?"

"I'm a junior."

"Great," he smiled. He didn't have a southern accent, and I worked hard to hide mine.

"Are you a junior?" I asked.

"Senior."

I was angry with Suzy for this. I didn't have the time to be put on the spot to meet guys. I told myself to get through the dinner, and he'd be on his way.

"Do you know Suzy from class?" I asked.

"No. We met when we were freshmen. The first time I saw her was at a party at Bolton Hall. She was louder than anyone there, so I thought she was drunk. But she wasn't," he smiled.

"That sounds like her," I chuckled.

He told me the jokes he and his friends had played on her. There were the parties they went to, the football games, and the clubs they danced at.

"Last year, Suzy and I won a disco dance contest at the Parrot Club," he laughed. My giggling was steady. "Won a hundred dollars."

"Hi, Peter."

"Hi, Roberta," he nodded as she flurried by with cowboy boots and purple hair. "Roberta looks ghastly today."

"Are you a resident advisor?" I asked.

"Used to be," he answered. "I'm head resident now. Over at Taylor Hall."

"Ah," I nodded.

"You ought to stop by sometime. We have *Miami Vice* night on Fridays."

"Miami Vice night?" I asked.

"Yeah. You know, Crockett and Tubbs."

"My dad likes that show."

"People come from the other dorms and watch it in my apartment. About fifty to a hundred people," he smiled.

"Sounds like fun," I said. Count me out, I thought. I looked at my watch.

"I know you need to leave. Can I have your phone number? I'd like to call you."

"Oh. Okay."

My mind went blank for a moment as I pulled out a sheet of notebook paper. I scribbled my number and handed it to him. He tore off a piece of the paper and wrote down his number and gave it to me. I put it in my purse and zipped it up.

"Do you ever go to the campus movies on Thursdays?"

"Sometimes," I answered.

He paused, his eyes showing that he liked what he saw when he looked at me. I, Annie Lee, actually had a conscious man staring at me.

"Your eyes match your hair," he said.

"They change color sometimes, from brown to green, sort of a hazel color."

"They're beautiful. I've never seen anyone with red hair like yours. It's the prettiest color."

"My daddy has red hair," I said. That was the only thing I wanted to inherit from him.

"You're definitely a true redhead. I can tell by your skin."

"People ask me everyday if I dye my hair," I said.

"Tell them, 'hell no'!"

"It's okay. I'm used to it."

"You have high cheekbones."

"I do?"

"Yes," he said as he viewed me closely.

"I guess I should go." I was trying to keep from getting too excited over the attention I was used to not getting. He grabbed my tray and his as I awkwardly stood up. On the way to my dorm, a dozen or so people disconnected our conversation to speak to him. We stopped on the sidewalk.

"I sure thank you for walkin' me," I said, my accent slipping through.

"Anytime, anywhere. See you soon."

As soon as I got off on fifth floor, I knocked on Suzy's open door. She hadn't unpacked from her weekend at home. Clothes covered her unmade bed, the desk, and the floor.

"Who's Peter?" I was out of breath.

"Isn't he adorable?" Suzy gushed.

"Yes, but—"

"And he's real smart," she continued. "He's an honor student."

"That's nice Suzy, but I'm—"

"And he's very athletic. He plays flag football. Oh, and he bikes. Last Sunday, he rode a hundred miles with his cycling buddies."

"But what does he want with me?" I asked.

"Annie." She closed her closet and smiled. "He wants a date."

"Why?"

"Because he thinks you're nice."

"He doesn't know me."

"Well, I told him about you."

I looked down.

"No, I mean, I wasn't matchmaking. He saw you in the cafeteria with me."

"So."

"He loves your red hair," she said.

"I'm glad someone does."

"Annie, come on. He told me you're the most beautiful redhead he's ever seen. Peter has a thing for redheads. He's a great guy."

Peter McBride began to appear wherever I was. He'd show up at breakfast, looking as though he'd just rolled out of bed. Staring into his bloodshot eyes turned me off, at first. Sometimes, he'd be with a group of friends from Taylor Hall, and they'd conveniently eat lunch and dinner with me. Denise and Suzy were thrilled, while I wallowed in embarrassment. I turned down his invitations to parties and a bicycle ride. I was terrified of crashing in front of a bunch of buff cyclists. I dreamed of being athletic and built like the models in exercise magazines. Why had I wasted all of those years in front of the television? Walking six miles almost every day had kept me thin, though not as toned as I wanted. Finally, Peter called and woke me at ten o'clock one night.

"I can't," I said. "I have some things to do."

"Are you going home again?"

"Uh, yeah."

"Oh."

"My mom, uh, hasn't been feeling well lately. So, I've been taking care of business things for her," I said carefully.

"Does she have her own business?"

"Sort of."

"How about the campus movies on Thursday. Sound good?"

"Sure." My heart began to pound. *What have I done?*

I went back to bed. My accounting classes had become difficult, and I felt intimidated by the professors. At the junior college, I breezed through the classes, and I had gotten used to making A's. Henry was used to me making good grades, and I wished I hadn't bragged about it. I was nervous about work-study, because I wanted to please the professors I worked for. There was Mama and Daddy to worry about. Then, there was the fact that I had never been out on a date. I had never been kissed, and I didn't want Denise or anybody else to find out. I was going to have to wing it.

Career woman or not, I had to confess to myself that I wanted to be wanted. I suppose it was Peter's physique that attracted me. When he ate supper with me on Thursday to remind me of our movie date that night, we stopped by the student union to check his post office box. I watched his long legs glide from side to side as he went to open his box. He was a six-footer, I was thinking. Muscular arms, wide shoulders, and a nice high rump. I liked tall guys. Neither Daddy nor Pop Price was tall or well built. Gloria's beaus were dwarfs. As Peter walked ahead of me, he cracked jokes about receiving a letter from a former resident assistant who had a crush on him for two years. I was beginning to see how anyone could be infatuated with him. He was twenty. His mustache was blacker than his hair, and I believed he'd grow more handsome as the years went by.

My palms sweated as I applied my makeup in the communal bathroom. I started to call Peter to cancel the date, but it was too late. I was feeling like Brother Buddy, my eyes wild like those of an animal in a cage. In the hallway, Suzy was complimenting Denise's new outfit, and my stomach began to burn. I owned only two pairs of faded blue jeans, and I was trying to decide if I should wear the pair I had worn all day or the clean pair in my closet. Losing weight didn't mean I could go on a shopping spree, so I hadn't the inventory my friends had to pick and choose from. I wore a purple blouse and my fake pearl earrings. My insides were turning flips, my empty stomach roaring, because I didn't eat much at supper.

At six thirty, Peter picked me up at my dorm, and we walked over to Baxter Auditorium. A movie date with him included half of Taylor Hall and most of the fifth floor of Borden Hall. Behind us, our dorm-mates were rowdy, with Peter occasionally joining in. He was so animated, and I hadn't realized how popular he was. It was his sense of humor that made him charming and attractive. The movie was *The Goonies*. I sat nervously, afraid to laugh at anything. I could feel Peter snickering next to me. Then, I felt his arm leaning into mine. *This isn't so bad. Maybe I am desirable.*

Back in my dorm lobby, women hugged him or squealed out his name.

"Peter!"

"Peter McBride! How's it going?"

He cracked jokes and nudged shoulders, while I stood beside him like a ghost. I wanted to get rid of him, because I didn't know what to do with him. I already felt attracted to him. At the back door, I waited for my first kiss, but he had other things on his mind.

"Are you going to the homecoming game?"

"Uh, I think so," I answered.

"I have an extra ticket. You could go with me, if you want."

"Oh, sure. I'd like that."

"It's a date," he beamed.

He put his arm around my waist. I nodded, forcing a nervous smile. He kissed my cheek.

I was in a trance as I washed my face, brushed my teeth, and slipped into my nightshirt. I wanted to talk to Denise and Suzy, tell them about homecoming, but they weren't in their rooms. Peter's laugh was stuck on replay inside my mind. Even lying in the darkness, I could still feel the skin on his arm touching mine.

I wouldn't be seeing Peter over the weekend, because he was going to New Orleans with some of his dorm-mates. I was disappointed, yet relieved. Mostly, I was disgusted with myself, because I couldn't let go of Mama and Daddy. At school, they pulled at me. When I went home, I regretted it. My desire to spend time with Peter was growing. He stayed on campus every weekend. Had more friends than a rock star. Could talk to anybody. He fit in with the fraternity crowd, and he also fit in with the Taylor Hall gang that rebelled against looking or acting like the frat crowd.

Peter's home was Austin, Texas, now, but he was born in Oregon. He could ski, and I envied him for it. Oregon might as well have been Europe. I questioned every day if I was ever going to get out of the deep South. Suzy had met Peter's parents at a football game the year before. She told me that they were devout Catholics. His mom had auburn hair, blue eyes, and a sense of humor. Compared to my folks, they were world travelers. Mama didn't venture and went no further than Ellisville to see Aunt Mooney. Since no legitimate church would let Daddy preach, he gambled on the rural tabernacles and drove far off to mite-sized towns such as Mize, Leakesville, and Tylertown to do his stints of holy-rolling.

Chapter FIVE

Knowing there wouldn't be anything to eat at home, I flipped my left blinker and drove through Arby's. I ordered the usual turkey sandwich and iced tea, and ate in my car while I watched the traffic go by on Highway 49. Behind the signs and billboards, the old Woolco store, another casualty of Tri-Mart, stood empty. It had been Aunt Mooney's favorite. I couldn't wait to get back to the campus on Sunday, because Peter would be calling me. Mama and Daddy would never grasp this. *Oh brother, Annie's in love. Don't get pregnant.*

I drove up the driveway, stopped my car, got out, and walked over to a black clump in the front yard. It was a garbage bag partially filled with trash. I picked it up, tied a knot in it, and took it to the ditch by the street. No one could be that lazy, I thought, and I sped to the back of the house. Mama's car and Daddy's truck were gone. From the back seat, I took out my books and a paper sack with my clean clothes and makeup in it. I petted Trudy and rubbed her stomach. Since the weekend before, the place had aged twenty years. I went on in the back door. The lock was broken. There was no need to worry about someone breaking in. They'd have to be complete idiots to burglarize this waste heap. The kitchen was kind of clean. Instead of a week's worth of dishes, there was just Daddy's breakfast and lunch mess. The rest of the house was a disaster.

The rattling and backfiring of Mama's '76 Nova announced her arrival. The color used to be sky blue, but now it was sun-beat blue denim. And it hadn't been in a demolition derby. Daddy was guilty of vehicle abuse, and Mama's car was the most abused one I'd ever seen. He thought he had to be braking or accelerating, pedal to the metal. He didn't understand a car could slow down by coasting. She was opening the trunk when I walked out in my bare feet.

"Mama? What are you doing with boxes?" I pulled a couple out.

"Annie's home!" Wiley yelled.

"Hey, Wiley! Okay, you can let me go now. Wiley, go on, I'm trying to talk to Mama."

She ran with Holly in tow, slamming the screen door. It fell off and landed on the ground.

"Shit! Well, that'll never get fixed," Mama said with a cigarette in her mouth.

I lifted it up and propped it against the back of the house. "I'll beg Daddy to fix it."

"Huh. Good luck."

"What are you doing with these boxes?"

She pulled out the cigarette. "Whew, you ain't gonna believe . . . we gotta move again."

"Why? What happened now?"

"Mr. Kelley told Burl to clean the yard a couple of months ago. Well, you see how clean it is." She tapped ashes in the grass and stumbled up the back steps.

"I knew it. He screws up everything. This is the nicest house we've rented, and now he's screwed it up."

"He'd fuck up a two-car funeral," she snapped. "It's not just the yard. He wanted him to keep the house up, too. He thought Daddy bein' a carpenter meant that he'd repair things. Ha! He was certainly in for a surprise if he waited on Burl to do anythin'."

She cracked an ice tray, put the ice in a glass, and poured herself some Diet Coke.

"I love this house, Mama. It doesn't have roaches. It could be fixed up nice."

"It's too late now. For over a year, I've begged Burl to fix up this place. It looks worse now than it did when we moved in. We have to get out before old man Kelley sues us. He's such a bastard. A rich bastard."

"He's not rich, Mama. He just hasn't screwed up everything the way Daddy has."

Mama thought everybody was rich, especially people who paid bills on time. She flicked an ash into the sink.

"I'd like to roast his balls for this."

"When do we have to be out?"

"By the end of October, or he'll charge us."

"Where? Have y'all found a place?"

"We found a place over on Fourteenth Avenue."

"Fourteenth Avenue? Mama, the houses are ugly and run down. Guess it doesn't matter. Daddy'd screw up a mansion."

"It ain't too bad. We can drive by this weekend, so you can look at it."

She was proud of it. Relieved to have a place to go, it seemed.

"I'll probably go see the Prices tomorrow. I kind of promised Henry I'd stop by. I'm not staying long. Can't take another all-day deal with them."

"You shouldn't feel that way. They love you. I wish I had some-one to spend money on me."

"Oh, yeah, they spend millions on me."

She sighed with frustration.

"You don't know what Henry says to me. He questions me about my weight. I get tired of it."

"That's just the way old people are. They're lonely and enjoy seein' you. It only takes a little bit of your time."

"When I'm there, it feels like an eternity. I just feel bad. My period started this morning."

"Oh, God." She looked up at the ceiling and shook her head. "I hope you rest this weekend. You shouldn't kill yourself cleanin'. You see how filthy the livin' room is? Every day, I drug myself in from work and picked it up. Burl and the kids destroyed it in five minutes."

"Don't let them."

"I can't kill 'em."

"You could kill Daddy."

I was agitated, my pad soggy, and I had changed twice at school. Couldn't keep any pads at home because Gloria would use them up and not buy any. I went to get one out of the paper bag. Mama was full steam ahead with the fussing, as she followed me.

"I'd love to knock him in the head. Oh! He makes me so mad, I feel like I'm gonna have a stroke."

I walked to the bathroom and unzipped my pants.

"Commode's stopped up again."

"Shoot!" I zipped back up.

"I think Holly threw a brush in it. Burl's bitched all week 'cause he's had the runs. Said he was gonna snake it."

"He always has the runs. That's what gobbling does to you," I said.

"I've plunged the thing until my arm's 'bout to fall off," said Mama. "You can use it, just don't put paper in it."

"He probably stopped it up. It'd be quicker to call a plumber than wait for him to fix it."

I eased the lid open feeling squeamish. The water was low, and the effects of Daddy's bowels were splattered all over the sides.

"We can't afford no plumber. They'd charge the hell outta us, outta me, just to come out here. I ain't got that kind of money."

"Ask Gloria for it. She lives here for free. What does she do with her money?"

"Don't start anythin' with her tonight. She's been on the warpath with her job. Please."

"I'm not saying a word to her, except you and Daddy support her and Holly. She should help out."

"If she offered to help, I'd think she was mentally deranged. Her idea of helpin' is throwin' a pair of her jeans and a tee shirt into the washin' machine. She wastes all the hot water."

Daddy grinned as soon as he hit the back door. "Mama? Where's Annie?" He peeked into the bathroom. "There she is. How's my two ladies doin'?"

"Mama said we had to move again."

"Yeah, ole man Kelley wants us to move."

"Why?"

"I think he's wantin' to sell this place. Mama don't think so, but I'm sure that's what the man's gonna do."

"Shit. You know damn good and well he ain't," she sneered.

"Why Mama, I'm not really sure . . ."

"If you woulda done what you told him you were gonna do when we moved in here, we wouldn't have to leave." She whisked around and stormed to her bedroom, with him following.

"Mama, I told the old man I hurt my back."

"He don't care!"

"Well, I know that. Uh, what are we havin' for supper?"

"Shit! I don't know! I'm tired!"

"I mean, I was gonna run up to the Jitney Jungle and get us somethin'. Annie, whatta you want for supper?"

"What, Daddy?"

He was standing on the other side of the doorway. "You wanna ride up to the store with your ole Daddy?"

I zipped up my pants. "Just a second." I opened the door. "I guess. I only have a little money."

The mere mention of money woke up his mind. With his hands in his work pants and his belly protruding, he said, "Okay!"

I flushed the toilet and prayed as the water rose up. Sluggishly, it went back down. I washed my hands.

"I gotta fix that stupid commode," he griped.

"I hope so," I said, not believing him.

"I'm gonna spank Holly about throwin' things in there." He stepped back to Mama's room. "Mama, whatta you want from the store?"

She was digging out the money. "Can y'all get me some BC powders. I'm almost outta my Diet Cokes. Gloria's guzzled 'em all week. Between her and the kids, I can't keep any. Have to hide 'em in my closet." Like a serpent, he slithered alongside her and strained to sneak a peek in the overstuffed wallet that was full of medicine receipts. She pulled a twenty out, glared, shoved it at him, and screeched as she ripped her purse wide open, "Get a good look!"

"I wasn't tryin' to look in your purse."

She plopped it down on her crowded dresser. "Yeah, you was."

"Ready to go?" I interrupted.

"We'll be back, Mama." He shoved the cash into his top shirt pocket.

"I know that," she grumbled.

I held my pocketbook and followed the dirt path that molded its way to the automobiles. Shoving aside several empty 7-Up bottles and a Kentucky Fried Chicken box of bones that had been picked clean, I climbed in and buckled up. His green Dodge was eleven years old and had never been washed. A colossal crack extended from one side of the windshield to the other. How he accomplished that, I didn't know. He'd said something about a chicken truck. As he backed up, the engine made unholy sounds, wheezing for breath and begging to be sold for parts. It was obvious that it burned oil like a factory, with the empty Quaker State cans in the backyard and in the back of the truck. Three cans of oil sat in a bag under my feet. He didn't see well at night, but it was daylight, and he swerved halfway into a ditch, grinding rocks under the tires as he veered back onto the road. Tools were rolling over the back bed, making intolerable sounds. The wind from the open windows blew my face and hair, and I cried without shedding a tear. I had very much to worry about. I didn't need my parents having to move again to be on my mind. As much as I fought it, I was painfully worried about them.

"How was your week, baby?"

"It was good."

"Yeah, I was tellin' Sister Campbell about you goin' to Eastern Mississippi. She said it was a good college."

"It is."

I turned toward the window and closed my eyes. *I swear death must have more life to it than living like this.*

"What kinda food do y'all get in that cafeteria at school?"

"Same thing I eat at home."

"I bet it's good."

"It's not all-you-can-eat."

He wasn't listening. "Yeah, pretty soon, you'll be an accountant. How much longer you got to go?"

"Two years."

"Two years. Yeah, you'll have a good education. You're the first one of our girls to go to college. I told Mama I wouldn't mind goin' to college some day to be a . . . oh, what was that?"

"A paralegal."

"Yeah, that's it."

That harebrained idea came from a lawyer he had painted for. He was always on his best behavior for strangers.

The Jitney Jungle was busy on a Friday afternoon. Every aisle we walked on, Daddy would stop to talk to someone he knew, telling about his illnesses. I tuned him out as I looked over the canned goods, occasionally smiling at someone who knew I was his daughter.

"I can tell she's yours, with that red hair."

It was a widow woman he piddled for. I hoped he hadn't made her angry, his tendency of leaving work incomplete.

"She's the one goin' to Eastern Mississippi," he bragged.

I wanted him to shut up. I picked up a can of tuna, then set it back on the shelf and left the aisle before she could question me. After five minutes, I walked back, grabbed a can of chili, chucked it into the basket, and gave him the wide eyes, meaning, "Let's go, Reverend."

"Ooh, me, well, I guess we better go. It was nice seein' you, Mrs. Hester."

"Good luck in school, honey," she smiled.

I couldn't take time to thank her when I saw where Daddy was headed. I was uneasy as I took two chickens out of the cooler. *We'd only need one if he weren't around.* I watched his burly arms lift a big pack of ribeye steaks and set them back. He was in search of something affordable. Mama and I together didn't have much money, and we were the ones who had anteed up. Mama never felt like cooking, and I wasn't about to, so I picked out a pack of sandwich meat for the night. I wanted to get a small block of cheddar cheese, but he'd eat it up, so I stuck with American cheese slices.

"Boy, this meat sure is high."

He moved down to the cheaper cuts, but he had to have a hunk of real meat. Screw the rest of us. We'd eat sandwiches. I was to the point of tears when he placed a roast in the top part of the cart. Then he was ready to leave, while I was hastily grabbing cookies, milk, and crackers for the kids. Pushing past several people, he steered the cart toward the cash register of a pudgy grocery checker with bleached fringe and craggy teeth. In the process, he ran into my heel.

"Watch it, Daddy," I growled.

"Oh, I didn't see you. And, how are you, Carol?"

She didn't look as thrilled as he was. "Hello, Mr. Lee. How're you?"

"Just fine. Yeah, my stomach's been—"

"Daddy, did you get Mama's BC's?"

"Oh, no, I sure didn't. You run get 'em or she'll be fit to be tied."

I went to the medicine aisle, picked up the largest pack of powders, and walked quickly to the front where he hadn't stopped running his mouth.

"And the burnin' ran up and down my arms . . . I was pure sick. . . . Uh, Carol, this my daughter Annie. She's the one goin' to Eastern Mississippi."

"Yeah, hey, honey. Your Daddy sure is proud of you. He talks about you all the time."

"That scares me," I said. He grinned and rubbed his eyebrow.

"He brags on you, and I would, too."

Her yellow teeth gave away that she was a smoker. Amazing, I thought. Mama said Daddy hated smoking, hated heavy women, and hated short hair on women. What was the appeal of this one?

"Yeah, Annie's gonna be an accountant. She'll be makin' more money than her ole Daddy and Mama," he boasted.

As we carried the bags to the truck, Daddy gave his lowdown on Carol.

"Yeah, that old gal sure has put on the weight."

"Who?"

"That ole Carol. She used to be a skinny woman. Then, her husband left her. She sure has ballooned up."

"Maybe *she* left him."

"No, no, she didn't leave him. She told me the other day that he walked out on her. Left her with a ton of bills. What kinda man would do somethin' like that? Must be pure trash."

I looked the other way, walling my eyes. Carol was another victim of his spiritual advice. For forty dollars, some mail-order place in Louisiana sent him a preacher's license. Hilarious. He had never been a regular churchgoer.

I felt every bump in the driveway as he pulled into the back of the house. Gloria's yellow Subaru was behind my car. We brought in the bags, and the kids tore through them.

"I got y'all some chips and dip. Mama, I bought them some cookies if you need to hide them until they eat a sandwich," I said.

"Oh. You got some turkey." She was holding it up. "Good, I'm sick of ham sandwiches. That's all Burl ever buys so he can gobble all of it."

Daddy's breathing had increased to panting, so he didn't hear Mama's bitterness. A ladle of cheap shortening made a thud as it went into Mama's largest black frying pan. Flour scattered across the floor as he coated the meat. He was going to fry a roast.

"I bought some cheese and lettuce, too," I said.

"We've been out of everythin'," Mama said. "I'm so tired of plain ham sandwiches. I'm glad you got a jar of mayonnaise."

"I got a couple of chickens for tomorrow. Maybe we can barbecue them."

She fixed Wiley a sandwich while I took care of Holly. I was starving, my hand shaking as I spread the mayonnaise. The vent above the stove didn't work, and the smell of scorching meat was making me sick. A thick cloud floated in the kitchen while Daddy hovered over his banquet of burning beef. Grease was shooting and sputtering on the floor, stove, and the side of the refrigerator. When he plunked his roast on a plate, it resembled a black tennis shoe.

"Mama, you want part of this meat?"

"Shit no, can't eat that tough mess."

"I wish we had some of that mushroom gravy you make," he said.

"Well, that's too bad. I'm tired." She threw her hand in the air. "You forgot to cut off the stove!"

He roughly turned the control. "I thought I did."

"You've burned up every pan I have," she snarled.

Before I could get anything, he brushed by me as if he were running a marathon. On his plate were the rubber roast, two sandwiches, and three slices of the loaf of wheat bread I had gotten for Mama and myself. I threw a piece of turkey between two slices of bread. Forget the condiments.

"I'm eating in your room," I told Mama.

I went in and sat on her rumpled bed. She came in with a plate.

"My legs are killin' me." She lifted one after the other onto her bed.

I had planned on keeping my mouth shut. Before I knew it, I couldn't harness my anger. "Mama, at the store, Daddy talked to a dozen people, then the first place he headed for was the meat counter to get himself a chunk of beef."

"I know it. That's all he studies is blabbin' to the moon and fillin' his belly."

"Guess whose line he went in?"

"I know, that ole ugly gal, Carol. He's pure thrilled over her. All he does is run his big fat mouth to that woman. She can't get away from him."

"She doesn't want him."

"Hell, no, but he *thinks* she does. He thinks every woman wants him. I wish they had him."

"Jesus, you'd think a hunk of meat would fill him up. I hope he doesn't eat up the sandwich meat."

"Oh, he will. He don't give a damn if any of us get anythin' to eat. The kids and me starve. He don't go without eatin', I can tell you that. You can look at his belly and see that he don't miss any meals."

"That Carol's not attractive. I thought Daddy didn't like women with short hair, because they look like dykes."

"As long as they have a hole to poke," she muttered.

Gloria came in holding the potato chip bag, chomping one after the other. She had a towel wrapped around her head, and wore only a pair of tight thong panties.

"When did you get back?" she asked.

"About two thirty. Are you going out tonight?"

"No, I'm too tired. That job's killin' me. Hey, I've been gettin' obscene phone calls at the store."

"From who?"

"I don't know, probably one of those old perverts that comes in to buy beer all the time."

"That'd make me madder than hell." In the same breath, Mama said, "Gimme a few of those chips."

Gloria handed her the bag and took one of Daddy's hole-ridden undershirts off the floor, sniffed it, and slipped it on.

"Please stop wearin' his undershirts. He bitches every mornin' about you losin' 'em," Mama begged.

The next morning I left the house at nine thirty to see the Prices. Driving down Fifth Avenue, I clutched my steering wheel in recital mode. *I'll pretend to love Henry this morning. I'll hang on while he criticizes and questions me. I hope he's in a giving mood. Darn, what does it cost to buy one stupid blouse? Twenty dollars? Forty dollars?* I was spending more time with them than my friends did with their real grandparents. But they weren't on a mission for money. I was.

It was coming into fall, and the weather brought back memories of Saturday morning cartoons. During the chilly winters, we had to stay in the house, and, if we were lucky, Daddy would be working somewhere and we could watch television. If he wasn't, we were stuck in front of the gas heater, broken-hearted.

Like a prowler, I drove slowly by the Prices' house. They were home, so I parked. Their side door was closed. I knocked and waited. I was feeling fidgety. *Just get on with it.* I heard the sound of the locks being opened, and it was too late to run. Henry appeared with tousled hair and an unshaven face. It took him a second to focus his eyes.

"Oh! Look who's here! Lordy me, come in, darlin'."

"Hey, Pop. Sorry I didn't call first. Hope I'm not disturbing y'all."

"Not at all, dear. You know you can come anytime you want." He hugged me, and when I tried to pull away, he wouldn't let go. When he did pull back, it was with a dejected expression. I waited for the usual facial inspection. It didn't happen.

I smiled. "I just wanted to stop by awhile."

"Here, sit over here on the couch. Mom's lying down. She's been dragging all morning. You know how she gets sometimes."

"Is she okay?"

"Oh, sure. She just gets confused, and you know how it wears her out. How's school? Did you have a good week?"

I nodded, folding my hands carefully on my lap. "Yes, I've gotten a lot of work done. Spent some time in the library doing my homework."

"That's right, honey. Get that homework done, it's very important."

"Pop? Well, our homecoming game's next weekend, and I'm planning to go. . . ."

"Oh, that's right. Who are they playing? I can't remember."

"Alabama."

"That's right. That's a tough team. Tough football players."

"Yes, sir, I've heard Alabama has a great team this year."

"Yeah." He nodded. "Well, I'm glad you're going to the game, honey. It's good to support your school."

"Yes, sir, I—"

"Who did you say you're going with, or did you?"

"Oh . . . my friend Denise and some of the girls from my dorm."

He looked exalted. "I'm so glad you've met some nice young ladies. You know it's better to socialize with people who have the same Christian values. You know what I mean? Now, this friend, Denise, what's her major?"

"She's pre-dent."

He lifted his hand without touching his hearing aid. "What now?"

"Pre-dental. She's going to be a dentist," I spoke loudly.

"Oh." A surprised stare. "That's wonderful. You can surely make a good living with dentistry."

"Yes, sir."

He leaned in and touched my knee. "Listen, give me her address. I want to write to her and tell her how much Mom and I appreciate her friendship with our granddaughter," he beamed.

"Oh . . . I don't have it with me."

"Bring it next time, you hear?"

He had awakened, and I cursed myself for coming over.

"Yes, I will. Well, since it's homecoming, I have to dress up. Most of the girls, my friends are wearing UEM sweatshirts," I said, faintly but deliberately.

"That's those jersey-type shirts?"

"Yes, sir."

"Yeah," he said grimly. I knew that look. I was wasting my time, I thought, and now I was trapped here. However, his expression changed as he gazed at me with what I thought was fondness. Then his brow wrinkled. "You look a little heavy. Have you gained weight?"

"It's my monthly cycle. You remember how it bloats me."

"Mom never had problems with hers," he shrugged. "Are you eating properly?"

"Yes, I eat in the diet line."

"You don't want to do that now, eat too much, gain a lot of weight," he grimaced, as he cleared his throat. "Pop is proud of how lovely you are and how hard you work to take care of your shape."

"I know."

Leaning closer, his coffee breath nauseated me. He took my hand. "Take care of yourself for me. Do it for your ole Pop, will ya, honey?"

Do I disgust you, old man?

I almost didn't ask, but then I smiled to shut him up, and zeroed in for the kill. "Pop, I was wondering if you could help me buy a blouse for the game."

Clutching my knee, his voice quivered. "I certainly can, dear."

Reclining, pleasure in his face, he nudged my foot with his slipper. "I know you want to look nice."

"Who's there, and who done it?" Pearl asked in jest. She stumbled from her bedroom in a silk gown. I stood and smiled while he hugged her.

"Honey, look who's here to see you."

"Hey, Mommy Junior."

"Well, well. You look so pretty today!"

"Thanks, Mommy, so do you."

"Not as pretty as you."

"Here, Mom, sit on the couch with your granddaughter," he said. "Honey, Annie's going to the homecoming football game next weekend. She wants to look nice. Why don't we buy her a new blouse?"

"I sure will. Get my checkbook."

"Okay, hang on, honey, I will. Now Annie, what else do you need? Maybe some makeup? Some new earrings? Do you still have that girdle we bought you?"

"Uh . . . it's at school."

Forgetting what he asked, his rampage of giving continued. "Hey, maybe some new tennis shoes. Mom, Annie walks a lot at college, she exercises to take care of herself." His attention turned to my feet. "Honey, those shoes look a little worn. Mom will buy you a new pair."

"I guess they are starting to look pretty bad," I said.

"How much do you have in your checking account?"

"Let me see." Nervously, I took out my checkbook. "Sixty-eight dollars and sixty-seven cents. I had to buy a few things."

He didn't hear me. "Okay, let me get Mom's checkbook. She wants to buy you the things you need. You and Mom talk."

I waited until he was in his room. "Mommy Junior, thanks for helping me, I mean it. I'll pay you back as soon as I can."

"Shutterbug! You don't pay back a thing. Anytime you need anything, you call me, you hear?" She squeezed my hand, making me feel the liability for my lies.

"Okay, Mom. I need you to sign." Her hand trembled as she signed, then he handed the check to me.

"This is too much," I said.

"Now, honey," he spoke sincerely. "We know you take care of the money. Good shoes are expensive. We want you to get some good ones. We want you to look pretty at the game. I know how it is when you feel bad about what you wear. I don't want you to feel that way."

Kneeling down, Henry started sobbing while clinging to me. I didn't want to hear this replay about his poverty-stricken childhood. Marrying Pearl had been good. She came from a family with money.

"Heavenly father," he began. "We want to thank you for your mercy and the many blessings, oh, how much we are blessed, with Annie, with each other."

Between each supplication, he'd inhale, lick his lips, and go on to the next. My eyes stayed open. Pearl's hand tightened around mine every few seconds, then she'd ease off. I studied the dirt on my tennis shoes, remembering the first time I smudged them and how disturbed I was about it.

"We don't always live the right way, but we try our best, we do, sweet Jesus. Annie loves you, Lord. She stays in your Word."

What a whopper. His voice was far away when I thought of Peter. *Please don't forget me.*

"And we ask these things in your name, sweet Lord. Amen." He squeezed my shoulder firmly. "Amen."

"Amen!" Pearl wailed, before one last hand squash.

The aroma of chicken roasting in their oven caught my nose, and I had better take the money and run. But he wasn't done with me. He was in his recliner, wiping his glasses, back to normal.

"Why don't you go to the mall, to, maybe to J. C. Penney's, to find a blouse. They have good clothes. I wouldn't get a sweatshirt. Get something pretty."

"Okay, Pop. I'll find one on sale."

"You see, Mom, Annie's so obliging. That's why we admire you, honey. Get you a nice blouse. Promise Mom you'll get something nice."

"I promise. Thank you so much, Mommy Junior, for the money."

"Oh, shutterbug!"

I didn't wait for permission to leave. I grabbed my purse and stood. I hugged them both, keeping my eyes on the door as I walked out.

"Let us know when you're coming home again, you hear?"

"Okay, Pop." I didn't look back.

"Love you!" Pearl yelled.

I drove toward town wondering why I should be bothered about his mentioning the girdle. I had lied. I'd thrown it away. Lying was becoming a habit.

The balance in my checking account had been a sham since the spring. Henry would ask to see my checkbook, and I'd tell him I'd left it at home, when it was snug in my purse. How much in it? Seventy dollars, I'd tell him, when I had twenty. Figuring he'd never quit asking, I decided to show him the damned thing next time and be done with it. I turned the corner and accelerated. That bad feeling was surfacing again as I passed through a traffic light. It was safer to lie.

At Penney's, I walked circles in search of the most breathtaking blouse, but I couldn't find it. The sales clerks were following me as if I were a shoplifter, until I took refuge between the nightgowns and robes. Feeling both foolish and offended, I came out, passing the lingerie section for the third time. I spotted a pair of small looped earrings, then stopped at a clearance rack. Hanger by hanger whipped by as I pushed aside every shirt. It had to be gorgeous. I had to wow Peter. I had to impress Denise. I had to please Pop. The pressure was mounting. I paid for the earrings. I was going to another store. . . .

The rush of my shopping spree subsided by the evening. I had sense enough to leave my new stuff in the back of my car. My family had a way of thinking anything I bought in a store was evidence that I'd found a gold mine, and they'd be jealous. Daddy was across town at Willa's house. He fed her ostrich birds for her, and I was happy he was gone. I just wished he had taken Mama with him.

"Darlene caught her husband with that whore down the road from their trailer," Mama said, casually. Darlene worked with her at the curb store. "She conked him over the head with a Coke bottle, and he had to have twenty-three stitches."

I ran my fingers through my hair, trying to focus on my accounting work. "She should've left him long ago."

"She had no money and nowhere else to go."

"I hear Siberia's nice. It's better than living with a loser."

"She has those two little girls."

"Yeah, and she shouldn't have had kids with a drunk," I said. "He didn't have a job when she married the thing." I looked up and stared at her. "Women shouldn't produce kids with bums, you know that. You're married to the king of the bums."

She took the cigarette from her mouth. "Well, what was I supposed to do with all y'all? I couldn't leave."

"Why not?"

"I don't got an education. I woulda had to get a job. Who woulda kept y'all while I worked?"

"We'd have been better off alone with a gas stove leaking in a slum area of a war zone than with him."

"You're crazy," she mumbled. "Wiley, don't roll your boogers, baby."

"I wonder why." I grasped my side.

She gave me the motherly eye. "Is it your stomach?"

"Just a cramp. I'm usually over them by now," I moaned.

"If your side's hurtin', it could be somethin' else."

"It's my uterus, Mama."

"You've had pain in your side a long time. I believe you'll eventually have chronic appendicitis."

"I didn't know you were psychic and could predict ailments."

CHAPTER SIX

Back at UEM, Marge wasn't in the room. Seeing a man, a handsome Irish stallion, lying across my bed was inconceivable. I was nervous when I escorted Peter up, but his free and easy nature somehow calmed me.

"I like Manilow's music," he said. "Which song is that? "Mandy"? I like that." He patted my bed. "Want to sit?"

I hadn't moved from the same standing position for ten minutes. He sat up and leaned against my wall.

"Where's your roommate?"

"Probably in her boyfriend's room," I answered.

I became unsettled when I heard Suzy coming in from her weekend at home. I didn't want to share him with her. I stayed quiet, as if I'd heard nothing. He was checking out my side of the room.

"You must've left a lot of stuff at home."

"I did," I said. "I have too much junk."

"What's there to do in Soso?"

"Nothing, I mean, Hattiesburg has more things to do, because of UEM being here," I answered.

"Want to see *The Rocky Horror Picture Show*? It's playing on campus Halloween night."

"Sure," I smiled.

"It gets pretty wild in the auditorium."

"That's okay. I need the excitement."

He smiled playfully and kissed my cheek. I didn't want the sensation of him being here to ever leave me. His jeans were faded, the knees worn, and his tennis shoes dirty. I adored this guy.

A recognizable knock. Denise was back.

"Guess I'll see who it is," I said.

He stood with me and squeezed my arm. "Tell whoever it is that we have something to do."

Denise's astonished expression told me how pleased she was. "Am I interruptin'?"

"No. We were just about to head out for a walk," I said.

Suzy wasn't far behind when she spotted us in the hall. Peter, by my side, broke out into joking.

"Here she comes, Miss America . . . ."

"Shut up," Suzy laughed. "I told you Miss Mississippi would win."

"She did?" I asked.

"Yeah. Susan Akin from Meridian won. Peter said Miss Texas was goin' to win."

"Well, I was close," he grinned. "Miss Mississippi's cool." He nudged me.

"Are you and the guys sittin' with us for homecomin' or what?" Suzy asked.

"I'm sitting with Annie," Peter answered.

Suzy was all teeth now, as she looked at me, my shoulder secured by Peter's arm. Denise's eyes were delighted.

"So," Suzy spoke, her voice raised up about an octave. "You're takin' Annie. Good. We'll see y'all there."

"I have to go unpack, so you two can do your walk," Denise smiled.

"A walk? That's great." Suzy was going to rupture if we didn't leave soon. I'd be accosted later.

"We'll see you later," I said.

"Call me." Her hand firmly held my forearm, and I had to pry loose. They went off down the hall. Denise followed her into her room, and the door closed while we stood at the elevator.

I wasn't going home on weekends any longer. Around campus I was known as Peter's girlfriend. People were speaking to me, people

I didn't even know. I was in a beautiful dream. So afraid that I would wake up, and it would turn out to be an unfulfilled dream, like the others. Dreams of having money. Dreams of living in the mountains. Dreams of having a brick house with central air and heat, and without Daddy.

Mama and Daddy weren't smart enough to be suspicious that I had a boyfriend. But there was Henry. He was the perceptive one, and he wasn't even blood kin. He phoned me every week. How much was in my checking account, he'd ask. How were my grades? How much did I weigh? Why did I sound nervous? When would I be coming home? I told him I had to study harder, which wasn't a lie. I just didn't tell him that I was going bowling, to football games, and eating out with Peter. Henry said he understood that I had to study hard, and that I needed the peace of my dorm room. But he'd still like to see me sometime. There were holiday breaks coming up, I'd repeat to him, and he'd let me go. A letter was in my box a couple of days later. He and Pearl were thinking about me, it said. Would I be home the upcoming weekend, he wanted to know, so he could plan. *I won't feel guilty Pop. I deserve my own life.*

I had entered into a contract with Henry Price. The day I let him give me money was the day I gave away a part of my life. Mama and Daddy did this to me, I thought. Why did I have parents like them? Suzy had normal folks. Denise's mom didn't smoke and actually drove two and a half hours from the coast to take her to dinner and see if she needed anything. I was too afraid to break off with the Prices. I loved Pearl. I couldn't tell this to Peter, and going home on weekends to see my family and the Prices was tugging at me again. Peter's life was full of friends and activities. His parents sent him money twice a month. I couldn't tell him about my parents. I wouldn't tell my parents about him.

"You can't go home," Peter said.

"Well, my mom—" I tried to explain.

"Nah, won't let you do it." He hugged me close.

"But I have to—"

He pulled away. "We're going to the game on Saturday and out with the gang. You don't want to upset the guys."

"No, I don't. It's just—"

He rubbed my face. "And you said you might, you know, stay over."

"Stay over?" I asked.

"In my room."

"Well," I stuttered. "I don't want to get into trouble."

"I'm the head guy. You won't get into trouble."

I stayed quiet as I sat on his couch.

"I'd never let anything happen to my redheaded babe," he said softly.

On a freezing Wednesday night, I received the second call of the semester from Mama.

"We hadn't heard from you. You comin' home soon?"

"I won't be home this weekend. I have way too much to do," I told her.

She paused. "Can you help us move Friday?"

"Oh, God," I groaned. "I'll have to come by in the afternoon. I can only help move a few things, because I really have a lot to do. That's why I'm here, to study."

"I can't depend on Gloria or anybody."

"None of my stuff's there. It's mostly Gloria and Holly's junk. Make her help out."

"I told her she had to help."

"Christ, can't anybody do anything? Did Daddy spray the house on Fourteenth for roaches yet?"

"Said he was gonna do it in a couple of days. I'll have to threaten him."

"That new house is horrible. It's the worst one."

"I know, Annie, but that's all we can afford right now. Daddy promised the landlord he'd keep it up."

"Oh, yeah, right. Like he did the last three that kicked us out. The landlord's getting the best deal for that hut."

"Well, when you don't have the money . . ."

"You make your husband get a job, or you leave the jerk," I snapped. "Don't start with the poor people nonsense. I can't take it."

"Is it time for your period?"

"No."

"Well, you sound like it."

"I'm under stress. College is hard. I need to do well."

"Well, it ain't worth it if it makes your health bad. Shit on that."

"I'm healthy. I just get tired from time to time."

She was lighting another cigarette.

"How's Trudy? Are y'all feeding her?"

"I feed her when I come in from work."

"Let me know if she needs any more dog food."

"She still has a lot left from that other bag you bought her. I give her scraps when we have 'em. Did I tell ya about Dessie Reagan's daughter?"

I rubbed my forehead. "I don't think so."

"She's been havin' grand mal seizures outta this world."

"I don't know her."

"The medicine costs over five hundred dollars a month. They're havin' such a time."

"I'm sure she gets Medicaid or something."

"I think she does, but that's a hard thing to have to live with."

"There are worse things."

I met Thomas Barnes at Peter's Saturday night appreciation party for his resident assistants. Thomas was the guy Peter always envied. The guy who sprinted faster, climbed harder, and outlasted anyone on a bicycle.

"So, you're Annie," he smiled.

He was strikingly handsome, which I had noticed in the hallways of the business building whenever I passed him. He ran his fingers through his thick black hair, his dark brown eyes still on my face. He was reaching to shake my hand.

"I'm glad to meet you," he said.

I nodded. Thomas seemed to have no accent, his voice smooth and smart. I'd be in trouble if I said too much.

"You're in accounting, I take it," he said. "I see you going into Dr. Sales' eight o'clock class."

"Yes, Accounting 301," I nodded.

"He's a great professor."

"Yuck," I moaned.

"So, he's a bit of an ass," he chuckled.

"Here's your Diet Coke," Peter said as he handed me a cup.

"How many miles today?" I asked.

"Seventy-five," Thomas answered.

"God, I wouldn't be able to walk," I said.

"You get used to it. Hey, Peter said you might be going out with us."

"Hold on," Peter said. "She's going to ride with me awhile before she rides with the gang."

"Can't I just stick to my walking?" I joked.

"Oops, got to change the music," Peter said. "Be right back."

Peter pushed his way across the room to his stereo. I couldn't move from my spot, so I smiled at Thomas, who wasn't moving either.

"Peter told me you're from Soso."

"Yes," I answered.

"I've been a couple of times when my dad's been down there on business," he said. "Nice town."

"Yeah."

"So, what do your folks do?"

"Oh, um, my dad's a builder. Mom's a bookkeeper."

"What kind of construction does he do?"

"Who?"

"Your dad."

"Oh, uh, lousy."

"How many siblings?"

"Four sisters."

"That's a lot of sisters. I have an older sister."

"One's enough," I said.

Peter walked me back to my dorm at two in the morning. Everything I thought I'd never do for a guy I was doing to accommodate him. I had been getting up early on the weekends to work on my homework, so I could see him in the evenings. I had eight o'clock classes during the week, but I waited up at night for his calls. Yawning as he cracked jokes, I pretended I was wide awake and studying. If Peter ate dinner at six, I waited until six, even when I was starving. I was taking extra showers and reapplying my makeup just to take late-night strolls around the campus with him. And I still wasn't going home on the weekends, and the guilt was eating at me.

Peter had backed off about me spending the night in his room, and I believed he knew. How could he not sense that I was a virgin? I'd never give it up until I married. Someone spectacular was going to come into my life and love me for being strong. And I was beginning to think it was Peter. He was sending me cards and notes just to let me know how "special" I was to him. He was everything I wasn't, and I didn't feel real any longer. My dreams were fading in the background, and Peter had become more important than anything. He was boundless energy, filled with enthusiasm, and I wanted to feel that way. Every Sunday night, Denise knocked on my door to be updated on my weekend. Something in her had loosened up, and I was spilling my deepest feelings about Peter, while she sat on my bed, taking in every word.

The following Friday night, Peter took me to see a movie, then to a Mexican restaurant. Back in his room, he locked the door and cut out the lights. We stood watching each other, and I went to him. We kissed while standing, then we fell on the sofa. He whispered in my ear. "What are you doing over Thanksgiving?"

"Oh . . . we're having company. What about you?"

He sat up. "Oh. Well, Tony invited me up to Jackson. I'm going up there, I guess."

He was disappointed, and I should have sensed that he expected to be invited home with me. But picturing my home made me do some fast-talking and fibbing.

"My aunt and uncle are coming from out of state. They stay with us every year," I said. "They refuse to get a hotel room. Won't you go home?"

"Nah. I'll go home at Christmas. I don't want to drive to Austin, then have to drive back."

"I understand. I hate having company." I was thinking up more lies. "We'll probably have twenty people staying in our house, with my cousins and all."

"Thomas lives in Jackson, so I'm going to ride with him. He invited a group of us over to his house on Saturday."

"That's great," I said. I was almost caving in.

He pulled me close. "I'm going to miss my redheaded babe."

"I'll miss you, too."

"I love you," he said tenderly.

Later that night, when I went back to my room, I realized I had arrived on the fifth floor with no memory of pushing the buttons or riding the elevator. The hall looked different. The moldy air now smelled luscious. Was it four or five times he said he loved me, and how many times did I tell him? Over and over, I played his words in my mind, milking out every syllable. I was in love with every inch of him. But Jesus, I was scared to death. How could I tell him that my family was totally insane? How could I tell him that he could never come home with me? I certainly couldn't introduce him to the

Prices. It would devastate Henry, and he'd accuse me of wasting my time and his money. He'd think I was sleeping around. All I could think of were his stories about the "type" of women he could tell weren't virtuous. Of course, he knew the women before he met Pearl, he said, so I guess he wasn't too wholesome himself. "You know, honey, a man can just tell these things." *Pop must have sampled the merchandise.*

A month earlier, I had helped Mama and Daddy move on a Friday afternoon. It was a nightmare. Boxes were half-packed, and Daddy hardly lifted a thing, causing Mama, Gloria, and me to do the heavy toting. Moving ugly junk to an ugly house overrun with roaches wasn't my idea of living. And I had to lie to Peter and tell him I had a doctor's appointment back home, with him asking if he could take me. So, I told him another lie to keep him from taking me. Then I lied to my parents and told them I had to be back Friday evening to work on a project, so that I could see Peter that night. My hands were so cut up and my body so messed up that I was afraid he'd catch me coming back to my dorm before I could take a shower. No, he'd never see my home. I was sure his best friend, Tony, lived in a nice house, and that made me happy for Peter's sake. Ed was going home over the Thanksgiving break with Marge. I'd met her parents once, and I knew her house was clean. One certainly didn't need much money to take care of what little they had.

Chapter Seven

My car seemed to rattle more the closer I got to Soso. I was elated to have a break from school, yet I was awfully troubled. It wasn't just facing another dump for a house. It was having to endure Thanksgiving lunch with the Prices. I knew I'd be drained by the indirect suggestions, the profound stares, the questions, the carping remarks. I didn't want any of it.

West Soso. Not an area he'd live in, Daddy used to say. Full of drug-heads, punks, and bums. The slums. Wooden roach traps were surrounded by overgrown weeds and bushes, with trash and beaten-up garbage cans in the streets and yards, and exhausted appliances sitting on the porches.

My stomach churned as I neared the corner of Chester Drive and Fourteenth Avenue. The house stood on blocks. The yellow paint was peeling, and most had come off. The front yard was sand and rocks with massive roots from an oak tree protruding through the hardened ground. Even the weeds refused to live there. I parked by Daddy's truck and took out my paper sack of clean clothes. Wiley and Holly ran out the front door onto the rotted porch. "Aunt Annie!" Holly screamed. Hugging my legs, they both held on as if they never wanted me to leave. *Hush up, I can't save you, little girls. I can't save anyone.* There was no escape from seeing their dirty and despairing faces.

Trudy's barking alarmed the Reverend, who stood at the ragged screen door, smiling.

"Hey, baby. Glad you got here. Mama and I was gettin' worried. You need to call us next time before you leave."

"I didn't have time. I had to work all afternoon."

"Guess what we got?"

"What?"

"A turkey. Gloria's boss man gave her one. It sure is pretty. It's eighteen pounds."

Again someone had taken pity. Didn't Daddy's gut give away his lack of starvation? Mama hollered from the kitchen. "Is that Annie, Daddy?"

He went inside, tromping over the trash and sand on the floor. "Yeah, she's out there pettin' that stinkin' dog. I hope she washes her hands."

The television boomed with gunshots and screams. A putrid stench nearly overwhelmed me. Daddy's underarm aroma was atrocious, but this was something else. I dropped my bag and held my breath as long as I could.

The boxes hadn't been unpacked, and they had been living out of them. What did they do with their time? I was thanking God, the angels, the heavens, and Mother Teresa that I didn't bring Peter home.

"What's that smell?"

En route to the bathroom, I tripped over a mangled box containing Mama's whatnots. The bathtub was an older model, and the shower plumbing was missing, leaving only a hole in the wall. The white linoleum was torn in places and rusted in others.

There was nowhere for me to sleep but in Mama's room, and it looked like it had been bombed. I put my bag and purse on top of her dresser and went to the kitchen. Mama took a pair of pliers, clenched her teeth, and turned on the cold water to rinse the dishes.

"Mama, what's that smell?"

"Last renter was an old lady with a slew of cats. If I'd known that, I wouldn't have moved in here."

"I think some of the cats died in this joint."

"Well, Daddy said the old lady died here."

"And he moved us on in."

"Well, hell, Annie, I didn't know. He didn't either, until Mr. Patel told him after we were already in. The house shouldn't stink. I mopped it good before we moved in."

"You mopped?"

"Yeah, Clarie helped me."

"Maybe something croaked under the house."

"You shoulda seen the rat shit I found on the shelves. Spent over twenty dollars on shelf paper."

"Rats?"

"Rats, roaches, termites."

"God. Are you working tomorrow?"

"Yeah, I get off at three."

"Who's going to cook Thanksgiving dinner? Not Daddy."

"Oh, I'll have to when I get in. He ain't gonna do a damn thing. He promised he'd put on the turkey. Hope the big bastard's thawed out by then."

"What about Gloria?"

"She has to work 'til seven."

"Great. I hope he doesn't burn the bird."

The garbage can was sticky with grease. I snatched a crumpled rag off the stove and began the wipe-down.

"You eatin' lunch with the Prices, aren't you?"

"Unfortunately."

"They look forward to seein' you."

"Oh please, don't feel sorry for them. Henry'll be fine after he belittles me."

"He don't mean anythin' by it, Annie. He's just interested in your college. He's lonely, with Pearl bein' sick."

"He should get a hobby."

"They're takin' you to a nice restaurant. Who wants to cook? I sure as hell don't."

"I just want to relax and be home. Not be interrogated over my weight, my grades, or my hair."

"He's just an old man. You know how old people are," Mama said.

Daddy heard the Prices' name and hurried to the kitchen. "You need to go see those Prices."

"I am," I snapped.

"Those old people are good to you," he continued.

"Please, I'm not stupid."

"They probably think we're a bunch of bums," he said, as he leaned against the sink near Mama. "Mama, you want me to make giblet gravy tomorrow?"

She sighed. "I don't care, Burl. No one eats it but you."

"Don't make gravy, Daddy, please," I begged.

"I think Mooney likes it," he said.

I perked up. "Aunt Mooney's coming?"

"Yeah, her and Tish," Mama said.

"How's Tish doing?" I asked.

"Better. She's goin' back to the doctor's next week."

"Yeah, that ole Tish is big," Daddy said, with his potbelly hanging out. "I saw her and Mooney at the grocery store the other day, and I didn't even recognize her, she's gotten so fat."

"Poor thing can't stop gainin' weight," said Mama with a cigarette hanging out of her mouth.

"She sure has. She must weigh close to three hundred pounds. She's a big thing," Daddy said.

"I think somethin's wrong with her, and those crazy doctors don't know what it is," Mama said.

"Aunt Mooney's heavy, too. And Tish sits around eating all day," I said.

"Well, she's depressed."

"Aren't we all. She needs to go to school or get a job so she can stay busy. Aunt Mooney spoils her."

"That's her only child. She loves her to death. They only have each other."

"I know, Mama, but Aunt Mooney's not helping by babying her. I know she's been upset since Uncle Melvin left, but she needs to go on and live her life."

"She said Melvin called and talked to Tish the other night and upset her so bad she cried. It's hard when your father marries someone else, especially someone so young," Mama said.

I sighed, wishing Daddy would run off with anyone, even a man.

He asked, "How old you reckon his wife is?"

"Twenty-eight, maybe," said Mama. "Melvin's always had his radar on for younger gals. Pervert."

"How old's Tish now?" Daddy asked.

"Twenty."

Uncle Melvin left Aunt Mooney when Tish was sixteen. I had never seen anyone so devastated as Mooney was when she lost the love of her life. Mama, however, prayed Daddy would walk out on her.

"I hope you'll fix the faucet," I said.

"Shit, I've waited all week," said Mama.

"I'll fix it. I have to go get a part for it," Daddy said as he rubbed his neck.

She scowled at him and threw a hand towel against the sink. You'd think he'd leave town and never come back, with the death looks she gave him.

"I'll cut up the onion and celery for the dressing," I said. I opened the refrigerator. It was barren, except for a few sticks of margarine and a saucer with a shriveled-up piece of meat and gravy stuck to it. "Do we have any eggs?"

"Mama and me are gonna get some tonight," Daddy grinned, as he pinched Mama's side.

"Quit, Burl! I'm gonna knock the shit outta you," she snapped. "I told ya to get the stuff while you were out burnin' up the roads today."

"Well, I didn't know what we needed."

"Hell, look in the 'frigerator."

"I wish someone woulda given us a ham. I like it better than turkey," he said. "I may price some at the store."

"Turkey's fine with me," I said.

"Shit, I ain't studyin' ham. Ain't studying nothin'. We need some groceries," said Mama.

"Well, write a list," he said. Leaning against the counter, he said faintly, "Mama, I ain't got much money."

"Hell, Burl, I don't either! You're not satisfied until I spend every fuckin' dime I have!"

"I have five dollars," I said. "That'll buy a few things. Are we out of cornmeal?"

She blew a puff of smoke and scratched her forehead. "I have a little bit, I think."

"What's Mooney bringin'?"

"I don't know, Burl. I thought you had some money comin' from Snookie Bush."

"I do have some moolah comin', but she don't get paid until next Wednesday."

"That don't help us now, does it. Too afraid to ask people to pay you."

"Oh, me," he said. He reached over and picked up a bottle of antacid and swigged it like water.

"Have you've heard about Vera's cousin's friend, Nicole?"

"No, I don't know Nicole, Mama," I answered in a tired voice. Her stories were tedious.

"She got hit by a chicken truck the other day. It hit her so hard it knocked the pins right out of her hair. Totaled her car and put her in a neck brace. It's been on the news."

"I don't know the girl."

"They oughta outlaw those trucks," Daddy added. "That's how I got that crack in my windshield."

"We know."

"Her Mama's been so worried about her. Poor girl just bought the car," Mama continued.

At seven o'clock, Mama and the kids rode with Daddy to the Piggly Wiggly. She got him off the ham patrol by making a run through Kentucky Fried Chicken. I guess she made some overtime, and having to use it for food put her in a foul mood. She'd face a firing squad before she'd let him see her pay stub, but Daddy knew.

My plans were to stay up late and cut up the onion, celery, and bell pepper to save time tomorrow. I walked to the dining room to clean. I didn't know where to start. Smudgy walls and threadbare curtains were all around, taunting me. Boxes were everywhere. Where would I put the junk? I voted to keep it boxed and burn it later. At home, a holiday was just another agonizing day. No merriment, since Daddy was usually watching a football game and pouting because his team was losing. No love, since everyone wanted to strangle him. One big meal, which was hell to cook, and listening to Mama bitch about having to cook. Then, it was eaten up in five minutes, and we were scrounging for food every other day of the year. The house was appalling, yet I'd rather be here than see Henry Price. I was beginning to resent him as much as Daddy. Tears welled in my eyes as I ran my hands through my hair. So what if I got a free meal. I'd rather drink water and be left alone with my thoughts.

Henry sulked for forty-five minutes. The ride to Shoney's was solemn and demoralizing. I didn't attempt to make conversation. I was dumbfounded. I had answered his letters and received his phone calls. Nothing had forewarned me of this behavior.

"We wish you'd come home once in a while," he spoke harshly. Pearl was staring blankly out the car window. She was onto him, I was sure, because she spoke with caution. He responded to her in a dejected voice. He looked at me as if I'd betrayed him. He had better get used to it. I was in love. But I was uneasy that he had caused Pearl to be upset with me.

At Shoney's, Henry gave the waitresses his spiritual attention. The sudden humbleness of his voice irked me until my emotions were raw. He and Daddy should win Academy Awards. Removing his hat, he pulled me ahead of him like a chastised child. We sat down. The place was swarming. Before he opened the menu, his eyes darted about to see if he knew anyone, his posture such that he was ready to vault and shake a hand in an instant. My heart was thumping a hundred miles a minute.

"Uh, Annie, get what you want now," he said.

"All right," I answered. I opened the menu, knowing I would order the baked chicken. Forget the turkey and dressing special.

"Get the turkey and dressing, you hear?"

"All right," I said, glad to oblige.

We ate in silence, while people at other tables laughed and enjoyed the meal. Henry was looking around the restaurant, more so today. He was punishing me, I thought. I could have easily told him a number of things going on at college and in my life, but I refused to. Let him pout. He sluggishly began to ease up. *Am I forgiven now?* I forced myself to smile, loathing him each solid second. *You won't make me feel guilty, old man. I didn't ask for help. I came to you for encouragement. How did we get this far?*

"Uh, honey, you want some pumpkin pie?"

"Yes," I answered, as I wiped my mouth.

"I think I'll let Mom have a piece today."

We got to Shoney's at eleven. It was a quarter of two when we puttered back into their driveway. I plunked down on their couch, with my mind working on a departure excuse. Henry was preparing his inquisition as he hastily opened the window blinds.

"I think I'll let a little sun in."

Pearl stumbled out of the bathroom, and he grabbed her shoulders. "Sweetheart, are you tired?"

"A little," she said sadly.

"Why don't you take off your dress and take a nap, you hear?"

"I think I'll do that."

"I'll visit with Annie. She understands."

As soon as he sat in his recliner, he was in full swing. "I sent Mom to bed. She seems to be getting worse and worse. Some days she has to go back to bed after breakfast."

I said nothing.

"When do you think you'll be home again?"

"Probably not until Christmas. Exams are coming up, and I have to get ready."

He nodded. "Annie, you never tell us about your church."

"What?"

"Who's the pastor at First Baptist in Hattiesburg now?"

"Oh, um, Dr. Brian Sharpe."

I hadn't been in months, and actually only twice, with Denise. And if it weren't for her, I don't know if I would have gone at all. His brow was furrowed while his fingers tapped his head. *Oh, Jesus, how long is this going to take?*

"I don't think I ever met Brother Sharpe. We knew Dr. Ralph Jones when he was there. Oh, what a good preacher he was. Let me see if I can remember. He transferred to a church in Dallas. First Baptist Church of Dallas. Great preacher, yes he was. Occasionally our church would go down for conventions. One Sunday during the morning worship, Brother Jones asked me to come up and lead the congregation in prayer. I was so surprised. Who was I, I mean, I was a little ole Sunday school teacher. He could've called one of his deacons or one of the important members of the church, but he called me. He's a great man. I'll have to write him sometime."

"That was nice of him to do that."

"It sure was. Pearl and his wife Gayle became close friends. When Pearl got sick, Gayle came up to see us. What a lovely woman." He turned his head sideways and grinned. "I'm so happy you're going to a good church. It's so important. And how's your friend Denise? I'd still like to write her sometime."

I had forgotten to bring her address. "Oh, sorry. I'll ask her for her address when I get back."

"How's your folks doing? How's the house?"

"Everything's fine."

"The other day I was coming from the bank, and I drove by there. Needs some work, doesn't it?"

"Lots of work."

"Let me see, the address is . . ." He snapped his fingers, "Oh, it's one forty-four South Fourteenth Avenue?"

"Yes."

"Do you have the same phone number?"

"Yes, sir."

"Good. Is the rent reasonable?"

"I guess. I don't really know."

"What were they paying at the last place?"

"I . . . I think two hundred a month."

"Surely they don't pay that much for this house," he grimaced.

"Pop, I don't know. I haven't been home in weeks."

"Oh, I know, honey." What he was looking for, I couldn't imagine. Maybe he thought I was helping them with their rent. I almost started the explanations when he continued. "Aren't you happy that we decided you should live in the dorm. Not that I'm putting your parents down, but you don't want to be involved in all that. How could you concentrate on your studies, having to move from one place to the next?"

"Yes, sir."

"Now why did they move from the place in the country? You never told me."

"Yes, I did."

He adjusted his hearing aid as if that was the cause of his forgetfulness. "Oh, did you? Haven't seen you in so long . . ."

"Mr. Kelley, the landlord, is selling it."

"Oh, I see. Well, that's understandable. Too bad Burl had the bankruptcy and lost the house on Third. I begged your Mama not to let him do it."

"I know."

"But they didn't listen," he scoffed, as if he wanted to ring Mama's neck for having the nerve to disobey him.

"Hey, I know what I wanted to talk to you about. Mom and I

would love it if you could go to church with us some Sunday. We never go anymore. I miss it, you know. I'm hungry for some spiritual feeding."

I stared into Henry's cloudy eyes and thought how much he'd adore Denise. She was thin as a rail, beautiful, frugal, and a regular churchgoer. What would Pop think if I told him I had been to Catholic mass with Peter?

When I left, I was wiped out, but I had promised Mama I'd help with our Thanksgiving supper.

The afternoon was gray with clouds, and Trudy began to bark. My cousin Tish opened the car door and grunted as she got out of the black Trans Am. Her cowlicked bangs pointed east, and the rest of her frosted hair was stiffened with hairspray. Her eyelashes were spider legs, and her blush two pink splotches. She avoided Trudy's greeting as if the dog were diseased.

"Come here, Trudy," I said.

Looking frustrated and tired, Aunt Mooney waddled out of the driver's seat. "Tish, honey, you have to help me with the food, now."

Tish stopped walking, sighed heavily, and stomped back to the Trans Am. Mooney handed her a coconut cake. I crossed the front porch and stepped into the sand.

"Hey, y'all. Need any help?"

"Hey, Annie. Can you grab this bag? Ooh, you look so thin."

"Thanks. Still walking." I carried the bag up the steps.

"You see how thin Annie is, Tish?"

"Yeah," she muttered, and handed me the cake to hold with my other arm.

"Aunt Mooney, this cake's beautiful. Did you make it?" I asked.

"Yeah. I had a time. I think my oven's goin' out. Tish wouldn't lift a finger to help me."

"You didn't ask me," she sassed.

"The cake's so pretty," Mama said. She held the screen door open.

"Hey, Penny!" said Mooney. Trudy was eagerly wagging her tail. "Well, hello, Miss Trudy. What are you so happy about? She looks so shiny. Annie musta given her a bath."

"She got her dipped a few weeks ago. She loves that dog," Mama said. "She gets fatter when Annie's around."

Bending down, Mooney baby-talked her. "Well, Trudy and I love our midnight snacks, don't we?"

Mama hugged Tish. "You look so pretty today."

Her pout faded away. "Thanks, Aunt Penny."

"There's my favorite pretty niece," Daddy grinned.

"Hey, Uncle Burl," she said distantly.

While our food simmered in burned-up pots and pans, Aunt Mooney's was presented in shiny nonstick pots with handles and Corning Ware. I arranged the cake, squash casserole, lima beans, and green salad on the table. I was proud to have it, as well as the three bottles of salad dressing and the several kinds of soft drinks Mooney had brought. Tish looked around the living room for somewhere to sit. She turned up her nose at the worn-out couch, and I didn't blame her. I had cleaned the house the night before, having stacked the boxes in the kids' room. I doused Lysol over as many surfaces as I could, to get rid of the grease-pit aroma and dead cat smell. She parked herself in the corner chair near Daddy, even though she didn't want to talk to him.

He leaned over, grinned, and said, "I bet Tish has been gettin' sugar from Joe."

"Leave me alone, Uncle Burl."

Joe was an old bum who lived down the road from Mooney's house in the town of Pendorf. Tish hated him.

"I think Tish is premenstrual. She's been drivin' me crazy all week," Mooney said.

"I know how she feels," I said.

"Nothin' satisfies her. I took her shoppin' for clothes yesterday, 'cause she can't wear anythin' in her closet. I hope she'll quit gainin' weight. Lord."

"Her clothes are nice," I said.

"Well, she wanted me to buy her a diamond necklace. I told her to wait for her birthday."

"Aunt Mooney, I don't think Tish needs to worry about jewelry right now."

"Oh, I know. We have to get her well. I wish those doctors could find out what's wrong with her."

"Ha! Not the quacks around here. You're shit out of luck if you're sick in this town," said Mama.

I waited by the oven to pull the dinner rolls out. I'd baked four packs, hoping that would be enough, since Daddy alone could wipe out a dozen in minutes.

My sisters, Clarie and Jessie, arrived at the same time with their husbands. Each had casseroles in their hands. Their husbands had pies in theirs.

"Where's Annie?" Clarie asked, as she walked in the front door.

"I'm in the kitchen." I came out with a dish towel in my hand.

Clarie was nineteen. The youngest for ten years until Wiley came along. She was short and stocky, with thick auburn hair cut in a page-boy style. She was a waitress at the Western Sizzler. Her husband Bill ran an auto parts store.

Jessie's husband Keith didn't talk much unless he had a few beers in him. He and Jessie lived in a trailer on his family's property. His parents owned a good bit of land with gardens and chicken houses on it. Jessie was twenty-one and the smallest of us older girls. She was just four-foot-eleven, one hundred pounds. With brunette hair, she favored Mama more than any of us. She and Keith worked on an assembly line at a factory in Ellisville.

"Sit down. Make yourself to home," Daddy said.

"You look so good," Jessie said.

"I feel pretty good," I smiled.

"Hey, Tish." Clarie walked over to hug her. Jessie followed.

Clarie and I walked to the kitchen with the food. She grabbed my arm and whispered, "Ain't Tish huge?"

"I was shocked seeing her," I said.

"God, I'm shocked, too."

"Yeah, Burl. I cleared about a thousand dollars' worth of merchandise last weekend," Bill bragged. He grabbed an ashtray and set it on his lap.

"Is that right?"

"Sure did. I had the biggest commission check in October."

Aunt Mooney came out of the bathroom, went to hug Clarie in the kitchen, then went to the living room to hug Jessie and the husbands. "Jessie, you stay so little, so does Keith. What do you two eat?"

"I can see that Tish has some more new clothes. She never does without, does she?" Clarie said sarcastically.

I lifted what was left of a large spoon out of the drawer.

"I guess Daddy's been cooking a lot," I commented.

"He melted my colander the other day," Mama whined.

As quietly as possible, Clarie and I went about fixing Wiley and Holly's plates. We put them in the back bedroom to dine, for safety purposes. The Reverend could knock down a bulldozer to get at food.

"Everythin's ready. Y'all come eat," Mama said.

"Y'all come on now and eat. Me and Tish'll leave a little food for the rest of you," Daddy joked.

"Leave me alone. Aunt Penny!" Tish hollered as she stood up, looking defiant. Keith and Bill laughed.

"Burl, quit teasin' her. She's sick," Mama scolded.

"I'm just pickin', Mama. Tish knows her uncle loves her," he said.

"Tish, come fix yourself a plate," Aunt Mooney told her in baby talk. "You wanna turkey leg?"

"Sure, if no one else wants it."

I leaned against the sink with a glass of iced tea in my hand. The food smelled heavenly, but I wanted to wait until everyone had something. There was a hole in the floor by the back door where one could look under the house. I just couldn't imagine Peter seeing this place. Clarie eased beside me. "Look over by the stove."

A cockroach was slowly creeping across the floor.

"Not another one," I moaned, as goosebumps popped up on my arms.

Clarie squashed it with her shoe, then swept it out the back door before anyone took notice.

"Annie, I'm glad you made your potato salad. I've been cravin' it," Mooney said. "No one makes it as good as you. I try and try, and it never tastes right."

"I love that blouse, Aunt Mooney," Clarie said.

She looked down and chuckled, "Thanks, it's old."

"It looks good with your black hair," I said.

"Yeah, it brings out my eyes, too. We stopped by the Piggy Wiggly on our way over here and the produce manager told me I look just like Elizabeth Taylor."

"He's a drunk," Tish said hatefully.

"No, he's not. He goes to that church over in Richton. You just forget about the diamond necklace, Miss Smart Ass."

The last of the women straggled in for a plate. In the living room, Daddy was scooping steaming food right into his mouth.

"He eats like he's havin' sex," Jessie said. Daddy ate with gusto.

"Shit," said Mama.

With a plateful in his lap, Bill mumbled to Keith, "Damn. I ain't ever seen anyone eat as much as Burl. He can pack it away. He and Tish need to join Overeaters Anonymous."

Mooney and Mama escaped to her bedroom. Thankfully, she had picked it up the night before. Still, clothes were piled on top of her dresser, and boxes were stacked against the closet door. I joined them, while my sisters stayed in the living room to eat with their husbands.

The pity party began when Mooney whined, "We went to the Social Security office, but I don't think they're gonna approve Tish for disability."

"They might, with you bein' on it. Burl ain't hurt a word from 'em about his bad back," Mama chimed in.

"Why does Tish need disability?" I asked.

"For her depression," Mama said.

"She's had such a struggle lately," Mooney said. "I pray she hasn't inherited it from me."

"Maybe she should try to go to college. I know she can get financial aid like I do," I said.

"Well, hon', Tish has a learnin' disability."

"They have developmental classes she can take. And she can get a tutor."

Tish walked in carrying her seconds. "I hate school."

"Look, Tish, I was afraid of college math. So, I took a developmental math class, and it helped me a lot. I made an A in college algebra."

"I hate school."

"Annie, Tish isn't as strong as you. Ever since her sorry Daddy walked out on us, she hasn't been the same."

We should all be so lucky.

"Annie, Tish has physical problems," Mama scolded.

"Mama, she's a young woman. Quit writing her off like she has one foot in the grave."

"I'm not. But when you have physical problems, it can affect you mentally."

"She can't roll over and give up and live on disability the rest of her life. She's only twenty years old. Tish, what do you want to do with your life?"

"I don't know," she said with no emotion.

"Oh, Lord. I wish she'd go to secretarial school or anythin'," Mooney said. She stared up at the ceiling as if she wanted to pray.

"Yes. That's better than nothing. It'd be a big help to you, too, Aunt Mooney," I said.

Mooney already had other things on her mind. "Annie, are there many blacks at your college?"

"Yeah, blacks, Asians, whites. Why?"

"Be careful. Black men love to rub against butts. One rubbed against mine the other day."

"Mama, please," Tish whined.

"It's true."

"I'd be careful around that school," Mama said.

"I'll try not to drink too much and walk around in the nude," I said.

"Dr. Vincent was so ugly to Tish the other day about her weight," Aunt Mooney said.

"I hate that old Dr. Vincent," said Mama.

"Aunt Penny, he told me I had to lose weight," said Tish. "He said I was too fat, and it wasn't from my thyroid. It was my eatin'. He said I was gonna blow up, and no man would look at me. I wanna get married some day."

"Guys are the least of your worries," I said.

"I wanna get married. Not all of us can be skinny and go to college."

"That's a lie and an excuse. You have plenty of ways to better your life. You have to want to do it."

Mama muddled, "I still think it's somethin' physical."

"Dr. Vincent stared at my cleavage while I—"

"No he didn't, Mama," Tish said to Mooney.

"Yes, he did. He couldn't keep his eyes off me. I was pure sweatin' in his office. Those deep blue eyes . . ."

"He wasn't lookin' at you. He was talkin' to me about my health. Why would he be lookin' at you?"

"He did stare at me, Miss Smarty Pants."

"Did he find anythin' wrong with Tish?" Mama asked.

"He said she was too fat. Then he proceeded to get on me for buyin' her Twinkies and candy bars. He said I should throw her television out the window. Shouldn't have wasted my money takin' her to him."

"I'm gettin' some more potato salad," Tish said.

Daddy barreled in behind her for his third plate. "Baby, you want some more lima beans?"

"I guess. Thanks, Uncle Burl," she said.

"It'll make you grow hair on your chest."

My hands were scorched by the running hot water as I scrubbed on the Dutch oven. I was too impatient to let it soak. Outside was cold, but the kitchen was toasty from cooking. As with every house we ever lived in, there was no decent ventilation. There was never central air or heat. Daddy's idea of cooling the house during the dreadfully humid Mississippi summers was to slap a fan in a window. His idea of insulation was to patch the broken windowpanes with duct tape.

Above the sink, I squinted through the smoky window and saw a small portion of the sky and the stars. Mostly what I saw was the house next door. It was in the same horrid shape as ours, except the yard had grass. Perhaps I had been dreaming for the past few weeks, and perhaps Peter wasn't my boyfriend. I left my hands in the soapy water as I studied my reflection in the glass. My face was sweaty, my makeup faded, and tiny lines were engraved around my eyes. Damage from the second-degree sunburn I had at age ten. I had no urge to be some poor white trash woman who was over the hill and used up at thirty.

I had done the right thing by not bringing Peter home, and when I got back to school, I'd tell him how busy I was, and that my grandparents took me shopping, and that my sisters—more lies. I finished the pot and drained the sink. I dried my hands and glanced at the bowls of leftovers. Aunt Mooney and my sisters had taken a ton of food home, and there was a ton left. The rich aromas of turkey and dressing tempted me to get another plate, but I couldn't afford to gain a pound, or Henry would notice. Besides, there wasn't a shred of turkey left. Every year, while other people had leftovers for turkey soup or sandwiches, all we had was a skeleton. Daddy was more efficient than a vulture.

I walked into the living room, where Daddy was parked in front of the television, drinking his antacid. I loved watching TV, but I didn't feel like listening to him belch and pass gas. The phone rang, and Wiley and Holly tore out of their room in a race to see who could answer it first. This time, Wiley grabbed it.

"Annie! It's for you! It's a boy!"

"Okay, I'm going into Mama's room to talk. Please hang up when I pick up," I told her, trying to sound calm.

I walked out of the living room without saying anything to Daddy.

"Hi . . . hang up the phone, Wiley . . . ." I heard a quiet click. "Sorry, Peter."

"That must've been your little sister."

"It was. Are you having fun at Tony's?"

"We're having a blast. I'm stuffed. Just thought I'd call and see how you are doing. Can you talk right now?"

I was whispering, so I raised my voice a notch, expecting Daddy to walk in and ask who it was. "Yes. My relatives are in the living room."

"I miss you."

"I miss you, too. I'm kind of bored. I can't wait to get back to school."

"Me, too. Tony and I are going to Thomas's tomorrow and Saturday to ride. What are you doing?"

I was sweating above my lip and rubbed it while I fought to get my brain to function. "Well, my grandparents want to take me shopping, and I'll probably see more of my sisters, and do some exercise myself. Burn off the turkey. I didn't know Tony rode bikes."

"Sometimes. He's not in the best shape, if you know what I mean. I thought I'd torture him."

I hardly remembered the rest of the conversation. I sat still on Mama's bed for five minutes. With weak legs, I got up, in need of a tub of hot water. I stopped in the hallway, where I saw Mama in the bathroom brushing her top false teeth over the sink. Daddy stood in the bathroom doorway, grinning.

"Have you got a fella?"

"No. He's just a friend from school. We're working on an accounting project next week. He had some questions to ask me, that's all."

"Me and Mama thought you caught you a fella at college," he said as he patted his stomach.

"I'm not going to school to catch guys, Daddy. I have too many things to do."

"Burl, leave her alone. It's none of your business," Mama said as she rinsed her teeth.

"I know, Mama. I wasn't bein' nosy."

"Ha! Your middle name's nosy."

"I was just askin'. Our daughter's so pretty, boys are bound to come callin'. I thought she might be gettin' a little sugar at school."

"Please, Daddy. I want to take a bath."

He snickered as he walked into the living room. I leaned into the tub and turned on the water. Mama washed her face quietly. I walked back into the bedroom to get my nightgown and some clean underwear. I took off my dirty clothes and lay them in a corner. Nude, I quickly walked back to the bathroom and into the tub. Mama continued wiping her face with a washcloth while I turned off the water faucets.

"Have you met someone?"

I leaned back to soak. "No, Mama. He's just a guy from my classes. He's real smart. He's helping me with my accounting."

"Well, I find it funny that he calls on Thanksgivin'."

"That's the way he is. A constant worrier about his schoolwork. He drives me crazy, calling me at school. You know, he wants to make straight A's."

"Yeah, you remember old man Patrick and how he kept pushin' his kids. He made his son Terry so nervous about his grades that he stuttered. I don't see the point in demandin' that your kids make perfect grades."

"Yeah, it's the same thing here. This guy's like that."

"Their kids couldn't even drip on the toilet seat without gettin' a lecture."

"Our family's way past that."

On Mama's bed, I stretched out my legs. Done with Henry for a while. Done with big meals until Christmas. Almost done with Mama and Daddy until Christmas break. Done listening, for now, to Aunt Mooney and Mama's whine sessions. They were alike, and ever so different. Mama was conservative. Aunt Mooney was wild with house decorations and her clothing. She'd spend money on something and wear it once, then decide she didn't like it and return it. Mama just wanted to be able to buy anything. Aunt Mooney spent money knowing Uncle Melvin would be angry. Mama let her money get piddled away at Daddy's discretion, then she'd bitch about it. And yet, they grew up together in horrible circumstances. Mama wouldn't talk about it much, the childhood beatings and all.

I pulled a rumpled green blanket up to my neck. Before I could close my eyes, I saw a huge cockroach crawling across the wall. My spine shivered, and I threw back the blanket. I couldn't sleep until that roach was dead.

"Mama! There's another cockroach in here! Come kill it!"

"Kill it with one of Daddy's shoes!"

I grabbed a shoe off the floor and flung it against the wall. The roach scurried across the wall close to the bed. "Please don't get in the bed!"

I hurried to the living room and sat on the couch, waiting. Mama was sitting in the corner chair with a glass of Diet Coke in her hand. Daddy was giving her his opinion on Tish's dilemma.

"All these doctors in Soso are quacks," he griped.

"I told Mooney she should take Tish to Jackson to see another doctor," Mama said.

"Mama, Dr. Vincent told Aunt Mooney the truth. Tish has to lose weight. I think that's why she's depressed. She used to be so full of life," I said.

She flicked her cigarette into an ashtray. "Well, I think she gained weight 'cause she is depressed."

"Could be. But, being that big will kill her if she doesn't slow down her eating. She and Aunt Mooney should go for walks together and quit dwelling on Uncle Melvin."

"They're not interested in walkin'. They're havin' a hard time."

"Oh, God. Tish always comes out smelling like a rose. So does Aunt Mooney. They have a lot more than we do. They always have. It's a funny thing that the both of them have never worked a job, and yet they have nice things. I tell you, I'm not going to sit around and wait for someone to hand me alimony or a Social Security check every month. There's more to life."

"Well, I wish you wouldn't make comments like that to Tish. Mooney looked funny when she left," Mama said.

"What comments? I was nice. I could've told her the truth. That Tish is an obese, spoiled, lazy, hateful brat."

"You shouldn't say things like that about your cousin. She's sick," Daddy said.

"She's bored. She needs a job," I replied. "That's why Uncle Melvin left. They ran him off."

Mama said, "Mooney's always liked fancy things. She spent too much money—"

I interrupted her. "And now, Tish is just like her and has expensive tastes. They sit around watching soap operas all day. That's not a good thing."

"Mooney's thinkin' about goin' to a therapist."

"Good," I said.

"I don't know why anyone would wanna go to a stupid therapist," Daddy said. "All it'll be is some ugly bag sittin' on her big butt holdin' down a chair wantin' to know personal things. Ten years down the road, you still got problems."

I was so sleepy. "Mama, can you come kill this roach?"

"I guess so. There's nothin' to be afraid of."

She set her drink down. I walked into the bedroom and stood with my arms crossed for protection. She came into the room with a broom in her hand and a cigarette in her mouth.

"Where's the damn thing?"

"Oh, no, where'd it go?" I moaned. "There it is!"

She swung the broom at the bug, and it scampered the other way.

"Don't let it fall in the bed," I begged.

"If it gets in the bed, I'll get it out."

Now it was running across the wall, and she had a clear shot. She smashed it, and it dropped to the floor. I shut my eyes as she took a wad of toilet paper, picked it up, and flushed it down the toilet.

Chapter Eight

Peter stopped calling me two weeks before Christmas break. At first, I just thought we were playing phone tag. On Friday, I had lunch with Denise, then I walked over to Taylor Hall and knocked on Peter's apartment door. No answer, and a dark, sinking feeling hit me in the pit of my stomach. I went to work-study, thinking he'd be waiting for me when I got off. He wasn't. I went to dinner and ate alone. When I emptied my tray into the trash, I saw Peter and his buddies sitting on the other side of the salad bar. He lowered his eyes when he saw me, and I knew. *You're being brushed off, Annie.* Outside, I waited in the cold for half an hour. I could hear his rowdy friends coming down the stairway. When they saw me, they became silent.

"Catch you later, Peter," Tony said. "Hi, Annie."

No one else said anything. They walked toward Taylor Hall.

Peter broke out into a charming grin. "How's it going?"

"Why haven't you called me?" I asked.

"Was I supposed to?"

"After we went out Wednesday night, you said you were going to call me last night when you got back from the computer lab, but you didn't."

"I got in very late." He wasn't making eye contact.

"What's going on, Peter?"

"What do you mean?"

"You know what I mean. Don't act like you don't."

He looked down. "I think you've got the wrong impression about us."

"You don't love me anymore?"

"I like you, Annie."

"You told me you loved me. . . ."

"Look, I like you as a friend. I didn't mean to give you—"

"Is it because of Christmas break? Is it because we'll be separated a month? What is it?"

He was shaking his head. "No."

"What did I do?"

"Nothing, Annie. You're a nice girl."

I walked away. He was coming behind me, calling my name, but I refused to turn around. I could barely breathe, then I was crying.

"Wait, Annie." He grabbed my arm. "I didn't mean to give you the impression that it was anything other than friendship."

"You kissed me so many times," I sobbed.

He didn't say anything. I saw the cracks in the sidewalk, and in my life.

I ran, and he didn't follow. Inside my dorm room, I backed into my closet doors with mascara dripping off my face. The tears were torturous. I couldn't stay on campus for the weekend. *Where's your independence, Annie? Can't you stay for yourself? Do you have to have a man?*

CHAPTER NINE

My Chevette had been parked for days, and I had to pump the pedal to get the engine started. I drove out of the dorm parking lot and off the campus along a service road. Not concealing the hurt, I wailed from the pit of my gut. On the entrance ramp to Highway 59, I floored it. Peter's face wouldn't go away. *I'm too inhibited, too nice, too boring, and that's why he dumped me.* Up ahead I saw the sign for Ellisville, and I exited. The town was small, but seemed even tinier after living in Hattiesburg. I coasted through a yellow light, turning onto old Highway 11. This used to be a busy two-lane, before Highway 59 was built. Both sides of the road were thickly wooded with pine trees, a house here and there. I turned onto Beacon Street and stopped next to a row of beat-up mailboxes, then onto Fountain Road to a shady dead-end. To the left was a house trailer. To the right was a brick home, and I pulled in and got out.

Aunt Mooney was all I had. The only person in my family who might listen to me. I knew what Mama would say: "Shit on him. That boy dumped you 'cause he wants a piece of ass." Daddy would call him a punk and a bum.

I walked onto a bricked walkway. Aunt Mooney and Uncle Melvin had lived in a double-wide until the last five years they were married. She pestered him until he built a two-story brick house.

The first time I'd stepped inside, it was paradise. It had carpet, central air and heat, and extra bathrooms. Through the front door, I could see her familiar leopard-print sofa. I was secure now. I knocked. Aunt Mooney came from the kitchen, chewing and smiling.

"Honey, come in."

A towel wrapped her head. Cotton was stuffed between her toes. In her arms, I fell apart.

"Honey, what's wrong?"

The sobbing clogged my throat. "Aunt Mooney, he . . ."

"Sit down." She pulled over an ottoman and sat down in front of me. "Is it school?"

"No. I mean, I wish it was."

She wiped my face and hugged me again. "Oh, sweetheart, Aunt Mooney's here. Take your time."

She brought me a box of tissues. I quieted down.

"I had a boyfriend. . . ."

She smiled. "You do?"

"I *did*. He broke up with me today."

"Oh, honey." She hugged me.

"He told me he loved me, Aunt Mooney. We've been going out, and then he stopped calling. When I asked him about it, he acted as if I had imagined everything, our entire relationship."

She leaned back with a disgusted expression. "I bet he was runnin' around. These whoremongerin' men. All they study is their dicks!"

"No, Aunt Mooney, no," I cried.

"I'm sorry, honey. I didn't mean to upset you. It'll be all right. Do you wanna tranquilizer?"

"No. Can I stay with you? I can't go home like this. I can't face going home."

"You know you're welcome here anytime. Tish is at her Daddy's, so we can just stay here."

She took the towel off her head. I stopped crying. "Aunt Mooney, your hair is purple!"

"I know. I don't know what I did wrong this time. I'll just keep tryin' until I get the right color." She smiled, touching my face. "You're so beautiful. I remember holdin' you when you were a baby. You're hair was so red and thick, more so than any of your sisters. I used to make a curl right in the middle of your head. I'd plaster your hair with hairspray until that curl stood straight up."

Ellisville wasn't a "happening" town, even with the junior college there, and I felt as if I were being swallowed up. The pain was unreal, and there was no escape. Aunt Mooney was lying on the sofa, eating ice cream, and watching reruns that I used to watch. In my mind, I'd be with Peter. We'd be walking the campus, watching TV, making out, or cruising up and down Hardy Street. Evidently, my being with him for company wasn't enough to make him happy. It had fulfilled me, though. I could see a few lines in Aunt Mooney's face. Like Mama, Mooney was attractive. But losing Uncle Melvin had almost destroyed her.

I didn't sleep much that night. Every few minutes, I was having conversations with Peter, and I'd awaken to find my mouth moving. My mind wouldn't stop the grueling replays. If only yesterday hadn't happened.

Aunt Mooney was a late sleeper, so I took a bath quietly and attempted to put on makeup. I couldn't, and I began to cry on the edge of the tub.

I smelled coffee, so I dressed. When I walked into the kitchen, Mooney had her black hair back, having stayed up after midnight trying different colors on it.

"Good mornin'. Did you sleep well, darlin'?"

"Not really. I kept having dreams."

"Dreams, oh, I know about dreams. When Melvin left me, I couldn't stop dreamin' of the way things used to be. When we were young, and when Tish was a baby, one big happy family. I still dream about him from time to time." Rubbing a tear from her face, she clung to the counter. "Honey, you're young. You'll get over Peter. You may not think so right now, but you will."

Like you got over Uncle Melvin?

I didn't want to get over Peter. I loved him.

She handed me a cup of coffee, and I realized Aunt Mooney was shaken up.

"Why did Uncle Melvin leave? I've heard Mama talking about it, but what really happened?"

Sipping from her cup, she sat on a stool next to me. "Well, precious, I wasn't the best wife, you know. I went through these depressions that'd last sometimes for months. I let the house go. I didn't cook. I wouldn't let Melvin touch me. He couldn't deal with it. Maybe you know this story, but I was seventeen when I met him. He was sixteen and so darned handsome. I always preferred men with hairy chests, but Melvin's bare chest made me happy. I was insanely jealous of him, and I said mean things to him in front of the family. In front of your mama and daddy. I belittled him for wantin' sex. I told him his penis was small. I accused him of sleepin' with every woman he looked at. Then, he really started messin' around."

"Where'd he meet Mary?"

"Mary." She turned her face. "She was the secretary for our insurance agent. Whenever we went in to pay our car insurance, she took the payment. And she took my husband. I guess if it wasn't Mary, it'd have been somebody else. She's not pretty. Wears no makeup. But she's young."

Aunt Mooney treated me to lunch at Bonanza Steak House, then drove us out to Lake Bogue Homa. We reminisced about the summers of picnics, and Uncle Melvin teaching me how to swim. Not once did Daddy go with us. He was sulking at home because Mama wasn't there cooking. By Saturday evening, Aunt Mooney had the blues.

"I tell ya, I hate screwin'. That's all men wanna do is screw. I told Marcia I wasn't interested in Lonnie Cole, but she set us up anyway. I thought he was gonna undress me with his eyes."

"What did you do on your date?" I asked.

"He took me to that fish place over on the Highway. The fish was good, but I ate more than he did. The stupid bird. He looks like a lizard with those green eyes of his."

"Is he good-looking?"

"Hell, no. His hair's thin. He's too short and skinny. I felt like a whale, standin' next to him."

"Well, he might like a full-figured woman like you."

"Tough shit. I wish he'd stop callin' me."

"Is he divorced?"

"Is he divorced? He's divorced, all right, with seven children."

"Seven children? With one wife?"

"Yeah. Her name's Rita. They're Catholic. She works at McRae's in the mall. I've seen her in there. She's not pretty, but her figure is better than mine, honey."

"Are his kids grown?"

"Most of 'em. The youngest is ten."

"My God, Aunt Mooney. He must pay some child support."

"A lot of child support. I don't want anything to do with him. You know what kind of work he does? He's an exterminator. He don't make doodlesquat doin' that. At least Melvin makes good money.

"Aunt Mooney, I hate to pry, but is Uncle Melvin having kids with Mary?"

She rocked harder, digging at her hair. "I don't know. From what Tish says, Mary don't want kids right now. Melvin wants . . ." She started crying. "I don't want her to have his baby, I don't!"

"Aunt Mooney, I'm sorry."

"I've played it over and over in my mind. That she'll give him the son he always wanted. I couldn't help it. They took my uterus out. After Tish was born, they gave me the shock treatments. Almost turned me into a vegetable . . . ."

For the next hour, she rocked and raved.

"He thinks he can walk out on me and dole out a little alimony here and there. I deserve more. Women get screwed out of everythin' in this world. If you remember anythin' from me, Annie, remember that. Take care of yourself, don't give your life over to some cocksucker that's gonna ruin it for you."

"That's why I'm in school."

"I pray that son of a bitch loses his hair. I pray his balls fall down to his knees. All those months he was screwin' me and pretendin' I was Mary. Wishin' I was thin like her. Wishin' my vagina was little like hers."

"Aunt Mooney, please take another tranquilizer."

"No. I wanna feel this pain. I wanna experience hate for him. I wanna wallow in it."

Chapter Ten

I came back to the dorm on Sunday evening to find a note from Marge on my desk. Mama had called. I panicked and called her back.

"Where were you? Your roommate said she thought you went home."

"I went home with Denise."

"Oh." She blew a puff of smoke.

"I didn't get a chance to call y'all." Tears began to flow. "I really need to study for exams, Mama."

"When are you havin' 'em?"

"Next week."

"Well, don't kill yourself. They're just tests."

I rubbed my face. "Has Daddy been working?"

"Fat chance."

"How's he going to pay the rent, then? He knows you don't make enough to pay it. I guess y'all are going to get booted out of that roach pit."

"He paid only part of it this month, and it'll be comin' up again, and he sits around here waitin' on the mail, thinkin' some money's gonna fall of the sky. Idiot."

"God, if he'd put forth some effort, any effort to work, and if Gloria'd pay a utility or two, it'd help a lot, Mama."

"She don't do shit around here. And if I even mention to Burl about callin' some of his old clients to see if they need any work done, he starts complainin' with his back. 'Mama, my back hurts.'"

"He's an old faker." I pulled off my tennis shoes and threw them across the room.

"Well, it does act up."

"Bull. Why don't you sue him for divorce?" I begged.

"Yeah, and he'll go around tellin' people that I ran off and left him, and they'll feel sorry for his ole ass."

"No, they'd give you a medal. And who cares what his holy-rolling buddies think? Don't you think they need to clean out their own backyards? Half of them won't work either. Sit around waiting for donations."

"Just like Burl. He lies around here eatin' and bitchin'. I bought a pizza for the girls last night, and he ate most of it. Then he stayed up sick all night with his reflux."

"Good. I hope he pukes his guts out."

In the background, I heard the front door slam. "Who's that, Mama?" Daddy asked.

"It's Annie."

"Did she call us?"

She screamed, causing me to hold the phone out. "Yes! Don't worry, you don't have to pay for it!"

"I'm not worryin', Mama," he said innocently.

"Can't even call Edna and check on her when she's sick for you standin' over me worryin' about long-distance phone calls. He calls whoever the hell he wants to."

"I'm not fussin'," he said.

She continued. "Jessie said Keith's been dead-drunk since last Sunday. He won't try to get a better payin' job. He forgot to pay their light bill, and she had to get an advance at work to keep 'em from cuttin' off the power."

Daddy cut in, "I'll tell ya one thing, I'd put his worthless butt on the road. He should help out."

She agreed. "That's right, women should put men's worthless asses out when they don't help."

"Well, does she wanna talk to me?"

"Hang on, he wants to talk to you."

"Hey, baby."

"Hey, Daddy, how are you?"

He started sniffing. "I got sinus drainage."

"Oh." I wasn't listening. "Are y'all feeding Trudy?"

"Yeah, I been feedin' her scraps from the table."

"Let me know if she needs any dog food."

"Alrighty. I sure wished you could've come to Brother Mosley's funeral."

"Why?"

"It was beautiful. About a hundred people showed up. The Campbells, the Jordans, me and Mama."

"Sounds like y'all had a party."

"Sister Willa's daughter was there."

"I didn't know she had one."

"Yeah, she do. She's a lawyer up in Tennessee somewhere. She's one of those . . .uh, well, she's kind of a know-it-all. She looks like a lesb'an. I believe she's one of those feminists, but she's married to this ole guy. . . ."

"Mama said your rent's behind."

"No, the rent ain't behind."

"Shit," Mama jeered.

"I'll have the rest of the money in a couple of days, Mama."

"What'll you do, borrow it from someone? Still puts us in a hole," she said.

"No, I'm cleanin' out some gutters for Sister Cooper. You remember Sister Cooper, don't you, Annie?"

"Vaguely."

"She got a new fifty-two inch TV. It's the biggest thing I ever seen."

"Isn't she about dead now? She must be eighty years old."

"No, she's . . . Mama, how old's Sister Cooper?"

"She's eighty-two."

"Eighty-two. My, oh my."

I wasn't off the phone five minutes when it rang. Thinking it might be Denise, I grabbed it.

"Been trying to get you for ten minutes." Henry was perturbed.

I gritted my teeth and squeezed my fingernails deep in to the palm of my hand. "I was on the phone with my mother."

"Oh, is everything all right?"

"Yes."

"Well, good," he said, distantly. "Did she call you?"

"No, well, she called earlier, and I called her back."

"Oh, I see. Y'all sure talk a long time. Can't they say 'hey' and let you go?" That made me angry.

"How are you, Pop?" I kicked my laundry basket against the door, seething.

"Just fine. Been thinking about you. We miss you. When did you say you were coming home again?"

"Christmas break."

"When's that?"

I didn't want to speak the words. "It starts the second week in December."

"Oh. Good. We just wanted to hear from you. Got your letter and card the other day. That was so sweet of you, sending Mom a beautiful card like that. She sure appreciated it."

"I'm glad." Each card I sent bought me more time.

"She's had a good week. Took her to get her hair done on Wednesday, and then we drove to Sandersville to see my sister Colleen. She just loves Pearl. We had the best time. We even thought about driving down to see you in Hattiesburg, but it was after four and getting late. We weren't sure where you'd be."

"I work on Wednesday afternoons."

He wasn't listening. "Well, I won't hold you. Just let us hear from you when you get home. We want to spend a little time with you. Oh, by the way, did you say you were working during the break?"

"Yes. I've already talked to the manager at Tri-Mart—"

"What's his name again?"

"Mr. Sikes."

"Who?"

"Mr. Sikes!"

"Sikes, that's right. Well, it really helps that you're doing that. Are you working the whole time you're home?"

"I'm working the two weeks before Christmas. That's when he needs me most. I'll probably get in some overtime."

"Really?"

"I'm sure we'll be busy."

"That's great. That'll certainly help us."

"Yes."

"The Lord has blessed us in so many ways . . . ."

I cried hard when I got off the phone with Henry. I was embarrassed that the Prices were even helping me. I was angry with Mama and Daddy for having the nerve to check on me. All I wanted was a phone call from Peter, yet I only got calls from the people I didn't want to hear from. Peter would never be calling me again, and I knew it. He'd go on making good grades and impressing the right people. He'd marry someone athletic and beautiful and live happily ever after. At the moment, I was afraid to look to my future. Being his girlfriend meant I was desirable. Now I was back to being one of the unwanted.

That night, I spent three hours evaluating my goals. I wrote down what I wanted to accomplish, how much money I was going to make, how much I wanted to weigh, and how toned my body was going to be after I took ballet lessons.

It was nearing twelve thirty, and I had early classes. Marge wasn't even in yet. I put my pencil down, then the sorrow returned. I couldn't face tomorrow. Seeing Peter in the cafeteria. Having to tell Denise and Suzy that he broke up with me.

I washed my face and brushed my teeth. The elevator door opened, and I thought it might be Denise, since she sometimes came in very late from home. I peeked out from the bathroom.

"Oh. Hey, Marla."

"Girl, you look like a ghost."

"Rough weekend."

"Uh-huh," she commiserated, as she carried in a laundry basket.

"You've been washing this late at night?"

"Girl, yeah," she groaned. "I didn't have any clean drawers."

Marla Jones was a loner. She lived across the hall from me in a private room. She was black and wore her hair long and ironed into a swoop. I had stayed clear of her, because she seemed so independent, and I was so insecure. Suzy said Marla had been a track star at her high school in Vicksburg. But the weight gain in her thighs and hips told me she no longer ran.

"What you doing up so late?" Marla asked.

"Oh, just writing some stuff down."

She was quiet, nodding her head.

"My boyfriend broke up with me," I said.

"Broke up with you? Why would he break up with a pretty girl like you? Is he a fool?"

"I guess I bored him to death."

"Mmmm, mmm, he's the fool. I saw him up here at times. Girl, you're better off."

"You won't anymore."

"Come on, now. You still walking the track?"

"Yeah. I'll be walking several days a week, now, that I'll have more time."

"I'm joining you. Starting this week. When are you going again?"

Marla's goal was to walk three evenings a week, no matter how cold it was. No longer would I be alone on the track. She was born in Detroit. Her mom and stepfather moved back up there when she was in junior high, and she opted to stay with her grandmother and do her track thing down in Mississippi. She didn't have to tell me she loved her family. I knew where her confidence came from when we checked our mailboxes, and she'd have a letter of encouragement from them, along with a check. She told me she'd be in the same room for the spring semester, and I eagerly told her I wouldn't be moving, either. We studied for our exams in the library. Before we left for Christmas break, Marla gave me her address in Vicksburg.

Chapter Eleven

On Christmas Eve, midnight was closing in, and I was still at work at Tri-Mart. My head hurt from the voices of irritable, last-minute shoppers demanding to know why we didn't have this and that in stock. My hands were filthy and cut from stocking shelves in the toy department earlier in the day. My nine-hour shift turned to fourteen.

We counted our registers down to fifty dollars. The twenty-eight-year-old manager was spouting off commands like a Nazi. Seeing my co-workers, grown women, have to snivel and bite their tongues during the indignity made me thankful I was at UEM so I could get a better job one day. We were commanded to clean the floor, as if we were servants.

I punched out after three in the morning. No thank you's, no goodbyes, no "Merry Christmas" greetings were exchanged. I was too exhausted to feel happy that I'd receive a decent paycheck, that it would help with my college expenses.

This was for Henry. To keep him off me. To buy myself some sanity. He came in the first day, the first hour I worked. He put the crossword puzzle on the conveyer belt where I was cashier, but he wasn't looking to buy. His eyes were fixed on me, dressed in my blue uniform. There were about twenty people in line behind him, and he wanted to chat. Times had changed, and Tri-Mart wasn't a five-and-dime where an old fogey could loiter with the cashier, talking about the weather and other baloney. He recalled in detail my working at Tri-Mart the summer of eighty-four. That was when Tri-Mart rolled into Soso offering excellent benefits, good pay, flexible hours, and stock sharing. Hoping they paid better than minimum wage, I applied and was hired to help set up the store. I was in junior college and worked the whole summer, becoming the manager's best cashier.

I was cold when I left the store, so I cranked up the heater, the only thing that seemed to work in my car. I held up my hands in the light to see the damage. I didn't know if I felt sorry for myself, or if I was just wiped out. I twisted the mirror to my face. *You look old. How could anybody love you?*

Christmas morning came too fast. Shoney's was closed, along with every other restaurant in Soso. Henry had been in panic about it since October. "It's hard for people like us to cook a holiday meal. We need somewhere to go. They shouldn't close up like that." Any other time of the year, Henry would be too cheap to eat out unless I was around. He was prepared, though, and it was lucky for me that he was. I had no desire to spend all day Christmas at their house while he cooked, and I wasn't offering my services. Weeks earlier, he had made reservations at the First Baptist Church cafeteria, where a holiday lunch was being served.

I walked reluctantly from my car to the Price's house. Henry's glowing expression and Pearl's clapping hands didn't help the headache and depression I felt. The clean clothes I brought from school were now foul-smelling with burnt grease and cigarette smoke, after hanging in my parents' home. Luckily, Henry had gone whole-hog with cinnamon-scented potpourri throughout the house. Below a fake silver Christmas tree were eight presents. In an orderly manner, Henry passed them out, and we opened them together to the sounds of religious yuletide music. Pearl cut up with the giggles, until he chided her for being too loud. "That's enough, Mom, you'll wear yourself out." Henry hit the road at a quarter to eleven, driven by his fear that the food would run out.

First Baptist was the largest church in Soso. Its membership had flourished, and in the early seventies they left their original chapel in West Soso and built a monumental red brick building on Fifth Avenue.

Inside the church cafeteria was a senior citizen showcase. The ladies, some of whom were almost fossils, were outfitted to the hilt in beaded necklaces and hats. I thought I looked pretty good in my navy dress pants and white blouse, but I was way underdressed. Pearl was gabbing occasionally with old friends. I was famished, but Henry gripped my arm and dragged me from one crony to the next, showing me off. What a way to spend Christmas Day.

I vowed I would never grow old this way.

By the time we reached the buffet line, I was ravenous. But I dutifully stuck to the healthy foods, turkey and salad, while watching Henry amass a plateful. Ham, sweet potato casserole, crescent rolls — foods he'd missed since he took on Pearl's diabetic diet. This was a feast. The tables of desserts were outstanding, with rows and rows of the pies and cakes of my dreams. Daddy would kill for this. Yet I relished nothing, with Henry around. Couldn't be too happy, couldn't be too sad, or he'd pick me apart.

"This is such a good deal, only two-fifty a plate, plus drink and dessert. Can't beat that."

After repeating it a few times and getting no response from me, he shut up. I chewed slowly while he watched every bite I took. Out of the corner of my eye I could see him and Pearl picking crumbs off the table as they ate. He was the first to finish.

"You want some dessert, or are you watching your weight?"

"No, my weight—"

"What are you, a size twelve?" Pearl asked.

"No, Mom. Annie's a five. She's small. We just don't want her to grow wider, do we." A piece of stuffing was stuck in the corner of his mouth.

"I thought she was a twelve," Pearl insisted.

"No, *you* used to be a twelve. Now you're a ten. You got all the way up to size eighteen at one time." He repositioned his glasses, giving her a disgusted look. She shrugged her shoulders. "Mom's always been a little, uh, chesty," he explained. Now that chest sagged and dragged.

Back at their house, Henry was absolutely content and practically lying down in his recliner, watching me. I was dead, legs aching, eyes stinging from lack of sleep. Between the job and home, I felt like a prisoner. Henry didn't care. Mama and Daddy didn't care. I yearned to leave the Prices, but I couldn't, since he had gone to the trouble of buying presents for me that I didn't want. I'd spend a little more time with him, even though I felt like he was sucking me dry.

"Mom and I hope you like what we got you. I know it isn't much," he told me in a low, tired voice. The fraternizing at church had worn him down.

"It's great. I really appreciate the pajamas and the slippers. And I need the perfume."

He touched my shoe with his toe. "I'm so happy to hear that. Mom loves the hummingbird. Thank you, sweetheart."

"I wanted to get her something."

"That's so sweet of you. You know, Mom and I decided that it's more important for us to spend the money to help you with school than for presents," he said as he crinkled his nose. I didn't need his explanations.

"I appreciate everything . . . ."

"Did your parents get you anything for Christmas?"

Does it matter? "They just bought a few presents for Wiley and Holly, since they're little."

"That's right, honey. Little ones believe in Santa Claus. You know, all we used to get was an apple, when I was a little boy. My father would lay it on my chest so I would see it in the morning. Didn't know any better or expect any more. That was it. Say, when do you get paid from the store?"

He was reviving, and I'd be stuck here if I didn't get myself in gear and leave.

"Next Friday."

"Good. I need you to bring me the check so I can put it in the bank for you."

"You know, Pop, I thought it'd be okay to put it straight into my checking account for when I go back to school."

"Well, let me see. I guess we can do that."

"That way, you and Mommy Junior won't have to give me any money. I'll use it until I get paid from my work-study job."

"Okay, honey, that's fine." His voice faltered, and I could tell he was thinking about it. "Are you still working for the same professors?"

"Yes. Mrs. Johnston asked me to come back."

"Isn't it wonderful that they want you to come back and work for them? They know you're a hard worker. I'm so proud of your grades, dear. In hard classes, too."

"The accounting classes are very hard."

"Just keep up the good work. Just think if you could've made straight A's. I remember graduating summa cum laude. My father, who was just a simple farmer, mind you, oh he was so proud." He touched his chest. "Straight A's, maybe a B or two." He shrugged as if it had been a piece of cake. Then he grinned and started patting his hands on his hips. "Have you gained any weight since I saw you last?"

"No. I'm in better shape than ever." *Except for sleep deprivation.*

"It's just that, during the holidays, people put on some pounds, all that rich food. I noticed when you were walking at the church, that you weren't as thin in the hips." His hands drew out the shape of a rump as wide as the Mississippi. "Next time you go to the bathroom, weigh on Mom's scale."

Feeling cowed, I glanced over at Pearl's hummingbird collection, trying to distract myself and wishing I hadn't bothered with buying her one more cheap thing.

"Honey, you seem down. Are you okay? You can talk to Pop about anything."

"I'm fine. I'm just tired. I didn't get off work until three this morning."

His eyes gleamed. "You must have gotten in some good overtime. How much did you get in?"

"I'm not sure." I was sweating, feeling an attack of diarrhea coming on.

"What you have to do is write your time in a small notebook, that way you can make sure they get it right. You never know if they might miss an hour or two." He closed in and touched my cheek lightly as my stomach cramped. "Your eyes are a little swollen."

"Because I didn't get much sleep," I said, with gritted teeth.

"Oh, I know, honey." He leaned back, feeling satisfied. He got what he wanted. Me for lunch. Me for his time. "Like I told you the other day, you could've come over here and spent the night, since you were coming for Christmas anyway. I wouldn't have minded picking you up that late. You could've called me. Pop would have driven right over," he reassured. "I didn't sleep well. I was so afraid of you getting mugged in the parking lot, not knowing who might be lurking around."

"All the employees leave together."

"That's good, honey, but always be careful. Park under a light."

"Pop, I need to go."

"Did I tell you? I wrote your friend Denise. Got a nice Christmas card from her. Want to see it?"

"I need to go and help Mama. "

"Aw, do you have to leave now?"

"I'll see y'all before I leave."

"Please let us know if you need anything for school."

I stood. "I will, Pop. You don't have to wake Mommy Junior."

"Mom gets so exhausted as the day wears on. Maybe I should've cooked for us today."

"No, I think Mommy Junior wanted to go out."

"I think so, too. I worry so much about her. You can understand, can't you?"

"She'll be fine. Give her a hug for me."

He hugged me too long. My skin crawled, and my eyes stayed wide open. His body was squashy and weak and aged. I tried to numb my nerves, not wanting to feel him. I tried to hold my breath, so I wouldn't have to smell his skin. He reeked of loneliness.

I walked fast to my car, carrying the gifts in a sack. I sensed that he was following me, and my innards were on fire. *No more hugs, for God's sake. I can't make you happy, Pop. I don't want to.* He pulled a pine straw out of the windshield wiper. Before I opened the door, he spoke, but his tone wasn't jolly anymore.

"Do we need to get your car serviced?"

"How long has it been?"

"Come next Monday, and we'll take it to my mechanic, you hear? We have to keep your little car running until you get through school. Could use a new paint job, couldn't she?" He was getting cranky. "But it runs, and that's what we're concerned about. Get here by seven o'clock, and we'll take it in. You can come home with me and have breakfast with Mom."

He kept tugging at pine straws. He yanked hard to get the very last one removed. We waved at each other through the windshield. I was in agony. I hadn't planned to come back here until the end of my break, but now I was stuck with having to spend most of Monday with them.

As soon as I was back in West Soso, the pain in my stomach passed. "Jesus," I pleaded. "Don't punish me like that."

I dwelled on everything Henry had said to me. The condemnation of my weight: "You look a little heavy." My hair: "Has you hair always been thin? Want to go to Mom's hairdresser and get a perm?" My grades: "Just think Annie, if you could've pulled it off, you'd have straight A's."

The season would be changing into spring, my favorite time of the year, and I needed clothes. My shirts and blue jeans were worn and faded. But my professors expected professionalism. If I had to depend on my clothing, I'd be out of the league, any league. UEM business students were notorious for their dress, especially the women, with their hairdos, suits, and briefcases.

The paycheck was history, every nickel going toward tuition and living expenses. If I asked Henry gently, tenderly, maybe he'd give me some money for clothes. Hitting him at the right moment would be pure luck, a gamble that might or might not pay off. The gospel truth, I didn't want to be beholding to him anymore. A visit to the Salvation Army store would have to do.

Back at home, Mama was standing over a steaming pot of red beans. Puffing, stirring, coaxing. Daddy was on the couch, sullen and furiously rubbing the back of his neck. He wasn't speaking to anyone, for some reason, which was a miracle. He was pretending to watch a cowboy movie, but his pea-shaped green eyes were watching Mama's every move. Her eyes were shooting death daggers his way, and she stomped out of the kitchen.

Our Christmas tree stood lopsided in the corner by the television. Daddy didn't try to put it in an upright position, just stuck it in an old paint bucket. "I know it's ugly, but that's the best I could do. I ain't got the money to waste on tree stands and decorations." And they never would.

Jessie and Clarie arrived early to help with dinner. Gloria was off work and stayed in everyone's way. Wiley and Holly were playing in the back bedroom with their new toys. Mama came back to the beans again, with one hand on her hip and a sour look on her face.

"These damn things are dryin' out. Hand me a glass."

I took one from the dish rack and filled it with water. She added it to the pot, watching and mixing as if she were working on science project. Gloria walked into the kitchen with a cigarette between her fingers.

"What's wrong with Daddy?"

"Who cares?" Clarie said.

"Mama, what's wrong?" I asked.

The spoon smashed on to the stove. "I hate fuckin'."

I stopped washing the dishes.

"Mama!" Gloria laughed.

"What happened?" Jessie asked.

"Aw, Burl's mad 'cause I don't wanna fuck."

I stared at her harried face. "My God, Mama."

"Well I'm sick of it. He always wants to fuck when we have a house full of people here. I'm worn out and don't want no one bouncin' on my belly. 'Specially a pot-gutted stinkin' skunk. I can't stand it."

"Tell him to leave you alone," Clarie said defiantly.

"I did! Now he's in there sulkin'. He's gonna ruin everybody's Christmas. I told him he shouldn't act ugly when we have company. He doesn't care."

"I'm used to his crazy ways. I know how selfish he is," I said.

"Just like his ole Mama was. He's one selfish son of a bitch. It's his fault we don't ever have a good Christmas. He won't work, and I can't buy you older girls anythin'. Hell, I barely got the kids somethin'."

"Christmas presents are the least of our worries, Mama, believe me. We don't need anything," I said.

"I don't," Jessie said. "I put the kids' presents on layaway months ago so I would be able to give 'em somethin'."

"I did, too," Clarie nodded, an ashtray in her hand.

Gloria had relented and bought them a doll after Mama begged her to, and after several cussing episodes. I held back five dollars a piece for them. The kids loved getting the cash.

"What did the Prices get you this time?" Jessie asked.

"They got me a pair of silk pajamas, same kind he bought for Pearl. A pair of slippers like she wears, and a bottle of perfume."

"They got her some nice things," said Mama. A carton of cigarettes was nice to her. Sweat beaded on my forehead. It had been a long day, and I wanted to put the walking wounded behind me.

"Annie, have you made a lot of friends at school?" Clarie asked.

"A few. Most of the girls I've met are on the same dorm floor as I am, so we hang out together."

Daddy walked in. "Mama, I have this pain that runs all the way up my chest."

If a glare were toxic, he'd be dead. She clenched her hand into a fist. "You probably got heartburn from eatin' all that fruitcake."

Not another word from him as he marched out of the kitchen, with Mama waving a spoon behind his head. Not speaking was his idea of punishing us, but he didn't know how overjoyed we were.

"I wish to God he'd drop dead."

"Mama!"

"Oh, Lord," Clarie snickered.

"It's his own damn fault. He'll be up all night again throwin' up 'cause of his hiatal hernia. Can't keep a garbage can in the bathroom for him. He's puked up the toilet."

"Gross," I moaned. "He's a good diet pill."

"Bastard's disgustin'," Gloria sneered.

"When's Aunt Mooney and Tish gettin' here?" Jessie asked.

Mama took a knife and dug thick chunks of margarine out of its container, piling it on each roll. "Tish ain't comin'. She's at Melvin's. Mooney said she'd be here at five."

I squinted into the greasy oven window. "I think the turkey's done."

"Yeah, it is," Mama said. "Let me get pot-gut in here to lift it out. Don't let him eat it up before the rest of the food gets done. Burl! Come take the turkey out!"

He didn't hear her. He was in the heat of giving one of his self-appointed editorials. "That's what's wrong with this country," he said, pointing a finger at the TV tube. "These women's groups. They don't have nothin' better to do than start trouble. Bunch of hairy lesb'ans. They're the reason TV's gone down the drain. There was this movie on the other night about this gay man . . . I tell you one thing, his parents didn't teach him the facts of life."

"You're so right," said Bill. "Burl, I may get a promotion to regional sales manager. I could make up to eighteen thousand dollars a year. Good money." He took a long puff of his cigarette.

"Whew, that's good. I'll tell you, if we didn't have Mama's income, I don't know what we'd do," he said.

"You'd have to work," said Clarie.

Mama ripped the cigarette from her mouth. "He ain't gonna do nothin' but what he's doin' now. Piled in front of that television, bitchin'."

Gloria sighed. "I don't know why you don't tell him to shut his mouth."

"He makes me sick," Clarie said.

Not one day at home was pleasant when Daddy was around, and he was always around. And Mama didn't do anything about it except complain. How could they settle for so little? I flung some utensils in the dish rack and stormed into the living room.

"Daddy, come take the turkey out *now!*" I was fuming.

He pulled out the turkey and quickly carved some hunks to shove into his mouth, slinging turkey juice over the kitchen floor.

With the knife still in his hand, Daddy resumed his editorial where he'd left off. "Did y'all see that news program about the, uh, gymnasts, those gals starvin' themselves. Little whores."

"Take some lessons from 'em," Gloria snarled on her way to her bedroom.

In front of Mama's rusted mirror, I ran my fingers over my clothes and the shape of my body. I could clearly see my collarbones and the points of my hipbones. My blue jeans hung loosely, and my stomach was sunken in.

When I walked through the dining room, Daddy stood with an Alka-Seltzer fizzing in a cup, and a thick slice of turkey in his other hand.

"I'm so proud of you for goin' to school," Jessie said as she rubbed my shoulder. I smiled. She wanted to go to junior college, but Mama had her believing she was a slow learner. She passed her GED the year before.

"Will y'all help a tired old battle-axe?" Aunt Mooney joked, as she lugged in a chocolate cake and a bag of sodas.

"Hey, Aunt Mooney. Are there any more bags?" I asked.

"One more. Ooh, I'm out of breath. You look so skinny!" she said as I passed her.

"Work," I replied. I brought in the last bag containing two meringue pies in pink cardboard boxes from the downtown bakery. "Mama, look what Aunt Mooney brought."

"Mooney, you didn't have to bring all that," she said.

"I needed to bring something so I could come my fat butt over here and pig out."

Mama called dinner. I waited in her bedroom to avoid the stampede. I thought of calling Kirby, my friend since junior high. Thought it'd be fun to go to a movie together while I had time. I could wish her a Merry Christmas and Happy New Year. There was so much to tell her. I could hear Daddy's heavy footsteps to the kitchen, and I got up.

"This turkey's so tender, Mama," he garbled, with food in his mouth.

"I haven't gotten to taste it yet, Burl. Save some for the rest of us."

"I am, Mama. Everybody's eaten, I think."

"I haven't. Annie hasn't. You don't give anybody else a chance."

She plunked a spoon of potato salad on her plate. He got up and opened the refrigerator. "Did you get some whupped cream for the peaches?"

"Bottom shelf."

I went to the stove with an empty plate and a fork. A ravine had been dug deep in the black-eyed peas, and I spooned a teaspoon helping, holding back as I did at the church. Food was everywhere. Turkey, dressing, black-eyed peas, red beans, potato salad, green beans, dressing, two kinds of pie, chocolate cake, peaches and pound cake, and a banana pudding. Mama griped about being poor, yet she managed to buy cigarettes, and Daddy always manipulated a banquet for holiday meals. It'd be gone by tomorrow. Scraps of food would trail from the kitchen to the television, with dirty bowls, saucers, and plates in the wake. I followed Mama into her bedroom to eat with Aunt Mooney. The rest of my sisters followed suit.

"Mama, Daddy acts like he's starvin' to death," Jessie said.

She stopped chewing. "I hope his stomach busts wide open."

"Mama!"

"I do. I'm so sick of him. I couldn't get anything done this afternoon, 'cause he kept comin' in the kitchen and standin' in my way."

"If I ate as much as Daddy, I'd weigh five hundred pounds," I said.

"If anybody else ate like Burl does, they'd be huge. He should weigh more . . . shoot, he weighs enough, the bottomless pit," she growled. "I'd love to shove a side of beef down his throat."

Mooney changed the subject. "How's school, Annie? Your Mama said you're makin' good grades."

"It's going well. I have to study real hard, because it's not as easy as junior college."

"Don't give up. Lord, how I wish we woulda went to college, don't you, Penny?"

"Yeah, instead, I married gobble-gut and got saddled with a bunch of young'uns."

"It's not our fault," said Gloria.

"I can't stand school," said Clarie.

"Lord, Tish hates it, too," said Mooney.

"It's not so bad," I said.

Aunt Mooney brought down her fork. "You look so tired and skinny, Annie."

Mama cut in, "She's spent her Christmas break workin' herself to death at that job and helpin' me with kids and cleanin' the house. Burl's been haulin' his ass out to the country, feedin' those stinkin' birds for Sister Willa. He don't even fix anythin' for the kids to eat."

"Does he still like Willa?" Clarie asked.

"Hell, yeah! I tried to tell her to be careful around Burl, and she don't listen. Let him grab her," Mama said.

"I can't stand Sister Willa," Gloria said.

"Aw, she's all right. They're just usin' Burl, and you know how stupid he is."

"Well, I couldn't get much for Tish this Christmas," said Mooney. "I got her that diamond necklace she wanted. I had to put it on lay-away six months ago. I got her those new designer jeans, I don't remember the name. Melvin bought her a stereo and some cassettes she's been wantin'. He always tries to outdo me at Christmas."

I fed Trudy what I couldn't finish, then took my plate to the sink. Daddy took a clean hand towel, wiped his greasy hands, and ran it across his mouth. As he walked out, Mama grabbed the towel and threw it on the floor with sheer hostility. I picked it up and put it in the dirty clothes. I patiently waited until everyone had dessert. I swooped through, stacking the dirty dishes. After washing them, I poured the leftovers into bowls and scrubbed the pots.

"Whew, Annie, you're so fast," said Mooney. "I was gonna help."

"No, I'm all done. Sit down and relax."

"Your Mama said you made some nice friends at school."

"Oh, I have. Really nice girls, from good homes."

"That's good. You need some friends." She was refilling her glass with Diet Coke. "Have you heard from Peter?"

"No. Doesn't matter. At least I won't have to worry about bringing him home. Imagine if he saw this place. He'd die."

"Honey, all that matters is that a guy likes you, not where you live and not who your parents are. You."

Aunt Mooney left by eight, afraid to drive alone at night. Bill and Clarie stuck it out, while Jessie and Keith split as soon as they finished dessert. Daddy's leg was hanging over the arm of the recliner, his mouth doing its nightly gibberish.

"And that's why people like me and Mama can't ever get ahead. Payin' taxes to a bunch of communist freaks in the Democratical party who waste our hard-earned money."

Bill nodded as he flicked his lighter.

"Mama, what was that movie that was on the other night?"

"I don't know, Burl."

"You know, the one with that gray-headed actor."

"You mean the movie with women gettin' raped in it?"

"That was a good movie, Mama."

"It was awful."

"I guess I missed it," Bill said.

"It sure was good. Maybe it'll come on again."

"You always say that when women are gettin' raped and tortured," Gloria said.

"I most certainly do not."

"You do, too. You like seein' women get abused."

"Well, a little rough lovin' don't hurt anyone, does it, Mama?"

"Shit," she replied.

"You make me sick," said Gloria as she stomped to her bedroom.

The New Year rang in as usual for me, meaningless. I was within an inch of going bonkers. I hadn't seen the Prices since the Monday my car was serviced for eight hours, no less, and Mama and Daddy pestered me about going back for a visit. "Are you going to the Prices' today? Call the Prices. The Prices are good to you."

I yearned to watch the New Year's Eve parties from New York, Europe, Boston, anywhere. But that wasn't Daddy's idea of fun. He switched channels until he found an old rerun to his liking.

1987
CHAPTER TWELVE

It was January the second. The TV was playing, but Mama and I didn't use Daddy's absence to watch anything. We were waiting for food. The Reverend came through the door carrying two Piggly Wiggly bags. He immersed himself in the bags, breathing heavily as he emptied the contents on the counter. I was praying he'd bought us some cheese, maybe some mustard and lettuce. I picked up a pack of some sort of lunchmeat.

"What's this?" I asked.

"Mama likes it," he answered.

"I don't like it, but I have to have it to take sandwiches to work."

"If you don't like it, don't eat it," I said. "Eat something healthier. Buy yourself some turkey and fruit, stick it in the fridge, and tell everyone to stay out of it. This crap isn't even good enough to have a name on it. No telling what's in it."

"Mama can have some of this turkey," he said.

"There won't be any left, after you wipe it out," she snapped. "Did you get anythin' for the kids?"

"I got the lunchmeat. They'd waste the turkey. I woulda got more, if I'd known you wanted some. Stuff's so expensive."

"Can't afford it if you eat four sandwiches at a time, Burl."

"Next time, I'll get some turkey ham, it's cheaper."

"I wouldn't eat that crap," I said.

"You would if you had nothin' else," said Mama.

"You have a job, Mama. Buy yourself some good food. Don't let anyone near it."

Daddy wadded up the bag and threw it on the floor. "I tell you, it's a 'bomination when you go to the grocery store and buy two or three things, and it costs you thirty dollars. Those rich politicians are the reason people can't afford to buy food." He shoved a hunk of meat into his mouth. The economy hadn't hurt him too much. Every item in the grocery bags was something he liked. Sliced turkey breast, a steak, a pack of bacon, some ham, a couple of cans of corned beef, a bag of rice, three loaves of bread, a few canned goods. Nothing for the kids. Nothing for me. Unidentifiable lunchmeat for Mama. Where did he get the money?

A slab of grease melted as he rocked the frying pan back and forth. I only guessed that he was having the steak with the turkey.

"I tell you, hell's gonna be full of rich people," he said.

"No it's not," I argued.

"It most certainly is."

"Why? You tell me why?"

"Because people are puttin' money ahead of God."

"God loves everyone."

"I know that, but a person'll burn in hell—"

"You mean people that work hard," I said.

"Lots of people work hard," Daddy said. "They don't all beat and cheat people."

Mama glared at him.

I was angry. "Not all rich people beat and cheat. You're putting every single rich person in one category and judging them."

"No, I'm not. The Bible clearly says—"

"Don't start, Burl. Can't even relax without you bitchin' about some shit."

I was uncontrollably angry. "Who's going to heaven, then? People like Brother Buddy, who has five kids that welfare supports?"

"Brother Buddy's a good man. He's sick," he said.

"Yeah, mentally."

"Just wait until you have stomach ulcers."

"I won't, because I have nothing to feel guilty about."

"The Bible clearly says—"

"Goodnight."

I walked to Mama's room. My heart was thumping rapidly. I ripped off my clothes and threw on my nightshirt. It was only seven o'clock, but I was going to bed. Walking and sleeping kept my mind off what I didn't have, and onto my future, and if I could make it through tomorrow, I'd leave early Sunday morning and get back to UEM. I'd never be homesick again, I told myself, as Mama's screaming started up.

"Burl, you ain't happy 'til you make everybody else miserable!"

"I'll just keep my mouth shut then," he sulked.

"That'll be the day!"

"Mama, I ain't real important around here."

"No! You think you're the only one that deserves to eat, deserves anythin'!"

I shut my eyes, and tried to shut out their voices. I hated him. He was going to live forever. So was Henry. I rolled over on Mama's bed, knowing there was no escape unless I got in my car and drove away. I hadn't the energy for that tonight. Tomorrow I was expected at the Prices, and I wanted so much to cancel. I could tell Henry I had a virus, and he wouldn't want me ten feet from their house. But I'd go, because there was still that chance he might offer money for clothes. I wanted new clothes. I wanted to feel beautiful. And I wasn't going to feel guilty about it. If Peter had raped me, I wouldn't have complained, because I was that lonely. Just one last showdown, and I wouldn't be seeing Henry for weeks, months. Schoolwork and my plans to leave Mississippi would fill me. I had helped at home as much as I could.

Mama's voice returned to its original softness. "You wanna sandwich?"

"I'm not hungry," I said.

"There's enough turkey for a sandwich."

"I'm too tired to eat."

"You've been sleepin' so much. I think you need to go to the doctor."

"It's working those long hours. There's never anything good to eat."

She sat on the bed. "I stay starvin'. I'm fat, but it's 'cause I live off that junk at the store."

"You want some turkey?" Daddy stood at the door.

"I'm not hungry," I answered.

"She's worn out. I'm worn out," Mama said.

"I've been so tired lately," he said.

"From what?"

He was acting gentle, the self-pity evident. "I wonder if I have low blood sugar. Brother Leonard got so tired, they thought he had leukemia. They found out it was low blood sugar."

"If you have anything, Burl, it's high blood sugar. It's a wonder you ain't went into a coma."

At the Prices' house, Henry was moody. In his hand was a letter from Social Security. I hadn't been there two minutes before he had Pearl wound up and in tears.

"It never fails. Think things are going well, then something like this comes and spoils the day." He shook his head, his skin flushed with anger. "They raised it on us last year. Now we have to pay out more, and they pay less on the doctor bills. It's not right. Well, thank the Lord we have that supplemental policy."

Pearl was wiping her eyes. "Damn government."

Henry adjusted his hearing aid. His speech deepened and slowed. "Been working on our estimated taxes the last couple of nights. That's a headache. Got to be done, though. They get you over each little thing. Oh boy, if you had more in savings, they'd suck the taxes off that." Looking at Pearl, he said, "But the Lord'll take care of us, won't he?"

"Yes siree," she smiled.

"He's blessed us so we can help Annie."

Pearl nodded and patted my leg.

"Even though we can't deduct what we give her, that's okay. The Lord will continue to provide."

He was still pissed off underneath that holy enthusiasm. *That's life, Pop. Nothing runs perfectly.* He put his hand over his heart.

"I know Annie won't let us down. She isn't lazy. She proved that by working on her holiday break. Most students do nothing. Go shopping. Spend money they don't need to spend. Spoiled. Not Annie. Mom and I are so proud of you."

He was in tears. Pearl was in tears. I was disgusted.

"Did you ever get your paycheck to the bank?"

"Yes, sir."

"How much does that give you to go back on?"

I took out my checkbook to look, but he was already reaching for it.

He studied it tenaciously. "Uh-huh . . . uh-huh . . . oh, what's this?"

"What?"

"Written on the twenty-eighth to Jitney Jungle for eighteen dollars, thirty-eight cents? Now, darlin', I know your family has it tough financially, but you can't support them, you hear."

"I'm not."

He shook my checkbook as he talked. "You need your money for college."

"Pop, I know that. But since I do live at home when I'm not at school, I have to eat."

"You can't help your parents out of their mess, you understand?"

"I wasn't. We needed food, and since I've been eating there, I thought I should contribute."

He gave me a brooding look through his glasses. "But you can give and give, and it never gets any better."

"I know that, Pop. I've lived it with my parents my whole life."

"You see, that's why I wanted you to bring me that check. It's tempting to spend money when it's there, but it doesn't—"

"I didn't spend the money," I said firmly. "I never get to spend any money. You know it's not one of those situations where I go home and everything's clean, and the food overflows in the cupboards. My family life is far from normal, and you know that. I've been home one month and haven't written but one check. I'm out of makeup. I need clothes . . ." I forced myself not to cry.

Henry looked hurt. "Darlin', you could've come over here and eaten with us every day. I didn't know there wasn't anything for you to eat."

"Poppycock! It doesn't matter whether Annie buys food. If she needs any money, I'll give it to her." Pearl was angry.

He touched his glasses. "Mom loves you so much."

"I know that, and I appreciate her very much." *Please don't try to make me feel guilty.*

"Honey, just call me anytime of the day or night if you ever need any money," she said.

"Okay, sweetie. Before Annie leaves, you can give her a little money."

"I certainly will," she said boldly.

"I'm going to fix us some lunch." He pecked her on the cheek, smiled at me, pecked my cheek, and strolled into the kitchen, shoving my checkbook into his sweater pocket. One second, a loving old man, the next, a Gestapo.

Their kitchen was small, with white appliances, white cabinets, and white linoleum flooring. It was spotless, no food or grease on the floor. Where you weren't risking your life cooking on a greased-up, clogged-up, burnt-up stove. Where it was a breeze washing the dishes and not having to scrub the pots, because the food wasn't engrained into the metal. Where the garbage can wasn't overflowing. Where you didn't have to fight off the roaches and Daddy. But even at times when I felt I was starving, I hated eating here. Here, savoring was sinful, eating rapidly, a crime.

Each meal was eaten at a small wooden table with an elegant yellow tablecloth and simple plastic placemats. In the larger dining room, the mahogany set went unused for years, as friendships dwindled away.

Two baked chicken thighs, fresh green beans, and mashed potatoes were neatly arranged on my plate. A yeast roll with diet margarine melting in the middle of it sat on a saucer. Sugar-free Jell-O with bananas was dessert. All on Pearl's plate had been precisely weighed, no more, no less, every gram of carbohydrate, protein, and fat dutifully tallied.

Fruit magnets held a calendar on their refrigerator. Doctors' appointments were methodically penciled in, and he never used a pen to balance his checkbook, in case he had to erase a number. He lived for his meetings with doctors, bankers, and lawyer, since it gave him a chance to have someone rational to talk to. His conversations with Pearl hadn't been rational in years.

"Saw Benny Jones the other day," Henry said. Benny used to be the associate pastor at First Baptist. "He's doing well. Still preaching in Louisville. He and Sandra were down visiting Lenora. Proud of that granddaughter."

"That's nice," I said.

"She sent us a picture last month. Such a pretty little baby." He picked up a crumb and set it on his plate. "I guess Lenora graduated last summer, yeah, last summer from a school in . . . oh, where was that school? Tulsa, it was in Tulsa. Graduated with honors. That was the most beautiful wedding I ever saw. Remember Lenora's wedding, Mom?"

She nodded.

He let Pearl wash up the dishes, which she made into a major event. She wanted to feel useful again. I dried, while Henry stuck the leftover chicken in the refrigerator.

I was preparing my exit, but Henry wasn't going to let me go so easily.

"You know, I've been thinking that you should probably work for a tax firm when you graduate. Don't you think that'd be good?"

"There are so many job possibilities in accounting. I'm not sure where I'll work, or who'd hire me."

"Well, tax firms are much more distinguished."

"Tax firms are fine. There are also oil companies and banks. Lots of places."

"Yeah, that's right. You do plan on looking for a job here, don't you, honey?"

"No, I'll probably have to look in Jackson, since there are more jobs there. I mean, Soso's economy isn't good right now."

"Jackson's a nice city," Pearl said.

"Yeah, it is. I just wish Annie would consider working for a tax firm."

"I'll go where I'm hired, to get the experience."

"Jack Thames' daughter got on with the biggest accounting firm in New Orleans."

"That's good. Mr. Thames knows a lot of people, since he's a CPA."

"Annie'll get a good job where she wants to," Pearl interrupted. She was getting flustered.

"I know, sweetheart," he told her softly.

He leaned to stand up. "I have some bookkeeping to do, don't I? Stay with Mom."

Thirty seconds later, he came out with her checkbook.

"Annie, honey, should we go ahead and give you what you owe in full on the tuition, or half?"

"Half is fine. I can pay the rest out of the work-study money." *Just let me leave!*

"No, darlin'. Mom wants to pay it. It would mean so much to her."

"I'm paying for it. All of it," she said firmly.

"Okay, darlin', you can. Now, Annie, I'll give you one check for what's left on your tuition, and another check for a little extra."

I watched him writing out the amounts. Perhaps Pearl's outburst did it. I got more than I bargained for.

"Okay. Seven hundred eighty to the school, and two hundred dollars for little Annie," he declared.

I took the checks, trying to remain calm. "Thank you, Pop, Mommy Junior. I love you very much."

It was four o'clock, the day gone. Had it been profitable? I was shocked at his sudden generosity, but it was the remarks of telling me where to work, wanting me to live in the same town as he that were traumatic. That would be almost as bad as living with Daddy the rest of my life.

CHAPTER THIRTEEN

On Sunday, January fourth, I checked into Borden Hall for the spring semester. Marge wasn't in from Mobile, and the fifth floor was still vacant. Suzy was busy helping the housing department in a neighboring dormitory. I took my clothes to the campus laundromat behind my dorm and re-washed every piece of clothing that had been in the vicinity of Mama and her smoking. I went back to my dorm and organized my side of the room, then waited for Denise and Marla to show up.

Denise came in at four thirty, carrying an extra suitcase full of new clothes. I sat on her bed and watched her slowly unfold and hang up each piece. She was a bargain-hunter. Wore something different each time I saw her.

"That's a nice color," I said.

"I love pink," Denise smiled. "Mama got this at J-Mack's in Slidell."

"I've never heard of that store."

"Aw, you'd love it. The clothes are cheap! Mama bought me a bunch of things there for Christmas. This would look good on you." She held a green long-sleeved blouse against my chest.

"I like green," I said.

"Guess who paid me a visit at home? Miss Leslie Lang. She came down with her mom to visit her uncle. He's in jail in Biloxi for stealin' cars."

"My word. Leslie said she was going to write me, but she never did."

"Heard from Peter?" Her tone was cautious.

"Nope."

"How are you doin'?"

"I'm doing just fine."

Denise sat on her roommate's bed and looked at me. "I have somethin' to tell you. I wanted to tell you last semester, but I wasn't sure how you'd feel about me if you knew this. I'm seein' someone."

"Who?"

"Christopher Wright."

I tried to place his face with the name.

"You met him in the cafeteria. Remember? He's a friend of Suzy's. He plays softball."

"Okay. But doesn't he have a serious girlfriend? You know, what's her name?"

"Linda. Yeah, he has a girlfriend."

I was stunned. "Denise."

"I know. I like him, Annie. I really like him."

"How long has this been going on?"

She sniffed. "Since October. Halloween night."

I was with Peter that night, I remembered. "What about Linda? Are they going to break up."

She shook her head. "I don't know. He says they are. He took me out durin' the break. He lives close by, in Pascagoula. My parents met him. Mama thinks he's a little rough around the edges."

"I can see her thinking that. He's a ladies' man?"

"I know he seems that way, but he's not."

Marla's parents had been down to Vicksburg to see her for three weeks, and she was anxious to get back to exercising. I met her on the track at seven o'clock. We were cold and needed to walk fast to warm up.

"Mmmm, mmm," Marla moaned. "That Denise is crazy for going out with some other gal's man. She'd better watch herself now."

"I'm shocked, Marla. You know how prudish she is."

"Prissy is how she is, and catty. Catwoman. She'd better take those long claws out of that guy or she's going to regret it."

"I don't think she will. She's in love."

"Lord have mercy. She just thinks she is." She smiled at me. "You look good, Annie. You don't seem to be as down as you were before."

"I'm okay, Marla. I'm moving to the mountains, remember?"

"That's right. You sure are."

On Monday morning, Nell dropped Dr. Dearman's cup of coffee in the copier, and the machine shorted out. A new one had to be ordered. By the time I got to work-study at one, Nell was frazzled.

"Take this to Dr. Katz." She shoved a memo in my hand.

"Do you want me to proof it, Mrs. Johnston?" I asked.

"Yes, do that first."

The first sentence had three misspelled words, and she had smudged some White-Out over part of a paragraph.

"Can I have Dr. Katz's notes, and I'll quickly retype this?"

"Oh, Lord, did I mess it up?" She handed me his two pages of notes.

"It's not bad, just needs some fixing."

I finished in five minutes and took the memo down the hall to Dr. Katz's office. He was busy and didn't look up.

"Tell Mrs. Johnston I need Dr. Clark's telephone number, please," he said.

"Yes, sir." I turned to leave.

"Annie?"

"Yes?"

"Welcome back," he smiled.

"Thank you, Dr. Katz."

Peter had wasted no time. He was dating the new graduate student in the housing department. Her name was Nancy Long, and Suzy didn't like her. She thought Nancy was snobby, because she was from a college in West Virginia. I thought Nancy was pretty when I first saw her standing in line with Peter in the cafeteria. She was wearing a long dress, flat shoes, and no bra. She was different, I thought. And I wanted to be different. What was even more surprising was Nancy was getting her master's degree in psychology, so her classes were in the education and psychology building where I did work-study. She stuck out like a sore thumb.

Peter was making it a point to speak to me whenever he saw me on the campus or in the cafeteria.

"Hey, Annie! How's it going! You look nice today."

I guess Peter thought he had to speak to me, this unfortunate "nice girl" whose heart he had broken. I began to dread the cafeteria.

"I can't go in there," I told Marla.

"Why? Is it because of Peter? Girl, that boy ain't nothin'. That bug-headed bastard. When you come into this cafeteria, you hold your head up high and shake that pretty behind of yours. And if he says anything to you, you look at him like he's dog shit. Don't let him intimidate you."

For some reason, out of the blue, Nancy started speaking to me. When she passed me in the ed-psych hallway, she smiled and asked how I was doing. I was doing fine, I replied. We both kept moving. She probably thought I was one of Peter's beloved followers. Perhaps she thought I was one of the many young women who had a crush on him. She was confident. Honey-blond hair, doll eyes, and a small pointed nose. She lived at Legion Hall, the best dormitory at UEM, but it was located off the main campus. Her red car was a frequent sight on the campus roads and in the parking spaces near Taylor Hall. I was really hurt, but I sensed that a resolution was emerging. If Peter and I had stayed together, he wouldn't have treated me well. At this point, I wanted someone to treat me like a goddess.

I had gone home every weekend since the beginning of the semester, and every weekend I regretted it. January had past, also Valentine's Day. Pretty soon, students would be talking about Mardi Gras and spring break. Marla and I were faithfully walking our laps. My weight was now one hundred fifteen. Marla was down ten pounds, her stomach firm. The body remembers that it was fit before, she told me. Sometimes Leslie would join us. She'd walk a lap or two, then stop and wait until Marla and I walked a few more laps, then she'd get up and walk again. Leslie tried to be a trooper.

"I think I'm allergic to the gravel on this track," Leslie said.

"Girl," said Marla, "you're not allergic to anything."

"Well, I know I'm allergic to nuts. Last night, I made some peanut butter cookies, and a rash broke out under my armpits and across my neck."

Marla shook her head. "Get walking, girl."

I finished my last accounting class for the day. I had to grab a quick lunch and be at work-study by one.

"Hey, Annie."

I looked up. "Oh. Hey."

To conceal my embarrassment, I walked toward the door. Thomas came up and walked next to me.

"I've been looking for you," he said.

"I've been here."

"You must still be walking. You look wonderful."

I stopped. "I'm still walking. How's the biking?"

"I rode ninety miles last Saturday. I'm doing some racing this spring."

"That's great."

"Yeah. You know, I heard from Peter that you two aren't seeing each other anymore."

"That's right."

"I'm sorry."

"Don't be. It happens."

He was quiet for a moment.

"Would you like to go for coffee sometime?"

"Sure," I answered.

"Friday night?"

"I'm sorry, I have to go home this weekend. How about Sunday? I'll be back by early afternoon."

"I'll pick you up at six?"

"Six is fine," I smiled.

As soon as Thomas was out of sight, I panicked. What had I done? Thomas Barnes was Peter's biking buddy. Thomas was a very competitive type, and I was scared of my own shadow. Without effort, Thomas made straight A's in honors classes, but I had to study hard to get good grades in undergraduate classes. Thomas was athletic, and I was a former couch potato. Thomas looked like he'd jumped straight out of a hunk-of-the-month calendar, yet I'd never be Miss America.

I woke up with throbbing muscles and a headache the following morning. Dead for sleep, I went to classes and listened to my professors drone about matters that wouldn't benefit my life now or ever. I drudged to the cafeteria with no appetite, but I stood in the diet line and got the tuna noodle casserole and a cup of coffee. I poured three creamers in the coffee and sipped slowly. Pushing the casserole away, I was trying to decide if I should call Nell and tell her I was sick.

At work-study, Dr. Dearman was on a copying frenzy, so I made three runs to the copier for her and one for Dr. Katz. Nell had me walk across the campus to the treasurer's office. Today would be the day every professor was in the office. Nell was having fits.

I left work at five, sweating and chilled. Denise walked me to the campus infirmary, where the diagnosis was a sinus infection. A quick shot of antibiotic, a bottle of pills, and I was in and out in ten minutes. With Denise practically holding me up, I worried about what it would cost me. My checking account was dwindling, and I couldn't complain to Pop. I had been going home, but I'd visited the Prices only twice. During those two visits, Henry wore me out completely, and I hated the way I saw myself when I left their house. I wasn't Annie, the someday-great actress. Or Annie, the someday-beautiful lady who lived in the mountains and accomplished great things and loved people. Or even Annie, the accountant. I felt like a worthless nobody. I wasn't at the top of the accounting classes. Henry made me question my intelligence, my spirituality, and my worth. So, the distance between visits meant no extra money. Didn't matter if I wrote Pop every week. Didn't matter if I called him every day. Not seeing him face-to-face meant the phone calls and letters didn't count.

Chapter Fourteen

I was still sick on Friday but went to my classes, and paid Henry and Pearl a visit late that afternoon. Henry was tired, and he showed no mercy.

"How's your grades?"

"Good," I replied.

"All A's?"

"No. Mostly B's."

His eyes were boring holes in my soul, and I knew he wasn't pleased. He pointed to his face. "You said your nose is stopped up?"

"My sinuses," I said.

"Need to go to the doctor?"

"I went to the campus doctor. I'm feeling better."

He folded his hands. "How much do you have in your checking account?"

"Let me see."

He studied my checkbook. "Whew, money don't last long, does it?"

"I paid my car . . ."

"What do you do with your work-study money? The money you got from Tri-Mart?"

"It's in my checking account. I had to pay my car insurance."

"When was that due?"

"February the twelfth. I had to buy some—"

"Well, honey." He handed me back my checkbook. "You have to watch what you spend."

I had over three hundred dollars in my account. Did he think I should have a million?

"I had to buy some underwear and a new pair of jeans."

He inhaled, and put his hand over his heart. "You see, Mom doesn't understand. She'll give and give, but she doesn't know there's a limit."

You happily wrote the check to me, old man.

"I haven't been feeling so well lately," he continued, as he switched off the TV with the remote control. "I'm going to see Dr. Wallace on Tuesday."

I nodded, forcing myself to hold in my cough.

"Hey. Where were you? You weren't in your room the other night," he said.

"Oh, which night, Pop?" *I'm going to cry.*

"Last Wednesday, yeah, I believe it was last Wednesday."

"I was washing my clothes in the laundromat."

"At night?" He shrugged and looked at Pearl. She was picking her fingernails.

"Yes, sir. I washed with my friend Marla."

"Who?"

"Marla," I answered with gritted teeth. My eyeballs were about to burst.

"Who's she, now?"

"She lives in my dorm."

"Is she majoring in accounting?"

"No, sir. Management information systems."

"Manage what?"

"Management information systems." I spoke loudly and slowly.

"Never heard of it."

"Computers. She's learning about computers," I said.

"Really? That's wonderful. She must be very smart."

"Yes, sir."

"Maybe she can help you with your studies."

I was about to lose my mind.

"I make better grades than she does."

He stood up. "I'll be in the little boy's room."

Pearl was humming as I heard the toilet flush. Henry came back to the living room with a stern expression on his face. He gave me a slight smile and sat down in his recliner. He touched my tennis shoe with his foot, but he didn't say anything for a while.

"Mom's nephew, Clayton, is moving to Clarksville to be the minister of the Second Baptist Church."

"That's great," I said. *I don't care!*

"I remember when Mom and I used to bring little Clayton over to our house to spend the weekend. He was so cute, and Mom would take him shopping for clothes and shoes. He graduated seminary school in seventy-five thanks to Mom," he beamed.

When I left, I felt like I had been violated. I considered it a blessing that Henry had never had a child of his own, because he or she would have ended up in a mental institution.

Chapter Fifteen

When I got back to Hattiesburg on Sunday, I bought a newspaper, scanned the classifieds, studied, and showered for my date with Thomas. I didn't really want to go, with Henry's words ringing in my mind: "You've got to watch what you spend." I knew I had to get a second job.

Thomas took me to Applebee's on Hardy Street. I picked at a grilled chicken salad as he ate a hamburger and drank a Coke.

"Eddy Merckx is the greatest," he beamed. "No other cyclist has ever come close to winning the races he has."

"What country is he from?"

"Belgium."

"What makes a person want to go through so much suffering and pain?" I asked.

He shrugged. "Passion. To some, he's an animal. To many, he's an artist."

"What made you want to ride?"

"Dad took us over to France when I was eleven, and I saw a stage of the Tour de France, and that was it. I was hooked."

Thomas glowed. Not a care in the world. He had it together. He had his own apartment and supportive parents. The support I got from my parents felt like standing in quicksand. Thomas's dad was a partner in a law firm, and my father was educated in the art of slothfulness. Thomas's mom was a registered nurse in an administrative position at a large hospital. My mom was a chain-smoking clerk in a dead-end position in a curb store. Thomas had been to Europe several times. I had lived in over thirty rent houses in my lifetime. Thomas had an undergraduate degree from Ole Miss.

"Did you have a scholarship at Ole Miss?" I asked.

He nodded. "I don't know why I'm getting a master's. I had job offers. You see, I went to Europe to ride after I graduated. My dad wanted me to work as a stockbroker, but he understood. He thinks cycling's a beautiful sport."

"Your dad seems like a great guy."

"He is."

"You're very lucky, you know, that he'll help you."

"He does. I worked for his accountant a year and saved some money, too."

I nodded with a smile.

"I bet your dad's proud of you, Annie," he said.

"I guess so."

"You know, since you're the only one of your sisters in college. What did the rest do? Get married?"

"You got it."

Thomas parked by my dorm. Behind us, a party was going on at Bolton Hall. Even the lawn was packed with students. Thomas turned off the ignition and moved his eyes toward me.

"I had a great time tonight," he said.

"So did I. Thanks for taking me out."

"Can I call you?"

"Sure."

"I want to see you again."

"That's fine," I nodded. "Let's just take things slowly, Thomas, as friends."

"As friends."

I didn't believe him. Especially when he leaned over and planted a kiss on my lips. And I let him. He pulled away and looked into my eyes and kissed me again. I pushed him away. "I have to go now."

He got out and walked me to the back door.

"I'll see you soon." He kissed my cheek.

As Thomas was walking away, a guy yelled his name. He slipped his keys into his pocket and walked into the crowd.

I had work-study on Monday afternoons, so I waited until Tuesday to look for a second job. I filled out an application at Tri-Mart, but the manager wanted me to work during the week and be on call whenever he needed me. I couldn't work those crazy hours. I had to go to classes and study, and I had to walk to keep my weight off. I cranked my car and drove back down Hardy Street. I stopped at stores, restaurants, and the C & R drugstore. C & R was a huge chain, and I convinced the manager that he needed me on Saturdays and Sundays. I told him I'd clean shelves, mop the floors, stock, and help customers. The store stayed busy, and the cashiers hadn't time to straighten up and run the registers. He hired me at three eighty an hour. My shift was nine until three. I was very happy to have the job, but my spirit dampened when I realized I wouldn't be able to go home on weekends.

Mama sounded depressed on the telephone, and I pitied her when I hung up. When I told her I was working the weekends, she just said, "Okay."

I was proud of myself as I read my newest list of goals. The main goal was to save my money to pay my summer tuition. I was the ever-so-busy Annie, and I felt as if I could do anything. I was helping to pay for my own degree, and I could see my future. Hard work goes a long way. I called Pop.

"Did you say three eighty an hour?" he asked. "That's not bad."

"I'll get in twelve hours on the weekends."

"What's your work?"

"I'll be helping the customers on the floor, mostly."

"That's good, helping people." He was tired, his voice flat. "How's your grades?"

I had just told him the Friday before. "They're good."

He didn't hear me. "How many hours are you working on the weekends?"

I stared up at the ceiling. "Twelve hours."

"Wow." He was perking up. "Yeah, now how many hours work-study?"

"Twelve hours work-study, so that's twenty-four hours."

On Thursday, I received a single, perfect, long-stemmed red rose from Thomas. It was waiting at the front desk of my dorm when I got in from dinner. Marla and Denise were with me and immediately started clucking like hens. By the time we got to the elevator, I was blushing. This was something I'd only seen happen on TV.

"I guess I'll call and thank him," I said.

"No, girl," Marla said. "You wait. He'll call you tonight. He'll want to know if you got the rose, and he's going to ask you out again."

"She's right," Denise agreed. She squealed. "Do you know how lucky you are?"

Strange to hear that, I thought. I never felt lucky.

Thomas called at eight o'clock and asked me to a movie on Friday night.

Watching the pavement along Highway 49, I felt rich, being escorted in luxury in Thomas's black Camaro. Not a speck of dust, paint, or motor oil was on it or in it, and he washed and waxed it himself. I found myself trying to name his cologne. Whatever it was, it was an aphrodisiac and made me feel aroused.

He took me to Chesterfield's, a restaurant near campus. I knew what I was going to order, but I continued to study the menu. Stealing peeks above the menu, I scanned Thomas's face and thick eyelashes. I hadn't noticed the natural curl in his abundant black hair. He looked up.

"Order whatever you want. Do you like lobster?"

"Well, not really," I answered. I had never tasted it.

"I love it," he said.

I was thinking like Mama. Wondering how Thomas could afford to take me out if he wasn't working a job. *Think big, Annie.* Did his parents just hand over money to him?

"The turkey sandwich sounds good to me," I said.

"Are you sure? Would you like a steak or fish?"

"No." I shut the menu. "Turkey's fine."

After we ordered, he placed his arms on the table, his eyes expressing his like for me.

"I'm glad we're going out again."

I smiled without saying anything.

"I've been thinking about you."

"Really?" I swallowed hard.

"I think about you a lot, Annie."

"What's there to think about?"

"What do you mean? You're intelligent and beautiful."

"Just wait until you get to know me." *The roach motel hell-babe.*

"I feel like I already do."

"Well, I don't know you yet, Thomas."

"I want you to know me."

I said nothing.

"Do you want to know me?"

"Yes. I want to go slow, though."

Later we sat in the dark theatre watching, of all things, a romantic movie. He'd planned this, I thought. At midnight, he drove me back to my dorm.

"Would you like to come over to my apartment sometime? I love to cook, and I want to fix dinner for you."

"That'd be nice."

"Next week?"

"Well, maybe Thursday?"

"Thursday it is," he beamed.

"I guess I should go. I have to work tomorrow."

"What are you doing for spring break?"

"Well, I have to see . . . um, I have plans with my sisters."

"I just thought you might like to come up to Jackson."

"Oh gosh," I said. "I already promised my sisters and grandparents I'd spend some time with them."

He smiled. "You must be close to your family."

"Yes, I am."

"Well, we may be going out of town anyway. My folks have a log cabin in Colorado."

"Colorado! I want to live there."

"Oh, have you been there?"

"No, but I've seen pictures."

"It's incredible. There's tons of cycling, rock climbing, skiing . . ."

"The mountains," I sighed.

"Lots of those, too," he smiled and reached for my hand. "I enjoyed seeing you."

He took my other hand, urging me closer. Then he kissed my mouth. I didn't fight him when he tightly brought my waist against his. My arms went around his shoulders. He moved his lips down my neck and whispered, "You make me happy."

Christopher Wright was coming by our dorm regularly to see Denise. They usually sat in the lobby and talked, or sometimes they'd go out for a soda. He was a physical education major. Large shoulders, and a dash of freckles across his nose. Suzy was jumping hoops about it, having constant gossip sessions with Marla and me about Denise's scandalous affair. I was disappointed, though. Christopher still had the girlfriend, who on several occasions had joined us in the cafeteria. While Denise and Christopher played footsie under the table, Linda sat next to Christopher, oblivious to it all.

Chapter Sixteen

Spring break came the third week in March. Marla flew up to Detroit to see her parents. Denise went home to the coast to wait for Christopher, who had promised to visit her. I drove home Friday after my last class ended at noon. I ran over several torn garbage bags as I parked in the sand. I jumped out and slammed my car door. The television was going strong inside the house.

"Daddy!" I yelled.

"Hey, baby! I didn't know you was here."

With my arms full of trash, he hugged me. I held my breath until he was far enough away. "There's trash everywhere. Why hasn't anyone picked it up?"

"I know. Those stupid dogs from down the street have been tearin' up everybody's garbage. I tell ya, when I catch one of 'em, I'm gonna shoot it."

"I need a garbage bag. Are we out?"

He hesitated. "Nah. Uh, let me go look. Mama burns the garbage in the back."

"In the back?"

Trudy followed me as I stomped around the side of the house. The air was filled with a foul odor. With tears in my eyes I followed the trail as it snaked its way through the backyard, streaming down into the ditch. Green slimy muck ran alongside the house, over and under anything in its path. Sewage runneth over. Imagining my friends seeing this was too much to endure. If that wasn't degrading enough, add on the sight of the burn pile, which was small to begin with, but now took up most of our tiny backyard. No matter where we moved, my parents created a burn pile. Mama said it helped save on the garbage bags. One windy day, she burned, along with the trash, several trees and part of the yard at the rent house in the country. Marching inside the Manor, I found Mama tediously stacking several days' of dirty dishes.

"The kids and Trudy are going to get in that gunk and get sick," I said.

"Mr. Patel told your daddy to get the stuff to fix the sewage line, and he'd take it off the rent," she said.

"He doesn't know Daddy too well, does he?" I said.

"Shit. I ain't got any money to buy any pipes. And he ain't gonna move from the couch long enough to dig up the old ones. Said he's gonna get Mulie to help him."

"Mama, Mulie's retarded."

"Well, he'll work, Annie."

"Jesus, even retarded people work. Why doesn't Mr. Patel buy the stuff, and Daddy can do the labor?"

"I told Burl to call him about it. He's too scared."

"Why? Don't tell me Daddy's still behind on the rent."

"Two hundred dollars."

"Darn! How much could pipes cost? Ask Gloria for some money."

"I ain't," she said, waving her hand.

"I'll ask her."

"Please don't get her started."

"I can't help, and when I do, Daddy just—"

"I ain't askin' you to."

I guess Mama wanted to have some mother-daughter time with me, so we cleaned the yard Friday evening while she cussed at the Reverend. He threw some junk on his truck, promising to take it to a real garbage dump later. I cleaned the house for two days. The only alternative was to burn the place down to the ground.

Food was scarce. Nothing you could grab and put in your mouth to tide you over. No bread for sandwiches. Nothing to put in the sandwiches. Wiley and Holly were puny, so I took them to

McDonald's for hamburgers, which was better junk than the junk they had been getting. I weakened with guilt and hunger pangs, giving Mama twenty dollars to buy some canned goods and milk and cereal for the girls. Gloria brought home some chicken, pork chops, and ground beef, apparently because I was there and Mama urged her to. Gloria made it clear that she didn't want to do it. I was furious at her for not caring for her little Holly, leaving the burden on everyone else.

I commuted to Hattiesburg to work at C & R on Saturday and Sunday. Since I was home, relatives were expected for supper Sunday afternoon. Relatives meaning my sisters and brothers-in-law, Gloria's new boyfriend, Aunt Mooney, Tish, and her new boyfriend. A house full of authentic lulus, I thought, as I drenched barbecue sauce on two fryers. Reaching for the salt and pepper, something my parents never used sat next to a can of shortening.

"What are y'all doing with olive oil?"

"That's Daddy's for his prayin'," Mama answered.

"He's buying expensive olive oil but won't buy pipes?"

"He's been prayin' and fastin' with Brother Buddy."

"I can tell by his gut he's been fasting. I can tell by the empty cabinets he's been fasting. I can see by all the empty cans we picked up the other day he's been fasting. I think he's got fasting and gorging confused. Must've gotten sick again."

"Those panic attacks are horrible, Annie."

"I hope they do scare the hell out of him."

"Well, they ain't done me any good. He kept me up the other night readin' Bible verses to him."

"He should be scared for his family, not himself. But no, Daddy's a man of the cloth—the tablecloth."

Dressed in a leopard print blouse and black polyester pants, Aunt Mooney was the first to arrive, carrying a tossed salad, chicken and dumplings, sodas, a green bean casserole, and a lemon Bundt cake.

"Let me help you, Mooney," Daddy said. He was barely able to pry himself out of his recliner.

"Ooh, Burl, thanks. These drinks are heavy."

Her short black hairpiece was attached on top of her cropped hair and had been teased unmercifully.

"Oh, Annie. You look so pretty, not as sickly as you did at Christmas, thank the Lord. Is that a new shirt?"

"No, I've had it for years. Clarie gave it to me."

"It looks brand new. You take care of your clothes. I wish Tish would. She just throws hers down."

"Where is Tish?"

"She's comin' with that beast she calls a boyfriend."

"Is he nice?"

"In front of me. But I've got him pegged, the trashy thing."

"Where did she meet him?" Tish never socialized.

"From her friend Rhonda. I wish she wouldn't hang out with her. Tish can't get involved with someone who's ambitious, no, she has to scrape the bottom of the barrel. Where's your Mama?"

"In the bathroom."

Daddy brought in the rest of the bags, with Clarie and Bill behind him.

"Come hug your Aunt Mooney, Bill," she gushed.

"Hey, Mama," Clarie said.

Mama walked in the kitchen rubbing her tousled hair. Even with her makeup on, she looked dreadfully exhausted. "Hey."

"The house sure smells good," Mooney said.

"Annie's cleaned up on it all weekend. She's the only one who lifts a finger around here. It stays a disaster," Mama said as she lit a cigarette.

"I know what you mean. Tish's room looks like a hurricane hit it."

"I can't wait to meet her boyfriend," said Clarie.

"He's not impressive, believe me," she said.

"You don't like him?"

"I hate him! He's sneaky. He won't work. Tish thinks he's a lump of gold."

"What's his name, Aunt Mooney?" I asked.

"Pepper Tisdale. He's kin to those Tisdales in Baysprings. They're all nothin' but trash. His Daddy's still in the pen for forgin' checks. Old drunk."

"Gloria has a new boyfriend, too," I said. "I can't wait to meet him"

"Me, too," Clarie said. "Have you met him, Mama?"

"No. All I know is he's in his forties and never been married. Don't know why Gloria goes out with losers. Shit, he lives forty miles away from here, way past Hattiesburg. Lives in a trailer. Gloria drives down to see him. He never comes up here to see her.

Instead of spendin' money on Holly, she spends it on goin' down and seein' some bum."

"Where are they now?" Clarie asked.

"She stayed with him last night, so they're comin' in together," Mama answered.

"What does he do for a livin'?" Aunt Mooney asked.

"He has a good job workin' for the telephone company. Gloria's half-starved herself tryin' to get skinny for the idiot. Piss on that. I told her if he don't like her the way she is, he's shit out of luck."

"Has he said something to her about her weight?" I asked.

"Oh, yeah. He lets her know he prefers skinny women. I can't stand that."

"Mama, Gloria will learn," I said.

"Sounds like Tish. I wish she'd wise up," Aunt Mooney added.

Daddy entered the kitchen. "Where's my niece?"

"She's comin'. How're you doin', Burl?" said Mooney.

"I tell ya, my hiation hernia's been givin' me fits. I stayed up all night the other night vomitin'."

Smoke bolted from Mama's mouth.

"I think I have one of those, too, 'cause sometimes I can't even breathe for the indigestion," she said.

"I thought I was havin' a heart attack. I mean, the pain in my chest almost smothered me. I thought I was gonna have to get Mama to take me to the emergency room."

"That's all I need. Haulin' you to the emergency room in the middle of the night just 'cause you overate again."

"I didn't eat that much, Mama."

"Yeah, you did. If I ate as much as you did the other night, I wouldn't be able to move, Burl."

"Well, you need a man with a big belly to love on you," he teased.

"Shit! No I don't!"

"What did you eat?" Clarie asked.

"I only had a little piece of Kentucky Fried Chicken."

"No, you didn't," said Mama. "You ate over half the barrel. Me and the kids got one stinkin' piece, and I saved a piece for Gloria, which I had to hide from you."

Childhood and the memorable rituals of eating. Having to slink around and hide out in another room to defend our servings. Having to swallow hunks of food as quickly as we could, not savoring a bite. No enjoyment of typical local fare, such as shrimp creole, a recipe Aunt Mooney had given to us. Mama cooked it once, maybe twice, when she had the extra money to buy the ingredients. I'll never forget the aromas, from the shrimp frying in her big black skillet, to the creole stewing in a huge pot until the smell of bay leaves and spices overwhelmed the air. Why didn't she buy more shrimp, I wondered, so there'd be enough to go around. In Mississippi, shrimp comes pretty cheap. Even so, it cost too much for them, she'd lament. Daddy was waiting and observing and pacing back and forth to the kitchen. "Mama, that sure smells good." Ultimately, with exasperation, Mama turned the heat up to boiling. Get it done so he can eat it up. We didn't exist, as we stood with a bowl and spoon in back of him, watching scoop after scoop disappear, until the lake was nearly dry. Another pot containing rice was dug deep like a war trench.

"Hey, girl, you look so good," Jessie said. Behind her Keith wore a drunken grin.

"Thanks, I'm still walking at school."

"It's shows. Don't she look good, Keith? Where's Aunt Mooney?"

"In the kitchen. Have you heard, Tish has a boyfriend. She's bringing him over to meet us today," I said.

"I know," said Jessie. "I bet he's one ugly sucker."

Back in the kitchen, I saw that Aunt Mooney was more upset about Tish's boyfriend than I realized.

"You aren't happy with him?" I asked.

"I think he's mean to Tish. 'Course, she hides it from me, 'cause she knows I'll cuss his ass out."

"How old is he?"

"He said he was thirty, but I found out he's thirty-seven."

When Mama came back into the kitchen, Aunt Mooney, who always said her daughter would marry someone of class, whispered, "Lori's neighbor, Teeney, told her that Pepper's been married three times and has seven kids. I told Tish about it and she went ballistic, cussin' me, sayin' it was none of my G-D business about her relationship with him. I don't know what to do."

"Oh, Lord," said Mama.

"Well, Aunt Mooney, she'll have to find out for herself. I think if you act like you don't care, maybe she'll come around, and he won't look so wonderful to her," I said.

"I hope so, but it's so hard. I told Melvin about it the other night, and he blamed *me*. Said it was *my* fault that she was rebellin'. He's just mad, 'cause his slutty wife said Tish stole some money out of her purse. Now, I don't believe that, 'cause I give her plenty of money, so does Melvin."

"What did Tish say about it?" I asked.

"She said Mary was a damn liar and a whore, and she was never goin' back to see her daddy again."

Daddy came back into the kitchen and stared at the stove.

"Damn it, Burl, the food isn't ready."

"I know, Mama. I was just gonna fix me an Alka-Seltzer."

Gloria looked like a country singer with her poofed red hair and gold belt around her blue jeans. Her weight was down about ten pounds. New clothes, new shoes, a new purse, all to impress some guy who'd be out of her life in no time. I met them in the living room, drying my hands with a towel.

Jed wasn't good-looking or distinguished like some people his age. "Cute" didn't even enter the picture. Gray hairs swirled around his sideburns. His hair was black and thin. Gloria had never dated tall men, and he wasn't. His clothes were neat. He was a bachelor who could do his own laundry, I thought. Hush Puppy shoes, jeans, a long-sleeved red checked shirt, and a blue jean jacket. He smelled of Old Spice cologne and was a little weather-beaten. Gloria was mad over this one, but stupid enough to bring him to the Manor.

After Jed was introduced to everyone, he sat down on the couch to chat with the men. In the kitchen, the women busily sized him up.

"He seems nice," I said.

"He's quiet," Clarie said.

"Looks like he's poutin' to me," said Mama.

"Mama, no he's not," Gloria said, not knowing whether to laugh or get angry.

"He's my age, isn't he?" Mooney asked.

"He's forty-two."

Aunt Mooney was thirty-nine.

"He's never been married?" I asked.

She shrugged her shoulders. "No."

"Probably no one can stand the old fart," Mama said.

"Mama, I wish you wouldn't talk like that. The house looks good, Annie. I was scared it was messed up."

"Yeah, well, you should've been here to help, since you were bringing him home," I said.

"I didn't have time."

"He looks good to me," Jessie said.

"Me, too," Clarie agreed.

Too bad I was too scared to bring Thomas home and show him off. My sisters would faint in ecstasy. Thomas would die of trauma.

"Hopefully, he don't have heart trouble or anythin' like that," Mooney said.

"Yeah, we don't want him dyin' on you," Jessie laughed.

"Please, y'all. I hope he can't hear you," Gloria pleaded.

"Probably hard of hearin', anyway," added Mama.

"Hey, there's my favorite niece!" said Daddy.

Tish entered the front door holding Pepper's hand. He came strutting in behind her like he was the main attraction, and he was. Mama, Mooney, and the rest of us peeked out of the kitchen. I started at his feet, and my eyes moved all the way up to his face. When I saw that he was missing two front teeth, I bit my tongue. What teeth he had left were rotten.

Jessie nudged me and whispered, "He's too damn ugly."

"Sssh, they'll hear you."

"He not only was beat with an ugly stick but the whole forest," she continued.

Mooney walked to the sink, took the pliers and turned on the faucet. She washed her hands. I walked up and hugged her.

"It'll be okay, Aunt Mooney."

"Oh, Annie. God help me get through this supper. Can't stand listenin' to that freak."

I heard introductions being made and Daddy teasing Tish.

"Tish loves to come see her uncle."

"Don't start, Uncle Burl," she glared.

"Hey, Tish," Mama said.

"Hey, Aunt Penny. This is my boyfriend, Pepper. Aunt Penny's my favorite aunt," she said proudly.

"Tish loves ya', yeah she does," he said with a thick accent.

When I walked into the living room, Tish brightened up as if she had something exceptional to show me. If she thought I thought

Pepper was special, she was right. I wouldn't touch him, firmly keeping my hands entangled in a hand towel. His hands were rough and cracked, fingernails longer than I could stand, with oil and dirt impacted underneath each nail. His hair was slippery and dingy blond. He wore it in a ponytail. He removed his black cowboy hat, and a ring of oil remained on the rim. His small head told me he had a small brain and could possibly be the product of inbreeding. We'd been called poor white trash, but this one seemed to be the real thing, and I wanted no part of it. Standing well over six feet and skinny as a flagpole, he towered over Tish. Mud had hardened onto his cowboy boots and the bottoms of his blue jeans. A silver chain drooped from the back pocket where his wallet was crammed. The other pants pocket was torn. His faded tee shirt had the picture of a beer can on it.

Mama brought out a couple of rickety wooden chairs for them to sit on. Then Aunt Mooney made her appearance. "Hey, Pepper. How you doin'?"

"Jus' fine, thank you, Miz Collins."

"Tish, I need your help with somethin'."

She sighed, got up, and followed her mom to Mama's bedroom.

I pulled the chicken out of the oven and set it on the stove. Mama whispered, "That thing was starin' at your butt."

"Who?"

"Pepper. He was starin' you up and down. Watch him."

"Please, Mama, I don't give a hoot about that rotten-toothed thing. I don't understand how three women would marry something like that and make kids with him."

"Probably a bunch of whores. Whores will go with anythin'."

Clarie walked in, laughing. "Ooh, ain't he ugly?"

"Where's Mooney?" Mama asked in a whisper.

"She's in your room talkin' with Tish. I know she's dyin' over this. All this 'Tish is marryin' a doctor, Tish is gonna marry a senator,' well, it looks like darlin' Tish is gonna marry the back end of a monkey's ass," Clarie snickered.

"Clarie, don't hurt Mooney's feelin's," Mama said.

Tish walked out of Mama's bedroom and plopped down by Pepper.

"Everythin' okay?" he asked.

"Mama wants me to be home early tonight."

"Is the food ready?" Gloria asked.

"Just about. I'm waiting on the rolls," I said.

"I was gonna fix a plate for Jed."

"Why don't you go ahead and fix y'all's plate before Burl gets his ass in here and knocks everybody down?" Mama said.

"I'm not eatin' anythin' today," said Gloria.

"Why? Everybody's got to eat."

"I'm cleansin'. I told you about it the other day. My friend Sherry does it to lose weight."

"Gloria, cleansing's only temporary. You'll gain the weight right back and then some," I said.

"I bought these new blue jeans. . . ."

"And they don't fit?"

"No."

"There's no way I'd starve myself to get into a pair of stupid pants," I said.

"Hell, I know it," Mama said. "Dumbo in there'd have to like me the way I am."

"Be quiet, Mama," she whined.

After Mama made the announcement that the food was ready, the herd stampeded in, with Daddy leading the way. It was disgusting. I left the kitchen and went into Mama's bedroom as Aunt Mooney was coming out after her talk with Tish. She had tears in her eyes.

"College must be fun," she sniffled.

"It is, sometimes. Other times, it's pure drudgery."

"You've always worked hard. It'll pay off, then, hopefully you can leave here. I know you're miserable."

Gloria walked out of the kitchen with a plateful of food and a glass of iced tea and handed it to Jed.

"Thanks, Gloria. I coulda fixed my own plate." He set the iced tea on the floor by his feet.

"It's okay, I don't mind."

I had never seen her act this generous before. She sat down by him, attending to his every need. Fuming, I fixed Holly and Wiley's food, encouraging Mama to fix a plate for herself.

Carrying his overloaded stash, Daddy looked around and asked, "Mama? Did Gloria fix her and that fella a plate?"

"She fixed him a plate. She's not eatin'. Said she's cleansin' to lose weight."

"Cleansin'?" he cackled.

Tish ate slowly, with only a bite of dumplings and salad on her plate, giggling like a schoolgirl whenever Pepper looked at her. With gulping sounds, he choked down forkfuls like a wild man. Mama, Mooney, and I carried our plates to Mama's bedroom. Daddy was leaning forward in his recliner, shoving the steaming food in his mouth. In two minutes, he'd be going for another round. He wiped his mouth with a clean dish towel and looked at Gloria.

"Gloria? If you wanna cleanse yourself, take two tablespoons of Milk of Magnesia. That'll cleanse you out fast."

"Shut your damn mouth!"

Jed laughed hard, and so did everyone else. Gloria stomped into Mama's room.

"Mama, why in the hell did you tell Daddy that I was cleansin'? It's none of his business!"

"What did he do now?" I asked.

"He runs his mouth! Don't tell him another thing about me."

After dessert, Pepper pulled a pack of cigarettes out of his jacket pocket. Tish worshipped him from her chair. Mama, Mooney, and I cleaned up in the kitchen.

"That chicken was so good, Annie," said Mooney.

"I'm glad everyone got some."

"I know. Did y'all see the way he ate?"

"Daddy or Pepper?" I asked.

"Pepper. I think he eats more than Burl."

"I don't see how," said Mama. "China don't eat as much as Burl."

Daddy was sitting on his throne, running his mouth to his court. No one was listening to him.

"And I told that woman I don't lie. I ain't gonna lie for nobody. And I don't expect anyone to lie for me. I ain't gonna lie," he declared.

From the kitchen, Mama snapped, "Shit."

On the television, the news flashed a story of a lady convicted of shooting her husband.

"Yeah, my last ole lady tried to kill me," Pepper blurted out. Tish nudged him to be quiet. "Well, she did."

Daddy said, "If a woman tried to shoot me, I'd sue the fire outta her."

"What if she actually shot you, Burl?" Bill asked.

"I'd . . . if I survived, I'd put that bitch in jail." He rarely cussed unless he was very worked up about something. "But no. You have these sorry good-for-nothin' feminists that have nothin' better to do than try to get some old bag out of jail that's a criminal."

"That's right, Mister Lee!" Pepper agreed loudly. "Women can surely turn on ya. My second ole lady got the law after me about some credit card bills, ain't even my credit cards. They're in her name."

"Is that right?" Daddy asked with curiosity. "They can't come after you for a little debt. Mama and I went bankrupt in eighty and eighty-one, and no one bothered us. They told us it'll only be on our record for uh, what, eight or ten years, somethin' like that."

"I guess that'll be what I'll have to do," Pepper said. "Go bankrupt."

"No you won't," Tish said.

"I ain't payin' her bills," he said.

"He's already been bankrupt," Mooney whispered to us.

"I wish Burl'd shut his fat mouth," Mama said. "I'm gonna knock him out."

"I mean, Mama and I was havin' a hard time. We didn't know what to do," Daddy said. "We struggled and struggled until we had no choice but to do it. Those bill collectors were breathin' down our necks."

"Didn't you tell Daddy not to get the new car, and didn't you also tell him not to mortgage the house again?" I asked Mama sarcastically. "Oh, and didn't you beg him to go to work?"

Bill asked, "What do hear from the Social Security, Burl?"

Daddy shifted his weight uneasily. "I'll tell you one thing, I'd hate to know that I had to depend on that bunch of bitches they got workin' at the Social Security office."

Gloria sighed. Jed found it amusing.

Daddy continued, "Think they're so smart."

"You blame everything on women," Gloria said.

"I most certainly do not," he said.

"You do too. I get so sick of it."

"Yeah, Jed, if Gloria gives you any problems," Daddy teased, "you can lock her in the closet."

"Ain't no sorry man lockin' me in a closet!"

Aunt Mooney waddled into the living room and sat in a partly dismembered chair by the couch. "Lord, I'm full as a tick on a fat dog."

"Mother!" Tish whined.

"What?"

"Don't talk like that."

"I'll talk any way I please. I'm grown."

"Don't talk back to your Mama," Pepper ordered.

"She needs to watch what she says," said Tish.

"Did ya hear what I told ya?"

"I heard you, and I'll talk to my mother any way I please."

"Shut your mouth!"

This was the moment Aunt Mooney was itching for. "Don't tell her to shut up."

"I'll tell her anythin' I want."

"No, you won't."

"Yeah, I will. Mind your own damn business."

"She *is* my business!"

"Not anymore, fatso!"

Weighing an extra seventy pounds didn't prevent Mooney from springing like a cheetah and standing over him. "You cocksucker! I knew you were no good from the time I laid eyes on your sorry ass!"

"Shut up, Mama!" Tish screamed.

"Yeah, shut up, Mama!" Pepper laughed.

"Now, hold on there, that's enough," said Jed as he pointed his finger at Pepper. He stood up.

"Mind your own business!" Pepper yelled as he stood.

"Don't talk to him like that, you ugly bastard!" Gloria shrieked.

"You keep your hands off my daughter!" Mooney screeched.

"You can't stop me, you fat bitch!" Pepper inched toward the front door.

"Now, boy, this is a Christian home," Daddy said calmly as he rubbed the back of his neck. "You don't need to be talkin' that way."

Mama and I came out of the kitchen.

"What's going on in here?" I asked.

"I'm sick of this piece of trash abusin' Tish. You're not goin' anywhere else with him!"

"You can't stop her!" Pepper yelled.

"Get out of our house," I said. "If you can't respect my aunt and my parents, get the hell out, or I'm calling the police."

"Gladly!"

Everyone sat silent for a few moments, listening to the rumble of his truck's loud muffler as he spun out and headed down the road.

Tish bellowed, "Pepper!"

Pointing her finger in Tish's face, Mooney was possessed. "You won't be satisfied until he beats your brains out!"

Tish ran into the bathroom and slammed the door.

"Jesus!" Keith said.

"I was about to kick his ass," Bill bragged.

Wiley's gentle hand woke me Monday morning. I uncurled my legs to get the kinks out and rolled over on my back.

"I'm hungry, Annie."

I tried to come awake enough to think. "I'll get you something."

She was out of the room before I could get up. Mama had gone to work to open the store by seven. Her bed slept awful. The mattress was lumpy and reeked of cigarette smoke. Cigarette burns marred the edges of her wooden nightstand.

Gloria's rage thundered through the wall. Nine o'clock was to early for her to be up, and I lunged out of bed. I thought she was after the kids for something, and I wanted to protect them. I stopped when I saw them playing in their bedroom. They were safe. I walked to the living room to see what the fuss was about.

"I don't know when he's comin' back home! Well, I can't help you with that. You'll have to talk to him. I'll give him the message, okay." She slammed down the phone, huffing and puffing.

"Who was that?"

"Some buildin' supply place. Daddy has a hot check up there. I don't know why Mama don't kick his fat ass out the door!"

On her way back to bed, the phone rang again. "I don't have all day to answer the phone! Hello! No, I don't know where he is! For how much? I'll give him the message. You'll have to talk to him. No, I'm not his wife. I'm his daughter!"

"Now what?"

"Another hot check. That's the fourth call this mornin' about a bad check. That son of a bitch has been writin' hot checks all over Jones County. Mama's gonna shit. I'm gonna call and tell her."

I rubbed my forehead, feeling the pulsing of my blood vessels. "I don't know if you should call her and ruin her day."

"Yeah, I'm tellin' her!"

"Let me go by and tell her, Gloria. I'm going to the Prices in a little while, and I'll stop by and tell her first."

"All right then." She was stomping away. "But don't forget. I hope she cusses him out about this." She slammed her bedroom door.

As I brushed my teeth, I recited my lines, preparing for the inquiry. *Pop, I've been very busy at school. My jobs keep me going. I'm learning so much from the professors. I'm learning so much about typing. I'm learning nothing about real life.* I lifted my hand to my nose. The stench of cigarette smoke had saturated my pores. I'd have to scrub my body and hair and immerse myself in perfume to get rid of the smell. *Do you smoke, Annie? You'll burn in hell if you do.*

I was staring at the kids. They were pitiful. In their bedroom, clothes and trash had covered every inch, until I cleaned it up on Saturday night. Their sheet was soaked with urine. I stripped it off and wadded it up. "Girls, did Daddy fix y'all any breakfast?"

Wiley stood up and grabbed the edge of my nightshirt. "No. I'm hungry, Annie."

"Get dressed, and I'll take you to Hardee's for a biscuit. We can't go in, though. I have to go somewhere today."

Wiley looked around for her shoes. Both were in their pajamas. Holly's were urine-stained. I wiped her down and found some clean clothes for her.

"Don't leave me," Wiley said in sorrow.

"I won't, baby. Get dressed now."

I found six dollars in my purse. As I helped Holly get her shoes on, Gloria came into their room.

"Are you gettin' somethin' to eat?"

"I'm taking them to Hardee's, since no one's fed them."

"Can you bring me some biscuits and gravy and a large Coke?"

The cleansing was out the window for her.

"I guess. I only have six dollars."

"I think I have a couple of dollars." She searched through the jumble in her bedroom. "Where's my purse? Did you kids touch my purse!"

"No they didn't," I snapped. "You misplaced it again."

I waited until she handed me three dollars. "Thanks," I said sarcastically.

The girls ran out the door and into the front seat of my car.

"Don't fight. You both sit there and be still, so I won't have a wreck."

Hardee's was a haven in this town, a hangout for people who needed to talk about stuff they knew little about—world topics, politics, government. The end result was always how unfair it was that other people had more than they did. They'd never left Soso. Daddy's kind of folk. Hardee's was where Daddy made daily breakfast runs for himself, never bringing anything home for anyone unless Mama gave him the money to get her and the girls something. I loathed this place. It was as bad as going to the church with the Prices. Wasn't Christianity about God-given happiness and living, and rewards for working hard and taking chances?

Twenty minutes later, both Holly and Wiley proudly came out carrying a Coke in their little hands. I was ravenous for anything—chocolate, potato chips, fried okra. But I only got a Diet Coke, appreciating the carbonation as I drove home.

When food appeared, so did the Reverend. Seeing his truck parked practically in the front door made me want to take the kids far away to feed them in safety. But time was running out. I was expected at the Prices at ten thirty. *Sorry I'm late, Henry dear, I was guarding over food at the roach pit.* Daddy greedily watched the Hardee's bags as I passed by, not offering him anything.

He pouted. "I wish I woulda known you was goin' to Hardee's, so I coulda gotten you to get me somethin'."

Pulling the girls' sausage biscuits out of a bag, I said prudently, "I thought you were working. I hadn't planned to go there, Daddy, but since no one fed the kids, I had to. Are you staying with them today, because I have to see the Prices in a little while?"

"Uh, I guess so. Lemme go get me somethin' to eat first."

The screen door slammed and his motor thundered up Fourteenth.

"Fat bastard," said Gloria, shoving half of a biscuit into her mouth.

"Did you tell him about the checks?" I asked.

"Yeah, he said he knew about 'em. You know what he's waitin' on, don't you? The income tax refund."

"He knows about that?"

"You know he does. They filed a joint return."

"I told Mama not to. He hasn't worked enough. Damn her. She does it to herself."

Eight hundred dollars and some-odd cents. Mama had big plans for that cash. "I hope I can get some new eyeglasses. I need a pelvic exam. Haven't had one since Wiley was born."

Daddy came back with three deli bags and ripped them apart with his rugged hands. A skinned chicken breast with a wooden stick through it fell out.

"What is that?" Gloria frowned.

"It's chicken on a stick," he answered.

High-on-the-hog eating. A Styrofoam container with potato logs and corn on the cob was in the second bag. A smaller bag had two soft rolls in it. He piled everything on a plate, then rubbed the grease off his hands onto his pant legs. Wiley and Holly watched the potato logs, but they knew their chances of getting one were slim to none.

"Daddy, what's going on with the bad checks?" I asked.

"Aw, it's only an error. I don't trust those crazy banks. I'm gonna call 'em as soon as I finish eatin'."

"Please call them," I begged.

Handy Pantry was two blocks from the Prices' house. I rarely visited Mama at the store, fearful that Henry might drive by. Many times I'd avoid visiting them and stay at home, and just clean and study. Once in a while I'd venture out to the grocery store with Mama always on the lookout for Henry and his car. Frequently, she saw him passing by and watching, but he never waved. I sensed a rivalry between Henry and my parents, and it came from him, not them. Through the glass front I could see Mama's disheveled hair and weary expression. She smiled as I parked my car. I went in and leaned beside the ice cream cooler.

"You gonna see the Prices?"

"I'm having lunch with them today. I took the girls to Hardee's and got them a biscuit."

"I guess Burl didn't cook 'em any eggs. I told him to."

"No, he didn't. They were starving." I rubbed my neck. "Have you talked to Daddy this morning?"

"Nah."

"Well, you need to. People have been calling. He's written some bad checks again."

She tensed up, her face contorted. "Oh, Lord! He's gonna spend that refund check. I can't ever get nothin'. I was gonna to buy us a bunch of groceries."

"You'd be buying *him* a bunch of groceries. Gloria was cussing all morning. She said four places have called. He blames the bank."

She sat on a wooden crate shaking her head. "It's not the bank. It's him. I don't know what to do. I'm gonna leave."

"Please leave. Go stay with Aunt Mooney a few days. Mama, make him work and pay those checks. Please don't spend your income tax refund on his mess. Please."

"I'll have to. He'll make life miserable for me and the kids, you know how he is."

"Life is already miserable. I know darned good and well that you can make life rough for him if you want to."

"Annie, no. I don't like gettin' that angry. I'm gonna have a stroke, and you know he won't take care of me if I'm a vegetable."

"Well, poison him, then. We'll tell the police that he's been abusing us for years. I don't care."

"Shit. You know he hasn't done a bloomin' thing since he found out how much that check was. He's sat around and gobbled and checked the mail everyday."

"He must've done something for him to write bad checks."

"I bet it's that work he was doin' for the rich lady. She's the one who's over the Catholic school. The one he has the flamin' desires for."

"Another one?"

"Yeah, she's has a college degree." She was scratching her head. "A doctoral or somethin'."

"Oh, she has her doctorate," I said. "Probably in education, for her to run a school like that."

"Yeah, and Burl is pure thrilled over her. She made the mistake of offerin' him some water one day, and oh, Lord, now he thinks she wants him."

"She wouldn't spit on Daddy. I'm sure she knows he's uneducated and stupid. And he stinks."

"Won't stop him. He hasn't done any work for her the last couple of weeks. I bet he made a pass at her, and she told him she didn't need him anymore."

"I hope he hasn't made a pass at her."

"You'd think he'd get arrested. But then I'd have to go bail his ass outta jail."

"I wouldn't. Pervert."

"Well, let me call him and find out how much damage he's done this time."

"Have you seen the checkbook? Don't you watch what he does?"

"He has it in his truck. Annie, I can't stop him."

"Someone should."

She took a long drag and blew the smoke out. "Your cousin Butch is in a halfway house for writin' bad checks."

"In a halfway house?"

"Yeah, he got arrested."

"That's not good enough. People should be put in jail for writing bad checks."

"Especially if it's someone else's checks. He stole his girlfriend's brother's checkbook."

"That's Daddy's side of the family. You need to take the checkbook away from him."

"He had hell gettin' that account open since we filed for bankruptcy. None of the banks would touch him but that one."

"He's not capable of having a bank account or being a man. Look, I need to go. I hated to tell you, but I was afraid he wouldn't."

She picked up the phone and dialed home.

"Gloria, let me talk to Burl." She squinted like Clint Eastwood. "How many bad checks have you written?"

I put my ear next to the phone and listened with her.

"Uh, only three or four, Mama. That crazy bank—"

"Uh-uh, no, don't start blamin' the bank."

"Well, guess what I have here?" he said.

Mama didn't say anything.

"I have a check from the U. S. government."

"The check came in?"

"Oh, yeah. I have it in my shirt pocket right here."

"Burl, I need to get some things done for myself," she said in a deep voice. "My teeth need fixin', and I'm not workin' if I don't get my teeth fixed, you hear me!"

"I know, Mama. We'll have enough for you to do that."

"You'd better find some work to do to pay those bad checks, too!"

"I am, Mama. I'm workin' for Dr. Pace this afternoon."

"Did she ever pay you for all of the work you've done for weeks now!"

"Uh, well, she would've, Mama. . . ."

"You . . . shit, I can't talk, a customer's comin' in." She hung up. "How are you, Mr. Lowe?"

"Just fine, Miz Lee, and you?"

"Bye, Mama," I whispered.

"Is that one of your girls?" he asked as I passed by.

I drove over to the Prices and parked my car. Through the glass storm door, Pearl saw me. "Looky there."

Henry turned, smiled, and placed the morning newspaper on the coffee table. He stood, synchronizing his hearing aid and unlocking the door. He embraced me for a long time. His body smelled moldy, old. He relaxed, then one last squeeze before he released and pushed me to Pearl.

"You look beautiful," she said.

"Thanks, Mommy. So do you."

"Oh, fiddlesticks, I'm a mess."

Henry's voice cracked as he spoke. "It seems so long since we've seen her, doesn't it, Mom?"

"It sure does."

"Here, sit down beside Mom."

"I've been so busy with my jobs and classes," I answered.

"How's your grades?"

"Good."

"You think you might get straight A's?"

"I'm not sure. It's too early."

He nodded his head, not too thrilled with my reply. "How's your new job coming along?"

"I like it."

"That's wonderful. And the professors you work for?"

"I've been helping Dr. Dearman out a lot."

"I'm so glad to hear that. It's good to get that kind of experience."

I nodded, deciding not to add anything else since it brought on more suspicion.

"Did you like the Valentine's card we sent you?"

"Yes, sir, thanks again."

"Started to send you some candy," he said. "But didn't want to be a bad influence, since you're watching your weight. Well, you look good."

"Thank you." I was sucking it in.

"We didn't have a good Valentine's Day, did we, Mom?"

She nodded agreement and picked her teeth.

"Mom felt bad all day. Wanted to go to the Western Sizzler, but she was too worn out. Not a good holiday for her or for me."

After lunch, I watched the clock. He used the bathroom and relaxed in his chair. I was on eggshells, not knowing which questions were coming. I could cry and make him feel sorry for me. I could get angry and walk out if he pushed. Maybe he'd forget everything and let me be.

"Did you bring your checkbook?"

He hadn't forgotten.

"Yes, I did."

"Let me see it."

He studied every transaction while I sat feeling like a crook. If he didn't like anything, I'd leave. He handed it back. "Do you have any cash?"

"A couple of dollars."

"I have some I'll give you. How you feeling after your sinus thing?"

"I'm better."

He wasn't listening. He got up and went to his bedroom. He came out and handed me twenty dollars.

On my way home, I stopped by Handy Pantry again, and found Wiley behind the Icee machine and Holly on the floor with a naked doll.

"Why are the kids here?"

"Burl got mad about the income tax check and left, so Gloria had to bring 'em here."

"I can't believe he got it so fast, because I didn't see it this morning."

"That's 'cause he stands watch over the mail."

"He needs to get out and work, then he wouldn't have time to check the mail. Well, I'll take the girls and get them a burger. Mr. Price gave me twenty dollars. It's embarrassing when he asks me how much money I have in my wallet, and I tell him two dollars. At least I got another job, and the extra paycheck will help. You want something from Sonic?"

"No. Mr. Evans brought us a sandwich from Tammy's." She was

quiet a little while. "Don't overextend yourself workin' another job. I'll give you some money out of the income tax."

"No, Mama, get your teeth fixed. Call the dentist as soon as you get home and get an appointment, or I'll call him myself."

I started a load of laundry before Mama came home. I pried open our ravaged freezer and couldn't find anything worth cooking. I dug out some frozen peas Jessie's mother-in-law had given us. I pulled out the pork chops Gloria had brought home last Friday. I planned on baking them before Daddy came home demanding that he wanted them fried. As soon as Mama walked through the front door, I pulled the IRS check from my purse. I had grabbed it from the kitchen table where Daddy had flung it in anger after Mama's call.

"Mama, I'll sign his name. The bank won't notice. Go cash this while he's gone."

"Give me a minute." She put her glasses on to look at the amount. "I wanna buy some groceries."

"Why don't we go, then?"

"I guess we can. He'll make my life miserable."

"Why hasn't he brought any money home if he's been working for that lady at the school? And why is he writing hot checks?"

"Well, you ain't gonna believe this. A few weeks ago, I was so broke I didn't have money for a postage stamp. While Burl was takin' a bath, I looked in his wallet. He had two hundred dollars in it. I was so mad."

"And he's behind on the rent? Why didn't you take it? I'm sorry, Mama, but I'd be a little more than mad. I'd take a meat cleaver and use it."

"I didn't know if it was for supplies or what."

"No, it wasn't, you know that. He's been holding out on you. No telling how long he's been doing it."

"Well."

"That's why we're going to go buy some groceries today. There's nothing here. Daddy's eating somewhere. He stops at every convenience store he sees, getting plate lunches and chicken on a stick. Come on, he's fat as a cow!"

"The other day he came in with some fried chicken livers and potato logs," she said, shaking her head.

"Maybe the grease'll kill him."

I wrote a grocery list while she went to the bank to cash the check. I took the clothes out of the washer and put them into the dryer. I put the peas and pork chops back into the freezer, since she decided to get us a dinner plate from Mac's Fish Place down the road. She came back from the bank as I was getting the girls ready. Then we heard Daddy's truck.

"He's back! Why in the hell is he home, now?"

"Great. Probably has to take an Alka-Seltzer," I said, as I combed Holly's hair.

He didn't say a word. He grabbed his Bible and sat in the corner of the living room where he had a piece of wood rigged across two other pieces of wood as a study desk. Mama went to the kitchen and took one of her BC powders, glaring at him as she walked out.

"He's needs to read the Bible," she sneered.

Her eyes were full of hatred for the man, and I bided my time until she jumped his case again. It didn't take long. With her purse on her arm, she walked to the living room.

"Daddy, if I give you some money, will you go by Mac's and get us all somethin' to eat?"

She wanted to save time.

"I don't want anythin'," he answered.

"Fine! I'll get it myself! Come on, Annie. I ain't puttin' up with his poutin'."

Mama's jaw was clenched, and her face was red. Like sweet little children, Holly, Wiley, and I followed her.

At the Jitney Jungle, I pulled out the list. "How much do you want to get? It's a long list."

"I guess everything we need. We've been outta so much for weeks now." She picked up a can of vienna wieners. "Holly loves these."

I studied the dried and canned goods for sales while the kids stayed under our feet, begging for candy and cookies.

"I'm gonna get 'em some goodies. They get enough junk, but I'll get some anyway," she said.

Her heavy mood had lightened. I went to the meat area at the back of the store. I wasn't crazy about ground beef, but Mama bought it because it was cheap and to stretch the meals. The meat market manager saw me and came out.

"How are you? Haven't seen you in a while. You still in college?"

"Yeah, I don't get home much."

"You need help with anything?"

I pulled a ham out of the basket. "Can you slice this for me?"

"Sure, sandwich-sliced, okay?"

"Yes."

"Stop it!" Holly yelled.

She and Wiley were kicking each other down by the chicken cooler, getting on each other's nerves like all kids do. Mama forcefully chucked a ten-pound bag of rice into the basket. I started sweating. She charged between them, grabbing Holly by the nape of the neck and shaking her like a rag doll. Then she grabbed Wiley by the back of her neck and shook her and pounded her back with her hand. Both the girls had long hair, and it was flying everywhere. The Coca-Cola man walked by pushing a load of Cokes and veered way around her, probably thinking she was deranged.

"I'm not puttin' up with your fightin' today. I've had it!"

I faced the glass and stared at the market manager while he sliced away at the ham. *Please God, don't let him see my crazy Mama beating the kids.* Holly sucked her hand and was on the verge of crying. She ran and hugged my leg.

"Anything else for you today?"

"No, thanks."

"Anytime." He smiled at Mama, who smiled back as if nothing ever happened.

"You embarrassed me," I whispered, as we went up the aisle.

"I can't help it. I'm under stress, and I'm sick of the fightin'."

"Go home and murder Daddy. You'll feel much better."

Mama had that destitute look on her face while the cashier pushed the items across the counter. It could be ten things or a buggy load, and she'd have that same expression. With several hundred dollars in her pocketbook, she was still struggling. I pushed a basket of bagged groceries to the car while Mama pushed the other cart. I put the bags in the trunk.

"Look who's parked over there." She lit a cigarette.

Daddy was watching from his truck. He got out and came over.

"What are you doin' here?"

"I had to get my stomach medicine at Tri-Mart. Uh, I'll go get y'all somethin' to eat, Mama."

"We already ate."

He picked up the last bag. "Mama, you sure got a lot of food."

I gave it a week until it'd be gone. From behind the dashboard, I watched and counted five twenties Mama handed over to him.

"I took care of those checks today, Mama."

She put her wallet back in her purse. "With what?"

"Dr. Pace paid me."

"She shoulda paid you weeks ago."

While she was driving us up Fourteenth Avenue, I made my move. "Why did you give Daddy a hundred dollars?"

"To get him off my back."

I didn't say anything for a long time. "I guarantee you that Dr. Pace has been paying him all along. He may have had money left after he paid his hot checks. You should have demanded to see inside his wallet."

"He's satisfied, now that he got a piece of my check. He's not happy until I'm broke."

"That's right. And I bet he has more money in his wallet than you do right now. He should be buying groceries. I don't think Daddy's human. You need to play hardball, Mama."

"Well, it's done."

"Oh, I know, and he wins again and you're miserable."

"Annie . . . I don't know how to be a bitch."

"Mama, standing your ground doesn't make you a bitch. You think that because some women get their hair done every week that they're manipulative. That's not true. They're smart. You work hard, so you should do things for yourself. Daddy does, believe me."

"I haven't had a permanent in my hair in a year."

"Go get one, now that you have your money, do that. Make an appointment this week, and I'll keep the girls."

"I need to."

"And your teeth, too."

Tuesday afternoon, Mama came in from the mall with her hair frizzed to her scalp after an inept hairdresser left her permanent in too long.

"What did you expect for fifteen dollars and ninety-five cents?" I asked? "You cheated yourself."

"Well, I didn't know the stupid woman was gonna give me some ole black gal to fix my hair. I told her it was burnin' my head. I ain't goin' back there."

"Niggers don't know how to fix white people's hair," Daddy said.

"I told you to go to McRae's, not some hole in the wall where the hairdressers aren't experienced," I said.

"I can't afford to shell out fifty dollars for a haircut and perm. That's too high."

"You get what you pay for."

"Baby, you know people like me and your Mama can't pay those high prices," Daddy said.

"Well Daddy, you can pay to have something done right, or go around griping when you look like shit."

By Wednesday night, Mama was a powder keg. She'd had to order a new set of upper false teeth. That was what she got for neglecting them, I told her. She waited so long to get them relined that nothing could be done to them. Luckily, she still had her own bottom teeth, because the upper plate cost close to three hundred dollars. She shouldn't have doled out a hundred dollars to the Reverend, I reminded her. I was sure he wasn't running low on cash.

Daddy had been working for several weeks for a Catherine Pace, building an extra room on her home. I'd pictured Dr. Pace as a classy lady in her thirties with blond hair, young, thin, just the way the Reverend wanted 'em. According to Mama, she was in her mid-fifties, squat and wrinkled. His working regularly was remarkable enough, but working late at night was scary.

Mama brooded for hours. At eleven o'clock, the Reverend wasn't home. By eleven thirty, I was in bed when I heard Daddy coming through the front door, whistling. Little did he know that a fire-breathing dragon lay in wait for him. Mama came from the kitchen and met him at the front door.

"Where have you been!"

"I been at Dr. Pace's."

"Nobody in their right mind works this late at night, Burl! Is that woman a fuckin' nut lettin' you work this late at her house!"

"Well, uh, Mama, she works durin' the day."

"I've had just about enough of your shit! I've put up with it for twenty-five years! I'm leavin', even if I have to walk outta here!"

"Mama, I don't know why you're so mad."

"I'm mad 'cause you want to fuck that woman! You ain't got no business over there at eleven o'clock at night! You fuckin' fool!"

"You're crazy."

"No, I'm not! I know you, Burl! I know how you think! A woman can't even be nice to you without you wantin' to fuck her!"

"You're crazy. That woman don't want someone like me."

"Aw, go ahead, feel sorry for yourself."

"None of y'all care about my feelin's. My own girls don't love me."

"Try bein' nice to 'em!"

Gloria and I were watching them.

"They don't respect me." Out of desperation, he picked up his Bible.

"Pick up the Bible, you bastard! You need to heed what it says in there!"

"Mama, please," he begged.

"I didn't ask to be born," Gloria said.

"None of you girls care about me."

"That's not true, Daddy," I said. It hurt me that he said that. I just wished he were dead.

"I don't wanna hear this crap. I have to work tomorrow," said Gloria.

"Then go to bed!" said Mama.

"I can't sleep with all this bitchin'."

I went back to bed. Between Daddy, Mama, and Gloria, there was enough madness for the entire world.

Mama and Gloria were off from work on Thursday. Mrs. Walker had given Mama an extra day, because she'd filled in for her and everybody else when they needed time off. Mama sure cussed about it enough. But she dealt with her job the way she dealt with Daddy. She should have quit them both.

Mama and the girls loaded into Daddy's truck for a ride to Sister Willa's, by way of Hardee's for breakfast. Watching them drive away, it was as if the beastly cussing had never happened. Gloria was up early, ten o'clock. Her makeup was on and her bag packed for an overnight stay with Jed. I was bored here, wildly eager to get back to UEM. Thomas had called twice from Colorado. He was eager, too. The phone rang and Gloria hurried to it.

"Hello! Fuck you!" She smashed the phone down.

I stared at her. "Why did you do that?"

"That son of a bitch was supposed to call me this mornin'."

"It is morning."

"No, earlier!"

"You didn't have to do that, Gloria. He could've gotten tied up at his job. You're impossible."

"I don't care. He's not lyin' to me."

"No, he's going to get rid of you."

Jed didn't call back. Twenty minutes later, I heard her mumbling on the phone in Mama's room. Then she left.

I didn't have to see the Prices Friday, because they were going to visit Henry's sister, Claudia, who had surgery on her hip. I celebrated by keeping the kids. Daddy was building shelves for Mr. George's liquor store. Gloria and Mama were working. I drove the kids over to my old junior high school where there was a park. I watched them swing. It was good to see them smile, and I was glad I was there.

I packed to go back to UEM and made sure my C & R smocks were clean for the weekend. I cleaned on the house until Mama came in, then I fell asleep. The contemptible sound of the Reverend's voice woke me. I rolled on my side and gazed at the dust on the smoky tube of Mama's broken television.

"They oughta lock up these punks and pill-heads, that's what they should do."

"What's wrong now?" Mama asked.

"A bunch of punks picketin' at a college in New York. They oughta deport 'em all. Communist freaks."

She got up from the gripe seat and went into the bathroom and closed the door. I stumbled to the door and peeked in.

"What's wrong with him?" I asked.

"Aw, he's sick."

"Again?"

"You know how he gets with his stomach. He decided to quit drinkin' the 7-Ups for the thousandth time 'cause he says they upset him. So, he started in guzzlin' the tea. This mornin', he set his glass down on the floor by the recliner and went to the kitchen lookin' for food. Then he came back for the glass and drank out of it, and there was a cockroach in it."

"Oh, Mama!"

"It must've crawled in there when he set the glass down. He's been gaggin' ever since."

I giggled as I walked into the living room. "Daddy, I hear there was a cockroach in your tea."

"There sure was." His knee was propped on the arm of the recliner, his face sullen. "Stupid thing crawled in my glass. I'm tellin' ya, I can't stand those stinkin' things. I been sick all day. No tellin' where the nasty thing's been."

"Probably came from under the house or the sewage, don't you think?"

He gagged and flew to the bathroom. Mama lit another cigarette and returned to the gripe seat. She looked hideous, worry etched deeply in her spirit. Just days earlier, she had been giddy over a few hundred dollars, and now it was gone. A flush of the toilet, and the Reverend returned to his recliner.

"Guess who I saw in town this afternoon?" he asked. "Mr. Price."

"You didn't talk to him, did you?"

"Yeah, he was comin' out of Mr. Whittle's office. He was real friendly."

"That's his lawyer," I said.

"You know what I think? I think he's gonna put you in his will."

"Daddy, he's not going to put me in anything."

"Why not?"

"Shit, Burl. Ole man Price ain't gonna do no such of a thing. He has some stepsisters who'll get it all. Believe me, Henry ain't that generous. Now Pearl'll give you the shirt off her back."

"Well I was just thinkin'—"

"I know what you was thinkin'," she said.

"You goin' to see 'em tomorrow?"

"No, Daddy," I answered. "I have to go to work. I might as well see if my dorm is open."

"I thought you wasn't going back 'til Sunday."

"I have friends I want to see."

"Well, they ain't gonna be back until Sunday, are they?" Mama asked.

"You can invite 'em over here sometime," Daddy said.

"I'm sure they'd love some cockroach tea."

"Burl, this house ain't fit enough for her to bring anyone home, and you know it."

"I can help clean it up," he said halfheartedly.

"Huh!" Mama snapped.

"Mama, this house ain't bad."

"It's a barn," I said.

"It's a shithole," Mama added. "I'm so sick of movin' from one dump to the next."

"Well, Mama, rent is high."

"I'm so sick of bein' broke and poor."

"Why do poor people smoke, if they need money?" I said sarcastically.

"I wish Mama'd quit."

She edged toward Burl. "And I wish you'd get up off your ass and work!"

"I been workin', Mama. I'm gonna paint Mr. George's shutters."

"Huh! You quit workin' for that Dr. Pace."

"My back was hurtin'."

"I don't feel so hot myself, Burl."

Chapter Seventeen

Spring break had put me behind. I had planned to use my time at home to study, but I didn't, not out of laziness, but because I let myself get sucked into cleaning and trying to hold things together. Why did I do it? Why did I waste my precious time when things just fell apart when I drove back to school?

The whole week was hectic, and I wasn't in the greatest of moods when I got off work on Saturday. Thomas picked me up at four for a drive to Johnson State Park. The park surrounds Geiger Lake, a man-made lake constructed by soldiers from Camp Shelby during the Second World War. The piney woods shared the park with magnolias, red maples, and several kinds of oak trees. One could take the short loop or long loop of the natural trails. My intention was to take the long hike. Thomas had other things in mind.

"I'd like to do more than computer programming, and the market's getting better for programmers right now. Maybe in the future, I'll design my own software, something oriented toward the sports industry," he told me.

I didn't hear a word. "That's nice."

"My dad wants me to help him in the law firm again this summer, but I'd like to . . . am I boring you?"

"Oh, no," I smiled as we walked over a boardwalk.

"I'm racing in Jackson next Saturday."

I slowed down. "You are?"

"Peter's going up with me."

I didn't say anything.

"I'd like to finish in the top ten." Smiling slyly, he said, "Or the top five."

"You will."

He touched my arm fondly, but I wasn't in the mood for holding hands. What worries did he have? I was going to pull a C in accounting theory. The professors didn't care that I was working two jobs. Then there was Henry, who had called at seven o'clock that morning to tell me that the Lord wanted him to call. I didn't mind the Lord calling me, it was Henry I didn't want to hear from.

"I want you to come with me," Thomas said.

"What?" I was getting agitated.

"I want you to come up to Jackson with me."

"I can't."

"Why?"

"I have a weekend job, remember? I can't just take off."

"Why not? Can't you get someone else to work in your place."

"No, Thomas. I'm the weekend help. I'm expected to be there."

He wasn't happy. "You just don't want to go with me."

"Thomas, yes I do, but I have to work."

"You work too much. Don't your parents help you out?"

The way he said it was sarcastic and it hurt.

"No."

He stayed quiet, staring out at the boggy area of the trail.

"I just want you to be there."

I looked down at my feet, guilt gnawing at my throat.

"I swear I'll be thinking about you. I want you to win." I meant it.

Before I took another step, I was in his arms, being hugged with more desire than I thought I deserved.

Christopher broke it off with Denise that Saturday night, and she came back to the dorm torn to pieces. Suzy got worried and woke me at midnight. I hurried to Denise's room where she was curled up like a ball in the middle of her bed, still dressed in her clothes.

"Lies! Everything he said to me was lies!"

I held her. "It'll be okay. We'll get you through this."

"What do I do, Annie? What do I do?"

"I don't know, Denise. Give it time. Give it some time."

"He told me he loved me. He said he was goin' to break up with her."

"I know."

"Then tonight," she gulped, "he said Linda was gettin' suspicious and he . . . why did he do this to me?"

It was after three in the morning when I left her asleep. I decided to sleep until six, get up and walk, eat breakfast, and go to work.

The next afternoon, I was sitting on Marla's floor, watching her dust her room. I had been in a tizzy, because when I got off work, I found Thomas waiting for me in his car in the C & R parking lot.

"At first he said he just wanted to say hi," I explained to Marla, "but that wasn't it. He was checking up on me."

"Mmmm, mmm."

"I've told him and told him to give me space. He says okay, then, he wants to know everything I do."

"Girl, you got this guy in love with you. You need to tell him you're not seeing him anymore if he doesn't back off. Just look at him and say back off, Leroy."

"Oh, God, Marla," I snickered. "I'm going to talk with him tonight when I see him. I need to go get ready."

"Where's he taking you?"

"Just out to dinner. I don't want to go back to his apartment. Last night, he cooked for me again. It was great, but he kept hugging me on the couch, and I couldn't even talk to him. I don't like that, you know, the hands everywhere."

"Uh-huh. Trying to feel you up was what he was doing. Next time he tries that, slap his face. Or you can grab his balls. Just reach down and squeeze like hell. He'll stop."

I laughed. "You should teach self-defense."

"Yes, ma'am. Miss Marla's been in too many sticky situations. How's Miss Denise doing? Still upset over that guy?"

"Yeah."

"Lord, have mercy." She looked at me compassionately. "You know, when Suzy hooked you up with Peter, she didn't mean for you to get hurt."

"I don't blame her for Peter. He did what he did because he chose to. Maybe he never really liked me, Marla."

"I'm proud of you for being strong, girl. It's so hard when these men act like fools."

"I hardly think about Peter. I have my dreams," I smiled. "Going out with Thomas helps a lot. He does turn me on."

"Honey, he turns me on, and I don't know the guy. Girl, you got you a hot one there. Sending you flowers. Calling you every day just to see how you're doing. He's a gentleman."

"What about the hands, Marla?" I laughed as I pretended to touch her all over. She slapped at my hands, pretending to scream.

"He can be a gentleman and still want to feel your titties. Like I said, squeeze those balls."

"He asked me to go up to Jackson with him to watch him race next weekend."

"Annie, you have to go."

"I work. You know I can't get off, I'm part-time. Thomas wasn't happy about it."

"Honey, he wants you there." She opened her closet. Her muscular legs were shining from lotion.

"Why did you stop running?" I asked.

She took a deep breath. "Because I got tired of being treated like a race horse. Being compared to other runners. Competing. The mind games the coaches play on you. I could've had a scholarship to any school I wanted, long as I ran track. I had to stop, 'cause it was killing me. I was so unhappy. I want to be happy, Annie."

"You did the right thing."

"I know I did. You and me are independent women."

It was Friday, warm with clear skies. I felt overwhelmed, imprisoned in my room with cumbersome books of such complexity I wondered who I thought I was, majoring in accounting. I thought of driving home, but I couldn't study there, and I had to work tomorrow, anyway. Denise was off campus working on a science project. Suzy had gone home, and Marla was in the computer lab. Thomas was in Jackson, preparing for his race. He had trained all week, calling me at night. I should be there with him. I wanted to be with him. Instead, Peter was with him. Suzy said most of Taylor Hall was going up to cheer Peter on. Peter could murder a nun, and he'd still have friends.

On Sunday, I felt more optimistic. I had my hours in at the drugstore. I had studied hard. Denise and I had gone to the movies Saturday night to see *American Tail*. Denise cried buckets of tears, and I knew it had nothing to do with the movie. Now, we met Marla and Leslie at Jerry's, where the buffet was two dollars and ninety-nine cents.

"Mmmm, mmm," Marla beamed. "I can't believe Thomas came in second at that race. That man has some strong legs."

"Second out of a hundred and forty racers," I added.

Leslie was blushing. "Ooh, Thomas is so delicious, a god with animal magnetism. He's got great chest hair."

"Leslie!" said Denise. "And how can you tell he's got great chest hair?"

"I saw it the other day when he wearin' his cyclin' clothes. I could even see his nipples," she giggled.

"Girl, you're crazy," said Marla. "When did Thomas call you?"

"Last night."

"Did he tell you how Peter did?" Denise asked.

"No, and I didn't ask," I said.

"Did Suzy tell you who went up to the race with Peter and Thomas?"

"No," I answered.

"Nancy Long."

Marla drove us back to the dorm, and I felt bad again, and I didn't know why. I was quiet while they talked and when we walked into the lobby.

"Someone's here to see you," said Marla.

Thomas was standing by the front desk.

"See you later, chick," Denise grinned.

They walked to the elevator.

"When did you get in?" I asked.

"About an hour ago. Want to ride around so we can talk?"

"Sounds good," I smiled.

We stopped by the IHOP for coffee. Thomas sat across from me, and I felt as if I were the only other person in the place. I was nervous.

"Aren't you tired?" I asked.

"No," he smiled.

"I'm sorry I couldn't come to see you race."

"It's okay." He took my hand.

"Did your parents come and watch you?"

"They came, and my sister and brother-in-law, my aunt and uncle," he chuckled.

I smiled, but inside I was jealous, because I felt left out. But whose fault was that? I was angry with myself for being afraid to call in sick.

"What are you doing for the break?"

"The break?" I asked.

"Yeah, I think we get two weeks before the summer session starts."

"Um, I have to . . . "

He quickly cleared his throat. "I have to go to New York with my parents. I think we're going to be gone a week. I don't want to go."

"Go, I mean, I'd go if I had the chance."

"My dad has business up there and he wants me to tag along to keep Mom company, mostly, to watch her shopping. I'd rather spend time with you."

"I want to spend time with you, too. It's just . . . things are so hectic at home right now. Dad's been so busy working, and Mom's putting in a lot of hours. Anyway, I still have to work on weekends, and I promised my grandparents that I'd run errands for them."

"Well, I'll call you when I get back, and we'll see if we can get together. I'll drive down and get you."

I was sick with worry when I got back to my room. *I'll drive down and get you.* It should be that easy. I sat at my desk and stared at the wall. He'd see our front yard that has no grass. He'd see the filth and the cockroaches. He'd meet Daddy. He'd smell Mama's cigarettes. How was I going to keep Thomas away? I had this fear when I dated Peter. But Thomas was a different creature. He was determined. I was angry at Mama and Daddy again. Then, I thought about Aunt Mooney. Perhaps Thomas could meet me at her house. But I didn't even want him near the town of Soso. It was too risky. No, I was going to make up some excuse to keep him away.

April was ending. Christopher had wooed Denise back with three red roses, and her state of mourning ended. Linda, though, was still in the picture. The day Denise asked to join me at the track, she was blissful and a little frail.

"Slow down," she said. "Can we walk slower?"

"I'm sorry. I'm used to walking fast."

We walked a full lap without talking so she could catch her breath.

"I'm movin' into an apartment at the end of the semester."

I stopped. "Why?"

"I want to see if it'll be cheaper than the dorm."

"Are you still going to eat in the cafeteria?"

"Sometimes. I'm not buyin' a meal ticket, though. But I'll eat with you when I can."

"I hate to see you move." I was heartbroken.

"I'm movin' close by, very close by. Right across from the campus. Carolyn's goin' to live with me."

"Carolyn? Carolyn Vickers?"

"Yeah, I didn't think you could afford an apartment, and I didn't want you to feel obligated. Anyway, you and I are best friends, and I don't want us gettin' on each other's nerves."

"Yeah, that's true. I really like living on campus, Denise."

I liked it because I could walk to my classes and not have to worry about parking. I could walk to the cafeteria and not worry about cooking. And yet, there was hurt. Why Carolyn? She lived at the end of fifth floor and was wild, compared to Denise. I'd understand her moving off campus with Casey, her quiet roommate, but Carolyn Vickers? She'd had more men than a porno starlet.

"I don't want you to be angry."

"Oh, I'm not, Denise, I promise. I understand about finances."

"I want you to come and sleep over anytime you want."

"I will. It'll give me a break from the campus rut."

"Are you goin' to see Thomas over the break?"

"I'm going home."

"You don't sound happy about it."

"It's a long story, and you wouldn't believe it if I told you."

"Is everything okay at home?"

Oh, Denise, are you up for this?

"It's just . . . you know how your father works a regular job and pays the bills. Well, mine doesn't. I mean, my mom works, but she doesn't bring home much of a paycheck."

"That's ridiculous. How does your mother put up with it?"

"She's on drugs."

"What?"

"She takes a nerve pill."

"What nerve pill?"

"It's called Elavil."

"Elavil is strong medication. I studied it in my pharmacology class."

"Well, if you were married to my daddy, you'd be on heroin."

"That's sad. I didn't know things were that bad."

"For them, not for me. I'm in college. I'm able to work and pay my expenses. So, it's okay."

"Still, I don't know what I'd do if my parents didn't help me."

"You're one of the lucky ones, Denise. I'm happy for you. Anyway, my adopted grandparents help out. I just don't want any more help from them. They've done enough already."

"Why?"

"I don't want to be beholding to anyone. I want to pay my own way."

"Annie, college is expensive. Not just the tuition, but the other expenses. Take their help."

"So far, I have. But I don't plan on doing it any longer."

As soon as I closed my door, the truth became clear. Denise was drifting away. Who'd blame her? I had never invited her home with me. Twice I had been to her house. It wasn't a mansion, but it was a real home with family pictures, flower arrangements, and her own room. She cooked with her mom and told me about their shopping trips, the time they made tablecloths, bought a piece of furniture, and the time she had lunch with her father while her mom was out of town. I'd said zip about my family life until today, and what a thing to confess. I kept a lot of secrets.

The semester had come to an end. I got up early on Thursday to pack my car, took my last exam at nine o'clock, and said goodbye to Denise. Marla had left the day before. Suzy was moving off campus to live with two girlfriends in a three-bedroom apartment. Borden and Taylor Halls were being renovated over the summer. I was moving to Beecham Hall with Marla. I'd be getting a new roommate. Marla was getting a private room again. According to Suzy, Peter was going to be the head resident at Bolton Hall, which was behind my new dorm. He and his friends would be attending the summer semester as well.

CHAPTER EIGHTEEN

When I got back to the Manor, Mama was trying to read Daddy's blood pressure.

"Hold your arm still so I can read the damn thing," said Mama.

"I feel so swimmy-headed," Daddy moaned. He closed his eyes.

"What's the matter?" I asked.

His eyes sparked, but he had to keep up the act until Mama finished taking his blood pressure. "Hey, baby. Your ole Daddy's sick."

Mama had owned many blood pressure cuffs through the years. Because of overuse and her impatient bedside manner, each one had quit working in short order. Mama pumped the bulb forcibly, her knuckles turning white, cutting the circulation in his arm. A cigarette hung from her pursed lips, and that, coupled with the scowl on her face, made her look fiendish. She released the gadget, letting the air discharge, and dropped his arm like a dead weight.

"Burl, it's normal. I knew it would be. It's probably your stomach again."

"I don't think so, Mama. My head spun in circles today when I tried to climb the ladder at ole man Carson's house."

"Your stomach can make you dizzy, Burl."

I stood looking about the Manor as a stranger might see it. Dirty clothes were scattered on the floor, along with trash and sand. Dirty dishes were stacked on the dining room table and in the kitchen. From where I stood, I could see the big black frying pan on the stove, no doubt full of old grease. The curtains were sagging on rusted rods. A washed-out green sheet hung over one window, and I swore it wasn't there last time I was at home. And they were worried over Daddy's normal blood pressure?

Mama pulled the cigarette out of her mouth. "What's wrong with you?"

A flicker of sunlight pushed through the bedraggled curtains, and the dust, lint, and smoke in the air became visible.

"Nothing," I sighed. "Daddy, can you help me with my boxes? I had to move out of the dorm and bring everything home."

"Uh, I guess so. I'm pretty sick though." Did he think I felt sorry for him, I wondered, as I walked out? He stood, rubbed the back of his neck, and followed me.

Mama picked up a box. "Why'd ya have to move out?"

"The dorm's being remodeled, so everybody had to move out. They wouldn't let us store our things at the other dorm."

I didn't have much, only four boxes. Daddy hauled in one box, grunting as if it was the hardest thing he'd ever had to do. He looked at Mama, wanting her to bring in the last one, but I grabbed it without waiting for him. He grinned and held the door open for me.

"How long are you gettin' to stay home, baby?"

"Two weeks."

"Well, good. Mama and I missed you."

I missed y'all, too. Like menstrual cramps.

"It's stupid that they made y'all bring everythin' home," said Mama.

"I know. It's a big hassle."

I gave them ten dollars to buy something for supper and to get them to leave. As soon as they left for the Jitney Jungle, I sat in the bathtub and cried. I hated myself for telling Henry I'd be by tomorrow, but the old buzzard wouldn't let up. The letters, the phone calls until he got his way. I washed off my makeup with deodorant soap. If it dried my skin brittle, I didn't care. I didn't clean the house. I threw on my nightshirt and shoved the clothes and trash from the gripe seat and lay on it. Daddy came back grinning, a bucket of Kentucky Fried Chicken under one arm and a bag of groceries in the other. The kids were rowdy, and Mama was trying to referee.

"Now why did you do that? I told you to stop kickin' her. Go outside and play."

"Get outside!" Daddy told them. They ran through the kitchen and out the back door.

"Are you tired?" Mama asked.

"Yes," I answered.

"Is it time for your period?"

"Next week."

"You're so pale. You're probably anemic."

I stood in the kitchen with her to eat. Daddy had slopped himself with two plates and was resting before the finale. I ate part of a chicken breast, a spoon of coleslaw, and a helping of mashed potatoes and gravy while he was complaining about the nightly news.

"That's what they do. They let anythin' into the borders of this country. Then we give 'em welfare. I tell you, I ain't supportin' a bunch of foreigners."

Mama glared at him. "I wished we could have one night at home without you bitchin' about some crap on that TV."

"I ain't fussin', Mama."

He was coming for more food. He picked up a clean plate instead of using the one he had eaten on fifteen minutes earlier.

"Save somethin' for the girls and Gloria, Burl," said Mama.

"I am. There's plenty left."

"Here." She slammed her plate down and grabbed a bowl. She butted in front of him, yanked three pieces of chicken out of the bucket, placed them in the bowl, and stuck it on top of the stove.

"Ooh, mercy me, Mama, my neck's hurtin' again." He wanted pity. "I need somethin' to kill this pain."

"Try Raid," she seethed.

I didn't work hard to look nice for the Prices. I wore a button-down top Mama had gotten from a rummage sale, my faded blue jeans, and old pair of tennis shoes. I was clean, and that was all that mattered to me. After the tears, hugs, and foot touching, Henry told me to go weigh myself. I thought he was concerned with my thinness. But I looked a "little heavy" he said. I stepped on Pearl's scale, and I weighed a hundred and twelve. I had lost three more pounds. I thought he'd be delighted to hear the news. It didn't matter.

"Where's your grade report?"

He studied it for a long time. Pearl was clueless as she held my hand in her lap. Henry's eyes were still frozen on my grade report. Clearing his throat, he handed it to me. "You have to do better."

"Pop, accounting theory is the hardest class in the department. Most of the class made C's. Some failed, and there were no A's at all."

"You could've given more effort and been in the B group, or been the only A. When I was in college, I worked hard on my studies. I wanted to be the best." Closing his hand into a fist, he continued, "I had to be the best."

I tried to shut out his words. The stories were replaying. "I remember when Dr. Jonathan McCrory told me I had made the highest score in my Latin class," he beamed. "It did so much for me."

I wanted to tell him that I didn't care about his accomplishments. I was wondering if he had some hair in college.

"Well, honey, let's hope you can do better," he went on in a slow, sullen voice.

"I thought I did pretty well, considering I was working two jobs. Better than a lot of the students who didn't work."

"I know, sweetheart. But the students with the best grades get the best jobs."

"But some of these students have never worked jobs in their lives. I wouldn't want to hire someone who hasn't worked before. I have a lot of job experience."

He frowned. "Grades matter."

I was giving up and ready to get up and leave when Pearl sternly shoved my hand aside. "Pooey on grades. Those C's are just fine. A's, B's, and C's don't make the world go around. It's hard work, and you know it." She crossed her legs defiantly. "I never went to college like you did, Henry, but I did just fine. I had my own beauty shop in the basement of this house, and I turned a good profit. I paid cash for every car I bought."

"I know, darlin'," he responded in a rankled tone.

"Just drop this grade business."

"You don't have to say it that way." His eyes were commanding. There was going to be a brawl, I thought.

"My hard work helped pay your sister Claudia out of some messes, didn't it?"

He adjusted his glasses. He looked like he wanted to choke the living daylights out of her. "Are you tired, Pearl? Do you want to take a nap?"

"I'm not tired. Why do I need to take a nap?"

"Okay. You've made your point." He pushed up his glasses, his face flushed. They sat staring each other down like two dogs standing guard over the same bone. Henry was bushed, though, and began to smile. Then he slid out of his recliner. "I just want Annie to get the best job."

"Annie will get the best job because she's smart, and she works hard. Just an ole C now and then don't mean diddly squat," she continued.

He pecked her cheek, then mine. "I'll go get lunch going."

As soon as he left the room, she leaned into me. "Have you ever met Claudia?"

"No, Mommy Junior, I haven't."

"She's a do-nothin'. Lazy thing."

After lunch, we were back in the living room, business as usual.

"You know, it'd be nice if that manager at Tri-Mart would let you work during your break," Henry purred.

"Pop, he doesn't need help this time of the year." *Don't I deserve a break?*

"Oh, that's right. They need most of their help during the holidays, don't they?"

I nodded.

"I got to use the little room," Pearl said. She tottered to her bathroom. Henry's expression was serious when he turned his recliner toward me.

"Mom seems to be getting worse with her memory. Some days, she asks me the same question over and over. It's exhausting. I'll be sitting here reading the newspaper, and she'll come in and repeat something. I could tell her to go leave me alone, but I can't. I love her so much."

"Poor Mommy Junior," I whispered, as I noticed his swollen ankles. How much had Pearl sacrificed for him? Which one was sterile? She loved him with more devotion than anyone I had ever seen. When he hurt, she hurt. In the old days, she made sure he had his twelve o'clock lunches, even though she was fixing hair in the basement. Roll one lady up, stick another under the dryer, run upstairs to fix Henry's lunch. He'd come home, eat in ten minutes, give her a peck on the mouth, and hurry back to the employment office to oversee his flock.

"You look a little tired, Annie. Are you taking any vitamins?"

"No, sir."

He gave me the look. "Don't you think you should take some?"

"I never thought about it."

"Hey, hang on a second."

He got up from his recliner, his hand automatically touching his hearing aid. He went into the bathroom. My thoughts were drifting.

Sacrifice? I wasn't going to do it. Not for a man. I didn't care if he was sent from the Lord. I didn't care how hard he worked or how much money he made. I didn't care if his penis was gold.

Henry returned. "I knew I had some vitamins somewhere. Here, honey. It's a brand-new pack." He sat down and read the bottle. "Centrum. Here you go. I bought them for Mom, but the doctor put her on something else. Take these, and see if you can get a little color in your face. I'm not saying you look bad, but we have to keep you healthy until you graduate."

Then what?

"Thanks, Pop."

I shoved them in my purse. Pearl came back and sat beside me.

"So, you're going to summer school. Now how much is that going to cost?" Henry asked.

"I got approval for more grants from financial aid. They'll cover a good bit. About seven hundred won't be covered. I can pay on it over the summer until I pay it off."

"You know Mom'll want to pay it for you, honey."

"I know, Pop. But, I'm going to try to pay as much as I can."

"All right, dear. It's good that you work hard, because, well, Mom and I have cut back on our expenses. Makes it easier to help you, you see."

I painted on a concerned look.

"We can't deduct what we give you on our income tax return. But," he smiled and wrinkled his nose, "it's okay." *Where's your faith in God today, Pop?* He touched my foot with his.

"As soon as I get a job after school, I'm going to pay y'all back."

Coming closer, he touched my hand. "No, honey. We don't want you to do that. All we want is your love, you hear?"

"I really want to," I said as I clasped my hands tightly in my lap.

"I know you do. But remember what we talked about last year? We agreed to help you get through school. We knew it would cost some money, but Mom and I stood fast and believed that the Lord would help us to help you."

Why can't the Lord give me a direct loan?

He touched my foot again and leaned back in his recliner.

"Are you still working for the same professors?"

"Huh? Oh, yes, sir."

"That's wonderful. How much do you have in your checking account?"

"I'm not sure."

I pulled my checkbook from my purse, automatically handing it to him. Opening it, he took a quick peek and nodded.

"Be right back. Talk to Mom."

Pearl's legs were crossed, with one swinging back and forth. She was rejuvenated.

"Mommy, do you like Claudia?"

"Shoot. That thing's so lazy, she doesn't even clean her house. We bought her a washing machine, and she's too lazy to use it." Then she whispered, "She's not getting another cent from me."

She winked at me as Henry came in with a smile and an unsigned check. She took it, signed very legibly and handed it to me. It was made out for a hundred dollars.

"Pop, I don't need this. I've been saving my paychecks."

"You take it," Pearl said. "You get you some clothes with that."

I hugged her firmly. "Thank you very much, Mommy Junior."

"Now get you some clothes with that, you hear," he repeated.

I put the check in my purse.

"Honey, if you need anything for school like a brassiere or some underwear, please get it. Or get you a blouse or two. Why don't you get a haircut?" he said. "Let us know how much you lack on your tuition. Mom wants to help you out with that."

Sometimes I wished I'd never been born. I had two old coots about to smother me, and a family of freaks lying around thinking good fortune was going to land in their laps because of their suffering. I drove around Soso watching houses pass by, trying to figure out what to do.

I had been home almost a week, and I was more than ready to go back to school and face difficult classes. At home, there was no food. There was no peace. I should have begged the manager at Tri-Mart for a job, so I could have a vacation from this.

Daddy had been up to his usual tricks. Mama caught him in her bedroom removing the doorknob off her closet door.

"What are you doin', Burl?"

"I'm gonna take this doorknob and put it on Mrs. Chester's door in her storage room."

"Why? Can't she buy her own damn doorknob?"

"Well, I just thought I could make a couple of dollars."

"Burl, I'll give you a couple of dollars to leave it alone."

I couldn't take it. I had money in my account, and it was my money, and I broke down again and bought some food. Pearl understood that I had to eat while I was at home. I spent more than fifty dollars on cheddar cheese, sandwich meat, bread, chicken, ground beef for spaghetti, and all sorts of canned goods. Mama was thankful for the food, although it wasn't much. I was fixed in the gripe seat feeling guilty, thinking about getting through school, and on the verge of biting my nails down to their bloody quick. The easiest thing would be to quit school. Then what? More minimum-wage jobs, and I'd be old before I knew it. I was too close. In a year, I'd be finished.

The thrown-open front door revealed the coming of summer. I was thinking about past summers, going swimming with Uncle Melvin and Aunt Mooney. I'd put on my swimsuit, lie on the hood of Mama's beige station wagon, and pray to God that they'd call us to go, and that they'd drive up with Tish to get us. I'd beg Mama to call them, until she'd threaten to beat me. Aunt Mooney always made the thin ham sandwiches with mayonnaise that I'd scarf down, for I wanted to eat, more than swim. She'd bring a cooler of sodas and splurge on potato chips, while Mama would bring Kool-Aid and the store-brand bag of lemon creme-filled cookies that I detested. She'd tell us not to drink up Mooney's drinks, drink the Kool-Aid. Uncle Melvin would slip me a Coke. Melvin taught me to swim. Mama said he had hang-ups. She'd tell us girls to "be careful" around him, that he might touch us in the wrong place.

We'd return home from our picnics to find Daddy in a mean mood, waiting for Mama to cook him supper, putting an abrupt end to our happiness.

I left the house and was halfway to Hattiesburg before I realized I had been going seventy, and I slowed to fifty-five. When I passed UEM, it was deserted. I turned onto a street in a quiet and modest neighborhood. I pulled close to a light-colored brick house and parked my car. I took my school schedule out of a notebook. I had diligently worked it over before the end of the spring term to get my jobs and classes together. Double-checking numbers, I compared the address in my notebook with the number on the house. I got out of my car and walked up to the door and knocked. A heavy-set lady with grayish hair pulled back in a ponytail answered. She looked tough.

"My name's Annie Lee. Uh, Cynthia Magee's a classmate of mine. She gave me your address. She said you needed someone to clean."

"Oh . . . yes. Come in."

Molly Perkins was in her early sixties. She hired me on the spot to clean every Wednesday afternoon. I held out for fifty dollars and got it. I didn't tell Mama and Daddy about it when I came home. They thought I had gone walking again.

"What, Mama?"

"You don't need to be walkin' so much, Annie."

"I know."

Summer was going to be busy for me, with three classes and three jobs.

Miraculously, the second week of my break was better, because Thomas's parents decided to extend their trip to Canada. I wouldn't have to think up another lie to keep him from visiting me. Best of all, though, Daddy was leaving every evening to go to a revival at a church in Ovette. It was way out in the sticks, where the level of education was below the fifth grade. He was getting to preach, so he was electrified. I was shocked that people were crazy enough to show up and listen to him, and content that I was getting to watch the television in peace. But, lo and behold, something was brewing. I didn't know what until the Friday afternoon of that second week.

Mama dragged in from her job in an ugly mood. I heard an ice tray cracking, and the slamming of the ice into a large plastic glass. I walked into the kitchen for some ice water. Before I could get a glass out of the cupboard, Mama began complaining.

"Stupid job's killin' me. Ole lady Walker wants me to work for her next week so she can go on another vacation. Burl's runnin' my car into the ground goin' out to the country every night, rompin' and stompin' in that church. I'm so sick of the shit."

"What's wrong, Mama? I thought you'd be glad Daddy's out of the house."

"I am glad his stinkin' ass is gone. If he wouldn't do the stupid things he does! Now I'm worried to death. He's after another woman."

"Oh, God. Are you sure?"

She paused with her "are you kidding?" look. "I haven't lived with him for over twenty-five years not to know his shit. I found some love poetry hidden in his Bible."

Mama knew the signs, especially his tendency to write poems declaring his love for some unwilling victim.

"He's been writing love poetry again?"

"Uh-huh. I saw him writin' the other night, and when I got close to him, he covered up the paper. Stupid fool."

He had rewritten verses from the Song of Solomon, but he didn't give the poem to the woman. He kept it for himself, why, I didn't know. Did my friends spend their breaks like this?

"Do you know who it is this time?"

"Not yet. But I guarantee you it's someone at that church in Ovette. He's been takin' two and three baths a day. I'm sendin' Clarie and Bill with him to find out who it is."

"Are they going?"

"Hell, yeah. Clarie's infuriated with him. They're goin' tomorrow night. Do you wanna go with 'em?"

"Mama, Daddy preaching is like a blind person doing surgery. His preaching 'don't ring my bell'."

"Shit, I know it. He can't preach worth a damn. His idea of praisin' is ravin'."

"And he doesn't have to commit every sin to preach about them."

"Mooney's goin' tomorrow night. So is Tish and Pepper."

"You mean all of them are going to listen to Daddy?"

"Yeah. Pepper says he wants to get saved."

"You're kidding? What does Aunt Mooney think?"

"She's tryin' to get along, for Tish's sake."

"Oh, my Lord. I'm going, then. If Aunt Mooney's going, I'm going. Are you?"

"Hell, no. He'll behave if I go, and I want Clarie to find out who he's hot after. Mooney's gonna keep an eye on him, too."

I grinned. "There's nothing like a night out with family."

With age, Mama had turned into a pack rat. The closets were crammed with clothes she had gotten from rummage sales, the bulk of which were out of date. I dug through her bedroom closet and found a spring dress, white with flowers. It was years old, but timeless. I washed and dried it, and went to the Piggy Wiggly and bought a pair of pantyhose.

I got off work Saturday and drove home. Daddy was in seventh heaven that some of his family members were attending. He had spent the day pouring over his Bible and writing notes for his sermon.

"Mama, how do you spell 'ability'?"

Splashing her fists in dishwater, she yelled, "A-B-I-L-I-T-Y! Stop worryin' the fatal hell outta me!"

A few minutes later, he was on me as soon as I sat down on the couch.

"Baby, spell 'predicament' for your ole Daddy."

"P-R-E-D-I-C-A-M-E-N-T. Why don't you use a dictionary, Daddy?"

"Uh, I can't find it. The kids lost it. D-I-C-A . . ."

I had to get away. It'd be bad enough listening to him tonight. Besides, I had letters to return to my friends. I got up and walked to Mama's room. There was nowhere pleasant to go in this house, which was hotter on the inside than it was outside. The humidity was unbearable. The cheap window fans ran day and night, but they didn't do much good. Heaven help us if we used the oven.

Gloria came through the front door, and he caught her.

"Gloria, spell 'arrangement'?"

"Shit, Daddy, I don't know."

"Don't start that cussin'. Uh, A-R . . . is it spelled with one R or two?"

"It's spelled with two, Burl," Mama answered as she walked through on her way to the bathroom. "No one can't even move without you botherin' 'em to spell somethin'."

He followed her and continued talking while she was on the toilet.

"Are you sure you don't wanna go, Mama?"

"No, Burl. I don't feel like it. I have to feed the kids."

"They can come, too. I sure wish the whole family could come."

Gloria screamed from her bedroom. "I ain't goin'! I'm tired!"

"I don't feel like draggin' 'em way out in the country to that hot church to listen to you preach for four hours," Mama said.

I tugged for the words to write in my letters. The heat and my parents' voices were more than I could stand right now. Every day this week had been uncivilized. It didn't let up. Tomorrow I had to work at C & R, then move into the dorm for the summer semester.

"Gloria, why don't you invite Jed, and y'all could come listen to your ole Daddy," he said sweetly.

"No! I ain't goin' and lookin' like those old hags you go to church with. Them and their long stringy hair."

"It ain't proper for women to paint their faces like jezebels!" Daddy replied.

"If I go, I'm wearin' my makeup. I'm not wearin' my hair long and wearin' those long ugly dresses to satisfy those damn Holy Rollers."

"Forget it, then!"

"Burl, leave her alone," said Mama.

Daddy left two hours ahead of everybody so he could pray and prepare. Aunt Mooney picked me up so we could talk on the way. Tish and Pepper were meeting us. Bill and Clarie were also.

Mooney walked through our door looking like a decorated hooker, wearing her long black hairpiece. Her eyes were outlined in thick black eyeliner, her lips painted pink, and her blush was a shimmering pinkish-red. She wore a black dress with gold horizontal stripes, black heels and pantyhose. She had a gold scarf tied around her neck, and gold loop earrings hung from her ears.

"I hope there's not a lot of people there," she said.

Mama blew out a puff of smoke. "There probably won't be. Usually only four or five people show up. Burl said seven showed up last night."

"I don't want people starin' at me," said Mooney.

"I think you look beautiful, Aunt Mooney," I fibbed.

"Not as good as you. I love that dress on your thin body. I look like a stuffed pig in a blanket in this dress. It shows my bumps and grinds. Nothin' fits me, I've gained so much weight."

I prayed that there'd be a full house tonight, because tongues would wag when Aunt Mooney entered that church, and I wanted the Reverend to squirm.

It would be dark soon. Mooney sped over the curvy country roads where scrub pines blended with impenetrable weeds. Houses stood far in the background, and I wouldn't want car trouble out here. I felt a world away from college, my friends, and Thomas.

"How far is this church?" asked Mooney.

"I have no idea. Mama wasn't sure."

She was humming along with a country tune on the radio.

"You still like Barry Manilow?" asked Mooney.

"Yes," I answered.

"You know who I love to listen to? That Butch Reeves. He has a voice like velvet."

"I never heard of him," I said.

She wasn't listening. "Lord, how does Burl find these churches?"

"Who knows. He runs his mouth to so many people."

"Have you lost weight, Annie?" Mooney asked.

"Eight pounds."

"Eight pounds! I can't even lose eight ounces. Is it because of your boyfriend Peter?"

"Peter's not my boyfriend anymore." I squeezed my hands together.

She kept her eyes on the road.

"You know, I wonder what it'd be like if Melvin wanted me back. Guess I'll never know. I'd take him back in a heartbeat."

For a moment, I thought of Thomas, and the tears came.

"It's so hard, Aunt Mooney. To be in love."

I was used to the brick cathedrals that seated hundreds and thousands. This was a small, white, deteriorating wooden building. "The Living Word Tabernacle" was crudely painted on a sign tacked to a wooden board that had been stuck in the grass next to the church. The parking lot was dirt. What was it about these churches that attracted land yachts like Buicks and Ford Gallaxies? Pepper's truck was there, and so was Bill and Clarie's Toyota. Aunt Mooney poured herself out of her car and tugged her dress down.

"Lord, I hope they have a bathroom in this place."

We walked up the fractured cement steps and entered the opened doors. No stained glass, just two plain windows on each wall. No cross or holy water. Hard wooden benches served as pews. People in the congregation were talking until they saw us, then a few eyes did triple-takes, and a hush came over the judgmental faces. The assembly stayed quiet while we found our pew. My eyes fixed on Pepper's small bald spot on the crown of his head. He looked like he'd just come off an oil rig, with his dirty shirt, torn jeans, and muddy boots. Clarie motioned for us to sit between her and Tish. Both of them were wearing sleeveless sundresses and sandals. Clarie wore very little makeup in order to appease the Reverend and convince him she was there for redemption. Tish's makeup was encrusted on her face, and her ash-blond hair teased several inches high. She did indeed look like a jezebel, with her gold jewelry and fake nails.

Cranky and uncomfortable, Bill pulled at his crotch as he scooted over. Daddy tugged at his collar, his eyes on Mooney. He was sitting on a bench up front with the preacher of the church. I tried to count the number of people—probably twenty-five. A turnout. An elderly black man holding a cane nodded at me, and I smiled back. Other black people were there, too.

What will you say about blacks tonight, Reverend?

Aunt Mooney brazenly scanned the church, looking at the women.

"I can't tell who it could be."

"I know. These women are ugly," Clarie giggled.

"Won't stop Daddy," I said.

Brother Buddy and his brood were in the front pew. Earlie Mae was a giant, built like a linebacker. She had stringy black hair longer than Denise's, a long-sleeved blouse, and a black skirt down to her ankles. Her shoes were work boots. Every piece of flesh was hidden, except head and hands. *No lust allowed, even though thou hast had five kids.* Brother Buddy had done his philandering, but now, with his weak stomach and panic attacks, Earlie Mae held the cards.

This wasn't like the Baptist church. No joyous choir singing, no huge pipe organ, no flowing robes. Just simple folk needing some peace, worshipping the best they knew how.

The preacher, Brother Woodrow Cummings, stood and led the congregation in prayer. Everybody's arms went up, except Clarie's, Bill's, and mine. I looked around, saw we were outnumbered, and held up an arm until it got tired. Brother Woody, as Daddy called him, was small-boned, maybe five-foot-six in shoes. He was in his fifties and had heavily tonic-slicked black hair.

"Let's sing praises to the Lord, people!"

"What a Friend We Have in Jesus" was the first song. The only accompaniment was a tambourine. After that song, we went to "In the Sweet Bye and Bye." In a soprano voice, Aunt Mooney sounded like Tiny Tim tiptoeing through the tulips as we sang "Holy, Holy, Holy." I caught the giggles in my throat. Switching over, Brother

Woody said, "'Amazing Grace,'"sweet people. He was playing minister of music, as well. People started clapping as Sister Hattie led us into "Give Me That Old Time Religion."

"Sing it, Sister Hattie!" Daddy was showing incredible zeal as he smiled at this elderly black lady. I'd had enough singing and just mouthed it from then on.

Brother Woody's arms swayed in the air. "Let's just give praise to the Lord!"

The screaming and wailing that came out of these people would terrify anyone who had never been to a Pentecostal revival. A competition developed between Mooney and Earlie Mae, until Earlie Mae landed on her back on the floor, writhing, praying, and crying. This made *The Exorcist* look tame. Wiping her eyes with tissues, Mooney held her arms up to the sky and bellowed, nearly deafening everyone until they stopped praising and listened. Brother Woody egged her on.

"Yes, sister! The Lord hears your prayers!"

"Amen, sister!" another man yelled.

She praised strenuously and damned anyone who got in her way.

"Lord, I am a sinner! I have lied! I have betrayed! I have vile and wicked thoughts! I've hated my ex-husband in his low-down, dirty, devil-possessed life! I've wished him dead every day! I've wished for him to get gonorrhea! I called his wife a slutty whore! But I know you love me and forgive me! Yes, Lord, thank you for your mercy!"

In the past, Mooney had actually spoken in tongues. The first time I heard her, I didn't know what she was doing or why she was talking that way. Mama and Daddy said it was a gift from God. I had never heard Daddy speak in tongues. Mama, as of two years earlier, had received the gift, though I had not heard her yet. The very first time we were taken to a romping and stomping church like this, Gloria and I walked up an aisle with Aunt Mooney to a long wooden altar. There, we knelt with others. Aunt Mooney cried her eyes out praying, while I didn't know what to do. I remember Gloria crying hysterically. She was six.

This was a circus. My father was dancing—no, he was jumping. I had never seen him this active, even over food. If the heat didn't give him a stroke, then I knew his ticker was in good form. I put my head down in revolt. My prayers were going to be silent. I wasn't showing off for anyone, including the Lord. I prayed for forgiveness for my wicked thoughts and sins. I went through my list of college friends, saying prayers for each. I gave thanks for Henry and Pearl and everything they had done for me. I prayed for Thomas's family—he would come later. I prayed for Peter. I even prayed for Linda, Denise's rival in her love triangle. I prayed for God's will in each and every situation, since I had no strength to deal with anything. When my family's turn came, I had to think it over.

Lord God, other people have hardworking and responsible parents. I don't know what mine are. I need lots of help here, please, right now. They break my heart every day, and my Daddy's hot after another woman while he's preaching Your word. Give me strength.

Lord God, I think I love Thomas. Please, can't you spare me a sign? Will it work out? Am I wrong for being ashamed of my parents? Please help me through this. I'll never cuss again. I'll let it slide about the red hair and freckles. Give me a sign, anything. Just take care of Thomas, please.

Clarie and Bill's heads were bowed, eyes open for protection from the loonies. Brother Buddy was on his hands and knees, sobbing. Earlie Mae was rolling on the floor. Their kids were climbing over and under the pews. A red-faced gentleman was turning around in circles screaming "Praise Jesus! Yes, Jesus! Hallelujah, Jesus!" His meek wife's mouth moved swiftly, as if she were chanting and strung out on drugs. Surprisingly, Pepper was crying, while Tish held his hand.

"I've cried. I've cussed. Now I can just laugh. Thank you, Jesus," Mooney said with closed eyes. She was winding down, thank God.

The praying died down, and people returned to their pews. When I looked up front, the Reverend was alone, holding his tattered black Bible.

He began with the Word. "Saint Luke, chapter sixteen, beginnin' with the nineteenth verse. *There was a certain rich man, which was clothed in purple and fine linen, and fared sumptuously every day. And there was a certain beggar named Lazarus, which was laid at his gate, full of sores, And desirin' to be fed with the crumbs which fell from the rich man's table; moreover the dogs came and licked his sores. And it came to pass, that the beggar died, and was carried by the angels into Abraham's bosom; the rich man also died and was buried, And in hell he lift up his eyes, bein' in torments, and seein' Abraham afar off, and Lazarus in his bosom. And he cried and said,*

Father Abraham, have mercy on me, and send Lazarus, that he may dip the tip of his finger in water, and cool my tongue; for I am tormented in this flame. But Abraham said, Son, remember that thou in thy lifetime receiveth thy good things, and likewise Lazarus evil things; but now he is comforted, and thou art tormented."

He continued with the prayer. His cadence was a well-rehearsed rhythm of heaving and breathing. "Dear Heavenly Father, tonight we pray that you will open our minds and our hearts, Lord, to understand these words. That you'll anoint us, Lord, to understand these words and to speak these words and to minister these words that others may know ya, Lord, and understand that there is a burnin' hell."

Next, the sermon. "So many people today don't really believe that there is a burnin' hell. If they believed, surely they would no longer commit sin, would no longer do the things that they do. There is a burnin' hell. The rich man here was a man that had plenty. All his life he enjoyed the great harvest of his labor, so to speak. And there was this certain beggar named Lazarus that was at his gate each and every day, full of sores, and the dogs came and licked his sores. Then, there come a time when this beggar would die and would be carried by the angels unto Abraham's bosom. And there come a time when the rich man would die, and the Bible said he was buried, and in hell he lifted up his eyes, and bein' in torment and seein' Lazarus afar off. So many people today don't think that we'll know each other or that we'll know anything when we get down into hell. But we'll know each other, and we'll see each other, and we'll remember the things that we done to each other."

Will you remember what you have done to your family, Daddy?

"And the rich man could see, could see Lazarus afar off, and he cried, 'Father Abraham, have mercy on me, and send Lazarus, that he may dip the tip of his finger in water and cool my tongue, for I'm in torment in these flames.' He was in flames. He was burnin', but never burned up. If after you've lived a million years, it'd be but less than a second in eternity because you would not even have begun, and the torment would go on day and night.

"The Bible says 'And the smoke of their torment will ascend up forever and ever,' and it would go on night after night, day after day, forever and ever and ever, and everything that you've done in life would no doubt come before you. You would remember all the people that you done things to. You would remember the people that you cheated, that you robbed. You would remember all the times that you violated the Ten Commandments. You would remember all the times that you, uh, would steal, cheat, and lie. You would remember the times that you committed adultery. You would remember all the lies that you have told. You would remember all of these things, and they would all come before you, and you would give an account over and over and over and over again."

Man, is he going to be busy in hell!

"When you could miss all of that by just simply getting down on your face prayin' and seekin' the face of God, turnin' from the sins and the iniquities of this world. It's so easy to miss hell. We have a Jesus. Jesus said 'I am the way, the truth and the life, no man cometh to the Father but by Me.' He sets upon the throne of mercy. He sets with outstretched arms in all that would hear his voice, all that would come to Him. He would in no ways cast out.

"I'm here to say tonight that Jesus is savin'. If you wanna miss this awful place called hell, come to him tonight, and turn from your wicked ways. Get a hold of him. He is savin'. He is savin' today, just as he was back in that time, and hell is just as real today as it was back there. Hell will be just as real tomorrow as it is today, and people that don't know God is goin' to hell. They're goin' to a burnin' flame. They're goin' to a place where you'll cry. The Bible says there shall be weepin' and gnashin' of teeth, and I tell you, praise God, that they're goin' to pay for their sins. They're goin' to pay for the way they live.

"We live in a society that has completely forgotten God. We live in a society of adulterers. We live in a society of fornicators. We live in a society of homosexuals and lesb'ans. We live in a society when all things are all right and just fine. This world has become a cesspool of adultery, of fornication, of abortion, of homosexuality. All of this wickedness is displeasin' God. I tell you, today is time to wake up. It's time for man to turn from his wicked ways. It's time for man to call upon the name of God. It's time for people to get on their face and seek God, to miss this awful place. It's time, it's high time."

I looked at my watch while Daddy ranted on, this need to hear his own voice. At home, Daddy imparted so much misery on his family so he could go to heaven. I wanted a better life and to enjoy life. He never preached on that. It was a cry for help when Mama took us to the Baptist church when we were children. It was air-conditioned, and the choir was huge, and there were pipe organs. Daddy wouldn't have lasted a second preaching in a church like that. I tried to shut out his sermon, and the temperature was rising.

Bill grumbled, "It's hot as a motherfucker in here."

Clarie nudged him, "Shut up."

He loosened his top buttons, his collar wet with sweat. "I can't help it. Next time I'm not dressin' up to come here. Fuck this shit."

Aunt Mooney fanned herself with her pocketbook and nodded every once in a while when Daddy said something she agreed with.

"Amen, brother!"

"Hallelujah!"

"Yes, Lord!"

Brother Woody took over. "Amen, Brother Lee. Anyone that has any special needs can come up front, and me and Brother Lee will lay hands on you."

Nearly everybody walked up. Tish followed Pepper. Pepper wailed like a wounded animal when his turn came.

"Lord, we have your son here who wants to repent from his use of women and drugs," Brother Woody prayed.

When he touched Pepper's wiry shoulders, Pepper hit the floor and didn't stir. Tish screamed and kneeled over him, crying. I sat, feeling lifeless. What a way to spend a Saturday night.

I watched the few people who were still seated while my sister did her research. There were two women, deeply crinkled from farm work, age forties to sixties, sisters, most likely. Could Daddy possibly be after one of them?

Another soul was being prayed for. "Jesus, we have a young lad, a lamb of God, who prays for a mended heart. His Mama's in heaven. Let's join hands and pray for him, people," Brother Woody said.

"Poor thing." Aunt Mooney cried as she pulled some extra tissue out of her purse.

She pulled herself to stand and went up front. People cleared a path.

"Lord, we have your sister who stands before you, askin' you to forgive her and to bridle her mouth!"

When Brother Woody touched Aunt Mooney, she collapsed into a black man's arms, and he slowly lowered her down next to several others.

"Sister Rosa! Praise Jesus! The Lord was tellin' me to pray for you!" Daddy wept loudly.

I turned toward the front, then Clarie and I looked at each other. Rosa, the Campbell's daughter. Daddy did work for them. Rosa kneeled while Daddy and Brother Woody prayed over her. My father worked passionately to save this woman-child's soul, as the Campbells came up behind her and kneeled. Mrs. Campbell and Rosa weren't the typical worshipers that Daddy wanted us to dress like. They had style and wore plenty of makeup. Rosa fell to the floor, while my sister and I watched our father rub the tears from his face. I wouldn't be the one telling Mama about Rosa. I had no desire to.

"Thank you, sweet Jesus," a black lady sang.

"Praise God!"

"Praise the Lord!"

"Amen!"

"Hallelujah!"

I stood to stretch my legs.

"Sweet Jesus!"

"We give praise to you, Lord!"

Thick with heat, the little church was about to detonate. The humid air stuck to my face. Beads of sweat covered my body. People continued to hold their arms up and pray to the Almighty. For a moment, I was afraid I'd pass out. *I fear God. Don't let me faint, Lord. The Lord is my shepherd. Lean not on your own understanding.* I loved God. He took care of me.

"Are you okay, Annie?" Clarie asked.

"I'm just so hot. It's hot in this place."

I picked up a tissue Mooney had dropped in the pew and wiped my forehead with it.

"Shit, it's hotter than hell," Bill said as he wiped his face with his hand.

"Be quiet," Clarie whispered.

"Next time, you can come by yourself and check up on your daddy," he told her.

After things calmed down, people got up off the floor. I left the pew and helped Mooney to her feet. She dusted off her dress and walked in a daze. Her hairpiece was crooked, and her makeup was smeared down her face. Her white leg bulged through a run in her black pantyhose. Pepper was bewildered and sat down.

"Go in peace now, and know that the Lord God loves you," Brother Woody said with grace.

Daddy grinned and motioned for me to come up front as the crowd scattered. Brother Buddy caught me on the way.

"Hey, Annie. How's your stomach?"

"Normal," I answered.

"Buddy, we gotta go by Mama's and pick up that pain medicine for my back now," Earlie Mae said sternly.

"All right," he responded quietly.

"Come on, Tulip! Roy, quit climbin'!"

Daddy beamed with pride when I walked up. "Brother Woody, this is my daughter Annie. She goes to Eastern Mississippi."

He shook my hand. "How are you? Thank you for comin'."

"I enjoyed it," I said.

"God bless you, child."

"I need it."

The Campbells were watching us.

"Now, which one is this? I know she's yours, with that red hair," Sister Campbell said.

Rosa was sulky. Her tears were dried, and she stayed tucked behind her parents. Her hair was long, blond, and curly. She looked like a sorority chick. This one, not so innocent. She kept secrets, I thought.

"This is Annie. She's the one in college," Daddy bragged.

Clarie stood back, so Daddy said, "This is another daughter of mine, Clarie, and her husband Bill."

"Look at all the red hair. It's so nice getting to meet you girls. Your Daddy sure is proud of you," Sister Campbell continued.

"This is my sister-in-law, Mooney Collins," Daddy went on.

"You're Penny's sister. I can tell the resemblance."

"Yeah, I'm the younger one, but Penny looks younger," she laughed. "Oh, I'm a mess," she said, as she brushed off her dress.

Sister Campbell smiled. "You look just fine."

Clarie was studying Rosa, getting down every detail.

"Brother Lee, you have some beautiful girls here," Brother Campbell said.

"Yeah, I have a houseful, and they won't let me get away with nothin'," he grinned.

If he only knew what Clarie couldn't wait to tell Mama. After some more introductions, we made it out to the cars. As soon as Daddy spun out of the parking lot full of glory, Clarie and Bill lit cigarettes.

"I feel like I died and went to hell," Bill said as smoke came out of his nose.

Clarie asked, "Did you see her, Aunt Mooney?"

"I'm not sure."

"It's Rosa, the one with the blond hair. Brother and Sister Campbell's daughter. Mama's gonna shit."

"Oh, Lord. She's a young thing. Are you sure?"

"I think Clarie's right," I said. "Daddy sure got excited when she walked up to be prayed for. I'm not telling Mama."

"Why?" Clarie asked.

"I just don't feel like it."

"I think your Mama should know," Bill said.

"I do too, Bill. But it won't change things," I said. "Go ahead and tell her, at least it'll keep Daddy from grabbing the girl."

"Why does Uncle Burl want other women?" Tish asked.

"'Cause he's full of lust and deceit," I said.

"Ain't that the truth," Bill laughed. "Remember that time we went to that church in Utica to watch him preach?"

"Hell, yeah," said Clarie.

"Your Daddy had the red hots for this woman," he continued. "You shoulda seen her. She looked like a big Jethro Bodine from the *Beverly Hillbillies*."

Mooney looked around. "I don't remember her."

"Hell, yeah. She was so damn ugly. Her teeth bucked out, and she was missin' two bottom teeth," Bill laughed.

"I'm going to throw up," I said.

"I know it. He's disgustin'," Clarie sneered.

"I love Aunt Penny," Tish said.

"I know, precious. She'll be okay. She'll cut your Uncle Burl's balls off," Mooney said.

Pepper's hands were in his pockets and his interest in the Reverend's lusty ways apparent, since he wasn't in a hurry to leave.

"Your mama's gonna blow a gasket tonight," Bill snickered.

"Why don't you tell her when I get back to UEM," I said.

"No, I'm tellin' her tonight before he does somethin'," Clarie said defiantly.

Pepper took hold of Tish's hand. "I'd better get you home. We'll see you in a little bit, Miz Collins."

"Be careful drivin'."

His truck backfired as they drove away.

"Pepper sure got into the Holy Spirit, didn't he?" I said.

"Yeah, but I still wish he'd leave Tish alone," Mooney replied.

When I got home, Bill and Clarie's Toyota was sitting in the front yard behind Daddy's truck. Before I opened the car door, Mooney said, "Come spend the night with me when you can."

"I will. Thanks for the ride."

"Bye, darlin'. Love you."

Her hairpiece was still crooked as she drove away. When I walked in, Daddy was beaming.

"Hey, baby. Did you enjoy listenin' to your ole Daddy preach?"

"Sure did."

Bill was nervous, with sweat beaded on his forehead and neck. Clarie's voice was lowered a few notches from behind the closed bathroom door. When I peeked in, Mama's one arm was propped against the wall, the other working back and forth as she smoked. She looked at me and her eyes looked satanic.

"Mama, it has to be her. You shoulda heard Daddy when she walked up," Clarie whispered.

"It is," she hissed. "What did he preach on?"

"A burning hell, because he knows it personally, because he's been getting invitations to it," I answered.

"Usually it's fornication, and believe me, that's all in the hell he has on his damn mind," Mama seethed.

The pot was about to boil over.

"Mama, Rosa's a pretty girl. I've seen her at the Western Sizzler," Clarie said.

She was adding fuel to an already fiery situation.

"Rosa left her husband to go live with some bum," Mama said. "Her husband's a nice-lookin' man, too. Has a good job. Hell, Rosa's Gloria's age. Just the other day Burl said he was helpin' the Campbells out 'cause they been so worried about her. They don't know what kinda help he wants to give her, though."

"You mean she had a good husband and left him?" I asked.

"Yeah, stupid bitch," Mama said as she flicked ashes into the sink.

I shut the door, walked to the bedroom, and changed into my nightgown. I didn't want to be home when my mama, now a lethal weapon, damned Daddy's ears to hell. I went to bed with the cockroaches.

The next morning I was in the bathtub, relaxing in hot water. The smells of dilapidation and yesterday's fried ham lingered through the house, along with the smoke. Daddy's truck roared into the front yard. I heard his door slam. Mama had given him the cold shoulder the night before, after Clarie tattled on him over his latest lechery. I was sure he didn't know why she was being hateful, since he wasn't brilliant and didn't consider lusting for women a sin. So, to pep her up, he offered to go to the grocery store to buy her Diet Cokes, cigarettes, and BC Powders, all of which kept her going. Little did he know that she was in the kitchen, coiled up like a snake ready to strike. I heard their voices move from the kitchen to the living room. I wasn't prepared for an early morning assault.

"I thought we could have fried pork chops for supper. I got us a pack at the store, Mama."

His perkiness was about to be annihilated.

"Fuck cookin'! You can root hog or die, for all I care! Why do you keep goin' to that church!"

"Why, Mama, Brother Woody asked me to preach the revival. I was helpin' him."

"Bullshit! You wouldn't leave the poor man alone until he let you preach. You don't know when to let up on people!"

"Uh, what's wrong?"

"Don't lie to me, you're supposed to be a preacher, Burl. Why do you keep goin' to that church?"

"I told you, Mama—"

"You're a fuckin' liar! A cocksuckin' fuckin' liar!"

I dried off and wiped the steam from the mirror. Did I come from these people's loins? It was a dismal thought.

"Mama, please, what are you talkin' about?"

"I know why you're tearin' my car up, drivin' way out there. You're after Rosa."

"No, I'm not. That's crazy."

"That's all you've talked about the last two weeks. Rosa. Poor Rosa. Rosa left her husband. Poor little Rosa. Well Rosa's a slut and a whore! She walked out on her husband and is shacked up with a fuckin' drug addict! Hell, you won't even talk to your own daughters! When Gloria was married to that bum, you never done anythin' about it! You never had a kind word to say to her after her divorce! You shoulda tried to counsel her! You've never supported any of your own daughters!"

"That's not true."

"It sure as hell is. You wouldn't know the fuckin' truth if it hit you upside your fuckin' skull!"

"Mama, please," he begged.

I hurriedly painted on my makeup. I'd planned to walk at the track this evening, and I needed a good long trek after all this.

"Don't 'Mama please' me! Are you gonna preach tonight?"

"Uh, I wanted to." His voice was shaky.

"Well, go ahead, then. And I'm gonna call Brother and Sister Campbell and tell 'em that you wanna fuck their daughter. See how they like that."

"Please, Mama. Don't call those people."

"I am. I am sick and tired of this shit. I'm sick and tired of worryin' about you rapin' some young gal."

"Mama, don't call 'em. I won't go to church tonight."

Gloria stumbled into the bathroom. Day-old mascara remained smeared under her half-opened eyes. Her red hair stuck up from left-over hairspray. She plunked herself on the toilet.

"I don't know why in the hell they have to do this when I'm tryin' to sleep," she whined. "I have to go to work today."

Selfish bitch.

"They're not on our schedule," I sighed, as I smeared lipstick on my mouth.

"I'm so sick of 'em."

She pulled her panties up without flushing and walked into the living room.

"What's the matter now?"

Chapter Nineteen

The university emerged before my eyes like a faithful friend. I threw a kiss at it as I passed by, then I turned on Hardy Street and drove to C & R. I pulled myself together in the stockroom and got to work. Saturday nights were busy, and the store was a mess. I straightened the shelves, picked up trash, and carried boxes of stock to proper aisles. At two, I was close to finishing.

"Excuse me. Would you recommend this toothpaste?"

My legs weakened when I looked up. Thomas was dressed in biking shorts and a light blue cycling jersey. I let out a giggle.

"Did you ride your bike over here?"

"I was out, well . . . actually, I couldn't stay away."

"From what?"

"From this redhead I know."

"When did you get back to Hattiesburg?"

"This morning. How was your break?"

"Oh, I got bored," I answered.

"Can I see you after you get off work?"

"Well, I have to check into my dorm first, but yes, I'd like that." I felt tingly as I watched him walk away.

I left at three, drove to UEM, and checked into Beecham Hall. I brought in one box and some hanging clothes. My other boxes I'd left at home, with Mama promising to guard them from the kids. I met my new roommate, Grace Wang, a twenty-five-year-old Asian who was working on a master's degree in computer science. I wouldn't be seeing much of her because she'd be spending her life in the computer lab.

Thomas picked me up at five and took me to his apartment. Though his place had two bedrooms, he lived alone. His furniture looked like it came out of a showroom, but it was his folks' old stuff. He owned quite a collection of pots and pans, handles intact. His dishes were a set, complete and without cracks and chips. The glasses were glass, not greasy plastic. The appliances matched, and the refrigerator had an icemaker—something I'd always dreamed of having. His zest for food was obvious as he whipped up a pan of lasagna.

"Where'd you learn to cook?" I asked.

"From my Uncle Jonah," he said. "I've also read a lot of cookbooks. Hand me one of those spoons."

I pulled a large spoon out of a clear glass container.

"What are you taking besides the management course?"

"Accounting 401 and cost accounting," I answered.

"Yipes. Some tough classes."

"I know," I sighed.

That got me to thinking about my jobs. I watched Thomas pour a glass of wine for himself. He was so cultured. He appreciated the good things in life. I'd always thought of wine as a fancy beer, another way to get drunk. How could I tell him I was cleaning a house? Then I'd have to tell him why I was cleaning a house. Next I was thinking about Henry, and my mood turned dark.

"You sure you don't want a glass?"

"I'll try some," I answered.

"When are you going riding with me? I have an extra bike."

"I know you do."

Denise's apartment looked like the Manor. It was a wooden structure located above an old garage, except it wasn't behind a house. It stood alone across Highway 49. It was made for one person, but she and Carolyn had crammed their junk into it. Suzy's apartment was located in a new apartment complex a few blocks from the campus. The place was spacious and pretty.

I worked my second Wednesday for my new employers. Claude and Molly Perkins were finicky folks living in a very dirty house. He was alpine in height, with a gut that hung a couple of inches past his belt. With bloodshot droopy eyes, he favored a basset hound. Molly was top-heavy, with stork legs. She reminded me of Mrs. Ziffel from the sitcom *Green Acres*. She suffered severe asthma, so I had to dust the walls, furniture, whatnots, and wash every curtain in the house. She hacked so much I was afraid she'd spit up a lung, so I steered clear of her mouth. They were closet drinkers. I stumbled upon the booze in their bedroom closet when I was vacuuming. I counted four cases of beer and three fifths of Vodka. They were nice enough people, though.

Molly hovered. Whether I was scrubbing the bathtub or mopping the kitchen floor, she was always behind me, sweating profusely. Wearing polyester shorts and flip-flops, with that long gray ponytail, I wasn't going to question anything she asked me to do. It was possible that she could whip three gangs at once. Claude sat in his recliner working on crossword puzzles, moving and speaking when she let him. When she was in another room, he stood watch over me until she came back and relieved him. I worked the majority of the afternoon.

"You want anything to drink before you go back to school?" Molly asked.

"No, ma'am, thank you." I picked up my purse.

"Annie, you clean better than anybody I ever seen."

"I've had years of experience," I smiled.

After a month of summer school, I was struggling. Between the classes, the jobs, and the drive to be some superwoman, I was bone-tired. Add dating Thomas to the mix, and the pressure was about to get to me. *I can't be everything to everybody*. I knocked on Marla's door in tears.

"I'm worried about my grades," I said.

"Now I know you're not failing," Marla said.

"No, but I can't keep getting C's in everything. I'm smarter than a C."

She lay a pair of pants on the unused bed. "I think you're pushing yourself too hard, Annie. One job's enough. You need to tell Thomas how busy you are."

"I can't tell him about the cleaning job. I just can't."

"Didn't you tell me his father worked several jobs before he became a lawyer?"

"Yes, but that's different. He probably didn't clean houses."

"You don't know that. He may have done janitor work, and there's not a damned thing wrong with doing janitor work. Cleaning a house just shows people how hard you're willing to work to get through college. And to tell you the truth, if it wasn't for my grandma and my stepdaddy, I'd be cleaning houses with you, and I wouldn't be ashamed of it."

Dr. Dearman told Nell to loosen up and close up shop, so Nell closed the office at three on Thursday afternoon and said that I'd get paid for a full day. Classes would not be meeting Friday due to the Fourth of July. I packed a few things, no hurry to get home. I still had to work the weekend at C & R. I grabbed a sandwich at Arby's and ate as I drove. My friends would be relaxing at home with their families. I couldn't imagine how I could ever relax around mine. Once again, I had gotten off the hook with Thomas, because he had gone to a bicycling training camp in Northern Mississippi.

CHAPTER TWENTY

By three forty-five I was hugging Trudy in the front yard. The sun shone brightly, and it was as hot as a firecracker. Daddy's truck wasn't there, but that didn't mean he was working. I walked to the house, kicking cans and paper from my path. Something green was sticking up from the sand, and when I kicked it over, I saw that it was rotting watermelon rind. Daddy had been celebrating the Fourth early.

When I stepped inside, I knew I didn't belong there. I had been at school so long that it felt like I was on a strange planet. I stopped in the dining room when I noticed the hideous green plastic chairs that Mama had bought to use around the dining room table. The other chairs had broken and were ashes in the burn pile.

Mama used to have good taste, I remembered.

The house looked like it had been turned upside down, shaken, and turned back up. Watermelon rind was on the table, on the floors and in the sink where Daddy had been slicing and dicing. Black seeds were stuck in the dried pink juice, and I got it on my arm and stepped in it.

"I thought you was gettin' home later," Mama said.

She drudged to the refrigerator for some ice. She put a cigarette in her mouth as she cracked the tray.

"Mrs. Johnston let me off early. Why does he get watermelon when he makes such a mess with it?" I asked.

"I told him not to. He's got the sticky shit everywhere. He's eaten so much of it, he's had the runs."

"He's not cooking out tomorrow, is he?"

"Yeah," she moaned as she threw her head back.

"Is anyone coming?"

"Mooney's comin'. Bill and Clarie said they're comin'. Bill wants to cook."

"I hope he does all the cooking."

"Well, Burl'll wanna do it. I don't know why."

"Mama, he burns up the grill. I don't think the last one's recoverable."

"Well, I ain't doin' it. He done went out and got a new one on sale at Rose's."

"Is it disposable?"

"Shit." She rubbed her forehead with the back of her hand. "You goin' to see the Prices?"

"Only for a few minutes tomorrow afternoon. I have to work this weekend."

"Shit, Annie. I thought you'd be off."

"No. I need the hours."

"Well, I thought they was helpin' you pay for school."

"Not if I don't work."

"Well, I think it's crazy to be killin' yourself workin' two jobs."

Three jobs, Mama.

I sighed and opened the refrigerator. "Where did the ground beef come from?"

"Gloria bought it."

"What caused her to do that?"

"I didn't ask her," she said. "I told Burl to get some potatoes and stuff for salad. You makin' it?"

"Yeah, I'll make it."

Temperatures reached the high nineties on Friday. The kitchen was Hades. My makeup was a blend of oil and sweat just ready to roll off my face. Daddy was in and out of the back door, grabbing utensils and dishes. Plates of raw hamburger patties were on the counter, and a convention of flies was feasting. I didn't do much housework when I came in the afternoon before. No longer was I embarrassed about Aunt Mooney coming into the filth. She had seen enough of it through the years, and she still came back.

"Daddy, did you put crackers in the meat?" Mama asked.

"No, I sure didn't, Mama."

"Damn." She slammed a rag against the counter.

Gloria wasn't any help as she moved around the kitchen fretful and teary-eyed.

"Men lie," said Mooney. "I think they'd rather lie than eat. That's all they know how to do is lie. I hate lyin'."

"Shit, lyin's what they do best, and screwin'," Mama grumbled as she chopped the heck out of a head of lettuce.

I rinsed a glass and set it in the dish rack. "Mama, those chairs are so ugly."

"Well, when you're poor, you have to get what you can. Those were only two ninety-nine a piece."

"Daddy could've fixed the other chairs."

"Shit. He wouldn't, and you know it."

"Ooh, God," Mooney spoke with gritted teeth. "Smokey, that dog down the road from us, has been out in my front yard screwin' every female dog in the neighborhood. I hate that dog."

"I can't stand that," said Mama.

"It's pure rape," Mooney seethed.

Out in the backyard, my sisters and their husbands milled around, smoking cigarettes and watching Daddy. Among the never-mowed grass lay oil cans, other rubble, and a tire where Keith decided to sit.

"Burl, I can do grillin' if you want," Bill said.

"I'll let you, 'cause I'm 'bout to burn up out here."

He doused the coals with lighter fluid. Before he could light them, Bill moved out of the way, as did Clarie, who went from sitting in an old rusted lawn chair to her feet in two seconds.

"I'm doin' the burgers or he'll fuck 'em up," said Bill.

Daddy came in the back door drying his wet glasses with a hand towel. "Mama, I got the coals goin'."

"Ain't you gonna stay out there and watch it?"

"Yeah, I was just lettin' the fire burn down."

Gloria's relationship with Jed was on the rocks. Really, it was out the door. That was one reason Mooney was fussing, because Gloria had cried nonstop about him.

"And he coulda at least told me to my face that he didn't wanna see me anymore, Aunt Mooney."

"Didn't have the balls, it sounds to me," she spouted off.

"That girl he's been goin' out with is younger than me."

"Ole Frieda Parker," Mama added.

I turned from the sink. "He's going out with someone else?"

"Hell, yeah," she cried. "The son of a bitch is gonna marry her."

"You know Frieda Parker. She used to go with that Mike, the one that got arrested for peepin' through the windows over in North Soso," Mama told me.

"She's been around," I said.

"She's a whore if she's alive, ain't she," said Mama.

"Is she pregnant?" I asked.

"No. I seen her in town the other day. She's fat as a whale, though," Gloria said as she rubbed an eye.

Mooney put her hand on her hip and joked, "Well, don't hold that against her, Gloria. We fat women have desires."

"I know, Aunt Mooney. But she's so damn ugly."

Mama eased up beside me while I had my hands in the dishwater. "That's all I've heard, Jed this and Jed that. I'm so sick of it. I wish she'd forget about him."

"I thought Jed preferred skinny women," I said.

Gloria wiped her nose with a worn-out piece of toilet paper. "I did, too. That whore. When I called, she answered the phone. I told him he coulda at least told me somethin'. He told me nothin'. He didn't say anythin' on the phone."

"Oh, Lord," Aunt Mooney sighed.

Mama placed the green salad in the refrigerator and slammed the door.

"I ain't never liked him in the first place. I knew he'd pull some shit like this. I told you not to be goin' down there. If he really wanted to see you, he'd have come up here. You were too easy."

"Well, y'all, I didn't know he'd do this to me."

"Gloria, you sound like a cat being tortured. Meooow! Meooow!" I said.

"Leave me alone."

"Leave her alone," Mama said.

"She should leave us alone," I said.

"She's upset."

"That's an understatement."

"Well, she's been hurt."

"She brought it on herself."

"I did not," she cried.

"Well, it still hurts bein' done like that," said Mama the therapist.

I stared out the window. Yes, it did hurt being done like that. Daddy caught the end of the conversation and started giving his advice.

"Gloria, now listen. . . ."

We all groaned. He put another empty plate in the sink.

"Listen to your ole Daddy. That man wasn't meant to be with you. I thought he was weird, didn't you, Mama? He was a little strange. You don't know, he coulda been a murderer. And with you goin' all the way down there. . . ."

"No he's not, Daddy," she whimpered.

"Shit, Burl," said Mama.

"He coulda been. He coulda slashed your throat, and we wouldn't have known about it. He coulda dumped your body in the woods where no one woulda ever found you. Those woods near his trailer are thick."

"Please, Daddy," she sobbed.

"Poor thing," Mooney said under her breath.

"Gloria, I tried to get you to go to church with me so you could meet you a nice fella," he said sweetly.

"I ain't goin' to some hole-in-the-wall church where those walleyed old bastards you hang out with make their wives wear dresses up to their eyeballs while they judge everybody and stare at other women. Holy Rollers!"

"There ain't no reason for you to be ugly," he muttered.

"Oh, brother. Leave her alone, Burl," said Mama.

"Well, she don't have to be ugly and cuss like that."

"Well, you know damn good and well that there ain't any young people goin' to the churches you go to way out in the boonies," she said.

"When he lit that fire, I got the hell outta of the way," Bill laughed, as he came in the kitchen when Daddy went back out to cook.

A few minutes later, Daddy came in and swiped his forehead. "Mama, the burgers are done if y'all want one."

Panting, he manhandled a patty and ate it in two bites. I was so hungry I picked up a paper plate and started with the potato salad. After I poured a glass of Diet Coke, I sat at the table. I didn't like beef too much, but I found a burnt meat patty and put it in a bun. I took a bite, chewed, and swallowed, thinking something was wrong with my taste buds. Bill took a big bite of his hamburger and stopped chewing. He swallowed and wiped his mouth with a paper towel.

"Damn, this tastes like lighter fluid."

"This meat tastes like shit," Gloria said.

"Ain't nothin' wrong with that meat," Daddy said.

"What is it?" Mooney asked, sitting across from me.

"How'd you like your burger cooked? Rare, well done, or soaked in lighter fluid?" Bill snickered.

I got to the Prices' at four, intending to stay thirty minutes. Henry flew to the kitchen and began cooking, and I was stuck.

"We missed you so much, honey."

"We sure did," Pearl said, wiping her eyes and glasses with a tissue.

"Do you have to go back so soon?"

"Yes, Pop. I have to work at C & R," I answered for the fifth time.

"She sure looks beautiful, doesn't she, Henry?"

"Yes, she does." Making the body-outlining gestures with his hands, he asked, "Are you getting to exercise, honey?"

"Actually, with the jobs and three classes, I'm getting to walk three days a week," I answered, hoping he'd get the point.

"It's just . . . well, I'm not saying you're fat. You just don't look as trim as you usually do."

I almost lost it.

"What size are you? A twelve or a ten?" Pearl asked.

"No, honey. I told you, Annie's a size five," Henry answered with aggravation. His tone told me it was too late for these old buzzards to be conversing with anyone. It was nearing seven o'clock in the evening, and I had never been here this late.

"How's your grades? You've never written me anything about them."

"I'm doing fine. I'm having a hard time in my accounting 401 class."

"Can your professor help you with it?"

"He has, but it's—"

"You're not failing, are you?"

"No, sir."

"What's your grade so far?"

"Well, a C."

His eyes almost popped out of his bald head. "Just a C?"

I nodded, afraid to open my mouth.

"Now, we don't need another C on your transcript. Surely you can do better than that. Well, honey, you'll have to do better. What about your other classes? You said you were taking three. How's your grades in those?"

"A little better."

"A little?" He frowned. "You don't sound too happy. Let's hope you don't get C's in those too. The students with the best grades get the best jobs."

"Pop, I'm cleaning a house on Wednesdays."

He touched his hearing aid. "What did you say?"

"I'm cleaning a house on Wednesdays. I make fifty dollars."

He frowned. "Did you quit the work-study job?"

"No, sir. I'm still doing it twelve hours a week."

He half giggled. "Isn't she a hard worker, Mom?"

"Yes, indeed," she smiled.

"Who are you working for?"

"Mr. and Mrs. Claude Perkins. The live near the campus."

"The Perkins," he muddled. "We used to know some Perkins. Willie . . . no, Wayne Perkins and his wife Rita. They moved somewhere."

"Yeah, Rita Perkins," Pearl added. "They moved to Cleveland."

"Cleveland," Henry perked up. "That's right."

"She wore the ugliest hats," Pearl grimaced.

Henry didn't hear her. "What do you do with the money they pay you?"

"I use it for my tuition," I answered.

"Oh, Lordy me," he said. "We haven't paid the rest of your tuition. I forgot about it, sweetheart. Now how much is it?"

"It's down to about five hundred dollars."

"It's down to five hundred dollars?"

"Yes, sir."

"What was it?"

"It was seven hundred seventy-two dollars," I answered carefully.

"Did you hear that, honey? Annie has paid her tuition down to five hundred dollars."

"I'm paying the rest," Pearl said as she tried to get up to get her checkbook.

"Mom wants to pay the rest of it."

"Please Mom, I can—"

"Are you able to save any money?" Henry asked.

"Yes, sir. I just keep my expenses to a minimum."

He leaned back and touched my foot with his. "You know, I've been thinking. Why don't you send me half of what you make from your job, uh, jobs, and Mom and I will match it and put it in a savings account for you. That way we'll have the money for the following semester. Doesn't that sound easier?"

"I guess. Thank you."

While he was getting Pearl's checkbook, my mind was running. Was he proud of me? Did I really look fat? For safekeeping, I kept my arms around my trunk, and Henry took notice when he came back.

"Do you think you need to join a gym, honey? If you're worried about your weight? Pop'll pay for it."

"I weigh one hundred ten pounds."

"Oh, do you?" He seemed surprised.

I said nothing, my face void of emotion. He shrugged and rubbed the short stubble on his face as he wrote out the check. He was very worn from taking care of Pearl, so tired he hadn't shaved. Too cheap to get a nurse to help him. I shouldn't be here and didn't want to be here. Pearl signed it, and Henry happily handed it over.

"Thank you, Mommy Junior."

"Anytime, sugar. You know you can come to me if you ever need anything."

"I appreciate—"

"How's your friend Mavis doing?" Henry interrupted.

"Marla is doing fine," I answered.

"Well, give her our love when you see her, honey."

Pearl was about to nod off, and that was my escape.

"I need to go, Pop. Mommy Junior's so tired, and I have to work tomorrow," I said, emphasizing the word "work."

"We're so proud of how hard you're working. The manager at C & R must be thankful to have someone like you who'll work on the weekends when most people want to play around," he smiled.

I stood to leave. Mommy Junior didn't move, and he didn't wake her. It was dark, and he stayed inside.

"Lock your car door!"

Chapter Twenty One

Christopher happened to be at Denise's apartment when Linda showed up and confronted them about their affair. Christopher walked out, leaving the two women alone together. Denise confessed everything, then she called me. I went over and spent the night with her. She cried most of the night. When the dust settled, Christopher made his last call to Denise to tell her he and Linda were getting married in August.

Thomas held me in his arms a long time. He was so soft-spoken and gentle, and when I thought about my feelings for Peter, they had been nothing like this. We got out of his car, and he held my hand as we walked to my lobby door. My head resident had her door open, and I could see Nancy Long inside with the other resident assistants having a meeting. I felt lucky that the lobby was busy and people could see who I was dating. We sat on the lobby couch.

"I'll call you tonight, after you've had time to study," he said.

"I'll be waiting," I whispered.

"When can I see you over the break? It'll be here soon."

My head lifted from his chest. "It's only a week."

"Yeah, I know, but—"

"I'll let you know."

"I want you to come up to my house."

"I'll try, Thomas, you know." I looked at my watch. "I'd better get to my room and study."

"Maybe I can come down."

"Uh, we'll see."

"Why do I get the feeling you don't want to see me over the break?"

"I do. I just have to get some things out of the way first."

He hugged me close. "We can ride, go to the movies, do anything you want. I can't wait."

He kissed my hand, and I felt so sorry for him. He rested his head on back of the couch, tired from riding and training. He could be anywhere with anyone, yet he was with me. Believing my lies.

"Thomas?" I swallowed hard as he stared into my eyes. "Would you tutor me? I'm not doing so well."

The summer semester was coming to a close, and Denise was in a wretched mood. Suzy had stopped calling her, and I would have, except she needed my friendship more than ever. Leslie and I met at Denise's apartment, because we were all going out to eat to celebrate our summer birthdays. But Denise's greeting was less than festive, as she paced up and down, throwing Carolyn's pillows against the wall and her cassettes out of her bookshelf.

"If she thinks I'm payin' all these bills, she's got another thing comin'. I'm ready to kill her. Look." She shoved several pages of a phone bill in my hand. "She hid this from me. Over three hundred dollars' worth of long-distance phone calls. She's been talkin' to some married man up in New Jersey. For weeks now, I've been gettin' phone calls day and night from credit card companies because she's not makin' payments, and she still owes me for half the water bill from last month."

"Where *is* Carolyn?" I asked.

She slung a cassette across the room, and it landed on the unmade daybed.

"She's off with some guy she met at a bar. The other night, she tried to drag him in here, and I made him leave. There's not goin' to be any screwin' goin' on while I live here," Denise raged.

Leslie was quiet, keeping her eyes on me for refuge. I had to confess that I was mighty amused, but my face was one of concern.

"I came back from class yesterday, and she was laid up in bed.

It was after two o'clock in the afternoon. I told her she'd better get a job, or I'm callin' her parents."

"What did she say?"

Denise kicked a pillow out of her way as she pushed rumpled clothes and the comforter off the daybed.

"She said her parents are sendin' her the money next week, and she'll catch everything up. Her dad's a friggin' doctor—he can help her out. I don't care. She'd better not be late with the rent. If she's late with that, she can move."

At Cuco's, Leslie and I looked at each other and ordered margaritas.

"Please order a drink," Leslie urged Denise.

"I'm the designated driver," Denise said, her prudish side coming to the surface.

The place was bustling, and Leslie's demeanor would perk up whenever a tray of food was passing by.

"Did y'all see that? I should've ordered the fajitas. I'm starvin' to death."

"Well." I held my drink up. "Happy birthday to us!"

A smiled moved through Denise's misery-lined face, and her tears sparkled in the colored lights. Her shoulders trembled, and her chin rested on her chest.

"If you need a new roommate, I'll move in with you," Leslie said.

Denise rubbed her face and giggled. Leslie was too naïve to know the joke. She ogled the tray of food that was being served.

"Ladies, would you like anything else?" the waiter asked.

"May I have a margarita, please?" Denise asked.

"Coming up," he said.

"Good for you," said Leslie. "We deserve this."

"Food and liquor," I laughed.

Swallowing a big bite of beef chimichanga, Leslie said, "I mean, look at us. Three beautiful women, and we should have dates."

I stirred guacamole in my taco salad while watching Leslie douse sour cream on everything.

"What about that guy Nelson you met in your archery class?" I asked.

"That's what I need to talk to y'all about." Leslie lowered her voice as she looked from side to side. "I need y'all's advice. What can I do to get him to notice me? I've flirted with him. I go out of my way to talk to him." She scooped some refried beans into her mouth, chewing and not missing a beat. "I wear sexy-smellin' perfume. He'll tell me he's comin' over on a Wednesday, but then he don't show up. I call his dorm room every day, and he's never there."

"He may not be interested. I mean, he could have a girlfriend," Denise said.

"No, he don't have a girlfriend." She was emphatic. "I asked his roommate, John. He said he knows he don't. I like him so much."

Denise took a sip of her drink, winced, and set it back down. I caught myself enjoying the food too much and slowed up.

"I think Annie's had a great summer," said Leslie.

"It's been a hard summer, Leslie."

"I'm talkin' about Thomas," she teased.

"Is he takin' you anywhere special for your birthday?" Denise asked.

"He doesn't know about my birthday."

"What!" said Leslie. "Annie, come on. He'll want to do somethin' special with you. I told Nelson about mine."

"Leslie, it's just another day," I said.

After work on Saturday, I checked my mail and, sure enough, a bland birthday card from the Prices was waiting. Henry had beautiful handwriting, and the words just flowed out of his Bic pen, but what was written was offensive. He went on to explain why he wasn't buying me a present and why he didn't send money, as if I expected cash and diamonds. I threw his note in the garbage can on my way out of the door. From Mama and Daddy, I got what I always got. Nothing.

Thomas picked me up at four thirty. He cooked dinner, and after we ate, he reviewed my accounting homework.

"The depreciation is wrong on this one," he said.

"I'll redo it."

"You're doing much better."

He was absorbed in my work, making notations in the margins of my paper. I made the corrections while he cleaned his kitchen. Then he went over it again. He was the most persistent individual I had ever met. It was nearing ten o'clock when I closed my books and set them aside.

"Did you like living in Europe?"

"I loved it."

He closed his own books. Thirty minutes later, I was still listening.

"Europe was grueling," he explained. "But it was such a great education. I can't wait to go back."

Learn from him, Annie. He has passion. Where's your passion for anything?

"When are you going back?"

"Probably next summer. Hey, what about the break? What are we going to do?"

I gulped. "What?"

"We get a week, so we can go hiking, or I can—"

"I, uh, can't come home with you, but—"

His eyes became intense. "Why?"

"Well, a week's not a lot of time. I was thinking that we—"

"You keep putting me off. Why?"

"I'm not."

"Do you still like Peter?"

"No."

"You act like it."

"No, I don't. What have I ever said about Peter?"

He got up and took his books into his bedroom. I couldn't move from the couch. After five minutes, I started to get up, then he came back and sat beside me.

"Do you care about me at all?"

"Yes," I answered. "More than anyone."

He stared into my eyes. I was ready to leave, but then I started talking.

"I was just thinking that we could, that I could . . . I think the dorms open up on Saturday, and I could get back early to spend some time with you. I have some things to do in Soso the first part of the week and—"

"Wait," Thomas interrupted. "Can you come back earlier?"

"I'm not sure."

"You could stay here. It'd be closer for you, you know, to drive. Let's meet here."

"Here, okay. I guess I can. Uh, what day? I have something to do Wednesday, then I can come here that afternoon or Thursday."

What am I going to tell Mama, Daddy, and Henry?

"We can meet here Wednesday afternoon," he smiled.

"I still have to work the weekend," I told him cautiously.

"That's okay. I can get in some extra riding."

"Are you sure you want to come back early? I mean, your parents probably want to spend some time with you?"

"They'll be fine," he smiled as he touched my face.

I placed my hand over his, and our lips met. He kissed me a long time, and whenever I pulled away, he pulled me back. I was embarrassed when he kissed my hand. I hated the freckles that covered my skin.

"I need you," he whispered.

As soon as I got home for the break, I told Mama and Daddy that I was meeting Denise in Hattiesburg on Wednesday, and that we'd be spending the rest of the week at Leslie's apartment. To really convince Mama, I told her that Leslie was depressed, and we were staying with her to cheer her up. Mama bought it right away. Then I told them I had taken a cleaning job.

"You're gonna burn out," Mama warned.

"I'm already burned out," I said.

"Why don't you quit the drugstore job, so you could come home on the weekends?" Daddy asked.

"No."

You two birds are crazy if you think I want to come home to this chaos every weekend.

"Baby, you shouldn't overextend yourself like that."

"She's crazy," said Mama. "Have you told Mr. Price that you got another job?"

"I sure did."

I saw the Prices on Monday. Henry studied my checkbook, but I couldn't tell if he was impressed that I had spent so little or what. Without fail, I had been sending him half my earnings to save. He made the usual comments about my weight and hair. "You're looking trim. How much do you weigh? Your hair needs styling. Did you bring your grade report?" I had pulled three B's, thanks to Thomas.

Henry was still feeling tired, so he was going to call Dr. Wallace to see if he'd run some tests. I asked if I could go grocery shopping or run errands for them, and he smiled and said no. Then, I broke the news. I told Henry that we had relatives coming from Nashville, and he reluctantly concluded that I shouldn't come back to see them that week. He repeated what I had told him, that I should help Mama out around the house.

As soon as I left the Prices, I went to Tri-Mart. Fall clothes were already out, so I dug through the sales racks. I bought three short-sleeved blouses, two pairs of shorts, and a pair of plain white tennis shoes to wear around Thomas. Mississippi stayed warm well into September, and I could use the clothes next summer.

By Tuesday afternoon, my attitude was veering, and I was beginning to feel disheartened. I heard Mama and Daddy talking in the living room while I was washing the dishes, and I began thinking about our house back on Third Avenue. I missed the happy times when Mama called us to supper. I missed playing outside in the yard with the neighborhood kids. I missed being a kid. It was easier, and I didn't know we were broke. I only knew that I enjoyed every second of the day.

"He was black, but he looked like a half-breed Indian," Mama rambled on. "He wired five thousand dollars through Western Union to his daughter in New York. Must be nice, havin' money."

"Probably drugs," Daddy said.

The phone rang, and Daddy grabbed it.

"Hello? Yeah, she sure is. Annie!" My eyes were met with his wide grin. "It's a fella."

"Shut up," I whispered. "Hang up when I answer it." I walked into Mama's bedroom.

A quiet click, then I could them chattering in the background like a couple of nosy birds. "Must be that guy that's worried about his grades. Poor thing," Mama said.

"You're calling early, Thomas." I sank into the bed.

"I couldn't wait. Are we still on for tomorrow?"

"Sure."

"Did you have a good day?"

Those polite questions.

Mama's unsightly room was stifling, and I felt my eyes welling up and my emotions on edge.

"It was wonderful."

"You sound unhappy."

"I can't wait to get back to Hattiesburg."

I need you so much. I was sobbing, my hand covering my mouth.

"We can go somewhere tomorrow night."

"I'd like that."

"What did you do today?"

"I, uh, helped my parents around the house."

"That's why I care about you, because you work hard."

I stared at the ceiling as more tears poured down my face. Yeah, I worked hard. I was a maid, and always had been.

"Are you okay?"

"Yeah. Can't wait until tomorrow."

"I'll be in my apartment by three. I won't leave until you get there."

After I hung up, I sat in silence. When I stood, I saw a cockroach racing across the wall. I swung the broom. "Die!" I smashed it to bits.

Daddy looked around. "What was that?"

I walked back to the living room. "I killed a cockroach."

"Was that the guy—" Mama started.

"Yes."

I walked to the back porch and put my clothes in the dryer.

"Mama, I wish we could get one of those satellite dishes."

"Shit, Burl. Those things cost thousands of dollars."

"I'm thinkin' about havin' the cable disconnected. You can't get nothin' good on TV anymore."

"We can't afford no satellite dish and you know it. I don't want the cable cut off. Hell, you know I love watchin' the preachers on that Christian station."

"Well, we could get a lot of those Christian stations if we had a satellite. Ray Levy got one financed, and I think his note's around thirty dollars a month."

"I don't care. I don't ever get to watch anythin' anyway. You're the only one who gets to watch the TV."

"The satellite would be for the whole family, Mama."

"Shit, it won't."

"Those satellite dishes cost too much," I said. "Pretty soon, the price will go down. Besides that, financing it will cost you more than the thing is worth."

"You got that," Mama added.

"I don't think it will, baby," he said.

"Daddy, Ray Levy has money. He has good credit. He probably paid a good bit down on it and got the rest financed through a bank."

"Uh, I don't know if he did or not."

"A satellite's the least of my worries," said Mama. "Hell, we can hardly scrape up the rent every month and pay for the cable. You can get the cable cut off, for all I care, since I don't get to watch anythin'.

Kids can't watch anythin'. . . ." She slammed the bathroom door, but her bitter voice could still be heard.

On Wednesday, Daddy had work to do for Snookie Bush, but he delayed leaving to do it because Mama was cooking chopped steak with rice and gravy. She wanted me to have a good lunch before I went back to Hattiesburg, and Daddy wanted to devour it all. I ate some rice and gravy with a little corn and black-eyed peas.

"You ain't ate nothin'," she chided when I carried my plate to the sink.

Rubbing his mouth with the back of his hand, Daddy was on his second plate. "Baby, you need to eat more than that. You're too skinny."

"I'm full."

"Did you eat some meat?" Mama asked.

"A little."

"What you girls gonna do tonight? You ain't gonna stay out late, are you?"

"No, Mama. We might go to the movies or just stay in. I don't know."

"I hope so. You need to leave us a phone number in case we need to get in touch with you."

"Leave us a phone number, baby," Daddy said. "Mama and I'll worry to death. . . ."

"Right." I left Denise's phone number.

"You call us as soon as you get there," Daddy said.

I cried as I drove away. I didn't want to have to go to the Perkins' to clean. I didn't want to stay home. I didn't want to see Thomas now, when I had been so anxious to see him the day before. Everyone wanted a piece of me, and I had nothing left to give. I didn't see God's point in putting me with my family. I didn't want to learn lessons from it. I would welcome reincarnation—better a dog or cat, than this.

I had purchased a cheap duffel bag for my clothes from Tri-Mart. Thomas came out to my car and carried it inside. I walked slowly behind him and sniffed my hands to make sure I didn't smell like cleanser and bleach after cleaning the Perkins' place.

"Would you like to go out for dinner?"

"Sure," I answered. *Would I be paying for my own? Did I bring enough cash? Just relax, Annie.* "What are we doing tomorrow?"

"Well, I'd like to ride, and . . . I'd like to take you with me."

"I knew you were going to say that."

"We'll take a short ride," he added.

"You've never taken a short ride."

"I promise that we'll do a short ride in the afternoon. I need to go to the grocery store. You have to tell me what you like to eat."

He placed my bag in his bedroom, and my heart began to pound. His other bedroom was where he kept his bikes, but I knew he had a bed in there also. Should I tell him that I wanted to sleep in the extra room or on the couch? I'd be spending four nights with him, and I was afraid I had gotten myself into something I couldn't handle.

After dinner at Cuco's, we rode around. Thomas could talk about anything. Whether it was a foreign country, politics, or the weather, he was up to speed. He had spoken French and a little Italian to me. I had seen photographs of races he had been in, and people he had ridden with. I knew nothing, had nothing witty to say, and I couldn't stand it. Couldn't stand who I was. My life was uninteresting, unless one enjoyed absurdity. As usual, I detoured the conversation whenever Thomas asked about my home life.

"So, your dad does carpenter work," he said. "Can he build an entertainment center?"

"Well, he can build anything, it's just, he's so booked up. . . ."

"I need a new one, and I can't keep taking my parents' furniture," he continued.

I smiled and kept quiet.

"You're not the oldest, are you?" Thomas asked.

"What?"

"The oldest of your sisters. Are you the oldest?"

"No. I'm the second oldest. How's your sister doing?"

"She's doing great. Been working on a huge case."

"She works in your dad's law firm?"

"No, another place. But the principal is a friend of my dad's."

We got home after nine o'clock. I showered in the bathroom adjoining his bedroom, while he used the shower in the spare bedroom. I nervously dried off and carefully hung his towel on the rack. I sprayed on an after-bath mist that I'd bought off a rack of discontinued products at C & R. I slipped on the same size-five panties I had worn for years. They were silk, with a butterfly stitched in the middle. Thomas wouldn't be looking any further than my knees, I told myself. I decided to leave my bra on, too bashful to be liberated. I brushed my hair and teeth and cut off the light. When I opened the door to darkness, I was disoriented.

"Can you see?" He turned on his lamp. He was under the covers. "Come over here."

He didn't have to beg. As soon as my head hit the pillow, his light was off again. I stayed on my back as he came closer. He kissed my cheek and stroked my arm.

"What so funny?"

"Nothing. I just get giddy sometimes." *Say something, Annie.* "Did you like going to Ole Miss?"

"It's a great school." He kissed my mouth. "I like it here better."

"I guess . . . you miss your friends."

"My best friend called last night, you know, Michael, from Chicago. He's in Los Angeles, working for an investment firm."

"Wow."

"Yeah, he's extremely smart."

"Does he ride?"

"Yeah, he does. I got him into riding with me. Now, he rides as much as I do. He called to tell me that he's getting married next June and wants me to be his best man."

"What an honor! Are you going to do it?"

"Sure."

"What do his folks do?"

"His dad's a corporate V-P. His mom's a shopaholic like my mom."

"V-P?"

"He's a vice-president of a textile company."

You're so stupid, Annie. "Exciting."

"Very exciting. Is Denise your best friend?"

"One of them. Marla and Suzy are close friends, too."

"What about Leslie?"

"What about her?" I laughed.

"Come on, you know you like her."

"I do like her, Thomas."

"I like her, too."

I rolled on my side and hugged him. His mouth moved from my forehead to my lips. I caressed his back, wishing his tee shirt were somewhere else. He was solid muscle, and he groaned when I kissed his neck. I lay back as my stomach tingled. He was busy kissing my face until his tongue was searching inside my mouth. I ran my fingers through his hair. When he moved to my neck, I pulled away.

"I want to hear more about Ole Miss."

He caught his breath and rubbed his hand through his hair.

"Okay."

"What dorm did you live in?"

"Tucker Hall for two years, Vann Hall for another year, then I moved off campus."

"Did you like the dorms?"

"I loved the dorms. I just wanted to get off campus."

"I love the dorms, too."

"Are you thinking about going to Ole Miss, I mean, for a master's?"

"No way. One degree is enough for me." I turned and stroked his stomach. I fell asleep listening to the beating of his heart. I awoke to the sound of rain hitting his bedroom windows. I sat up.

"What time is it?" I asked in a panic.

"It's, um, five."

"I have to go to work soon."

"It's Thursday. Just relax."

His hand went up my back, and I really wished he wasn't touching me, because I liked waking up next to him. He kissed my forehead while his fingers stroked my disarrayed hair. I was uncomfortable and aroused and couldn't help it when my leg ended up between his. I didn't go back to sleep and waited as the light penetrated through the darkness. Thomas's breathing was gentle as he slept peacefully.

At a quarter 'til seven, I eased out of his bed and went to the bathroom. I cringed as I stared at my reflection. Splashing water on my face didn't help me feel pretty, didn't wash away the freckles, so I hurriedly put on my makeup, dressed, and fixed my hair. When I came out of the bathroom, his bed was made up. Thomas was in the kitchen making omelettes with the expertise of a chef. Comparing that with my skill of making potato salad, I'd never offer to cook for him. He had as many spices in his cupboards as a grocery store. No generic labels, either. At my house, Girl Scout cookies were considered haute cuisine. I couldn't believe Thomas had cooked for as many as twenty cycling buddies. He set a plate in front of me and handed me a glass of orange juice. I wasn't used to this. Daddy never fixed anything for us.

Why did I have to get up and paint my face? *Always be prepared, Annie.* Why did I have to be a pale and stinking redhead? *If I'm ugly now, will I be beautiful when I'm thirty?* What could Thomas possibly want with me? He was used to women who cycled without mascara and lipstick. He was smiling as he sat next to me.

"How's the omelette?"

"It's great," I smiled back.

I savored the Swiss cheese, ham, and onions, edibles that wouldn't last a day in my home. I tried to eat slowly while Thomas was reading a cycling magazine. Was my ambition gone? I missed the years when I used to read magazines from New York and Los Angeles. When the mail came, so did the guilt. I shouldn't be wasting money on stupid magazines, they'd tell me. In his hand, Daddy'd be holding my magazines. *My magazines.* "I don't know why she's wastin' money on crap like this." *My money, Daddy.*

Cycling with Thomas was the most frightful experience I ever had. It had taken me years to wear shorts because of the brown birthmark behind my right thigh. Having Thomas ride behind me was worse than going to the gynecologist. He moved in front of me so fast, the wind nearly knocked me down. Hardy Street turned into a long stretch of woods, and I was beginning to worry at how far we were riding. We were on roads I'd never seen before, and then we were back at his apartment. I got off the bike and pulled off the helmet. Thomas took off his helmet, and he looked refreshed.

"How do your legs feel?"

"Like Jell-O," I gasped.

"You'll get used to it."

"Do you think I'm going to ride with you again? You went too fast."

"I'll go a little slower next time."

"Please, I won't survive a next time."

"That was forty miles."

"Forty miles!"

My back and legs were sore that night, and I wanted to stay in. But I didn't want to disappoint Thomas, so I agreed to go to the movies and a late dinner. He was happy, gushing with affection whether we were in his car or standing in line at the theatre. On his couch, I was dying for sleep, but he was restless. He turned off the television and leaned in to me.

"Tell me about your childhood."

"What?" I asked.

"You never say anything about it." He took my hand. "I don't even know when your birthday is. I want to know everything about you."

"My birthday is . . . oh, not for several months, and I have told you things about myself. I have four sisters. . . ."

"No, I mean, did you grow up in Mississippi?"

"Yes."

"And?"

"And what?"

"Why do you want to live in Colorado? You said you want to live in the mountains. Why?"

"We don't get snow in Mississippi. I need a change."

"But why?"

"I don't know, Thomas. I guess I'm sick of living in a flat state. There's nothing to do here. Nothing I want to do."

"What do you want to do? I know it's not accounting."

"I like, uh, I'd like to be involved in the entertainment business," I told him faintly.

"Doing what?"

"I'd like to . . . create stories."

"I didn't know that. I think that's wonderful."

He kissed my cheek, and I hugged him.

"Do you want to be a professional cyclist?" I asked.

"Sometimes. But sometimes I want to, I don't know, own companies. You know, invest money, play the stock market."

"Take risks?" I asked softly.

"Yes."

"That's great, Thomas."

"Would you be upset if I told you I love you?"

"I'd be very happy."

I bought my books early Monday morning. My classes didn't start until Wednesday, so I walked to the education office and offered to work. The place was in an uproar. The ringing phone was going unanswered, and Dr. Katz wanted Nell down in his office pronto.

"Oh . . . oh, Annie," she stammered.

Dr. Katz walked in and grabbed me. "Good morning, Annie. It's great to see you. I need you to type this for me, please."

"Oh yes, do that first," Nell said.

I typed the three-page class synopsis and took it to his office so he could proof it, while Nell answered phone calls. She passed me in the hallway like a streak of lightening.

"Dr. Purvis is on the phone again."

As soon as I sat at Nell's desk, she rushed back in. Her fingers were furiously moving through unopened mail and papers.

"It hasn't let up since I got here this morning."

Dr. Dearman came in.

"Hey, Annie, did you have a good break?"

"Yes, ma'am."

She went into her office. Nell remembered what she had to tell me.

"Dr. Katz said the synopsis was perfect. He wants you to make him one hundred fifty copies today."

I walked to the copier room and started the copying. I completed that task and took the first of four armloads back to the office. Nell was having a "quickie" morning gossip session with Dr. Dearman in her office. When I dropped a paper clip on my work table, she rushed out.

"Oh, it's just you. I thought it might be Dr. Katz. Need any help with those?"

"No, ma'am. I got it."

I loaded the stapler and stapled the papers sideways in the upper left-hand corner, the way Dr. Katz had taught me. Nell had certainly revived, laughing as she came out of Dr. Dearman's domain. She sat at her desk and watched me.

"I'll be finished with these soon," I said.

"It's almost noon. You go on to lunch, since you've done the worst part. You can finish after lunch, you hear?"

I picked up my purse. Outside, the campus was swarming, all parking places taken, and a long line was out the door of the bookstore.

Just about every table was full inside the cafeteria. I stiffened as I walked to a small table in the back. Remembering what Marla had told me, I held my head up, walking with bogus confidence. I had nearly finished eating when I saw Peter, his flock of followers, and Nancy Long sitting a couple of rows over. Before I could be embarrassed, Thomas placed his tray on my table.

"There you are."

I looked up as he kissed my cheek. "Hi."

"I was just at your dorm looking for you."

"I was working in the education office."

"I thought you were off today," he said.

"I wasn't scheduled, but I offered, and they needed me."

"You're too nice."

I was taken back by his tone. Should I have done nothing today?

"There's Peter. I have to ask him something about this weekend. Do you mind?"

"No," I answered.

Thomas took a swig of milk, got up, and walked over. I could see Peter joking with him. *Are you telling him to dump me just like you did?* While Nancy was laughing with them, I was sitting like a rock, too afraid to move and socialize. Nancy was wearing one of her long dresses. Why didn't I buy some fall clothes? Thomas looked back at me and smiled. I remembered the last few days, and I smiled back.

"Okay," Thomas said as he sat down. "Got that squared away." He touched my arm and leaned closer. "I want to bike to Columbia and back on Saturday, and I wanted to make sure Peter was up to it."

I stayed quiet.

"We're thinking about going to Jackson in a couple of weeks to train on the roads up there."

In early October, I received a dismal three-page letter from Henry. That pulled muscle sensation he had been having in his chest wasn't heartburn. I skimmed his summarization of the day he had gone to the doctor. The diagnosis was angina. The prognosis was good, as long as he wore a nitroglycerin patch. The Lord would take care of whatever may happen, he said. I pitied Pearl. Sending her to a nursing home was the last resort, but keeping a person with Alzheimer's at home without help was not the solution. They had been blessed. Pearl still had control of her bodily functions. She slept through the night. But she had to be watched around the clock. I folded the letter and leaned against the post office boxes. I had to call on them. Friday afternoon was good, and I could get back to UEM that evening. Explaining this to Thomas wasn't easy. When he didn't ride Friday afternoons, he was glued to me after my last class ended.

"When do you think you'll be back?"

"I hope by seven. If I tell them I want to leave before it gets dark, they'll let me go.

"Are you going to stay with me this weekend?"

"If you want."

"Yes I do."

Chapter Twenty Two

When I arrived at the Prices, Henry didn't get up from his recliner. He pointed at the unlocked glass door, and I walked in. I wouldn't have hugged him, but his arms came up. Since he didn't stand, Pearl stayed seated, so I had to bend to hug her too. Henry seemed down. But Pearl was bright, giggly, forgetful that her beloved was ailing, until he started in on me. He unbuttoned his shirt to show me the patch, then he pulled from his pocket a round gold pillbox containing tiny nitroglycerin tablets.

"It's a good thing this is your last year, sweetheart. If you had another year, whew. Well, we might not be able to help you out."

"Now this is high school?" Pearl asked.

"No, honey," he answered, too tired to explain it again. "You look well. Very trim," he told me, barely making the outline gestures he usually did so skillfully. "New diet?"

"No, sir."

"Whatever you're doing, keep it up."

"What size are you, a ten or a twelve?" Pearl asked.

"Pearl, she's a five, remember?"

"Yeah," she nodded.

"How's your grades?"

"They're good. So far, two A's on two tests."

"Really? Wow."

He seemed not to believe me, though, as he leaned on his elbow. He was whipped. Taking care of Pearl was like taking care of an infant. A seventy-eight-year-old had no business doing it.

"Want to stay for supper?"

"I have to get back to school to study, and I can't at home, so I'm going back."

"Isn't it something that you can't even go home and study in peace and quiet. Well, at least we did the right thing by putting you in the dormitory," he said. "You going to stop and see your parents?"

"No, sir. I want to leave before it gets dark. Maybe around five."

"That's a good idea, honey. You don't want to be driving at night. So many mean people in the world. I just wish you could stay for supper. Hey, maybe around four thirty, if you wouldn't mind, could you pick us up a hamburger from Peggy's Place? It's over by the shopping center."

"Sure."

"I don't want to cook tonight. Mom and I ate in there yesterday, and the food's pretty good."

"I'll be glad to."

"Would you like something?"

"No, sir."

"I'll cook us something," Pearl said eagerly.

"No, honey, you can't."

"Yes I can."

"Pearl. Let's get a hamburger, okay? Do it for me, please."

I thought I had done my good deeds by coming over and by getting the bag of hamburgers, and I was ready to leave. Henry took a bowl of canned fruit from the refrigerator, slowly scooped a helping into a small dessert bowl, and set the bowl before Pearl, who was seated at the table. He put a hamburger on her plate and told her to go on and eat. She hesitated.

"It's okay, honey. I'll eat in a minute." He said the blessing for her while I was standing with my purse over my shoulder. "Amen. Uh, Annie, honey, before you go, would you mind helping me with something?"

"Not at all."

I glanced at the clock, and it was after five thirty. He reached in the dining room closet and brought out a stepladder and a cleaning bucket. *Shoot.*

"If you could . . . Norma won't be here this week. She's gone out to Utah to see her daughter at school." He touched his hearing aid. "Did I tell you that her daughter's an honor student?"

A hundred times! "Yes, sir."

"She also volunteers at the fire department. Real smart girl. Anyway, I need you to dust the lightbulbs, if you don't mind. I'll hold the ladder."

Couldn't it wait? I dropped my purse on the floor.

Chapter Twenty Three

I sped down Highway 59 toward Hattiesburg. It was nearing seven o'clock, and I was ridden with anxiety. I was tired, and I felt as if I had dust all over my hair and clothes.

"I was getting worried," Thomas said.

"I made it." He kissed me and took my bag to his room.

He flicked off the light with a bashful smile.

"What's this?"

"Dinner by candlelight." Slender blue candles flickered in crystal candleholders.

"I see."

"I wanted to have a special night with you, since I'm riding most of the day tomorrow. Sit over here."

I was turned off, didn't want anything to do with him. Perhaps I was sick of feeling suffocated by people.

"What did you make?" I asked.

"Shrimp creole."

"I haven't had that in years. It must've taken you a long time."

The creole was tangy and loaded with shrimp and extras we never had in our cupboards. Mama used grease. Thomas used olive oil and spices I was sure we couldn't afford. I could have had as much as I wanted, but I ate a single helping. He talked about who he'd be riding with tomorrow and the schedule of races. He wanted me to go with him. *When could I go?* I got my clothes ready for my bath and planned how I was going to tell him that I needed some breathing room.

I lay in the darkness of Thomas's bedroom as he moved around his apartment. In my mind I was going over what I was going to say to him, just as I always did before seeing Henry. As soon as he got into bed, my heart rate picked up.

"Are you sleepy?"

"Not really," I answered. "I need—"

"Come closer," he said softly.

I moved over and met him in the center of the bed. He kissed my neck and then my face.

"I need to talk to you, Thomas," I whispered.

He was holding me against his chest. "I'm listening."

"I want to stay in my dorm tomorrow night. I need to be by myself."

He loosened his hold. "Did I do something?"

"No," I quickly answered. "I just need to be alone. I'm tired, that's all."

"Okay." His voice was strained.

"I have some personal errands to run and—"

"I understand," he interrupted. "I know, I tend to be demanding. I must be driving you crazy."

"No, I—"

"I'm sure you'd like to go out with your friends sometime."

"Not tomorrow night."

Thomas seemed distant when I left him the following morning. I worried about him all the way to work and most of the day. I looked for his car in the parking lot, in case he might have decided to drop by. I drove by his apartment, but his car was gone. Where was he riding today? What did he tell me last night? I had been so tired from Henry that I hadn't paid much attention.

I walked laps with Marla, and we had supper in the cafeteria. Then I showered and studied. My roommate Grace came in to change clothes and left for the computer lab. Thomas called at nine.

"You don't mind me calling, do you?"

"Of course not. I was about to call you. How was your ride?"

"Wild. I rode with Bob Lancaster, Peter, and a bunch of other guys I don't really know, and we got lost. Peter wasn't paying attention to the map, and we had to stop and ask directions." I could hear him washing dishes, then he sighed. "Did I do something wrong, Annie?"

"No, Thomas. Don't even think that."

I regretted that I had even opened my mouth.

"You'd tell me if I did, because you can talk to me. You know that, don't you?"

"Yes. Thomas, I . . . don't even like being away from you. If I didn't have . . . never mind."

"What is it?"

"I just wish my life were a little more relaxed.

Near the end of October, I was running on empty. My professors were piling on the work. The jobs were wearing me out, but it wasn't just the jobs themselves. It was the time they took from other things I wanted to do. Telling myself this was only temporary wasn't helping any longer. Thomas wanted what was left of my time, and I gave it to him, but I felt I was never really there for him. I decided to talk to him, be truthful about my life. I just didn't know when I'd quit chickening out until he showed up one morning in the cafeteria.

"I forgot to tell you on the phone last night that I'm doing another race next weekend," he said.

"You tracked me down to tell me that?"

"Yes, and to see you."

I smiled. "Where's the race?"

"In Mobile."

"What day?"

"Saturday. I wish you could come."

"I want to. I mean, I don't know."

I was so good at fibbing, I was contemplating calling in sick to C & R.

"Is Peter going?" I asked.

"He said he is. So is Nancy. She's really nice."

That bothered me. That had been bothering me. Nancy, so pretty Nancy. So different Nancy. So much freedom Nancy had.

"Are we still on for Halloween? We can watch some scary movies," he smiled.

He was so handsome, I wanted to kiss him. But I had to leave soon, and anxiety was crawling up my spine. *For once, Annie, be strong.*

"Thomas, I've been working a lot of hours."

"Can't you cut back?"

The concentration of his eyes was terrifying. It was like facing Henry, and I was close to giving up.

"I've been working for a couple on Wednesdays. Okay, I've been cleaning a house every Wednesday for the extra money."

His eyes narrowed. "You're . . . how many jobs are you working?"

"Three."

He leaned back. "When did this happen? How long have you been doing this?"

"Since the beginning of . . . for several months."

"Why didn't you tell me?"

"What's wrong?"

"That's why . . . that's why you never have time to do anything."

"Thomas, I'm in college to get a degree. I work to pay for it."

He wasn't talking now, and I felt hurt and flushed.

"It's not that I don't want to see—"

"No. It's always going to be something."

"It won't always be like this. Next semester I plan—"

"I want more."

"More what?"

"More out of this relationship."

"I want to give you more. It's just . . ."

"What?"

I looked into his eyes.

"What is it, Annie? Tell me."

"It's . . . nothing."

He stood and picked up his tray.

"Where are you going?" I asked.

"To my apartment. I think we need some time apart."

"No, if you'd just listen—"

"Why? You don't tell me anything."

Thomas didn't call me for days. I was in a stupor. Whenever I ate, the food went right through me. I called, but Thomas never picked up the phone, and he had turned off his answering machine. Why should he put up with me? I decided that I had nobody, with the exception of Marla. I rewrote my list of goals, adding a few more such as learning to ski, though I had never even seen a real mountain. I was going to show up in Colorado someday—thin, rich, and on skis.

Armed with my deodorant, dirty clothes, and makeup case, I was coming from the shower when the phone rang. I hoped it was Thomas, wanting to take me to dinner.

"We may have to move if Mr. Patel stays pissed at Burl. He's done threatened him once this week about the rent bein' behind," Mama said.

"Will y'all be there when I come home for Thanksgiving?" I asked.

"I hope so. I ain't got the energy to hunt another place to live. And we ain't got the money to pay another deposit."

I opened my closet.

"I've had diarrhea since Tuesday. That's a sign that my gall-bladder's goin' out," she said.

"Not necessarily."

"It can be," she said defensively. "I want you to know I went to that doctor . . . ."

"Which one?"

"Dr. Harper. He gave me the same stupid medicine he gave me before. I told him he already gave it to me. He said that's okay, try it again. That shit didn't do one thing to help."

"Help what?"

"My arthritis."

"I didn't know you had arthritis."

"I do. Between my legs, I think it's my tailbone. It hurts so bad, I can hardly sit. I know that's what I got, but none of the crazy doctors around here seem to think so. Guess I'll have to keep eatin' BC's. I didn't get the prescription filled."

I was pulling up my blue jeans, holding the phone out while I slipped a shirt over my head.

"Are you there?"

"I'm putting on some clothes."

"Are you goin' out?"

"I'm going somewhere."

"Well, I won't hold you. Just wanted to see how you're doin'. Burl's been buggin' me to call." She sighed with aggravation. "I fried eight pork chops the other night. You'd think that'd be enough for at least two meals. Gloria and I ate one, and I split one between the kids. Your daddy ate the rest."

"I thought pork upset his stomach."

"It does. Let him have another spell."

"He doesn't believe in spreading out his meals, does he?"

"Shit. I'll stand on my feet cookin' for two hours, and he gets his ass in the kitchen and stands over the pots until it's all gone."

"Jesus. Isn't gluttony a sin?"

"You ain't gonna believe what he said the other day. He thinks he can start his own church. He says, 'Mama, you and I oughta quit our jobs and be in the ministry full-time."

"He quit his job years ago."

"I ain't startin' no church with him so he can chase women."

"Chase the congregation. But hey, maybe Gloria can sing in the choir. Has she found another man yet?"

"No. She's been too busy bitchin' about that confounded job. Oh, damn, guess who's home?"

I could hear Daddy complaining in the background. "I'm so nervous with all the bitchin' Gloria does around here. I think that's why my stomach stays so upset. I can't stand it."

Mama growled. "You can't stand it! I wish she'd find herself an apartment."

You two never ask me about my classes. Never ask me anything that matters to me.

"Jessie's got a tumor on her left ovary. Big as a grapefruit." Her tone was casual.

"A tumor?"

"It's not cancer or anything. It's a huge cyst."

"I hope it's not cancer."

"I know it's from those tannin' beds she lays in. Crazy things will cook you. She's never looked right since she started layin' in those things."

"Does Daddy want to talk to me? I need to get off the phone."

"Daddy, you wanna talk to Annie?"

"Hey, baby," he said happily.

Calls from home left a bad taste in my mouth. *I'm so lonely*. I drove to Denise's apartment and watched her make a lemon pie.

Leslie Lang had disappeared. She had taken a job at the Beverly Drive-in, and she was running with a group of kooks she worked with there, and still pursuing the guy she met in her summer archery course. She had gotten him a job at the drive-in. Of course, he screwed her every chance he got, and she gave him many chances.

His name was Nelson Hyde. The only time I had eaten with them, I wasn't too impressed. He was friendly toward me but obviously didn't care about Leslie. Three times at the table he ignored her questions, and once he told her she shouldn't wear horizontal stripes. But she thought he was the one, her future husband. Nelson looked better than Pepper Tisdale, in that at least he had all of his crooked yellowish teeth. He was gangly, his hair and complexion oily. In the cafeteria, Marla almost cashed it in when she saw him passing by our table.

"That guy is doing her?"

"That's what she told me and everybody else," I said.

"Ooh, it's too gross to think about."

To celebrate Halloween, I went with Marla and Suzy to see the *Rocky Horror Picture Show*, which I'd seen the year before with Peter. Denise opted to stay in her apartment and do her toenails. Peter showed up, acting arrogant and speaking only to Suzy. Why he was snubbing me, I didn't know. He joined a few guys in the first row of the balcony. We were in the last.

"Peter said it was 'guys night out.' No women allowed," Suzy said.

A group of women from Stanton Hall came in and seated themselves in the same row with the guys. In the midst of the movie and commotion, I was watching Peter parody the actors, but I was missing Thomas very much.

Two weeks into November, it was a clear and crisp Saturday, after an all-night rain. Marla and I walked five miles, stopping after five o'clock to go get supper. At the table, I was still out of breath, so I waited until I was breathing normally to eat. Marla looked at me.

"Lord, I'm so tired. I sound like Leslie don't I?"

"We have good reason to be tired," I said.

Steam was rising from the thick slices of boiled cabbage on my plate, and I sluggishly cut into them. I had been eating regularly in the diet line. My personal life had gone down the drain, but I was feeling healthier. I didn't mind paying Henry a visit to show him my lean lines and to tell him I was down to a hundred and eight pounds.

"You sure do amaze me," Marla said.

"I do?"

"No matter how much pain you go through, you keep trucking along. You work a lot, but you just keep going. You're one courageous woman, you know that?"

"It's funny. I've never felt courageous. When I first started UEM, I thought everybody else around me was so much stronger, so much more confident. I thought Denise was, even crazy Leslie."

Marla shook her head. "Not those two, honey."

"Truthfully, I'm so depressed right now, I could scream bloody murder."

"When I get depressed I don't feel like getting out of bed. I just want to hibernate in my room. At least you got the will to get up in the morning and put on lipstick."

"Some days, I feel like I'm hanging on by a thread. I pray to God that the thread doesn't break."

"It won't break. You can handle anything, girl."

I was on the edge of crying.

"I'm really upset about Thomas."

"Men can cause you some unmerciful pain." She seemed so sad, I nearly hugged her.

"Why did I even tell him about the cleaning job?"

"He needed to know the truth, Annie. If he cares about you like he said he does, he wouldn't be acting like a two-year-old. He'd understand why you have to work. He'd be a man about it."

"I have no life here anyway."

"Yes, you do. This is your life. Right here and right now. Enjoy it while you're young."

"Oh, God, why are you always right?"

" 'Cause I'm an intelligent woman."

The following afternoon, I drove to Denise's after work. She had called. Had to talk to me. I was eager to provide an ear. When I sat on the daybed, I braced myself, wondering if it was about Christopher.

"Nothing bad, is it?"

She smiled. "No. Nothin' bad. I took this entrance exam for dental school, and I passed it."

"That's great, Denise."

"They want me to enter the school next semester."

"You mean, you won't be graduating with me?"

"No. I'll go on and start dent school early, you know, instead of next fall."

"Where will you go?"

"The University Medical Center in Jackson."

"I think that's great. I mean, I'm going to miss you so much."

"I'll be so lost without you," she said. "I dread goin'. It'll take the next four years."

"Four years," I moaned.

"It's a long time."

"It sure is."

"But, Miss Annie, you can come up and spend weekends with me from time to time."

"I will. I won't be working weekends next semester. I'm quitting after the Christmas holidays."

"It's about time. I don't know how you've done it." Her smile was genuine, her voice caring. "I hope you'll work things out with Thomas. He really does love you."

"I just want to graduate and get out of here."

I spent so much time thinking about Thomas and what he was up to. I hadn't seen him in the hallways of the business building. Every evening I had been studying in the library with a struggling group of accounting majors, but my thoughts were on Thomas. *Maybe he met someone else. Oh, God, he wouldn't?*

Chapter Twenty Four

On the morning after Thanksgiving, I was sitting on the gripe seat, not really watching a talk show, but the noise was keeping me company. Being home made me feel isolated and depressed. Daddy came through the front door and eased his head around just enough to see what was on.

"I wished they'd put a stop to stupid shows like that. But, no, they have to have freaks like him all over the television."

"Who are *they?* Are you talking about the communists or the National Organization for Women?" I asked.

"I'm talkin' about that bunch of trash we got runnin' the networks."

I stood up, wondering why he was such a bitter person. I walked to the bathroom as Mama was coming out.

"The Reverend is home."

"I heard him," she mumbled with a cigarette in her mouth.

The fact that Daddy didn't believe in providing for us didn't make me feel rejected. I was bothered and annoyed as hell, but not deserted. He didn't leave like a lot of men do when things are bad, but he was the primary reason things were bad.

I went to the kitchen. My stomach had rumbled since the day before, when I didn't eat much of anything. Mama and Aunt Mooney had eaten pieces of pecan pie, telling me I looked anorexic and that I looked better with a little weight on my bones like I did in high school. In high school, I wore size eleven. I wasn't called fat, I was called "plump" by Felicia Tate, who meant well. *You're not fat, Annie, you're plump.* There was some leftover dressing and potato salad in the refrigerator, but I needed protein. I looked for the turkey leftovers that had been carved and wrapped on a plate. The aluminum foil was on the table. The plate was empty.

From the living room, Mama and Daddy shared their usual intimacy.

"Mama, the rent's due next week."

"I can't shit it up, Burl!"

He rubbed the back of his neck with worry, since he didn't get the response he wanted.

"I know it. I was thinkin', uh, maybe ole lady Walker might let you borrow—"

She threw her arm up in the air. "I ain't borrowin' nothin' now! I don't make enough to borrow any money. I'm too busy buyin' gas for your truck so you can run out to Sister Willa's every day! What happened to all that work you supposedly had to do?"

I brought my plate into the dingy dining room and didn't look at them.

"Uh, well, Mama, I'm still doin' it. Startin' next week. The man told me—"

"I knew it. You'll worm outta that work."

"No, I ain't doin' that."

"If you don't build those chicken houses, I'm goin' to leave."

Do it! Leave now and make him sweat.

If it wasn't a utility bill past due, it was the rent in arrears or the simple need for a loaf of bread. Mama walked to the back porch to put some clothes in the dryer. I didn't finish my food. I washed the plate and listened to Daddy opening the refrigerator.

I went to Mama's bedroom and put on my tennis shoes and grabbed my coat and car keys. She was back in the living room, smoking, while Daddy was gobbling in front of the television.

"I'm going walking."

"Ain't it too cold?" Mama asked.

"I'll walk in a blizzard."

"I thought maybe you'd wanna go to the Salvation Army store with me. They're supposed to get a new shipment in this mornin'."

"Mama, it's too crowded. The people that go in there don't use deodorant."

"I thought you could find you some shirts. Clarie found some pretty ones the other day, and they only cost a quarter a piece."

Daddy wiped his mouth with his hand. "I'll go with you, Mama."

"I don't want you goin' with me. I can't even go rummage salin' without you up my asshole. You start that complainin' about your feet burnin', and I can't even look."

"I'll go after I walk."

"It's stupid to walk in this weather," she argued.

"But not to shop for used clothes? Let me go, so I can get back," I begged.

"Well, be careful," Daddy said.

I was freezing on the track. After three miles, I drove back home. I pulled into the sandy yard, and the cats scattered. Cockroaches weren't the only creatures we acquired with this shack. Most of the cats were wild and wouldn't let me and the kids pet them. Of course, Mama and Daddy forever bitched about them, but Trudy didn't mind sharing the porch with them. On those cold nights, the cats wrapped their furry bodies next to her, making me feel less guilty that she had to sleep outside. Daddy showed no mercy on her. I'd show him no pity when he reached his golden years. I'd stick him in a nursing home without a second thought.

With all the sand around, the cats had a front yard litter box, and therefore, another reason for Daddy to fuss.

"I'm gonna shoot those stupid cats. No one can step outside without smellin' that cat crap."

"Plant some grass," I said.

"I ain't plantin' no grass so they can dig it up."

Mama looked up from reading a Christian novel by Billy Graham.

"I'd have a heart attack if you fixed anythin'."

"Well, Mama, it wouldn't do any good to fix this place up since we're rentin' it."

"Uncle Grover's renting his house, and he fixed it up very nice," I said.

"He built Twilla some pretty cabinets for her canned goods," Mama told me.

"And he has cancer," I added.

Daddy rubbed the back of his neck. "If I catch another cat crappin' out there, I'll shoot it."

"No you won't. If people would neuter their animals, there wouldn't be strays," I said.

"Haul 'em off, for all I care," said Mama.

"No. I love animals more than humans."

I walked to the bathroom and slammed the door.

"That's crazy," Mama said.

"Lots of people are crazy!" I yelled. "Especially parents."

When Daddy hinted around about wanting a bucket of fried chicken, I left the house. On impulse, I drove to the mall, not realizing it was the first official day of Christmas shopping. But I wasn't Christmas shopping. I was trying to forget Thomas, plan my future, and save my sanity at the same time. My mood was desperate again, and I searched through the self-help section of a bookstore. When would I have time to read anything besides accounting? I picked out two new books to read during Christmas break. Passing a hair salon, I turned and walked in.

"Cut it off," I told the stylist.

Henry had been telling me to get my hair done, so I did. It was a short style, and I looked like a pixie because I was so thin. My cheeks were hollows and my eyes sunken in. My teeth even seemed larger without the fullness I used to have. But I was happy as I touched my hair. *You're a new woman, Annie Lee.*

I went to bed at nine o'clock that night. Mama was in her usual position in the gripe seat, a cigarette in one hand and a glass of Diet Coke in the other. Daddy was in the recliner with his leg hanging over one of the arms. The television was blaring a rerun of *The Waltons*. Quite a contrast to this family, I thought. I ignored the ringing of the phone.

"Uh, yeah, she's here," Daddy said.

I sat up with large eyes.

Daddy peeked into the room. "I think it's that fella from your school."

I cautiously picked up the receiver in Mama's room as Daddy went back to the phone in the living room.

"You got it, baby?" Daddy asked loudly as the television blasted.

"Yes, sir," I answered. Daddy hung up. "Hello?"

"Hi, Annie. This is Thomas."

I squeezed my eyes tightly.

"Hello? Annie? Are you there?"

"Uh, yes. Uh, how are you?"

"Miserable. I'm in Colorado."

"I wouldn't be miserable if I were in Colorado," I said.

"I just needed to talk to you. I had to hear your voice."

"How did you do in your race? I thought about you that weekend."

"I won."

"Oh my God," I whispered. "You won."

And you weren't there, Annie.

"I'm sorry for being angry with you and for what I said."

"No, Thomas. I'm sorry for not telling you about my extra job sooner."

"I should have understood, and I do understand now, and I can't wait to see you, if you want to see me."

"You know I do."

Chapter Twenty Five

Daniel and Maggie Barnes were coming to Hattiesburg Thursday evening on business, Thomas said. As long as they were in town, I might as well meet them. I took Marla with me when I rushed to Tri-Mart in search of something to wear. I hoped that Mrs. Barnes didn't think I was cheap for wearing a body-hugging green sweater dress. I was down to a size four. Marla insisted that I get good pantyhose, and good meant paying more, so I went all out on an expensive barely black pair that shimmered. I had black heels in my closet. As for accessories, less was more.

"You are gorgeous, girl. Thomas will fall out when he sees you."

"I hope he does fall out for putting me through this," I said.

She was sweeping her floor. She kept it cleaner than an operating room.

"Girl," she giggled. "Don't look so horrified."

"I feel like I'm facing a judge and jury."

"Get outta here. Girl, do you know how lucky you are? Do you know how many women would love to be in your shoes? Me, for one."

She went down to the lobby with me. She said she needed something out of her car, but I knew she wanted to check out his folks. My stomach gurgled as the elevator went down, and I prayed it wouldn't make a racket tonight. On my watch, it was six o'clock on the dot. I walked out of the elevator expecting to see Thomas.

"Not here," Marla said. "Take it easy. Relax."

She walked out the back door of the lobby. I ended up waiting in a chair by the front desk. Soon Thomas was getting out of a dark blue Lincoln Continental. He was wearing dress clothes. I waited until he came in, then I stood and wrapped my arms around his neck.

"You look beautiful."

He squeezed me firmly and led me to the car. He opened the door, and I slid in. Mrs. Barnes pounced.

"Hello, honey. How are you?"

"Mom, this is Annie Lee," Thomas said.

She slipped on some reading glasses without taking her eyes off of me.

"Annie's such a beautiful name."

"I'm Dan Barnes. Do you like steak, Annie?"

"Can we go now," Thomas interrupted.

Mr. Barnes smiled and backed out and drove off the campus.

"Thomas says you're from Soso," Mrs. Barnes said.

"Yes."

"I had an uncle who lived there. He died ten years ago. How long have you been going to UEM?"

"This is my second year. I went to junior college for two years."

"Which one?"

"Jones County."

"Good school," Mr. Barnes said quickly.

"Remember Dan, my friend Betsy went there. She majored in nursing with me. We worked together at Saint Thomas."

"I hear you're an accounting major," Mr. Barnes said.

"Good major," Mrs. Barnes said.

"So, you're a junior or senior?" he asked.

"Senior. I graduate in May."

"So does Thomas," she said.

"Accounting's a good field," he added.

"Annie's very smart," Thomas said.

While Mrs. Barnes told Mr. Barnes she'd left her keys at home, Thomas was rubbing my hand, reassuring me that I was safe. At Conestoga's, he opened the door and pulled me up. Then, he opened the door for his mom.

"Thank you, sweets," she said.

Aunt Mooney would've loved to be able to fit in the red designer suit, but it was made for Maggie Barnes, who could pass for a star of a soap opera. She wasn't skinny, but thin, compared to Mama, in the sense that she had a shape. From her shoes to her fingernails to her lipstick, everything was red. Her bracelets weren't the fake silver kind that Denise wore. I counted five on one wrist. She had a diamond bracelet on the other. She wore several diamond rings, along with a simple gold wedding band.

Daniel Barnes was completely gray, and the first thing that came to my mind was "Sugar Daddy." His blue suit looked impeccable, not like the old polyester duds Daddy wore to romp and stomp at the churches. Maybe it was in his gene pool to be handsome, but it was also in his nature, his attitude.

When we were seated, Maggie let the cat out of the bag while Thomas acted as if he didn't hear her. This wasn't a business visit. They had driven down to meet me.

"The traffic was horrendous," she chattered. "It started at two, then by four . . ."

For a moment, I wondered if she was on drugs like Mama. Except she was happy. Thomas held my hand tightly.

"Annie, now that I can see you in the light—your hair's just gorgeous. Remember when I had mine red five years ago? But it was never that beautiful."

"I hated your hair red," Thomas said.

"Yeah. I do look better with blond hair, don't I?" She opened her menu. "Thomas, I don't know what to get, help me. Annie, what are you going to get?"

Before I could open my mouth, Mr. Barnes tried to help. "Well, I'm having a ribeye. How about that?"

Thomas put his arm around me. "Get whatever you'd like."

After we ordered, Maggie smiled at me. "Is your mother a redhead?"

"No, my father is. My mom's a brunette."

"That green goes so well with your skin and hair," she added.

"Annie's a Christmas tree, all in green," Thomas smiled.

Maggie laughed. "She's prettier than a Christmas tree, son."

"Thomas said you're a nurse."

"Yes. I'm an RN, for eighteen years now."

"I think that's so great."

"Oh, I love it, dear." She took a sip of water.

"So your classes keep you busy, I bet," Mr. Barnes said as he tried to get a word in.

"Yes, they do. I work, too, so my schedule's full."

"Oh, you work?" they said at the same time.

"What kind of work?" Mrs. Barnes asked.

"I work for the professors in the education department. I do secretarial work mostly."

"Interesting. I bet you're learning a lot," Mr. Barnes said.

"I work for five professors, so I've become a very good typist."

Maggie was older than Mama. They were a couple who had their children when they were in their later twenties. They chatted with Thomas about his classes and his life in general.

"You can go by Stanley's, and he'll check your car for you," Mr. Barnes said.

"I'll go after I finish with my exams."

The food came out. Thomas turned his attention over to me while we ate. He whispered, "Guess who I saw in her little red car the other day?"

"Who?"

"Leslie."

"Who are you talking about?" Mrs. Barnes asked.

"A friend of ours," he said.

"Do you have the same friends? Is that how you met each other?"

"Yeah, we hang out with a lot of the same people. But I first saw Annie in the business building last year."

Maggie smiled. "He had his eye on you."

I looked at him.

"You were coming out of Dr. Fowler's statistics class, and I had a class down the hall. That's when I first saw you."

"And I'll be he couldn't take his eyes off you," she said.

"When was this?" I asked.

"The first day of classes," he smiled.

I went to the bathroom. A brief look at my face in the mirror made me realize I looked tired. Coming back, I caught the end of their conversation.

"Now Maggie, that's his business," Mr. Barnes said.

They grinned at me as I sat back down. She pretended to close her mouth with her fingers whispering, "My lips are sealed."

I knew they had been sizing me up.

"Would you like any dessert?" Thomas asked me.

"No, I'm too full."

"That's why she's so thin, she doesn't eat dessert like I do," Mrs. Barnes said. "I want that chocolate cake with the ice cream on top." When it came out, it did look tempting. "Ooh, it's so big. Dan, help me eat this."

"I can't."

"Thomas, help your mama eat this now," she offered.

He picked up a fork. "She does this to me all the time."

She picked up an extra fork and handed it to me. "Come on, Annie. Help us."

I took a bite. "It's so good."

"You see what you're missing, Dan. Annie loves it, too."

"Now you know why I ride my bike a lot," said Thomas.

"Isn't he something? Riding that bike from town to town, miles and miles," she said.

"He's in great shape," I smiled.

"Annie rode fifty-five miles with me," he bragged.

"Lord, you must be in good shape. Well, you are, I can see that," she said.

"It was rough," I admitted.

"She's in great shape. She walks, too," he said.

"Oh, I do, too. And I go to an aerobics class sometimes. How far do you walk?"

"About six miles."

"Heavens. I can't walk that far."

Mr. Barnes paid the check and talked to Thomas while Mrs. Barnes held my hand by the door.

"Honey, we really enjoyed meeting you. You'll have to come up and see us sometime. I've been telling Thomas to bring you up. What are you doing for the holidays?"

"I'll probably spend it with my grandparents. They haven't been doing too well, health-wise, and they look forward to seeing me."

"I understand. It's wonderful that you're close to them. They need that," she said. "But you come up for a weekend sometime."

"Thank you."

"Ready to go?" Thomas asked as he took my arm.

On the way back to the campus, he changed his father's course.

"Dad, can you take us by my apartment? I'm going to drive Annie back."

"Thank you for the dinner," I said.

"Oh anytime, dear," Mrs. Barnes said.

"It was our pleasure," Mr. Barnes agreed.

Thomas let me inside while Maggie was telling him their agenda for the next six months. I took off my coat and shoes. I wanted to lie on his couch but forced myself to sit up. He came in with a smile, locked the door, and took off his jacket.

"Can you stay awhile?"

"Sure. I really like your parents."

He sat close. "Yeah, they're pretty great. They like you a lot, too."

I was too tired to be in love with him tonight. But he was so damned desirable.

"I hope my mom didn't drive you crazy."

"No, I enjoyed her. She loves you a lot."

"I know."

"Your dad's so sweet and quiet."

"That's because Mom doesn't give him much time to talk."

"It's the opposite with my parents. My Daddy never shuts his mouth. Mama's the quiet one."

"Would you like to listen to some music?"

"Yeah."

He didn't get up, and I didn't leave his apartment until after one in the morning.

Daddy told Mr. Ford he broke his foot so he could get out of building him two chicken houses, sending Mama into another outburst of profanity, disgust, and depression. She called, crying, when Marla was in my room, and I had to ask Marla to leave so she wouldn't witness my distress. Mama told me in detail what she wished would happen to the Reverend, then raged about the new family that had moved in across the street. The woman had a controlling husband, wild kids, and suffered depression. It didn't stop Mama from calling her a blooper-cootered bitch.

When Suzy found out that I had met Thomas's parents, rumors of marriage rippled from her to Marla to Denise to Leslie. When Marla and I met up with Leslie and Denise outside the cafeteria, both were grinning as wide as the Grand Canyon. We got our trays and found a table.

"A guy doesn't introduce you to his parents unless he's thinkin' of somethin' serious," Denise said.

"We're just going steady, girls. I'm not in a hurry to be that serious."

"Lord, I've been dyin' to be very serious the last three years," Leslie whined.

"How's it going with that guy you've been . . . uh, dating?" Marla asked Leslie.

"It's goin' okay. It's just, he never calls me."

"He doesn't?" Marla tried to show sympathy.

"No, and I think this girl that works at the drive-in with us likes him."

"Who's that?" Denise asked.

"Her name's Rhonda, and I can't stand her."

"The important question is, does he like her, Leslie?" Marla asked.

"He's nice to her and all, but he does that 'cause he doesn't want to hurt her feelings. Nelson is like that."

"Mmmm, mmm," Marla moaned.

"Her hair's dyed blond. It's not natural like mine," she continued.

"Do you think Nelson may like her?" Denise asked.

"Hell, no. She's a slut. She flirts with him, and I just want to knock her on her ass."

Leslie swung her fist in the air. Marla put her fork down.

"Honey, Nelson may be calling that girl. You don't know if he is or isn't. He's telling you that he isn't, yet the girl and him seemed to be friendly with each other at their job. He's lying."

"Nelson wouldn't lie to me. We're too close."

"Screwing don't mean you're close," countered Marla.

"You're very easy to find in here," Thomas smiled. He set his tray by mine and sat down.

"She sure is," said Marla. "I can always find Annie."

"That's right," Denise agreed. "Thomas, congratulations on winnin' that race."

"Thanks."

"How many miles did you have to ride?" Marla asked.

"One hundred thirty-four."

"Mercy! I'd drop dead," she laughed.

"I can't believe you rode that far." Denise was shaking her head.

"He's very strong," I bragged.

"I wish Nelson would ride a bike," Leslie said.

Thomas opened his milk, giving the drama queen a deadpan expression.

"When are you going biking with me?" he asked Leslie.

"Well . . . I haven't lost enough weight yet."

"You can still ride. I have a couple of extra bikes. You and Nelson can ride with me this weekend."

"I'll have to ask him. We both work on the weekends."

"Only at night," Denise added.

"Yeah, but we have to study before we go in to work."

I mailed a stack of letters for Nell at the post office and walked over to the education department mailbox. I bent down and had entered two numbers of the combination before I was distracted.

"Hey, Annie. You look nice today."

I turned around.

Peter grinned. "How are your classes?"

"Busy. Guess you're looking forward to graduating."

"You better believe it."

"Well, good luck in finding a job." I was about to turn back around.

"I *have* a job. In Jackson."

I paused. "Jackson? I thought Texas would be a better choice for you. I mean, there are more jobs there."

"Yeah, but I've grown attached to Mississippi. I've lived here for five years now. Besides, I need to get some job experience. Jackson's a good place to start."

It's where I may have to start.

"Well, I wish you luck."

"Hey." He put his hand on my shoulder. "Why don't we keep in touch? I'll send you my address in Jackson as soon as I get settled in."

Thomas gave me a gold necklace with a small gold heart as my Christmas present. Guilt-ridden, I accepted it. I hadn't bought him anything. Long before Christmas he'd asked me to promise not to buy him anything. "Does it look like I need anything?" he asked as he looked around his apartment. He was right. I decided I'd write him a love letter and enclose it in a beautiful Christmas card when I got home for the break.

I opted to spend Saturday night with Denise to help her pack up. Carolyn had already moved out. Leslie was hobbling stiff-legged around the apartment, not helping us. Denise made her get off of a box, and she plopped on the floor, rubbing her legs.

"Do you have any Bengay?"

"No," Denise answered.

"I can't walk. Thomas almost killed me on that stupid bike last week. I started to go to the emergency room last night. I didn't get a wink of sleep," she whined.

"Leslie, I have to hurry," Denise said. "Mama and Daddy will be here in thirty minutes."

She rolled her eyes, seeking sympathy from me. She rotated to all fours and stood up with a red face.

"I'll never ride a bike again."

"Thomas told you it'd be hard," Denise reminded her.

"Not *that* hard. I'm just about dead."

I loaned Leslie five dollars for gas to get her to leave. I didn't want to be there when Denise's parents were there. I hated goodbyes, and I had to go see Thomas. He could have left days ago but stayed because I stayed. I stayed because Denise didn't finish her last exam until Thursday and didn't start packing until Friday night.

Chapter Twenty Six

In the midst of commuting six days a week to work for C & R and working Wednesdays to clean the Perkins' house, I had to survive living at the Manor. I had a good paycheck coming from C & R, and I'd give it to Henry to put in our savings account. It had built up nicely, and I had more than enough to cover my tuition for my last semester. I decided to keep both the work-study and the cleaning jobs to make money to live off of while I looked for a job after graduation. Still dressed in my C & R smock, I drove over after work in the cold evening to discuss my plans with Henry.

"Pop, I was thinking that I should keep my other two jobs so I can save some money for after I graduate."

He didn't hear me clearly. He nodded his head and adjusted his hearing aid. "I'm so happy you want to keep working. Most students would lie around, do nothing their last semester, relax," he said as he crinkled his face. "But not our Annie."

Not as long as you and Daddy are in my life.

"I tell you what. If you want to do the same as we did last semester and send us half of what you earn each week, we'll match that, too. That way, you'll have a cushion to live off of until you get your first job."

First job? What do you think I've been doing for the last ten years, vacationing?

"Pop, that's great. I earn fifty dollars a week cleaning, and eighty dollars every two weeks for work-study, so I can send you forty-five dollars each week to save."

His eyes were pointed up at the ceiling as he was figuring it out. "That's right, honey. Mom'll put in her forty-five, and that'll be ninety dollars."

"Mommy Junior, thank you."

"Anytime, darlin'. You come to me whenever you need anything," she said.

Henry smiled lovingly at Pearl. "Mom loves you so much."

I held her hand and leaned back. He would always drive me nuts, but he was looking out for my best interests. I had learned a great deal from Henry Price.

I made one B and three A's that fall semester, and I owed to Thomas—that, I didn't share with Henry.

When I got home, Mama started in about the new family across the street—the Spencer clan from Magee.

"Just as soon as I get home from work, Renee calls and keeps me on the phone for hours," she griped. "Ooh, her husband David. He watches everythin' she does. He goes to the grocery store with her and dictates everythin' she buys. She told me she stays so nervous when he's home."

"Where does he work?" I asked.

"At one of the banks. He's a maintenance man."

"At least he works."

"He don't make shit. They do pay their rent and utilities, but there's nothin' much left for groceries. Renee has to buy that cheap macaroni and cheese to feed 'em all."

"How many kids?"

"Three. God," she groaned. "I can't stand those loggerheads. All of 'em have big basketball heads. And the boy, Joey, they think he's a lump of gold. But he's a little sneak. He gets in here and eats up the cookies and crackers. I can't keep anythin' for the girls."

"Tell the brats to stay out of the kitchen."

"I do, and they don't listen. Renee sits on the couch talkin' my head off and lets 'em tear my house down."

"It's already torn down."

"I know, but I don't want 'em destroyin' what's left of it."

"Then put them out."

"I can't be rude."

"They're rude, and she's rude for not making them behave in other people's homes."

"I feel sorry for her."

"Mama, feel sorry for yourself."

On Saturday, I came home from work, and Renee met me at my car. She wanted to borrow a stick of margarine, so I gave her a stick that had been in the refrigerator since last Thanksgiving. When she left, Mama screamed obscenities and took a BC powder. I asked how old she was, and Mama said twenty-nine.

After lunch, Renee was back at our door with her spawn. They ran to the kitchen, climbing on the counter in search of glasses and Mama's Diet Cokes.

"Go outside and play," I said. "Now."

"We're thirsty," Joey said.

"Honey, you just drank some Kool-Aid. Go outside or we're goin' home," Renee said.

"I want somethin' to drink," Tina whined.

"Go now," she snapped.

I had to leave. Renee was just a few years older than I was, and seeing her dowdy appearance terrified me. Why would a woman let her front teeth turn black, and cut her own hair with a razor? I wasn't going to stay around while she and Mama conversed. I went to the Jitney Jungle for sandwich meat, milk, bread, and cereal for the girls. I took my time, gassed up my car, and rode around. Remembering that I had cold cuts in the car, I drove home and carried in the bags. I took a pack of cookies and slipped them on a shelf. Joey was rifling through a bag, and I took it away from him.

"Wait," I said. "If you want a sandwich, I'll fix it for you. You ask me first."

"I'd like a sandwich," he said.

"Okay. You want a sandwich?" I asked, as I stared at Renee's seven-year-old, Tina.

"Uh-huh," she mumbled.

Missy, the oldest, was sitting in front of the TV. I made her one too, to keep her out of the kitchen. They ate on the floor. With food in their mouths, they asked for another. So, I made up a plate and gave it to them.

"Told you," Mama whispered as she put ice in her glass.

"Shoot, I should've bought some peanut butter," I whispered.

As soon as I finished cleaning the kitchen, Joey slinked back in.

"What do you want, Joey?"

"I want some Diet Coke."

"No. You can have iced tea. You don't need Diet Coke. It's not good for you."

"I want it."

"No. Tea or nothing."

"Tea," he said, staring at Mama's Diet Cokes.

After they left, Mama took to bitching some more.

"They come over every day. Renee watches for my car, and she hits the door before I can even set my purse down."

"I don't see how she can afford to feed those kids," I said.

"She doesn't have to, 'cause they're comin' over here eatin' up our food." She took a deep puff and blew out a stream of smoke. "They're all fat. Except Tina. Oh, God, she's a monster. Tiner is what they call her. Renee says, 'Tiner, don't make a mess now. Tiner, don't get into Miss Penny's drinks. Tiner, you can't take Holly's doll home.' Ooh, I can't stand Tiner's cryin'," Mama seethed.

"Well Mama, they're just kids," Daddy said.

"I don't care, Burl! You don't clean up after the bastards!"

Gloria walked in and set her purse on top of the television, with the strap dangling in front of the screen.

"Don't set your purse up there!" said Daddy.

She snatched it up. "Shit."

"What's wrong with you, Gloria?" Mama asked.

"I'm tired," she whined.

"You're not the only one," Mama said.

"Don't tell me those brats have been over here again?"

"All afternoon."

"Damn."

"Now don't start that cussin'," the Reverend interrupted.

"I don't care, Daddy. I hate those bastards."

"Well, there's no need to be cussin' like that."

"I'm not puttin' up with the bubble-headed bastards," Gloria spouted as she stormed off to her bedroom.

"I wish she wouldn't be so ugly," he said.

"Well, I feel the same way, Burl," Mama said.

At three o'clock on Christmas Eve, I left my C & R life behind. It had served its purpose, and I was tired of it. I handed in my smocks, punched out, and ran through Arby's on the way home. At four thirty, I was taking off my tennis shoes and planning to call Thomas, but he beat me to the punch.

"I'm so glad you're not working at C & R anymore. What did the manager say?"

"He offered me a raise."

"Forget it. You need the weekends free."

"To spend with someone, perhaps?"

"To spend with me. Do you have to keep the other jobs?"

"For now."

"I want to drive down and get you."

"No! Uh, it's too busy here," I said as I kicked a piece of paper across the grimy wooden floor.

"How are your parents?"

"They're fine. They're at work."

"I can't wait to meet them."

"Oh, I can't wait for you to see them, too."

I was staring at the full ashtrays scattered about the house.

"Mom, I'm on the phone," he whispered.

I heard Maggie in the background.

"Is that Annie?"

"Yes. Now go away!" he laughed. "No, you can't talk to her!" I heard her giggles fading away. "Sorry, I'm in the dining room."

"Your mom's so much fun."

"Our living room's full of shopping bags. I wished she'd put the stuff away."

"My mom's been shopping, too."

"As soon as Christmas is over, you're coming up, or I'm coming down," he said.

I didn't respond.

"Is that okay?"

"Sure."

"I can't wait for you to meet my sister."

"I can't wait either."

I paced about the mud, smoke, and trash. My stomach erupted and I flew to the bathroom. My nerves again. *What am I going to do? Thomas is going to make me go up there. Dear God, he is my boyfriend. Aren't I permitted to enjoy him?* After my innards settled, I walked to the screen door. Trudy smiled at me from the broken steps, always happy when I was at home to feed and protect her. I had wasted my time cleaning the front and back yards. Again, trash was everywhere. I got a garbage bag out of the cupboard and walked outside. My most dreadful nightmare was to see Thomas drive up and catch me picking up trash. Especially if he then walked inside and saw not only the dirty environment but also the tacky furnishings. He would never come here if I had my way about it. If he pushed, I could tell him my parents were suddenly killed on a church bus going to a Pentecostal crusade. Tomorrow, a houseful of insane people would be here, and that was enough punishment. Pepper Tisdale was bringing his mother. Aunt Mooney hated her.

On Christmas day, I spent the morning with the Prices. Henry got me a new Bible with my name engraved on it. They bought me a salmon-colored nightgown, a pair of matching slippers, and an elegant teal-colored bathrobe. Pearl received the same nightgown and slippers in bright blue. I bought Pearl a glass redbird, which impressed Henry so much he decided that she could start a collection like the one she had of the hummingbirds.

By the afternoon, I was back at the Manor. I boiled a dozen eggs and cut up the red potatoes for the potato salad. The turkey came from Mr. George—Daddy was still doing odd jobs for him. Mama had gotten off work at noon and came right in and put the bird in the oven. Daddy was planted in the living room watching old reruns of cowboy movies. The banging and shooting noises were driving Mama crazy.

"Daddy, cut that TV down! It's too loud!"

He got up. "I turned it down once. I can't hear."

"You're deaf," she yelled back. She turned to me. "That Bible the Prices got you is nice. Now Daddy says he wants one."

"Well, he can go buy one," I said.

"He wants his name engraved like yours."

"I'll get him one with the verses underlined that he doesn't obey."

Aunt Mooney arrived gussied up, with a chocolate cake, a pot of lima beans, a green salad, and four bottles of salad dressing. Daddy brought in two bags of colas for her.

"I didn't think to get any ice, Penny," she said.

"Burl bought two bags."

"Aunt Mooney, I love that outfit on you," I said.

"Thanks, I bought it on a clearance rack at Tri-Mart."

"You look beautiful."

"I had to dress up, since Pepper's mom's comin'. She's such a loudmouth. But, honey, she's skinny."

"Just because she's skinny doesn't make her attractive."

"Oh, she's not. Her complexion's ugly. Her skin's red, looks like she has a rash."

"It's probably a fungus," Mama added.

"How old is she?" I asked.

"She's fifty-six and thinks she's the cat's meow. She's a bar-hopper from back yonder and goes with men younger than her. Her nose looks like it's been broken several times, but Pepper said she was born like that. Look at it when you see her."

"Have you heard from Lonnie Cole any more?"

She rolled her eyes.

"Oh, Lord, he calls me all the time."

"Do you still go out?"

"Yeah, we still go out."

She acted like she didn't want to talk about him, so I shut up.

"I want you to come spend the night with me this weekend. I don't wanna go out with Lonnie."

"Sure, Aunt Mooney, I'll come."

"Your mom said you quit workin' at the drugstore."

Mama blew through her smoke. "Thank God."

"Yesterday was my last day."

"How did you do it? Workin' those jobs and goin' to school?"

"I just did. Now I have the money to pay for next semester."

"She needs to rest," said Mama.

I smiled. "One more semester to go."

"Bet you thought it'd never get here."

"Are you and Tish coming to my graduation?"

"We wouldn't miss it."

My sisters poured in the front door. Keith stumbled in with a long glass dish in one arm.

"Be careful Keith," Jessie warned.

He handed her the dish.

"Those dogs have torn up the trash again," Gloria spouted off.

"I'm gonna shoot those mangy things," Daddy growled. He didn't budge from the recliner.

"Mama, those dogs tore up the trash again," Gloria repeated.

"Damn dogs," she groaned.

"I cleaned up their mess yesterday," I said.

"Well, I'm not cleanin' up the shit, gettin' my clothes messed up," said Gloria.

"I know that."

I got another garbage bag and walked outside. Aunt Mooney and Clarie followed.

"I can do it, Aunt Mooney."

"I need the exercise, precious."

Mama walked into the living room with a clenched fist and stood over Daddy.

"Burl, get out there and help 'em. Mooney don't need to be bendin' down like that with her bad back."

"I'm tellin' you, I'm gonna fill those dogs full of buckshot," he griped on his way out.

"Whose dogs are they?" I asked.

"They're from down the road. They need to pen 'em up."

Trudy was lying on the front porch with her head down. Daddy yelled at her so much she was scared to do anything.

"Well, I know Trudy doesn't get in the garbage," I said.

"No, it's not her," he said. "It's that big ole black dog and the spotted one."

"No, Trudy don't bother the trash, do you?" Mooney told her in baby talk. "She lays around gettin' her beauty sleep."

We were done in five minutes. I double-bagged the old bags and tied them tightly. Daddy was sweating as he walked into the kitchen. He picked up a hand towel and wiped off his glasses.

"That wore me out, Mama." Coming up behind her, he grabbed her around the waist. "Santa Claus is comin' to town—"

"Stop it, Burl," she hissed as she pulled away.

"Yeah, I haven't gave Mama her present yet," he grinned.

"Leave me alone," she said hatefully.

"You're so disgustin'," Gloria said.

"Gloria, you need a man to give you some hot lovin' and you'd feel better," he teased.

"Hell no I don't!" She stomped to the bathroom and slammed the door.

"Don't get her started," said Mama.

Loud, thick country voices came from the front door thirty minutes later.

"Hell no I didn't," said Pepper.

"Yeah you did," Jewel argued.

"You a lie."

"Y'all come in," Daddy said.

Jewel Tisdale was divorced from her husband of thirty-five years. After raising six kids and working hard on a farm all of her life, she found her calling: younger men and bars. She was wearing extremely tight blue jeans with a silver belt and silver three-inch heels and no hose. She was thin as a Popsicle stick but had belly-hang. She was either brave or plain stupid, wearing a long-sleeved red blouse that was unbuttoned just enough to show her creped cleavage. We watched her from the kitchen.

"Her hair's whiter than snow," Jessie whispered.

"When you get closer, you can see sores on her scalp 'cause she bleaches it so much," Mooney whispered back.

"I thought blue eye shadow and pink lipstick went out with the sixties," I said.

"Oh, God, y'all watch Burl around her," Mama said.

Gloria was introduced and came into the kitchen.

"What a whore."

"No it ain't, hell no," Jewel was arguing with Pepper.

"Yeah it is," said Pepper.

"You lyin' son of a bitch."

"Uh-huh."

"Hell no."

"Hell yeah."

Daddy, the Reverend, said nothing while they cussed at each other.

"Y'all be quiet. Y'all promised not to fight," Tish said.

"That's right, maw. No fightin'," Pepper said.

I pulled some plates down from the cupboard. Jewel began her bar-hopping tales.

"And that bartender tells me I sure don't look fifty-six years old," she said.

"God," Aunt Mooney moaned.

Mama called for everyone to come fix a plate. I kept my distance, standing against the sink while watching the clowns heap masses of food on their plates. I wanted to be in Thomas's arms, and I truly regretted that I didn't spend Christmas with him. Christmas at my house was a celebration of dementia, and Mama and Daddy were happy. As long as food was around, and people—no matter how screwed up—were around, they were fulfilled. I had enough to worry about with them. Having trashy people I didn't even know in my home on Christmas day was testing my temperament.

Aunt Mooney was polite but cool to Jewel when she walked into the living room to talk to Tish.

"How're you doin', Miz Collins?" Jewel asked.

"I'm fine, Jewel," said Mooney. "What about you?"

"I'm better today."

"No hangover," Pepper noted. "Stay outta those nasty-ass bars."

"It's none of your damn business now, is it?"

I ate alone in the back bedroom, then I cleaned a little in the kitchen to kill some time before I headed out the door to walk. The foolish arguing continued. *My house may be a roach motel, but it's too good for them.* I laced up my tennis shoes and left while everyone was going for dessert.

I walked five miles on an empty track in the cold. When I returned home, Pepper, his mother, and Tish had left. Aunt Mooney was whining about Tish not spending what was left of Christmas with her. Daddy was raging about the news. Last but not least, Mama was fuming because Renee Spencer and her three kids were eating in our living room.

That night I heard from Thomas. We had a lovely conversation, and I got to hear his happy tales about his family. He had finally gone through his mail and found the love letter I had written him. But it had started something I had been avoiding.

"You didn't give me your address."

"Oh, I forgot again," I said.

"I want to write letters to you, too. Where in Soso do you live?"

"Uh, the western part."

"I believe my uncle lived in the north side."

"What did he do?" I asked, changing the subject.

"He was a lawyer. Mom said he owned some oil wells."

"Soso has a lot of oil wells."

"I heard it was an oil town."

I wasn't listening anymore.

"Are your sisters as pretty as you?"

"Prettier."

I got off the phone without giving the address by telling him Mama had to use the phone. I prayed that I had convinced him to stay in Jackson. He was stupid, I thought. If he came down to see me, he'd be in for the shock of his life. He should stay at home and enjoy his marvelous lifestyle.

The next evening, I was sitting in the gripe seat reading one of my new self-help books and trying to keep a sound mind. Since Daddy practically worked for free or didn't work, he had time to drive thirty miles a day to the other side of town to feed Sister Willa and Brother Leroy's ostriches. They were nice people. They just didn't pay Daddy much money for doing it. He just wanted an excuse to have someone to talk about the Bible with, really someone who would listen to him.

"Mama, you wanna go feed the birds with me?"

"I ain't goin' way out to the country with you. I'm tired. Why didn't you go this mornin' and feed 'em?"

"I had to do that work for Snookie Bush. I won't be gone too long."

"Shit, you always say that."

"My truck's been makin' a funny noise."

She threw an arm in the air. "You smell when I have gas in car! You ain't usin' it!"

"Why do you drive way out there, Daddy?" I asked. "They don't pay you enough to cover the wear and tear on your truck or your gas."

"I know it. They wouldn't spit on your asshole if it was on fire," Mama put in. "I don't know why you haul your ass way out there just to run your mouth."

"Sister Willa has heart trouble," he said.

"So does Mama," I said.

"Y'all don't know how sick Willa's been. She can't feed those birds by herself."

"The exercise would do her good," I said.

"She can't stress her heart like that. You need to be more sympa . . . sympathetic towards people," he said.

"Gee, I wonder why I don't understand that."

"When's Leroy gettin' back? He shouldn't leave her alone if she's so sick," Mama said.

"He has to work, Mama. They have a ton of doctor bills."

"Well, they don't need ostriches then," I said.

Mama stood up, changing her mind. "Will you run me by the store on the way back?"

"Yeah, we can go by Piggy Wiggly," he said.

"I'm outta my BC's, and we need some bread."

"You wanna go with us, baby?"

"No way. I'll stay here with the cockroaches."

"Maybe we can stop by that store over on Highway 28 and get some of those chicken tenders, Mama."

They took the kids and left. Gloria was at work until ten. I was sweaty from cleaning, and I longed for a hot bath, so I walked to Mama's bedroom to strip. The phone rang, and it was Thomas.

"Did you ride today?" I asked.

"Only a couple of hours. Anyway, I'm over here at Shoney's."

"Are you eating out with your parents?"

"No. I'm here in Soso at a pay phone. I'm kind of lost. . . ."

I couldn't move. My shirt was lying on the floor, and my jeans were around my ankles.

"I know you said you lived in the western part . . ."

I still couldn't move.

"So I pulled off here at Shoney's to call you."

My mind focused on Shoney's, which was half a mile from my home, just across the highway.

"I thought I'd stop by, if you're not too busy."

"I, uh . . . God, I wished you would've called. Let me see . . ."

I was staring at Mama's flowery threadbare curtains.

"I'm here at a bad time?"

"No, let me see. My, uh, my parents aren't here. And our house is . . . Daddy's been painting the inside, so everything's a mess."

"I can come by and get you and we can talk over here at the restaurant."

"No! No, don't come here. I'll come over there and meet you, okay? Don't go anywhere, all right?"

"I'll be right here. Is everything okay?"

"Yeah, just give me a few minutes."

"No hurry. I'm not going anywhere."

I knew he wasn't going anywhere. My worst nightmare was unfolding, and I thought I was going to die. It'd be much easier to jump off a bridge and end it all. I pulled up my jeans and zipped them. I rushed to the bathroom and looked at my oily face. "Jesus." I took some toilet paper and patted it, then dusted it with powder. I scrubbed my teeth quickly and reapplied lipstick. I ran a brush through my hair, happy that it was short and easy to manage. I changed my shirt and sprayed perfume over the top of my clothes. I ran out onto the sand, passing Trudy. I stopped, turned, and petted her. I hurried to my car.

When I reached Shoney's parking lot, I parked in the first parking place I saw and got out of my car. Thomas was standing by the door with his hands in his pockets. When I saw him, I wanted the whole town of Soso to know he was my boyfriend.

"Hey, you look beautiful," he said.

I didn't want him to touch me, but I couldn't stop him. He hugged me, then kissed my mouth before I could talk. He took my hand, kissed it, and held it until we were seated. I wasn't hungry, but he made me get something. I didn't know how I was going to force it down. After we ordered, he reached over and held my hands across the table. He was so happy to be here and, truthfully, I was happy to see him. It was a stroke of luck that the Prices never went out when the sun was down. The thought of running into them while I was with a guy was surreal. Henry had this idea that I was a nun and didn't have lust in my heart. I scanned the place to see if any of the waitresses had waited on me while I was with the Prices, but it looked like a new crew.

Thomas was wearing a purple button-down dress shirt with black Levi's and black shoes. He didn't belong with me. He deserved better.

"Soso looks like a nice town."

"It's small."

"When I was about fourteen, my father came down on business, and I rode along with him. We actually ate here at that booth in the corner."

"There's not much to do here. Be glad you live in Jackson."

"Yeah, I like living there."

"Well, you've been busy. I can't believe you drove all the way down here."

"I'll drive anywhere to see you. I just wanted to surprise you."

"You did."

I smiled. I looked up and saw the red Piggly Wiggly sign reflecting off the car windows outside. The store was across the highway from the restaurant. Were Mama and Daddy there? That was enough to kill any passion.

"Are you okay? You're not mad at me?"

"No. I'm glad you're here, I really am."

He squeezed my hands. "Me too. Where's your necklace?"

"Oh! Actually, I left it at school. I thought it'd be safer there." The concentrated expression on his face was unnerving me. "I didn't want anything to happen to it."

Stroking my arm, he stared seductively into my eyes. "I've missed you."

"I've missed you, too."

"How are your parents?" he asked.

"They're okay. They're visiting some friends tonight. What about yours?"

"They're home. My mom's been hitting the after-Christmas sales all day."

"One of my aunts does that, too."

"You said your house is being remodeled?"

"Oh, it's a mess. Daddy's been painting and building stuff."

"Does he need any help?"

"No. He's almost finished."

"Maybe your parents can come up with you to Jackson and we can all go out to dinner."

"Well . . ." I answered nervously.

"Maybe before we go back to school."

"Oh, I have to see, Thomas. One of Mom's sisters is sick and in the hospital."

"Is it serious?"

Please don't make me lie. "She has cancer."

"That's terrible."

"Yeah, so she's been visiting her a lot and . . ."

"I should take you home with me tonight."

"I have to see my grandparents some more. Are you still working with your dad?"

"Yes. I've been doing research with a couple of his paralegals. When would be a good time for you to come up?"

"I'll let you know."

In his car, he held me close. I had to get away from him. I felt dirty and unprepared. My parents were probably back home and wondering where I was. Oh, God, I was so sick of being on a time clock with my own life. I prayed Thomas would never do this again. He had to give me a warning, like ten years in advance. He pulled away, and I knew he wanted to kiss me.

"I love you."

"I love you, too."

His mouth touched mine, and I forgot about the ostriches, chicken tenders, and cockroaches.

Nineteen eighty-eight was closing in, and I hadn't heard from Thomas since his surprise visit. The television was blasting away with Daddy watching another dreadful movie. A woman was screaming – it was usually that or the sounds of gunshots or karate fights. His version of a good movie was one that didn't have much dialogue but had a lot of pointless behavior. I was sitting on Mama's bed, dressed in my nightshirt. I hadn't seen any cockroaches, so I figured they had given me the night off, or maybe it was the cold weather. I kept watching the green phone and Mama's wall clock, which read ten o'clock. I began to feel the walls closing in on me. Did I stink that night? Did I say the wrong thing? Did he actually see where I live? I drifted off to sleep.

When I woke up, it was two in the morning, and Mama was lying beside me. I turned over on my side. I feared Thomas might be angry. I didn't hear from him the next day. I waited impatiently until eight o'clock that night, then I called his home.

"Mrs. Barnes, this is Annie."

"How are you, dear? How was your Christmas?"

"My Christmas was wonderful."

"Thomas was so thrilled about seeing you the other night. We sure wished we could've seen you, but he wouldn't let us come along."

"Is Thomas home?"

"Guess where he is?"

I became afraid. "Where?"

"Riding that bike. Every day after he comes home from working with his Daddy, he gets on that bike and rides for hours."

"He's so amazing."

"He is. Dan was athletic like that, so I guess that's where he gets it. Certainly not from me."

"Will you tell him I called?"

"I sure will, honey. He'll call you back."

I waited an hour with my leg bobbing up and down in nervousness. It was after nine when the phone rang. I yelled before Daddy could grab it.

"I've got it! Hello?"

Thomas was out of breath.

"I just got in."

"You're riding this late?"

"Yeah. Bob's visiting."

"Bob's visiting?"

"He drove down for a couple of days. I'm sorry I haven't called you. I wanted to give you some time to visit with your family. I know I've been bothering you."

"You haven't been bothering me."

"The other night, you seemed . . . I know you don't like it when I pressure you. I don't want you stop seeing me. I love you too much to drive you away."

"Thomas, you're not. I was just tired the other night. I'd been helping my dad, that's all."

His voice was fading in and out. He was undressing.

"My clothes are soaked. Okay, that's better."

"I didn't mean to give you that impression," I said.

"I know I can be pushy."

"I love your pushiness."

"Good, because you're coming up for the weekend."

I was thinking fast but too tired to think of a quick lie.

"Hello? Annie?"

"I hear you. Uh, what day?" My heart was racing.

"Thursday. I want you here with me for New Year's Eve."

"What are we going to do? Are we going out?"

"My parents are. You and I'll have the house to ourselves, or we can go out if you want."

"Well, I'll have to get to packing, then."

"You're folks won't mind if I steal you away?"

"No, they have things to do."

I lied to Henry. It was Wednesday morning, and I told him I was leaving Friday for UEM. I had to get back early to get ahead.

"Isn't it wonderful that our granddaughter is conscientious enough to get to school early and prepare ahead of schedule?"

"It sure is." Pearl winked at me.

"Need any money, honey? We have plenty in the savings."

"I'd like to buy a few clothes, if it's okay."

"It sure is," Pearl said. "Let me buy 'em for you, darlin'."

Henry smiled at her. "All right, Mom. We'll let you buy Annie some clothes. Isn't Mom sweet to do that?"

"She's an angel," I said.

He gave me a three-hundred-dollar check. I cashed it and went to the mall. I'd have to keep some cash on me for gas to get up to Jackson and for an emergency. I decided to keep fifty in my wallet. For three hours I looked for in-style blouses and pants. I bought a pair of brown dress shoes and a pair of tennis shoes. I had the new robe from the Prices, so I didn't have to buy one. The gown they had bought me was beautiful but motherly. As much as I wanted to be a "hot mama," I thought something between sexy and girlish would do. I found a pink sleeveless gown at Penney's for fifteen dollars. Two hundred and fifty dollars gone so quickly, but I had something to wear for this weekend.

I lied to my parents. I told them I had to get back to UEM early because registration was starting on the weekend for students in the dorms. They bought it, though Mama complained about how crazy college was to have such stupid rules. I finished my laundry and packed it a small blue suitcase Aunt Mooney had given me a few days ago. Her old bag looked newer and better than my duffel bag. I took my car by a car wash Wednesday evening.

At six o'clock Thursday morning I bathed, saturated my body with cologne, and kept my distance from Mama's smoking. If I could just get through the next four hours at home. . . .

Mama had griped so much the past week, I wanted to sock her. They were behind a month on the power bill, and they talked about it repeatedly. I had bought food, helped to clean, and cooked some meals. Giving them money was like putting it in the Titanic on its way down.

"I'm so sick of bein' broke all the time. It's depressin' not bein' able to buy anythin' or get groceries."

If I really listened to her, I'd run out into the street screaming. I'd learned to tune out most of it.

"Mama, you've got to make Daddy help support the family. Leave him, or threaten him with divorce. Better yet, file for divorce."

"I can't afford no lawyer, you know that."

"There's legal aid and places to help women like you. You have to try. And you and Daddy both need to make Gloria pay rent, instead of allowing her to spend money on clothes and dating losers. She has a child that y'all support."

"I ain't askin' her for nothin'."

"Then she has a rent-free place to sleep and eat. She has 24-hour-a-day babysitters."

"I can't throw 'em out in the street, Annie. Holly's our grandbaby."

"I know that, but Gloria'd be paying rent somewhere else if she didn't live here. Tell her to give y'all a little money each week, or she can pay a utility or bring food home. Anything would help."

"Shit. The last time I asked to borrow twenty dollars from her to buy some food for supper, she bitched so horribly I couldn't stand it."

"You can out-bitch her any day."

"You know I have high blood pressure and don't need to get that mad."

"Be a doormat all your life."

She didn't want to hear it. She wanted to bitch.

"Burl don't do shit. He worked all last week for Snookie Bush and didn't bring home but a hundred dollars."

"I believe it."

"I don't know what he charged her, but somethin' ain't right."

"No, it's not. He's holding back again."

"No, Annie, he's stupid. He don't charge enough. Now he won't even work this week 'cause he says his back's botherin' him." She blew a puff of smoke. "I did feel sorry for him last night, he was in such pain."

"He doesn't feel sorry for you when you have to work extra hours just to pay the health insurance so he can go to the doctor. It sucks."

"I don't know what to do."

"Mama, even animals work. They hunt for food. They build their own nests or dens. They dig tunnels. What does Daddy do? He has no honor."

"He had a conniption fit the other day when I was sick with my tachycardia. So afraid I'd have to miss work. He didn't even offer to call Mrs. Walker and tell her I was sick. Hell, I'd rather work and get away from him."

He was cheerful as he walked in with a bag of Diet Cokes.

"How's my two ladies doin'?"

We moaned and rolled our eyes. He was living at the Jitney Jungle now that they had a bingo game, and I was sure the cashiers loved to see his stinking body coming through the automatic doors. He checked the game sheet, throwing the unusable numbers on the floor.

"Did you get my BC's, Daddy?"

"I sure did, Mama," he answered as he peered over a simmering pot.

"That's the chicken Annie bought the other day."

With a fork, he dug out the liver, then swallowed the steaming organ without chewing. Then he took a cup from the cupboard and dropped two Alka-Seltzers into the water. I turned so I wouldn't have to look at him. Mama was revving her engine, and I was ready to run.

"Annie shouldn't be spendin' her money on food. She needs it for school."

"I know, Mama. Mr. Thompson wants me to paint his bathroom in a couple of weeks."

"Shit, a couple of weeks. We need money now, Burl. I don't why you won't find a steady job. You can even work in a liquor store like Jolene's husband does. At least he brings somethin' home each week."

He looked stunned. "You want me to get a job, Mama? I won't get my disability."

"Shit," she spouted off. "No Burl, I wanna live in fuckin' poverty the rest of my life! So stupid. Hitch up a trailer to your truck and mow lawns, anythin'."

Daddy's face dropped. I looked out the kitchen window and remembered when I overdosed on the baby aspirins. Was that a clue? Mama told me about it enough. I had thought about slicing my wrists to hell and back, but I wanted to overcome this mess. I calmly dried the dishes while Daddy rubbed the back of his neck. Mama continued fussing while slamming pots and pans.

"I'm outta my blood pressure medicine. I need my Quinidine."

"I don't have no money, Mama," Daddy said.

She spun around with homicidal eyes. "You a lie!"

"No I'm not."

"Then how did you buy those brake pads for your truck if you have no money?"

"I, uh . . . brake pads don't cost that much."

"Shit, they do too."

Her knuckles were clenched white as she wiped around the dish rack. I never knew how she kept from dropping dead from a heart attack. Daddy stood near but knew to keep his distance. These two people put me on earth, and it was horrifying that they even reproduced.

"Well, Mama. I called Mr. George about buildin' those shelves he wanted," he said sweetly.

"No, you didn't. You sit around here every day in front of that TV waitin' for the mail. Thinkin' some money's gonna fall outta the sky. Don't fill out another one of those sweepstakes, orderin' shit we can't pay for. I'm so sick of gettin' notices for bills for some crap you've ordered."

"I ordered that foot massager and those potholders for you."

"I didn't want 'em!"

He left, rubbing the back of his neck. The TV was now blaring, and I sighed with misery. I had to leave by eleven to meet Thomas, but Mama began another bitching session.

"I don't think it's fair to make me work ole lady Ritchie's hours and mine."

"Mama, you have to tell Mrs. Walker that you don't want to work Mrs. Ritchie's hours. Just tell her, or she'll keep taking advantage of you," I said.

"I don't know what to do."

"Tell her. That's what you do."

She idled down. "I love that shirt. Did Mr. Price buy it for you?"

I was wearing a long-sleeved orange and black shirt I'd gotten on sale for seven dollars and ninety-five cents.

"No," I answered. "I bought it with the money I've been saving."

"Are you registerin' today?"

"No. Saturday."

"It's stupid that you have to go back on New Year's Eve."

"Why, Mama? We don't ever celebrate anything."

Chapter Twenty Seven

I wore the new tennis shoes and kept my older clothes in the duffel bag hidden in the back of my car. My new things I organized in the blue bag. I was insane but on the road by eleven. Thomas was meeting me at an Exxon station on Highway 49. He said he'd be there at one o'clock, and he was. He opened my door as soon as I parked. I stood, and he hugged me hard and long.

"Do you need any gas?"

"No. My car's good on gas."

"We live about twenty miles from here. I'll go slow."

Thomas's driveway wasn't sand and rocks, like ours. It was neatly paved, and a brick walkway led to the front door. The house was made of gray stones and was larger than Aunt Mooney's. The yard was spacious. Not acres of land, but the grass had been fertilized and mowed, the bushes pruned. Thomas pulled into the garage and jumped out.

"Just leave your car behind mine," he said.

I turned off the ignition as he grabbed my suitcase from the passenger side.

"We can go in through the garage."

All my life I'd wanted a kitchen with an island, and they had one. The cabinets were cherry, and plentiful. A wine rack was beside the black refrigerator, and shelves of cookbooks were above a counter that was built into the wall. A few dirty dishes were left on a small dining table, and I almost picked them up. Thomas breezed through, while I wanted to stay and look around.

The hardwood floors were shiny and clean, adorned with colorful rugs. Thomas was sifting through some mail that was left on a glass coffee table, taking what belonged to him.

"I'll show you to your room," he said. "It's right next to mine."

I followed him up the stairs, amazed at how clean the carpet was. Maggie Barnes deserved a pretty house like this, I thought. Eighteen years of nursing. Down the hall, I could see the master bedroom, but I pretended not to look as Thomas placed my suitcase on a full-size bed.

"The bathroom's in here," he said as he switched on a light.

I was awed by the matching bedroom suite. *Is all of this for the guests?* Thomas turned and stared at me.

"We have one more room down the hall if you don't like this one."

"Oh, no, this is just fine."

"Come on, Maggie. We're going to be late," Dan called.

"I'm coming. Whoops! Forgot my purse," she laughed as she retrieved a black sequined bag from the coffee table. "Have fun, you two. We'll be at the club if you need us."

"Fine. Bye, Mom," Thomas said.

Dan was already in the garage.

"You're really too nice, Annie. Listening to her telling you all those boring stories about her shopping trips and how the cab left her in Paris. She got left because she was talking to one of the tourists, and the cabbie got tired of waiting."

"I enjoy her stories. And I loved having her show me the pictures of you when you were growing up. You were a beautiful baby."

"Well, I wouldn't encourage her. Mom has tons of photo albums. If she doesn't have a picture of a vacation or event, it didn't happen," he said.

He took me to Steak and Ale for dinner, then to a movie. We were home by ten. I went up to my room and took off my shoes. I had a beautiful guy in my life, but I was too tired to stay up to ring in the New Year with him. Thomas eased in.

"Can I come in?"

"Sure."

I was lying across the bed thinking of ways to tell him I wanted to go to sleep. He lay next to me and brought his arm around my waist.

"Want to watch TV?"

"Maybe later. What time are your parents getting home?"

"I don't know. Probably by one. They only stay until midnight 'cause they think they have to. I wish they'd stay out all night."

"Are you sleepy?" I asked as he yawned.

"No."

I had the feeling he'd be asleep if I weren't here. He kissed me, and I moved over to him. We were in the heat of passion when he sat up.

"Damn!"

"What's wrong?"

"They're home." He looked at his watch. "It's ten thirty. What are they doing back?"

"Maybe they're tired."

"I doubt it," he grumbled.

"Should I get ready for bed?" I asked.

He looked at me with empathy. "I know you're tired."

"Does it show?"

"Yes. I'm going to turn in too, before Mom gets wound up. I'll tell them we'll see them in the morning."

He kissed me and closed the door. I undressed and took off my makeup. Maggie's voice radiated throughout the house.

"Does Annie have everything she needs?" Maggie asked. She was coming up the stairs. *Please don't let her come in here.*

"Yes," Thomas answered in an agitated tone.

"Maggie, let's go to bed," Dan said.

"How's your headache, sweetie?" she asked, as their voices drifted to the other end of the house.

"Goodnight," Thomas told them in a whisper as he passed my closed door.

I stared at the doorknob as I unfolded my pink nightgown. I slipped it over my head, cut out the lights and went to sleep as soon as my head hit the pillow.

- 1988 -

I awakened to darkness and movement in the room. I lifted my head and leaned on my elbows.

"What?" I asked.

"Are you awake?"

"Yes," I whispered.

Thomas's hand slid across my stomach as he shifted his body next to mine.

"What time is it?" I asked.

"It's after midnight. Happy New Year."

He kissed my lips and my face delicately. I didn't need this right now, but I mumbled out "Happy New Year" and closed my eyes.

"I want to talk to you."

"Okay," I whispered, my eyes sealed tight.

"What do want to do tomorrow?"

"Anything you want."

"Want to ride?"

"It's too cold."

"I love you."

"I know."

He didn't really want to talk. I concluded this when his hand made its way down my leg.

"You're skin's so soft," he whispered.

I tried to ignore the sensation of his palm under my gown. My mind was running in so many directions. *Is this foreplay?*

"Can I take my shirt off?"

"Okay," I whispered.

I could see the shadow of his back as the shirt went over his head. He dropped it to the floor, and I was about to hyperventilate. He kissed me hard. I didn't resist. His fingers were underneath the elastic of my panties. I pressed my eyes closed as he gently massaged my pubic hair. He was pulling at my panties and they were sliding down my thighs. His hand moved across my hipbone until he was squeezing my left buttock. I caressed his back as he moved on top of me. My gown was up to my neck and he was kissing my breasts and stomach, then he was kissing my mouth again. His pelvis was pressed hard against mine. The image of Henry's face came to mind. *Pearl doesn't need to be spending her money on a slut.* I moved away from him.

"Thomas, I'm waiting until I get married."

"I don't expect you to do anything. I just got carried away. Do you want me to leave?"

"No."

At eight o'clock the following morning, Thomas cooked breakfast for his parents and me. We ate in their morning room with windows surrounding us. The sun was bathing my face, and it felt fantastic. *This is living.* Dan and Maggie were smiling, mostly at each another. She kissed Dan's cheek as she got up to get him another cup of coffee, and I began to feel strange. They did it, I thought. Thomas's folks still made love. I was thinking of their large bedroom, the king-size bed, the silk sheets, and their separate bathrooms. Then, I was thinking of Mama's ashtray-smelling bed that didn't even have a spread on it.

"Want another cup of coffee, Annie?" Maggie asked.

"No, ma'am, thank you," I answered.

"What are you two up to today?" Dan asked.

"We're going to the mall," Thomas answered.

"You know, I need to exchange—" Maggie began.

"Not today, Mom, please," Thomas interrupted.

Before we left, Thomas organized his bedroom while I looked at the posters on his walls.

"Is that Eddy Merckx?"

"Yeah. He was racing in the seventy-three Giro."

"Giro?"

"The Tour of Italy."

I nodded. "How many trophies do you have?"

"I don't know. There's some in the attic, too. Mom won't let me put any more away. She likes them out. I don't know why."

"She's proud of you," I smiled.

He shrugged his shoulders as he threw away a magazine.

"You did a lot of sports," I said as I picked up a baseball trophy.

"Yep," he sighed. "Baseball, track, soccer, and cycling."

I set down the trophy and stared out his window at the trees. Why did I stay in my bedroom for years? Why didn't I do sports? Why didn't I try out for plays?

"Are you okay?" Thomas asked.

"Yes," I smiled.

We were going to meet Thomas's sister Kim for dinner at the country club, but he wasn't pleased.

"I don't like going over there, listening to a bunch of snobs complain about everything."

"I haven't heard your parents complain about anything."

"It's their friends, Mom's friends. Most of them don't work. They live at the country club. They eat and drink too much, they complain about their workaholic husbands ignoring them. They're bored and boring. I don't even like to be around them."

I didn't tell him about my first job at the Soso Country Club. The job that I loved. Bussing tables, getting free delicious food, and making money to buy magazines and dreams. He turned into a gated area.

Kim Barnes was now Kim Yates. She was four years older than Thomas. Her baby brother got the looks in the family, that was for sure. Kim was gangly and flabby, a younger version of Maggie with black hair and very little makeup. Her clothing was simple, and she wore a single wedding band.

"Did you go to Ole Miss?" I asked.

Kim nodded. "That's where I got my law degree."

"Thomas said he enjoyed going there. Has he always been so smart?"

"Yes. He hardly cracked a book all through school and made good grades. Our dad's like that. I guess I took after Mom, because I had to study hard."

"I think she's great."

"She is. She drives Tom crazy. He gives her a hard time."

Her husband Kenny was sitting across the table talking to Thomas. Maggie was at another table, gossiping with one of her friends, and Dan was on the phone at the bar.

"What does Kenny do?"

"He's a civil engineer with the city," she answered.

"You ready?" Thomas asked as he looked at me.

"What?" I asked.

"Are you ready to leave?"

"Now Tom, we're having fun," Kim teased. "When are you leaving for UEM?"

"I guess we'll decide tonight," I answered.

"We have to go," Thomas said, now standing behind our chairs.

"You'll come up again soon?" Kim asked.

"Yeah, she will. Tell Mom and Dad we'll see them at the house," he said.

That night I showered and hopped into bed. Thomas knocked, came in, and locked the door. He got under the covers close to me.

"Kim just called. She's excited that she got to meet you, and next time you come up, she wants you to come over to her house for dinner."

"Are your parents home?"

"They're still at the club." He was on his side facing me. "I'd like to leave tomorrow. We can go to my apartment, and you can stay until you have to check in. Is that okay?"

"I'm having fun here."

"I know, but I'm tired of it. We can go grocery shopping. I can cook. We can relax."

The next morning, getting away from Maggie was almost as hard as escaping Henry.

"Mom, we *have* to get on the road," Thomas said, and threw another suitcase in his car.

"Please come up again, hon," she told me.

I smiled. "I will."

"What are you doing tonight?"

"That's the fourth time you've asked!" Thomas was getting peeved.

Before she could reply, Dan spoke. "Take care, Annie. We certainly enjoyed visiting with you this weekend."

"Bye," Thomas said as he pulled me to the car.

I stayed at Thomas's apartment until Sunday, then drove back to my dorm and checked in. I unpacked my bags by turning them upside down and making a pile in the center of the room. I really wanted to do the wash, but Thomas wanted me to ride, and I was going. I was keeping him happy. I ran to the post office to check my box. A letter from Denise was waiting, and I read it on my way back. She gave me her new address and phone number in Jackson and asked if I could come up the third weekend of January.

This semester brought into our office a new professor, and Nell was bending backwards to impress her. Dr. Rosemary Camp was thirty-four and a breath of fresh air. She was a lawyer who decided she loved teaching, so she got her doctorate in education. She was married to a political science professor. Dr. Camp flaunted her opinions on rape, violence, divorce, and university issues. She was warned by Dr. Katz not to take things so seriously, not to work herself up over matters she couldn't change. He was one to talk. I loved her almost on sight, and she immediately took me under her wing. She told me the short story of her life. She was a divorced mother with a young daughter when she met Alex, who was newly divorced and fifteen years older. Perfect for an idealistic graduate student in

North Carolina. Their busy lifestyle meant they lived in an apartment and ate out.

I was working fourteen hours a week on Tuesdays and Thursdays, since I had only one class on those days. A freshman named Irene was hired to work Mondays and Wednesdays, and I was happy to pass the baton to her. But Nell didn't like Irene, and from Dr. Dearman's sulky attitude, I knew she didn't care to share her authority with Dr. Camp.

Except for a small airplane painting a trail of white clouds, the sky was perfect. Leslie picked me up at one. Our drive was a straight shot up Highway 49 to Jackson. She was a good driver, keeping her eyes on the road. We went in halves on the gas.

"I wonder if they'll be any good-lookin' future dentists around."

"I'm sure there are," I said.

"I wouldn't mind marryin' a dentist," she grinned. "Does Thomas live in a mansion?"

"Not really."

"I want to see where he lives."

"Another time. Right now, let's see where Denise lives."

Denise came down to let us in with a tissue in her hand.

"I'm going to cry," I said.

"Go ahead, so am I." She already was.

Leslie was holding her other hand.

"I'm so happy to see you."

Her dorm room wasn't much bigger than the ones at UEM, but she had it to herself. Two day beds, a vanity, a closet, and desk. Denise and I would be sharing her bed, and Leslie would sleep in the other. A kitchen and the bathrooms were down the hall. A cheap mustard-yellow piece of carpet covered most of the floor.

Dollar signs were showing in Denise's eyes when she spotted my necklace.

"That necklace is so gorgeous."

"I love it," Leslie said.

"What time do you have to call him?"

"Now, I guess," I answered.

I used the pay phone in the hall. Thomas answered the first ring.

"I knew it was you," he said. "When did you get in?"

"Three. Are you riding today?"

"Maybe. I'm going to call around and see who's in town."

"Do you want me to call you later tonight?"

"Yes. As soon as you can."

"Are you okay?"

"It's hard to be in the same town with you and not see you. But I know you want to see Denise."

"I'm seeing you tomorrow."

"I'll come and get you. And them."

I returned to find Leslie in a fretting fit.

"Thomas cooks for you. He calls you. He buys you flowers and gifts. He took you home to meet his parents. He loves you."

She was in tears over Nelson.

"Well, Leslie, Thomas is like that," I said. "One day, when you're not looking, you'll meet someone who'll treat you like that."

"That's right," Denise agreed.

"That Rhonda. She's a whore. She's flirted with him and flirted with him," she said.

"Has he been flirtin' back?" Denise asked.

Tears poured down her face, and her voice shook.

"Yeah."

"Don't see him anymore. Don't let him come over to your apartment for sex either," I said.

"It's not the sex. I love him."

"No, he wants sex. That's all he wants. He's using you, and you're letting him."

"I need to take a shower."

She gathered up her clothes and a towel and left. Denise was fired up, jerking the covers back as she got the beds ready.

"She'll keep on lettin' him use her."

"I can't believe she'd just sleep with anybody like that," I said.

"Oh, she does. Believe me. There have been plenty of guys like Nelson through the years. And they all pull the same crap on her, and she whines about it."

"When she saw my necklace, she worried me to death to find out where Thomas bought it. I'm not going to ask him that. That's tacky."

"She'll ask him. Just wait."

She was quiet a long time picking at the foot of her knee-high stocking.

"I miss Christopher, but at the same time, I feel over him," Denise said.

"You're on your way."

"Oh, Annie . . . "

"What is it?"

"My parents are separated." Her eyes teared up.

"Separated? They seemed so happy. When did this happen?"

"After Thanksgivin'."

"I'm so sorry, Denise. I didn't know. I mean, at your apartment they seemed okay. Your mom did seem sort of upset."

"She was," she said.

"Did your dad leave?"

She turned, staring hard, and it scared me. "He got a perm in his hair, Annie. He came up here to see me two weeks ago, and I almost died. He looked awful."

I stayed quiet.

"He's been seein' this woman at his job. She's a secretary for one of the buildin' inspectors. She's ten years younger than Mama. I saw her waitin' in the car when he was here, and I made him leave. How could he bring her to my school, to my dorm?"

"Are they getting a divorce?"

"They need to. They're in counselin'. He said he's goin' through a bad time. Some bad time. And Mama wants him back."

Next afternoon, Thomas was peering through the glass door with a smile when we walked through the dorm lobby to greet him. As soon as we came out, he kissed me and put his arm around my waist. Leslie turned three shades of red.

"Did you decide where you want to eat?" he asked.

"Leslie wants steak," Denise said.

"Denise!" she blushed.

"That's easy," he smiled as he opened car doors for us. "Primo's. It's a great steakhouse."

Thomas reached for my hand.

"What did you do today?" I asked.

"I rode six hours."

"Six hours!" Leslie put her hand over her mouth. "I'm still sore from ridin' last semester. I think I pulled a tendon."

Primo's was crowded. Leslie grabbed the only available chair while we stood waiting to be seated.

"Mr. Barnes, your booth is ready," the hostess said.

"I'm glad they gave us a booth," said Leslie. "Those wooden chairs hurt my rear. I don't know what to get."

"What are you gettin', Annie?" Denise asked.

"I think the grilled chicken."

"Not me. I'm gettin' the ribeye," Leslie said quickly.

"What would you like to drink?" the waiter asked.

"I'll have iced tea," I said.

"I'll have the same," Denise added.

"Coke, please," Thomas said.

"A screwdriver, please," Leslie said.

Denise looked at her.

"Thomas said I could have a drink."

After we ordered our food, Leslie started with her customary complaints. She fanned her face with her hand.

"It's so hot in here."

"It's crowded, that's why," I said.

"I hope I don't pass out."

"You won't," Denise said.

"Thomas, I don't know what to do in this stupid computer class I'm takin'. I don't know why I have to have it in the first place."

"What class is it?"

"Introduction to computers."

"Leslie, come on, that's an easy class," he chuckled.

"For you, maybe. But I don't understand it. The stupid professor won't help me at all."

"Okay, when we get back to school, call me, and I'll see what I can do. Who's the professor?"

"Dr. Livingston. I hate him."

"He's a good teacher. He'll help you if you ask him."

Leslie had two drinks in her and was on the third when the food came out. Denise finished her plate at her usual pace, but I actually ate more slowly than she did. I blamed stress for her being thinner than ever, and I was jealous, though I still weighed under a hundred and ten.

Leslie ordered dessert, a whopping piece of Snicker's pie. Before Thomas could ask for the check, she got wound up about her life tragedies. Being polite as he was, he ordered more coffee for himself and me. Denise sat silently and cautiously like a cat, while the drunken drama queen driveled about the love life she didn't have.

"I don't understand why he'd want a skinny bleached-blond bimbo like Rhonda. I've cooked for him and everythin'. Is it because of my illnesses? I can't help havin' all these allergies."

Thomas was squeezing my hand under the table.

"And another thing, her breath stinks."

Thomas laughed. Folding her arms on the table, she focused in on him.

"Thomas, tell me now. What do guys look for in a woman? What do you want?"

"Well." He was rubbing the edge of the coffee cup. "I like women who work hard."

She nodded her head. "Like me."

"And that are ambitious . . ."

"Yes! I'm ambitious."

He looked down as he thought more about the subject.

She looked at him intensely. "And you like them skinny, like Annie."

He asked, "Is Nelson dating her, the other woman?"

"I don't think so. No, he can't be."

"Then why are you upset?"

"Because he talks to her a lot. And she won't keep her nasty hands off him."

"He must like it," Denise said.

"So you and Nelson do go out?" Thomas asked.

"Yeah, well, he comes to my apartment. I'm so sick of his shit."

She gulped down another drink. That was when Denise and I became uncomfortable. Denise thought she was going to ask him where he bought the necklace. I thought she was going to ask him something sexual.

"He's not like you, Thomas. You know how to treat a woman. The way you take Annie out and buy her things. I want him to do that for me. Why doesn't he?"

"Because he's a jerk. You should stay away from him," he said as he pushed his cup away.

"I love him so much."

Denise rolled her eyes in disgust. Only she'd forgotten she had been in the same boat a few months earlier.

"Thomas is right, Leslie. Don't waste your time on him anymore. Focus on your degree and getting out of school," I said.

"That's very easy for you to say. You have a boyfriend."

"Leslie, shut up," I said.

"Please, Leslie. We're ready to go," Denise begged with gritted teeth.

"Y'all don't care about me," she whined.

A waiter came by with another drink.

"No more drinks," Thomas said firmly.

"I'm never goin' anywhere else with her," Denise whispered.

"Take my arm, Leslie, so we can go now," Thomas said calmly.

"Sure, baby," she slurred, nearly pulling him down.

In his car, Denise dug through her purse so she wouldn't have to look at Leslie, who was sleeping on her shoulder. Thomas helped us lug her into the back door of Denise's dorm, then he waited outside. When I came out, he was looking down at the ground with his hands in his pockets. His dark hair was glistening in the moonlight. We sat in his car.

"Those things Leslie was saying—it's not like her to be mean," I said.

"It was the drinks."

"I've learned so much being around her. I've learned how I don't want to live my life." I was listening to his heartbeat. "I'm so happy you're here."

Leslie had amnesia about the night when Denise and I pulled her out of the bed the following morning. We walked her to the showers where her retching almost caused us to throw up ourselves. She was so hung over that I had to drive her car back to Hattiesburg. I parked by Beecham Hall and took out my bag. She lugged herself out of the passenger side and fell into the driver's seat.

"Are you sure you can drive yourself to your apartment?"

"Yeah, I feel better now. Thanks for pullin' over and lettin' me throw up."

"Go home and sleep it off some more."

"I will." She looked in my eyes and grabbed my hand. "Annie, you're too good to me."

"You're nice to me, too, Leslie."

"I'd better get home before I puke again."

I shut her car door and watched her drive away.

"I can't believe Leslie got drunk and showed off in front of Thomas."

"She was mean, Marla."

"People like that shouldn't drink. Thomas was polite enough to buy y'all dinner, and her drinking like a fish. She should be ashamed of herself."

"She's upset about that guy."

"That guy ain't upset over her."

"I saw Nelson Friday morning when I was going to class. He told me that he and Rhonda are engaged."

"Mmmm, mmm. Maybe that's why she got drunk."

"No. He hasn't told her. I told him he had better tell her face-to-face. I didn't even tell Denise, because she's at war with men right now, and she'd tell her. I want him to do it. All he'd say was he can't get rid of her."

"Yet he's over at her apartment screwing her."

"He's just as bad as she is. Except she thinks it's love. I bet ole Rhonda would have a cow if she found out."

I closed my closet door. "And Denise . . ."

"Uh-huh. Her folks got some bad shit going on, Annie. That's tough now. Can't believe her Daddy got a perm in his hair."

"He's going through the middle-age thing, I guess."

"He's whoring. He'll go back to her Mama as soon as that young thing spends his money and dumps his ass. You said they got some money?"

"He has a good job. They're frugal people. Denise's truck's paid for. They had a nice car when they came to pack her up."

"Well his dick's done got him to spending some money on a honey."

Daddy had cut his thumb building shelves at Mr. George's liquor store, but the emergency room didn't give him stitches. Mama was threatening to leave him because he was back on the couch twenty-four hours a day. I wasn't going home until graduation.

"Disney World!" Marla exclaimed.

"When?" Leslie asked.

"Spring break," I beamed.

"You're so lucky."

"Just you and him?" Marla asked.

"No. We're meeting his parents down there. We're going to stay in a condo their friends own. His sister's coming, too."

"Lord," Marla shook her head. "I haven't been to Disney World in years. You're going to love it, Annie."

"I wish someone would take me anywhere for spring break," Leslie said. "I hear weddin' bells for Annie."

"Don't say that. I'm not ready for that. I have things to do."

"Well, do them with him, honey," Marla said.

"But he's very demanding. He wants me with him for practically everything except his training rides. That's the only time I have to myself."

"Oh, Annie," Leslie whined. "I wish to God that Nelson wanted me around all the time. I'd do anything he wanted. I'd wash his car. I'd cook for him. I'd clean his apartment, do his laundry—"

"Leslie," I interrupted. "Thomas is a grown man. I'm not his servant, and he isn't mine. We're just dating."

"Shoot, Annie. It's more than datin' to him," Leslie said.

"Where is he, anyway?" Marla asked.

"He's doing a training ride, then lifting weights," I answered.

"Ooh, I'd love to watch him lift weights," Leslie moaned.

Wednesday was hectic, and I had two tests. It was raining, and I waited inside the business building for Thomas until time ran out and I had to get to class. When I didn't see him at noon, I went to lunch, then to my room to call him. I left a message and rode to the Perkins', working until four forty-five. At Beecham, I parked and walked quickly to the cafeteria for dinner. I waited, and it was a quarter of six when I went in and got my tray. I ate alone, my eyes searching about. I checked my mailbox, pretending not to be concerned, but I ran to my room and called Thomas again.

"It's Annie. Again. Hope you're okay. I'm in from dinner. I'll be in the rest of the evening. Call me. I love you."

Grace came in at midnight, showered, and went to bed. I hadn't left my bed for hours, and it was after two. I showered at five and got dressed. Grace was sleeping, and I quietly dialed Thomas's number only to listen to his message machine.

I stared at my breakfast for an hour. My stomach felt like it was being mutilated. I waited outside the business building until I was late for my only class. As soon as it ended, I ran upstairs to Thomas's classroom. He wasn't there. I took my books to my room, called him again, left a tearful message, and walked to the ed-psych building. I started to go back to my room and call in sick, but Nell always needed me.

At noon, I looked for Marla. When that didn't pan out, I got a tray, but I didn't eat. I had ten minutes, so I went to a pay phone downstairs and tried him again. Anger took over as I hung up without leaving a message. I went back to work, and we were so busy Nell didn't take her afternoon break. At five, she was still in the office and released me from duty.

I was going to the cafeteria to use the pay phone again. I needed Marla to help me sort this out, or I was going to call his friends one by one until I found him. As I walked around the corner, I spotted his car parked at the main entrance. I picked up speed as he got out. I hugged him so forcefully I nearly knocked him off his feet.

"Please," he whispered. "Don't." He pushed me away.

"Where were you? I've been so scared."

His eyes were vacant.

"Are you sick?"

I touched his forehead to see if he was feverish, and he promptly removed my hand.

"What's wrong?"

His jaw tightened, and he cleared his throat.

"Just say it," I said.

"Can we go for a walk?"

I didn't say anything as he moved ahead of me. I followed until we were near the small pond in front of the campus.

"What's wrong?"

"Is there any reason why we should see each other?"

"What is this about?"

"It's about you keeping me away."

"I haven't . . . what?"

"Why didn't you tell me that you and Peter were writing each other?"

"Oh, God, is that what you're worried about? He wrote me two letters. I didn't even write half a page back to him."

He stayed quiet.

"Who told you this?"

"That's not important. You should have told me."

"Thomas, I forgot about it, because I don't give a damn about Peter. He has a girlfriend."

"Then he shouldn't be writing to you," he said angrily.

"I'm sorry I didn't tell you."

"Why don't you want me like I want you?"

"I do. I swear it. You know that."

"No, you don't."

I bit my tongue and clamped my mouth tightly.

"Annie, it's tearing me up when I don't know what you're thinking or what's going on with you. You're so secretive."

"Just give me a little more time, and I'll explain it all to you. It's a long story." I was frightened of losing him. "Leslie told you, didn't she?"

"You told her about the letter. Why couldn't you tell me?"

"Thomas, she was with me when I got my mail that day. She ate supper with me."

He wasn't buying it and turned his back to me.

"I just want to finish school," I said in desperation.

"Am I in the way?"

"No, I promise, no."

"I'll just back off, then. I'll leave you alone."

"I don't want that." He wouldn't look at me. "I'll never write him again."

"I've missed two days of classes because of this," he said.

"Why didn't you just ask me about it?"

"I shouldn't have to. You'd go back to him if you could."

"No I wouldn't," I begged.

"And I love you." He stroked my face. "Bye, Annie."

He walked away.

Thursday night was hell. I paced the floor, despising Peter for this. He was up in Jackson with a good job, seeing Nancy on her weekend visits and also dating a marathon runner he'd met at a gym. He had to write letters, and I didn't say no. *You're too nice, Annie.* I was up all night. In the morning I showered, covered my puffy face with makeup, and went to breakfast. I ate a piece of toast, went to classes with my head down, and skipped lunch. I spent the weekend by the phone and in the bathroom, sick to my stomach. My only source of strength was Marla. She soothed me by walking laps with me.

"I've called three times today, and he doesn't answer."

"Annie, I'd give it some more time. He may have gone home. Give him a few days to cool off. Then call him. He's hurt, and he thinks you've betrayed him."

"I haven't. God, Marla. I should've ignored Peter."

She kicked a rock off the track. "Men have these big egos. He and Peter are buddies, and they've been competing with each another with the cycling, and you."

"Not over me. Nobody would compete over me."

"Listen, Annie. Peter may have a little bit of feeling for you, but it's much more of an ego trip for him to see if you'd take him back. That's why he started with this writing you and you writing him. He's something else. On the other hand, Thomas is really in love with you. I'd make sure I was careful about what I said to him," she said. "He's taking this hard."

I didn't wait. Monday evening, Thomas answered in a drowsy voice.

"Why won't you talk to me?"

"I'm not going through this again, Annie."

"Okay. Do you ever want to talk to me?"

"Not now. No."

I didn't know what to do or what to say. I was on the brink of begging when I got a hold of myself.

"When you decide you're not angry with me, I'll be here. I love you very much."

"Whatever you say. I have to go now."

Tuesday was long, and I hid my sorrow under the magnified effort to work my tail off for the professors. By five o'clock, I was the number-one queen of work-study, while poor slow Irene probably wouldn't be asked to work the following semester. Marla wouldn't let me skip classes on Wednesday. I was angry with her for making me go to breakfast, walking me to the business building, and for making me go inside. When classes ended, I was going to the Perkins', but she came from the tech building to see me to lunch.

"You're going to eat," she said adamantly. "If he's in there, he's in there. You're not pulling that shit you did with Peter."

"I'm not hungry."

"Girl, you don't need to be cleaning a filthy house without some nourishment. You need some food." She stopped giving me her serious-to-the-bone look. "If I'm working out with you, you're going to eat. I'm not toting your ass off the track."

Marla made me feel weak, but at the same time I was happy she cared about me.

When I got to the Perkins', Molly was slipping into her beige dress shoes, and Claude was shoving the checkbook into his back pocket.

"My blood pressure's kickin' up again," she said. "We'll be back before you leave."

I was sure of that. Three times I stopped cleaning and sat on the toilet seat to cry. *Well, Annie, how are you going to get over this one?* I could go over to Thomas's apartment, force myself on him, but I couldn't stand him sending me away. I got up, swept and mopped the kitchen, and scoured the sink until it gleamed.

"Annie, you outdid yourself today," Claude smiled.

"I think she's deserves a little bonus, don't you, Claude?"

She handed me a check for sixty dollars.

Thursday night a tornado was seen in the area. I was lying down, but I had to dress and go downstairs. The lobby was full of worried women, and I found Marla.

"You look terrible, girl."

"I feel terrible," I said.

"Want to stay in my room?"

"No. He might . . . he probably won't."

She rubbed my arm. "Don't wait on him, Annie. You're strong. Get busy."

We were let back in our rooms at nine. The head resident told us to sleep well and apologized about the inconvenience. I couldn't sleep now. I wiped my eyes above my opened accounting book. My grades were good, but this could send them spiraling. Thomas had been my faithful tutor. Now I'd have to go it alone unless I could find someone in the accounting department to donate time to help me. The phone rang, and I grabbed it.

"Yes."

"Uh, Annie?"

"Yeah, Mama," I cringed.

"Did you hear about the tornado?"

"Yes. It's over."

"You sound upset."

"Uh, no. I'm studying."

"Oh."

"What's going on now?" I asked with dread.

"I'm so depressed, Annie."

"Okay, Mama. I'll come home tomorrow."

CHAPTER TWENTY EIGHT

Daddy shouldn't have pushed Mama's buttons Friday afternoon. She wasn't in from work yet when he gave me the usual drill while I boiled water for tea. The light bill was two months past due, and it was everybody's fault, especially the power company's. Sister Willa was having another electrocardiogram, and Daddy was approved for disability but wouldn't start receiving checks until June, and it was an abomination that he had to wait until June after waiting so long. The house was in horrendous condition. The landlord was still demanding that they catch up on the rent or get the hell out. Mama stumbled in carrying her trusty plastic cup, her purse hanging from her arm. She was happy to see me, so I had to move Trudy from my lap, get up, and hug her smoked-up body.

"Mama, Mrs. Walker just called," Daddy said.

I stood back as her eyes ignited, Daddy too stupid to leave it alone.

"She wants you to work tomorrow for Mrs. Ritchie," he said.

"God damn!"

"Why Mama!"

The cup of ice flew across the room, and I backed up to the gripe seat and sat down. *Welcome home, Annie.* Wiley and Holly ran to the back bedroom. Mama's fist was pointed to the ceiling, and she ranted to the kitchen.

"That fuckin' ole bitch! I just left there, and she's gotta call before I can even get my shoes off!"

"Well, Mama, uh, maybe ole lady Ritchie's sick," Daddy stuttered behind her.

"Fuck! She ain't sick! Sawed off son of a bitch! I guess the ole bitch decided to take off and run errands for that pussle-gutted son of hers. Fat thing ain't even workin'."

"I'll call and tell her you're not feelin' well," he said.

"No! Fuck it! I'll work 'til I'm fuckin' dead. That's what you want me to do anyway, so you can charge more high-priced fuckin' shit on my tab. Ain't got enough sense to tell her I'm busy tomorrow. No, you want me to drag my ass in and work."

"No I don't, Mama."

"Shit."

"Sister Effie, uh, she wants me to come do an estimate for her."

"Huh," she grumbled as the smoke flowed.

"Well, don't go in," he said.

"I'll have to. Ole lady Walker ain't gonna do it."

"Maybe ole man Ritchie's in the hospital again."

"No he ain't. He's too busy bein' a bastard to be sick. Puttin' her down. Tellin' her she don't need to be gettin' her hair fixed or buyin' herself somethin' she might need. That overgrown mule-headed son's just like him, bastard fool! His wife's done suin' him for divorce 'cause he won't get a job."

"I'd put him on the road, too," he said.

She turned her burning glare his way, but Daddy still didn't get it.

"A man that don't work shall not eat," he went on.

"You should be an anorexic," I said.

I was wishing I had bought some magazines at the bookstore in the student union. At least I could look at the pictures.

"I'm tellin' ya, Burl, if I don't get some help around here, I'm leavin'," she said. "Did you feed the kids?"

"Uh, I cooked some rice and gravy."

"Shit!"

"Uh, Annie gave 'em somethin'. . . ."

"I brought them a 'Happy Meal'," I said.

She wasn't listening as she drudged to her bedroom, Daddy following.

"So fuckin' tired of this shit. Tired of comin' home to a filthy kitchen. . . ."

"Mama, you know my SSI's startin' in June. They said I'd be gettin' my back pay, should be several thousand dollars."

It'll be gone in a day.

It was hell trying to get to sleep that night, and hell to drag myself out of bed in the morning to the smell of burning pork and the sound of Daddy's loud talking.

"You need to check on ole man Price," Daddy said.

"He's fine," I said. "He called the other night and said he's feeling better."

"I still think you should pay 'em a visit. They're good to you."

"Daddy, I'm going to pack up and go back to school if you don't leave me alone."

"Leave her alone, Burl. She's tired. You on your period?"

"No!"

"You got dark circles under your eyes."

"She's too skinny," he said.

"I know it," said Mama. "Stupid dietin'. It ain't normal to be sleepin' three and four hours a night."

My face was unveiled. Wearing makeup around here would be wasting it, and I needed to conserve as much money as possible for my escape. I was a vat of nervous energy as I picked at my skin in the bathroom mirror. I lifted my bare foot, and the sole of it was black from the dirty floor. I walked outside and sat by Trudy on the steps.

Our house sounded like a bar on Saturday night, with the kids screaming, Daddy ranting, Gloria telling him to shut up, and Mama yelling at everybody. Nothing could stop the vision of Thomas's dejected face, and the smell of this rat trap. This joint needed a complete makeover miracle. I hadn't the time, money, energy, or stupidity to make it better. I had given up, just like Mama had years ago. Hopefully, I didn't have situational depression.

Daddy had a job to do for Mrs. Percy Pritchett that day. Except he had bought the wrong type of sausage, and the Cajun spice made him sick to his stomach, and the smell of the bathroom was asphyxiating us. Mrs. Pritchett called twice and grilled Mama about where he was, putting her in a bloodthirsty mood. I heard another flush, and he came out carrying his Bible. He stationed himself on the couch again, feeling for his neck pulse, the gates of hell calling him. From the gripe seat, Mama glared with murderous eyes.

"Mama, I feel so swimmy-headed."

"Well, try movin'. Why don't you call the old bitch and tell her you'll do the work tomorrow?"

"I'll call her in a minute. Oh, Lordy me, when I sit up, the acid comes up through my throat."

She sighed. "You need to do that work before Mr. Patel makes us move."

"I wish someone could lend us some money until I get my SSI."

"There ain't no one gonna lend us a dime, and you know it."

He rolled off the couch and back to the bathroom.

"Uh, Gloria . . ."

"Shit!" Gloria screeched.

"I'm in a bind," he begged.

"Hurry up. I have somewhere to go," she griped.

She walked from the bathroom to the kitchen in just her bra and panties. She came out with a glass of iced tea and went to her bedroom.

"All Daddy wants to do is borrow money, which he never pays back. He's like the government," I said.

"Shit," Mama grumbled. "I ain't gettin another advance at work. It took me two months to pay off the last one."

"I guess a budget's out of the question?" I was feeling mean.

"Years ago, when he drove a truck, we could make it a week on his paycheck."

"That's because he stayed gone," I said.

"I'd pick up his check on Friday and get groceries. I paid the rent and utilities."

"I remember," I said.

There was a ruckus brewing. Mama threw up her arms. "Now what?"

Daddy and Gloria were battling again.

"Don't know why you're in a hurry to go hang out with that bunch of trash," he said. "That ole Kayla Carpenter goes with niggers."

"No, she doesn't. You don't know! I'm gonna be late now. It stinks like shit in here! I'm gonna leave." The door slammed.

"I tell ya, Gloria treats those friends of hers better than she treats me," he pouted. "She treats me like a bastard child."

"You drive everybody crazy with your gripin'," Mama said.

"I don't gripe that much."

"Huh! The only time you don't gripe is when you think you're gonna drop dead."

Mrs. Pritchett called a third time, and Daddy lamented about the number of times he had used the toilet, so she settled on him working in the morning. When he started frying chicken livers, I called Aunt Mooney and high-tailed it to her house to spend the night. Tish had gone with Pepper to the Tisdale family reunion in Bay Springs and would be gone a day or so.

Aunt Mooney and I went to the mall so she could exchange a blouse at McRae's. She bought me a bottle of White Linen perfume, a pity present, I suppose. We ate at Bonanza and went home in time to watch the Saturday movie of the week.

"I have begrudged myself and starved myself on that stupid diet until I had to eat some chocolate cake, but that didn't fill me up," Mooney said. "No, I had to go to Shipley's and eat six chocolate-filled donuts without stoppin'."

"Talk about a sugar high," I said.

"I coulda eaten a dozen. But then I got started in on the donut holes. Thought I'd save 'em for later, share 'em with Tish. But no, I ate two dozen of 'em in the car, and my stomach got upset. I flew to the bathroom, then Lonnie Cole showed up at my door. I told him my kidneys were actin' up, and the fool stayed anyway. I used a whole can of air freshener."

"Aunt Mooney?" I wanted to tell her about Thomas, but I cut myself off. "You said the Tisdales are having a family reunion? I didn't think they were family-oriented."

"They have one every year. About two hundred people come. Half the young'uns are illegitimate. His Daddy just got outta jail after throwin' a drunk and knockin' his girlfriend around."

"I thought he'd been forging checks."

"He got out for that two months ago. I'm scared to death for Tish bein' around them."

"Tish isn't thinking about marrying Pepper, is she?"

"She told me she isn't. Said he had to get outta debt and get a steady job."

"Yeah. That's two big ones. And his kids. Does he support any of them?"

"Nah. That's why he don't work. They garnish his wages."

"Well, Lonnie does pay for his kids."

Her mouth quivered. I had said too much.

"Oh, precious. Your ole aunt has really messed up."

"What's the matter?"

"I'm a sinner and a slut. I had sex with Lonnie."

"Oh, my God!"

"I couldn't help it. You know, we've been seein' each other a long while. He is a good kisser. And . . . we've been pettin' heavily lately or for months now. God, it's been so long since I had any."

I put my hand over my mouth. "Aunt Mooney."

"We were just kissin' passionately on the couch, and somehow we ended up in my bedroom. Whew! I'd be a bald-face liar if I said I didn't enjoy it. But I'm gonna go to hell for committin' fornication."

"No, you're not."

"I am. God!"

"It's okay. Just one time."

"No! Seven times."

"You're kidding?"

"No. I'm gonna burn in hell."

"Have you told Mama?"

"No! You know how she is about sex, and I don't want Burl to know. He already thinks I wear too much makeup."

"His opinions don't mean anything. Are you in love with Lonnie?"

"No, I don't think so. I care about him."

"You're just lonely."

"A big fat lonely fornicator."

Chapter Twenty Nine

Nell gave me a letter to hand-carry to Mary, a cashier at the business office and one of her campus friends. They gossiped on the phone during work hours. Mary recognized my red hair and thanked me kindly as she took the letter. In the student union, I mailed a stack of envelopes and checked the education department's mailbox. In my purse I carried my heart in a red envelope. It had taken three hours and tearing up twenty-seven sheets of paper to tell Thomas how much I loved him and why I loved him. I was being punished for wanting space, but I didn't want distance. I dropped the card into the mail slot and walked back to the office.

Leslie found me in the cafeteria at dinner.

"Hey, Annie. Where've you been?" She placed her tray down, dropped her white cloth bag on a chair, and sat down. "Whew, my computer class is killin' me. I'm so exhausted."

I chewed, listened, and waited. Pretty soon she would come up for air.

"My feet are so swollen. I'm gonna have to go the doctor and get some fluid pills. I think I'm having circulation problems again. I still don't have any health insurance, and the stupid doctors demand the money up front. I don't know why they do that."

Mama should adopt her.

"Leslie, tell me something. Why did you tell Thomas that Peter wrote me?"

"I told him what?"

"That Peter wrote me a letter. You did tell him that."

"I could have . . . I don't remember. Is somethin' wrong?"

"He broke up with me."

"Oh, Annie, no!" She grabbed my hand and held it across the table. "I didn't know. Why did he break up with you?"

"Never mind." I took back my hand and placed it in my lap.

"I'm so upset." Her face was red. "I love Thomas. I wanted you two to get married. You'd have beautiful children together. The last time I talked to him was on the phone. He was helpin' me with the computer class," she said cautiously. "Oh, Annie, he didn't break up with you 'cause of Peter's letter?"

The tears came. "Yes, he did."

"I didn't tell him on purpose." She was afraid and thinking fast. "Let's see, I remember tellin' him I got a letter from Denise. Yes, that's what I said. You and I got a letter from Denise on the same day. Then I said that Peter had written you, but I didn't think anythin' of it. I was just talkin' out of my head."

I wiped my eyes with my napkin. "Leslie, it's fine. Don't worry."

"I hate myself for this. Do you want me to call him?"

"No. Just leave him alone." I took her hand. "Hey, it's okay. I'm not mad at you."

"I'm so depressed. Everythin's a mess in my life. Nelson won't talk to me. I'm failin' two of my classes. I don't know how I'm goin' to pay next month's rent."

I'd finish school whether Thomas spoke to me or not. I was a liberated woman, for God's sake.

"Last weekend, when Nelson came by, I thought everythin' was fine. Then, when we're at work, he avoids me. He won't even say hello."

"He's still coming by your apartment?"

"Every weekend."

"And you're still screwing him?"

"Annie, please. Why are you askin' me this?"

"Do you know that he's engaged to marry Rhonda?"

"No . . ." She was losing the color in her face. "No, he's not. . . ."

"He told me that they're engaged. You're screwing a liar."

She looked at me, then across the cafeteria. "Why that skinny bastard."

I started shopping. Marla and I went to Hudson's Salvage and looked for three hours. I hit the jackpot finding shorts, shirts, pants, and shoes, and spending under a hundred dollars. The stuff smelled like smoke, some had been wet, but I'd wash it and wear it. I wrote Henry a letter and asked if I could take some money out of the savings for clothes in case I had interviews. He called the day he got the letter and happily agreed. Marla's parents sent her a check, and we went back to Hudson's.

The spring outfit, new makeup, and my hair growing out a little invigorated me. I sprinted to class and stayed afterwards to ask a question of Dr. Hodgins. When I came out, Thomas was passing by my classroom with another student.

"Talk to you later," he told his friend. "How've you been?"

"I've been . . ." I was humiliated about his not responding to the Valentine's card. "Doing just fine. How are your folks?"

"Good. They're in Europe right now."

"How's the biking?"

"I have another race next week."

"Where?"

"Jackson. I need to go." He walked away.

I knocked desperately on Marla's door.

"Y'all have classes in the same building. You were bound to run into him," she said.

"He was so distant. I'm nothing to him."

"Girl, you're seeing things at their worst level 'cause you're hurting. He spoke to you first, didn't he?"

"So?"

"You know what, he didn't have to say a damn word. The best thing you can do is look good, which you do, and he knows it. If I was you, I'd find myself a date."

"I don't want anyone else."

"I don't mean that. I mean go out and have fun. Look at Suzy. She's has lots of guy friends. Is there anyone in your classes that interests you?"

"Not really." The thought of it was making me sick.

"I'd open up my eyes. You're too young for this, waiting on him to get off his high horse."

Henry sounded twenty years younger when he called and woke me Saturday morning at seven. He was updating his address book. Needed Denise's in Jackson so he could write her. Grace was on the coast with friends, and I took full advantage of the privacy. I kicked my chair across the room, slammed books on the floor, and broke a pen in half.

"Just a second, Pop."

"If you're busy, you can drop it in a letter, you hear?"

"No. I'm already up."

"Been walking a mile a day now," he purred. "Got up at five this morning and walked until Mom got up. I sure feel better. Dr. Wallace wants me to walk five days a week."

I was damning Dr. Wallace for this.

"I found it," I said.

I read it. Stopped. Read it to him again and again and again. Then, I had to wait until he read it back to me.

"When you coming home?"

"Pop—" I was about to scream. "Maybe in two weeks. I have to eat breakfast."

"What's that?"

"My friend Marla's meeting me for breakfast!"

"Oh, okay. I know you have to get going. Eat a good breakfast. Starts the day off. Say a prayer for me, will ya, honey?"

Reggie Walters was blah. For the last year and a half he had been in my accounting classes. I didn't care for him because he sat up front in every class, and I never liked students who did that. He wore a mustache and had brown curly hair that fell just above his ears. He was tall, six-foot-one. We had a chance to talk in a study group and, fortunately, it was made up of mostly straight-A students, and he was one of them. We went for coffee on Thursday after the group broke up.

"I think he's probably the most brilliant accounting professor in the department."

"I don't care for any of them."

"Annie, your attitude's goin' to get you in trouble."

"It already has."

"I like you. You tell it like it is."

I smiled, his compliment curdling my stomach.

"Well." He glanced at his watch. "Guess I'll drive you back to your dorm."

I picked up my purse and stood. "Thanks for your help. Again."

On the way across campus, he nervously cleared his throat.

"Want to meet in the cafeteria for dinner tomorrow?"

"Sure. I'll see you at five. Thanks again."

I think Reggie was attracted to me last spring, but I had been too consumed with Peter to chat whenever Reggie asked to talk about the day's lecture. Sitting across from him in the cafeteria was abnormal. I had never played the field, could never juggle more than one guy. I could have fallen for him, had I not dated Peter. He was somewhat handsome, and his nerdiness felt safe and inviting. He was from New Orleans, and his Cajun accent was much stronger than Denise's. He was too timid to question me personally, which led to him telling me everything about himself. He had an older married brother. His dad was a pharmaceutical salesman, his mom a nurse. He didn't work, concentrating fully on his studies. Had a job waiting in June with an accounting firm in New Orleans. Boring, I cringed, when I had dated an athletic genius. After supper, we strolled around the campus, but I cut it short, telling him I had to get back and call home. I went to bed with a heavy heart.

Back for an encore, panic attacks were plaguing Daddy, and he wouldn't stray too far from the house. Mama called to tell me, because Daddy wanted her to. He was terrified to be alone, so he took to hanging out at the Handy Pantry with her while she was working. Drinking sodas and scarfing down snacks out of the box, his chomping and smacking making her madder than a wet hen. Her tab at work that was supposed to be for her gas and food was reaching the national debt and about to give her a heart attack. *Who are these people, that not one of my friends has ever met?* I never talked about them, because it'd open a can of worms, and I was so sick of falsifying my world. I was a phony from the word go. Ambitious on the exterior, but inside I was too chicken, and it was because of them. Why was I even in college, only to be faced with the unbearable reality that I might not escape my roots?

Leslie's mom had taken ill with pneumonia, causing Leslie to miss some classes. Catching up seemed impossible, but common sense kicked in, and she hired a fellow classmate to tutor her in the library every afternoon and evening. The grin wasn't there when she flagged down Marla and me on the way to dinner.

"Girl, you looked like someone beat the shit out of you," Marla said.

"I'm so exhausted," she said. "I have to eat supper and get back to my tutor, Charlie."

"Where is he?" I asked.

"He's eatin' supper with his girlfriend."

"How much you paying him?"

"Seven bucks an hour. He wouldn't take five."

"Girl, pay him," Marla said.

"I have one more lesson in TV production, then I'm up with the rest of the class."

I received another letter from Peter on Friday. It was a page long. His job was stressful, and he didn't like his boss. He was riding with some guys he met at the local bike shop and was considering moving out west. His sister was expecting her second child. He had heard about the breakup, and how sorry he was. That Thomas was a great guy, and I was a wonderful person, and on and on. If I wanted to talk, I could call him anytime of the day or night. I slammed my notebook on top of the counter in the student union and wrote down his address. I ripped his letter into tiny pieces until my fingers cramped. I didn't want to keep in touch any longer, I wrote, and I didn't give justification. I bought a stamped envelope, shoved my scribbled note inside and mailed it.

During the two weeks that followed, I was an actress. Valiant before my friends. Pretending I was enjoying Reggie, getting on with my life. Only Marla knew of my deceit—she could read it in my eyes. Spring break arrived, and Reggie went home in bliss.

Denise had invited me to go home with her, but I did it again. I went home.

Chapter Thirty

"You don't know shit from Shabuta," Mama griped from inside the house.

"Why Mama!"

Our kitchen was mass destruction. Dirty dishes piled high. Food in the sink. A torn loaf of bread on the floor. Tools, nails, mud, and water everywhere. Daddy had brought in the old dishwasher and put it in the kitchen. He created an aqueduct made of narrow copper piping that ran along the walls above the sink.

"What is this doing in here?"

"Shit, Burl drug that filthy thing in here last week. He jury-rigged the damn thing and put another hole in the floor. It don't even clean the dishes. I still have to wash 'em."

"Why didn't he cover up the pipes? They shouldn't be showing like that. It's certainly not a Good Housekeeping installation," I said. "Make him take it out."

"I ain't done it. He'll tear the house up, gettin' it outta here."

"Who'd notice."

Lonnie had proposed to Aunt Mooney, but she was dragging her feet. I wanted to call her, but Mama said she had gone out of town with him. Wouldn't be back until Sunday.

"Mooney needs to get married," Daddy said.

"No, she doesn't," I said. "He's got seven kids and a low-paying job."

"He don't do bad."

"Aunt Mooney would kill him, Daddy. She likes spending money."

"Mooney said he brung over three of his kids, and they messed up her whole house. Spilled drink on her sofas, and Lonnie wouldn't even spank 'em," Mama said, as if she had never witnessed such incivility.

"Exactly," I said. "He feels guilty over screwing around on his wife and leaving the brats. If he screwed around once, he'll do it again."

"I was just sayin'," Daddy said, "that Mooney don't need to be alone."

"Yes, she does," I snapped.

Mama was irate about starting supper, and it would have taken two days to clean the kitchen, so Daddy drove off to the land of high cholesterol to get us a barrel of chicken. I managed to clear the table and set Daddy's tools on the porch, then I quit for the rest of the evening.

I spent two hours with the Prices on Tuesday and was off the hook the rest of the week. Henry had so much on his mind that I could relax and help them pack for a trip they were taking to Tupelo with his half-sister Harriet. They were leaving early Wednesday morning to see distant relatives they hadn't seen in years. When he sat down, he caught his breath and smiled.

"Thank you for helping Mom pack, sweetheart. Mom, doesn't she look beautiful?"

"Yup!" she replied, poking my thigh with her index finger.

"You're so trim. And that outfit! Pink is your color," he said.

"Thanks, Pop. I've been trying to dress well. Since I'm graduating, I want to look better."

"You certainly do," he said. "Pearl, can you see how flawless Annie's skin and makeup are?"

"Yes, indeed," she nodded.

"Did you get any clothes with the money you took out?"

"Yes, sir. I found a couple of suits and some shoes for interviewing."

I had only taken out a hundred dollars.

"Good. Need anything else?"

"I might."

"Well, I think Mom might like to give you something before you leave."

Pop couldn't handle more than one thing at a time, and when something was on his mind, his life was in suspension. He was so distracted by the pending trip that he forgot to ask for my account balance. He got up to get her checkbook.

I lifted my hand to admire my long pink fingernails. My makeup was the same old Cover Girl, but I was taking longer to apply it. Rising earlier to dress. I wasn't me, and it was tearing me apart. This preoccupation with my body. Drinking eight glasses of water a day. Anyone who wasn't thin and toned was a target for my backbiting thoughts.

"I hope that lazy thing isn't coming."

"Who, Mommy Junior?"

"Claudia. Henry's sister."

"Isn't she still recovering from her hip surgery?" I asked.

"Did she have hip surgery?"

I was home by three. I took off my good salvage store duds and threw on my gray stretch shorts and a tee shirt. At the sink, I filled a glass with water, wishing I had some lemon to put in it.

"Do you wanna go with me to the store to get somethin' for pusslegut?" Mama's voice was raspy from sleep. "Burl gave me ten dollars to get somethin' for supper."

"Wow. What did he do? Win the lottery?"

"At least he gave me somethin'."

There were days when she defended him, and I hated her today.

"I may go to the movies tonight."

"What you gonna go see?"

She was aggravated, didn't want me to go.

"I don't know."

The theatre was at the mall, and I wanted to walk around, to let people see me, and not waste my looking good here.

"You ain't hangin' around with Kirby, are you?"

"No."

"I wouldn't start callin' her now."

"I'm not, Mama."

She ripped the cigarette from her lips.

"What's the matter with you?"

I glared.

"I'm so sick of coming home and there's nothing to eat. It's so filthy, it nauseates me. I can't even invite my friends to come home with me. We have sewage running in our yard. People think we're trash."

"I'm doin' the best I can," she said.

"That's all I ever hear. Y'all expect too much out of me. I can't do it all. I can't live my life while trying to fix yours at the same time. I can't."

"Well, I can go to the store by myself," Mama puffed.

"Yeah, go buy him something to eat. To hell with us. The damned hog."

She sighed. "Annie, he eats like that 'cause he was starved when he was a little boy."

"Then he shouldn't starve his family. You need to get a better paying job, and he needs to get a job."

"I can't help it. He ain't educated. I'm not educated. You don't know what I went through, growin' up, bein' called stupid and a whore all my life.

"Mama, your father's dead. And you can help it. You need to do something, go to school, do anything."

"Well, I ain't gettin' started with goin' to college. Then he'll wanna go, and you know what that'll lead to. Him tryin' to fuck the students," she said. "He'd fuck anythin' that moved."

"Not him. Just you."

"I ain't got the energy to go to some college. It's all I can do to hold down a two-bit job."

I carried two boxes to the burn pile, struck a match, sat in the dirt, and watched the paper turn to ashes. Letters, the self-help books that had gotten me through my most desperate moments, and the Barry Manilow books of songs I had memorized in case I ever got to go to one of his concerts. Incinerated. Mama came towards me with a cigarette in her hand.

"Why are you burnin' your Barry stuff?"

"I kept the albums."

"Why, Annie?"

"I'm tired of lugging it around. I need some space."

Maybe they were right, I had wasted my money.

"We coulda stored 'em here. We have the room."

"It doesn't matter. Anyway, y'all will never know if—or when—you'll have to move again. I don't want you to have to bother with it."

CHAPTER THIRTY ONE

I felt stranded when I returned to my dorm. Stuck in Mississippi like a fish in a dried pond. Thomas could go anywhere, do anything, because his parents had money and he was so smart. I paced the floor. Why had I burned the self-help books? I needed a passage, something to pick me up, get my adrenaline pumping. . . .

Remember the good things, Annie. Winning second place in the art contest in first grade. The certificate for taking shorthand at eighty words per minute. Honor roll in high school. *Who's Who* in high school. Why did I feel so inferior to him? To Reggie? And to Peter? I needed a strategy. I got up and dialed Reggie.

"Want to study tomorrow—no, Tuesday?"

"Uh, sure." His voice picked up. "What time?"

"How about . . . can you do it after supper?"

"Sure. In the library?"

"Yes. I'll meet you, say around six?"

"I'll be there."

Reggie was just asking for it. I finished breakfast at seven thirty Monday morning when he sat down across from me with a wide grin.

"Good mornin'."

I looked around. "Uh, I was about to leave. I have to go over some notes."

"Oh. What time do you get in here?"

"Early."

I stayed fifteen more minutes out of guilt. I didn't let him walk with me to the business building. I told him I had forgotten something back at my dorm. I ran from the building at noon before he could catch me for lunch. Marla was in the diet line looking for me, and I waved her down.

"Hey, girl. What's got you looking so stressed?"

"Reggie. He's been following me. Now he knows when I eat breakfast."

"That's okay. Y'all are just friends. You're having breakfast with a friend."

"It's not friendship to him." I picked up a tray. "But he's going to be helping me more with my accounting. Shoot, I may even pay him like Leslie's doing with Charlie."

"He probably won't take it, Annie," she said.

"Well, it's only business, as far as I'm concerned."

After lunch, I napped an hour and a half, still mending from spring break. Marla and I walked at three and went to supper a little before five. In my room, I opened my closet and picked up my toiletries. I was going for a shower, but the phone rang, and I was summoned to the campus infirmary.

"Yes, ma'am. A nurse called me, a Miss Simmons?"

"That's me. We have Leslie Lang here. She asked that we call you. She came in two hours ago complaining of chest pains. The doctor checked her out. She had an anxiety attack. A Nelson Hyde brought her in. She's in the room down the hall and to your left. Room three."

I walked down the hall, stopping at the door when I heard the doctor's voice in the room and Leslie telling him every major disease she thought she had.

"And I think it's the Fasty-Sweet . . ."

"As I told you, go to the psychology department and talk to Dr. Winger. She'll set you up an appointment with one of the grad students, and it costs almost nothing."

"Will they give me some medicine if it's my heart?"

"Leslie, your heart's stronger than mine. You've had a panic attack. Do you know how many students we get here during the week with panic attacks? About a hundred. You'll be fine. Just take it easy the rest of the evening. Call me if you need anything."

He came out, and I went in. She was lying on an examining table.

"Annie, am I glad to see you."

"Do you feel better?"

"Not really. My head's been spinnin', and I threw up. I was nauseous all night. I knew I should've gone to Forrest General instead of this dump."

"Where's Nelson?"

She turned her head toward the wall.

"Did he do something to upset you, Leslie? Did he say something?"

"No," she sobbed.

I rubbed her shoulder, and she brought her hands to cover her face.

"It's okay. You want to come to my room and talk?"

Marla met us in my room. Leslie lay on my bed.

"Would you rather rest or talk?" I asked.

"Start talking," Marla said.

"Well, you see . . . " She eased her eyes from Marla's sober face and looked up at the ceiling. "I was upset, okay. I was up sick to my stomach half the night. I slept late and got up, and I didn't take a shower. I put on some clothes and went to class. As soon as I came out, I saw Rhonda walkin' across the lawn, and I lost it. I got in my car and drove back to my apartment. I paced and paced, but my feet started hurtin', so I sat down to watch some TV, but all that was on was soap operas. I couldn't bear to watch people on the television makin' love and bein' in love, so I cut it off. And there was the phone, and I couldn't ignore it. I called Nelson, and I must've woke him up 'cause he started screamin' at me. So I told him I'd swallowed a bunch of sleepin' pills."

"You did what!" Marla yelled.

"I did, so he'd come over, and he came right over. Before I opened the door, my chest felt so heavy I felt like I had actually taken somethin', but I knew I didn't, so I opened the door. He made me go to the infirmary."

"He left you there," I said.

"My life is such a mess," she sobbed.

"So is mine," I said.

"No, you're smart. You work hard. You're loved."

"You are, too. I love you. Denise and Marla love you."

"I wanted *him* to love me."

"You don't need him to love you," said Marla.

"No one wants me. I'm fat and useless. I caused Thomas to leave you, Annie."

"God, it's not your fault about Thomas. It's mine. I should've told him about the letters. I should've been more open with him. I caused him to leave me, you didn't."

"I called him a few weeks ago. I told him not to be mad at you, Annie. He told me that he wasn't goin' to talk about you with me. He said it was his business."

"You just don't know. I've gone through most of my life feeling like nobody. Feeling like I had to work harder and harder just to prove myself. Just to make my parents love me. Guess what? They love my sisters just as much, even more."

"Guys fall in love with you."

"Not until I came here to college, and you know, it hasn't been so rosy as you think. They've been more trouble than they'll ever be worth. Including my daddy. Leslie, you have to take care of yourself. Save your own self. Don't wait for someone else to do it."

"It's too hard."

"No it's not. It's really easier."

"I'm so fat and ugly."

"No you're not, girl," Marla said.

"You're unique. It's like me with my red hair and Marla with her white uncle. We're all unique."

"You're so beautiful, you two."

"So are you," I said.

Marla interrupted. "Girl, don't you ever pull this shit again. You almost gave us a heart attack. No man is worth this. Do you hear me?"

"I do. I'm feelin' so much better." She sat up. "Startin' Monday, I'm takin' charge of my life, honey. I'm goin' to be a new woman."

We made a pact. Marla, Leslie, and I would be career women. We'd get through this semester by sticking together.

Reggie was calling frequently, leaving messages with Grace. In class, I was friendly in a distant way, and I could see that he was confused. By the time I was in my room again, he'd call. I reluctantly agreed to meet him for dinner in the cafeteria on a Monday. I made Marla go with me.

"Oh, God," she moaned. "He's waiting at the door."

My arms were crossed, and I nearly retreated. But I wasn't going to be a coward. I had started this, and I'd finish it.

"Good afternoon," he grinned as he opened the door for us.

"I like those shorts," Marla said.

His legs were shapely, covered in light brown hair, though not as muscular as a biker's legs. That bothered me.

"Are you going to the movies this week?" Reggie asked.

"No," I answered.

"What about study group on Wednesday?"

"I'll be there."

Our cards were scanned, and he went to the main food line. Marla and I went for the diet line. I sat across from Reggie, but he moved next to me. I was ready to kick him.

"Don't do that," I said as he stroked my arm.

In the lobby, Reggie was anxious, making forced conversation, but the undertone was telling me I had better be honest before he went off the deep end.

"I'm sorry I haven't been very sociable lately. I have a lot of my mind right now," I said.

"I've been the same way."

"It's just—I want to be friends."

"Oh, I do, too."

"Just friends, I mean it. Reggie, I can't be serious with anybody."

"Have I done anything?"

"No," I told him firmly. "It's not you, it's me. I'm leaving the south as soon as I graduate."

He moved uncomfortably. "Well, if there's anything I can do to help you, you know, findin' a job. . . ."

"That's my responsibility. I'll do fine," I said.

"Can we go out? Can I take you to dinner sometime?"

"Yes."

"I really like you, Annie."

"You're a wonderful person. I'm not in a girlfriend-boyfriend mood right now. I'm going to work on my career."

"I hate myself," I told Marla later that evening. "I'll never do this again. I'll never lead someone on like that."

"Aw, he'll get over it Annie," Marla said as she rubbed lotion on her arms. "You didn't lead him on. You didn't even kiss him."

"Yes, I did."

"You didn't tell me that. Was it good?"

"It was okay. Not with passion, Marla. I wouldn't let him."

"You know, I've been thinking. We should get us some bikes and go riding."

"I'm too afraid to go it by ourselves. I don't know anything about changing tires. What if our chains break?"

"We're not racing, Annie. We can ride around the campus like other people do."

"I wonder how much a bicycle would cost?"

Chapter Thirty Two

Daddy had backslid. With one phone call, Brother Buddy had rekindled the flame. Close to home was Faith Assembly of God on Fifth Avenue in the cruddy part of North Soso. Brother Billy Speck needed assistance with a two-week revival of romping and stomping, and who had more time than two out-of-work Jimmy Swaggart wannabes. Daddy and Buddy were trading off nights preaching, a duet of grotesque illiteracy. But it was different this time. Mama was going. Back in the swing of religion and renewing her faith. Staying in the Scriptures when she wasn't working and while she was resting her feet. Her understanding of the Word was beautiful at times, causing Aunt Mooney to weep over her sinful secrets and break out into tongues. Mama was ever so pious until Renee crossed the street with the bubbleheads.

"I'll just be damn!"

"What now?" I asked.

"Here she comes, and I hadn't even went to the bathroom. Yesterday, Joey tried to beat the door down when I was in there."

I got up. "I'm getting rid of them."

"Don't be mean."

Renee was out of breath and smiling on the porch.

"We're fixing to leave," I said. "Got to go run some errands."

"Oh. All right." She was looking around outside. "Can I ask your Mama somethin'?"

"I'll get her." I didn't let them in.

When she left, every prayer Mama had spoken went down the drain. Welcome back, Satan grinned.

"Shit! I'm gonna fuckin' leave!"

"Wiley, take Holly outside to play," I said. I turned to Mama. "What did Renee want?"

"Wants me to take her to the store today!" She shoved a cigarette into her mouth and lit it.

"Don't you do it."

"She ain't got no way to go. Her car's a piece of shit. That fuckin' bastard's she's married to won't fix it. Now she'll be after me takin' her here and everywhere! I can't do it. I can't come in from work and haul her and them big-headed young'uns around. They won't behave, and she won't make 'em behave! I'd beat their brains out!"

"Why can't David take her when he gets home?"

"Aw, he ain't gonna do it. He don't do nothin' when he gets home but lay in front of the TV. Expects her to have supper done at five or he makes her life a livin' hell. Pot-bellied, pappy-suckin' son of a bitch!"

"Let me take her. But I'm not taking her kids."

Renee was agonizing like Mama did when she went to the grocery store. I didn't know how much she had to spend, but the woman was counting pennies and sweating blood. Mama was correct about the macaroni and cheese. Renee bought ten boxes of it and six cans of the cheapest tuna. I got Mama's usual cocktail of cigarettes, BC powders, and Diet Cokes. Ground beef, Hamburger Helper, three cans of green beans, and a loaf of bread was going to be our supper. I didn't worry about gaining weight, because Daddy would make sure our portions were small. I paid first, then waited at the end of the counter. Renee smiled nervously at me but kept looking inside her black change purse. Her total of eighteen dollars and seventy-one cents didn't break her bank, and she took out a twenty-dollar bill. On the way home, she thanked me graciously while I felt I was the rich one.

I wasn't looking forward to seeing the Prices, but the visit proved rewarding.

"Isn't it wonderful to have a granddaughter who takes pride in her appearance the way Annie does?" said Henry.

"Sure is," said Pearl.

"Do you want to get the bicycle here or in Hattiesburg? I betcha Hattiesburg has better stores, don't you think?"

"Yes, I do," I answered.

"How much do you think you'll need?"

"I'd say about three hundred dollars for the bike and a helmet."

"Uh, yeah," he nodded. "We want you to get a helmet, don't we, Mom? Safety's important. Mom, you want to give our granddaughter a little money so she can get a bicycle?"

"I sure will," she said as she tried to get up.

"Don't get up just yet, honey." He looked at me. "You said you have a friend you're going to exercise with."

"Yes, Marla. I told you about her."

"Marla, that's right. Does she have a bike?"

"Uh, yes, sir. She's bringing it from home this weekend. She's lost weight since she's been exercising with me."

"Is that right? You see, honey, Annie's had a positive effect on her friend Marla. We're so proud of you, sweetheart. You look beautiful."

I was on the edge of super thinness, and it wasn't all from exercising. I flat out didn't have an appetite. I was full of anxieties, from Thomas to Reggie to classes to worrying about the Manor and graduation and job-searching.

Chapter Thirty Three

Marla and I rode our new bicycles around the track area for a while, then ventured out to the campus roads.

"We're soaring, Annie!"

Friday afternoon was a good day for riding. Many students had gone home, and traffic was light in the campus area. We rode to the auditorium and around the parking lots. After an hour, I stopped.

"I'm bored."

"Come on, girl. Let's do some more."

"Where? We've been over the whole campus."

"Let go out in the street."

"I'm afraid."

"You went with Thomas. You can go with me. He showed you the hand signals."

I knew I wasn't going to run into him, and I wanted to. We rode off, and I made another important decision in my life. I was going to ride for me. I was going to be a biker babe. We rode to Rax, got a soda, and rode back to school.

"That was fun," Marla said. "Let's go out tomorrow afternoon."

"Let's do it," I smiled.

"I'm getting up and going to the lab early."

"I'll get up early, too."

We locked up our bikes and went up to our rooms.

Work-study was becoming a burden. As she scribbled her signature on a memo, Dr. Dearman pointed out that Dr. Camp thought she was that woman lawyer from *Hill Street Blues*. It was trying whenever Dr. Camp and Dr. Dearman needed me at the same time.

"Just a second, Dr. Camp. Annie," Nell whispered, "go see what Dr. Dearman wants in there first."

"Go get me coffee with lots of cream," said Dr. Dearman.

"Oh, Annie!" Nell called as I was walking out the door. "When you get back, Dr. Camp needs you to type something for her."

Dr. Camp's encouragement had led me to confide my family life, Thomas, and my dreams. She had even met me in the student union grill one afternoon just for "girl talk." She bolstered my hope that someday I'd look out and see mountains. Denver was too big, she said. Move to a small town where I could do big things.

I had to fill in for Irene Monday afternoon. Nell was frantic when she told me Irene had called in sick, and Dr. Katz wanted a class synopsis typed for the summer session. I put my plans to study with Reggie on hold until after supper. I wanted the night off to listen to my cassette player, but it was better I kept busy and quit dwelling in the past. At five, Marla met me in the food line with a grim expression.

"Thomas is in there."

"Where?"

"At a table by the salad bar."

I couldn't move.

"No Annie," she said. "We're not sitting on the other side."

She made me walk tall across the dining room to the diet line. I don't remember what I got to eat and drink. We walked to a table against the back wall and sat down. I was thanking the angels above that I was wearing my Hudson's Salvage purple shorts, purple top, and that I had taken the time to put on lipstick.

"How do I look?" I asked.

"Beautiful," said Marla. "He's right over there, and he saw you. Keep eating. Everything's going to work out."

"You sound more nervous than I do."

"Girl, I'm fine."

I recognized the faces at the table with Thomas, and my nervousness turned to irritation.

"He'll sit with them, but he acts like I'm a disease."

"Girl, him sitting with them has nothing to do with you. He was friends with them before he met you."

"Then why can't he be my friend?"

"'Cause he can't handle it right now."

"It's been weeks, Marla. Hell, it's been two months."

"And it could be longer. Annie, he may never come back. You need to think about that. You need to get that heart of yours ready. He may not come back to you."

I overslept the following morning and had to skip breakfast. After my last class, I had to get to work-study. With that in mind, I hurried down the hall of the business building.

"I hear you've been riding?"

I stopped. "What?"

Thomas was holding a load of books under his arm.

"I hear you have a bike."

"Yes, I do."

"You've lost too much weight."

I looked down at my legs. "Have I?"

"Yeah." For a moment, he seemed to care. "You need to eat more protein, if you're going to be riding a lot."

"I'm only riding on weekends. And I'm only riding for fun," I said.

He nodded. "That's the best way to do it.

I stared into his eyes, wanting to forget him. But he was making it so hard. He let out a smile.

"I have to get to the library."

In the cafeteria, I was exhilarated, ready to jump mountains and sky-dive.

"Now I wouldn't jump to any conclusions," Marla said.

"I'm not. I have to be cautious."

"You still letting Reggie take you out on Saturday?"

"Yeah, Lord. Why did I tell him I'd go? I don't want to."

"Go and have fun. That's what goddesses do. And if you're queen of the goddess club, you got to act like one."

"He said I was too thin."

"Who?"

"Thomas. Said I needed to eat more protein."

"That means he's been looking."

Denise called Sunday night. She was going to the coast the upcoming Friday, and since she was passing through, she wanted to spend the night with me. I eagerly said yes, and she rattled on.

"I've been in the lab all day."

"You're working on dead bodies again?" I asked.

"Yes, the body is so fascinatin'."

"What's wrong with you?"

"Nothin'."

"Denise, you're either drunk or you've met someone."

"No, everythin's fine," she said, trying to sound composed.

"Okay, now tell me what's going on."

"Christopher called me last night."

"What the hell did he want?"

"He said that Linda left him, and they're gettin' a divorce."

"When did this happen?"

"A couple of months ago."

"Why are they divorcing?"

"He said she's been havin' an affair."

"Well, it looks like she got even with him."

Her voice grew a little faint. "Yeah, I guess so."

"Why did he call you?"

"Well, he wants to come and see me."

"No. Don't let him. He put you through enough."

She kept quiet.

"Why? Why does he want to come and see you?"

"He said he regretted hurtin' me."

"Oh, God," I groaned.

"He wants us to see each other again."

"Please don't do it."

"I don't know what to do."

"It's your decision, Denise, but I'm telling you, he doesn't deserve another chance. He never gave you one."

"I really want to see him, Annie."

"How do you know if he's telling you the truth about Linda? They could get back together."

"She filed for the divorce. He said she's pregnant by this other guy."

"I'd think long and very damned hard before I'd look at him again."

"You don't understand. I can't help how I feel about him. I'm not like you. You just go on like everything's fine. You don't seem the least bit upset that Thomas broke up with you. You act like it's not a big deal. I don't want to miss this chance."

"Denise, you wouldn't even have a chance if his wife hadn't left him. I love Thomas more than you or anyone will ever know, but I can't change him. I have my own life and my own goals. Tough if he walked away. I'm not waiting for him or any man."

"I love him, Annie. I love him."

After we said our goodbyes, I moped around the room. She was surrendering to Christopher. I was jealous of her, resentful that she was finally getting the guy she always wanted.

Reggie was waiting outside the business building Monday morning.

"Good mornin', sunshine," he grinned.

"Don't call me sunshine."

He walked next to me, opening the door. "Can I call you beautiful?"

"Call me Annie."

"Enjoyed studyin' last night."

"I'm glad. I don't enjoy studying, myself. Want to join us for supper? Leslie will be there."

"Does she have to be there?"

"Yes," I said. "She's my friend."

Being mean to Reggie had made him want me more. I sat at the end of the table with Leslie in the middle. Marla took the chair across from me. Reggie slowed, then moved to the seat beside Marla.

"Hey, Reggie," Leslie grinned.

"Hi. Annie, are we studyin' in the library or where? You didn't tell me."

"Oh, yes, the library. How about . . . let's see. Let's study from six until eight."

I loved making A's. I enjoyed the competition I used to run from.

"What do you do after you study?" Leslie asked him.

"I don't know," he shrugged. "Listen to music."

"Do you ever go out?"

"Sometimes." He turned to me. "Hey, by the way, Annie, you never said if you wanted to go to the campus movies."

"I'm going with Marla."

"She's going with me," Marla said.

"Can I come along?"

"Sure," Leslie chimed in.

We met outside the auditorium and waited for Reggie to show up. The campus movie was *The Karate Kid, Part 2*. I had wanted to see it last year when its theme song, "Glory of Love," was a nightly request favorite on the radio. Reggie wasn't the person I wanted to see it with.

"I like your new glasses," I told Leslie.

"Thanks. They're Sophia Loren."

"They look good on you," Marla said.

"There he is!" said Leslie.

"I almost didn't make it," said Reggie.

He caught his breath and moved to my side. I crossed my arms, watching Marla's observant face. In the auditorium, he was cemented to me, and I didn't know where to go.

Marla was creative. "Annie, move to the end." She sat beside me, and Leslie sat beside her. Reggie didn't know what hit him when he had to sit next to Leslie. During the movie, which I didn't even watch, he kept moving his head in my direction.

After the movie, Leslie whispered in my ear, "I need to talk to you."

When we talked in my dorm lobby, Leslie's blue eyes glistened. "I got a crush on Reggie. But I think he likes you."

"No. We're just study partners, that's all."

"But he likes you, Annie," she said. "I mean, he didn't even pay attention to me. He was tryin' to make you look at him."

"Leslie, I don't like Reggie." I looked down at my hands. "I'm using him to get good grades. Thomas used to help me. Oh, God, I miss him so much."

Reggie called on Sunday afternoon.

"I'm busy right now," I said.

"What about studyin'? Want to do a couple of hours?"

I needed to. "Okay. Two hours in my lobby, and that's it."

"Have you worked through those problems Dr. Fall gave us?"

"All but three," I answered. "Look, I need to get off the phone."

"Okay. I'll be by at seven?"

"Seven's fine."

It was four. I had to use the bathroom. I needed to wash. I wanted to check my mailbox. I was planning to go to eat at Rax with Leslie and Marla at five. Just ten minutes later, the phone rang again, and I was ready to bite off Reggie's head. It was Leslie.

"I just talked to Reggie," Leslie said.

"Really?"

"He's goin' to eat with us."

"What?"

I sat on my bed and threw my underwear across the room.

"I called him and told him we were goin' to Rax, and I asked if he wanted to come, and he said yes!"

At Rax, Marla wouldn't let Reggie get next to me. She kept near, causing him to stay behind Leslie.

At the salad bar, Reggie was watching every move I made. Leslie was holding a plate, watching every move he made. I looked up and smiled at her happy expression and walked back to our table. I sat beside Marla.

"Is there any hope?"

"Possibly," she whispered.

Leslie's plate wasn't piled high, and I'd never seen her so nervous.

"Did you guys like my spaghetti the other night?"

"Girl, we sure did," said Marla. "You're a good cook."

Leslie looked at Reggie. "Annie and Marla ate dinner with me at my apartment Thursday night."

"Ah," he nodded, as he looked my way. "That's where you were. I called and called."

Leslie lifted her Coke, her eyes watching me.

"Can't study all the time," I said.

"I don't." He was offended.

"Hey. When are you comin' over for dinner?" Leslie asked him.

"Give me a call," he answered.

He was mad at me, but I smoothed things over with him. I still needed his help to get me through exams, which were coming up in two weeks. Again, my goals were at the forefront of my mind, and I was getting back to being a career woman.

CHAPTER THIRTY FOUR

Aunt Mooney married Lonnie at the Soso courthouse on a rainy Saturday afternoon. Tish stood in as maid of honor. Mama, Daddy, and I were witnesses. It was the highlight of their year. None of Lonnie's children were present. Aunt Mooney didn't love him. She had a mean streak and told Mama everything he'd said about us, like she was too good to belong in our family. She'd brought him over for supper to show him what a dump we lived in. Why she had been jealous of Mama for years, I never understood. Was it because Mama was thinner than she was? Was it because Mama's hair had no gray in it? I wanted to tell Lonnie that Aunt Mooney never held a job, treated Uncle Melvin like dirt, and would boil his balls over money. I knew my relationship with her would never be the same.

I stayed over until Sunday just to see the Prices. I was relaxed, willing to give some of myself now. I could withstand another round of Henry's needling, since I'd be out of his clutches after graduation.

"I was telling Mom just the other day that I sure wish our granddaughter would stop by."

I smiled.

"I wish we could go to church together sometime," he continued, "but I don't think Mom would be up to it, you know what I mean?"

"I can go to church, Henry," said Pearl.

"I know, dear. You remember what we talked about. It would be better if we didn't go."

"I can go," she insisted.

"Pearl, I know that," he said, getting flustered.

He looked at me, not smiling, then he looked back at her. She continued looking him straight in his eyes.

"I've been goin' to the Baptist church for over forty years, and I'm goin' to keep a-goin'."

Henry's face turned red. "There's no reason for you to be cross, you hear me?"

"I'm not being cross. I'll get in my car and drive myself," she replied.

He glared, pursing his lips a good while. "Okay, you just do that." He touched his hearing aid. "Now Annie, how long do you think the graduation ceremony will take?"

"I have no idea, Pop."

"Well. Doesn't matter," he shrugged. "I just think it will be too hard for me to take Mom out late at night. You understand, don't you?"

"Sure, Pop. Don't worry."

"I can go, Henry," Pearl said.

"Honey, you know how tired you get. By seven in the evening, she gets so tired. She gets disoriented. Pearl, honey, it'll be crowded there. We'll have to do a lot of walking. Annie understands."

"I'll be fine," she begged.

His face showed empathy as he made eye contact with me. Pearl poked my thigh.

"I wouldn't miss Annie's high school graduation."

"No, honey. She's graduating from college. Remember?"

She nodded her head with a blank expression.

"She's graduating from Eastern Mississippi. Two years ago, we promised to help her until she finished. You've helped her every semester with her tuition."

"And I'm goin' to keep helping her, you hear?"

"Pop, Mommy Junior, I'm very grateful for everything you've done for me," I said. "I couldn't have done this without you." I gave them each a hug.

"Thank you, darlin'. That was so sweet of you to say," he said. "We love you so much, don't we Pearl?"

"We sure do!" Pearl squeezed my hand.

"You know," said Henry. "I was thinking. You need a dress to wear for your graduation, don't you?"

"I have the dress you bought me a couple of years ago. The one with purple in it." It was two sizes too big.

"No, dear." He leaned over and touched my knee. "We want you to have a new one. Why don't you go to the bank this week and take out some of the money we've saved so you can get some shoes and a dress. How about that?"

"All right, Pop."

"I'd love to go with you and help you, but you know I can't."

"I understand. I'll go this week."

"Good," he smiled. He touched my hair. "Your hair is lovely. Let's get it fixed, too."

"I can cut it for her," Pearl said.

"No, Mom," he chuckled. "You don't do that anymore. She can go to a salon."

"I can certainly cut hair," she snapped.

"I know, Mommy Junior," I smiled.

He bent down before her. "Honey, you've done your time with hairdressing. Okay?"

"Okay," she said as she rubbed her dress. "I know I can cut hair."

At Shoney's, Henry said a quick blessing, and we started eating our salads.

"Honey, did you see Lester Moffett over there?"

She stopped chewing. "Where?"

"He's sitting over there with his wife, Ramona."

"Is she still livin'?"

He adjusted his hearing aid. "What?"

"Is she still alive!"

I put my head down.

"She's right over there," he answered.

She turned to me. "Ramona used to wear the tackiest wigs to church. She looked awful."

"Thank you, Tammy," Henry said, while he watched her pour him another cup of coffee. When she left, he started. "Her husband is in jail."

I nodded.

"She has three little kids to support, too."

"Now, why would a man go get put in jail and leave his kids," Pearl said.

She took off her glasses, dabbing a tear from an eye. I wasn't touched. The woman was stupid for marrying a creep and breeding with him. Pearl put her glasses on, abruptly forgetting her tender side.

"Lordy, Lord. Would you look at her hair? That's the ugliest mess I've ever seen."

The lady's hair did look like a bird's nest.

Henry whispered, "Mom doesn't like to see anyone overdone like that."

"Now, if I was fixin' her hair, I'd cut that mess off."

"Eat your salad now, honey," he urged.

After we ate, he put three dollars on the table and walked up to the cashier to pay. Pearl grabbed the money and shoved it into my hand.

"That's for the waitress," I whispered.

"No. You keep it," she whispered back.

I closed my hand.

Back at their house, Henry decided to go ahead and give me a check for the dress and whatever else I might need for graduation. He wanted to save me some time, and I appreciated it.

Chapter Thirty Five

When I got to the education office on Tuesday, every professor was standing in the reception area.

"Hey, Annie!" Nell smiled.

"Look at her face," said Dr. Dearman.

"We wanted to thank you for all your hard work," said Dr. Camp.

"Annie, on behalf of the professors in the education department, I present you with this money tree," Dr. Katz announced.

"Thank you," I said. "I don't know what to say."

"Just count the damned money," Dr. Dearman laughed.

They each hugged me, wished me well, and went about their business. My eyes were on the money tree, which was made of ones, fives and a couple of tens. With Nell's help, I took the bills off and counted a hundred dollars.

"You're the first student they've ever done this for," she confided.

Dr. Camp and Dr. Katz said their final goodbyes. The professors dribbled out.

"Come in here, Annie," Dr. Dearman said.

"You need me, Dr. Dearman?"

"I'll miss you, dear."

I sat in the chair next to her desk. "I appreciate everything you've done for me, and the advice you've given me."

"It was my pleasure. If you need me for a reference or anything, let me know."

"Yes, I will."

We hugged goodbye. When I walked out, Nell was pretending to read something on her desk.

"Was the memo okay?" I asked.

"Oh, yes. Perfect."

"You need anything else?"

"No." She looked at the clock. "It's almost five."

"I'm going to miss you so much, Mrs. Johnston."

She shook her head and was unable to speak. I picked up my purse because I wanted to leave.

"I guess I'll get back to the dorm and pack up."

She cleared her throat. "Take care. Call us and let us know what you're up to."

"I will. Bye, Mrs. Johnston."

I smiled as I backed away, walking out of the ed-psych building for the last time.

Marla had left the night before. I wasn't sad about it, because we promised to stay friends, and her promise was as good as gold. Grace's side had been abandoned, devoid of her computer printouts. I stripped my bed, throwing my last few things in my basket. My family wasn't coming to see the campus. They wouldn't be taking pictures or seeing what room I lived in. I loaded my car and drove out of this part of the campus for the last time. I saw the Arby's sign.

"Got to eat."

CHAPTER THIRTY SIX

Trudy ran off the porch barking and wagging her tail. Daddy had been watching at the door. He unloaded my car this time, happy to move me in. I called Henry with my final grades, which was the first thing he wanted to know. Three A's and one B, I told him. I wanted to tell him what it had cost me, getting those grades.

I was fearful of being alone, and I was even more fearful of crowds. Friday night, I'd be facing the largest crowd ever. If it weren't for Marla calling me at the house, telling me where to meet her, I'd have my damned degree mailed to me.

On Thursday, I had no appetite. Mama swore it was a virus, but I knew it was stress. When the sun came up on Friday, the jitters grew worse. I got up with raw eyes and took a bath. I left my face bare. Daddy took off, leaving me with the kids while Gloria and Mama worked. I took them for burgers at Wendy's, and listened to them fight the rest of the day. Renee called, looking for Mama, and I got her off the phone in less than thirty seconds. At three thirty, she was at the front door. Her kids were huddled on the porch with prying eyes. Joey's forehead was pressed deeply in the screen while I stood on the other side of the locked door.

"I have my graduation tonight. We're all going."

"I bet you're so happy to be finished with school," she smiled.

To be in your twenties with three kids and a dominant bum for a husband would be hell, I thought, as I stared into Renee's vacant eyes.

"I have to go get ready before Mama and Gloria get here, because they have to get in the bathroom. I'll tell Mama you came by."

"How long did you go to school? Stop it, Tiner."

"Four years. Sometimes, it takes longer."

"Four years." She was looking somewhere as she twitched her nose. "I been thinkin' 'bout goin' to the junior college and takin' some classes."

"You should. I'm sure you can get financial aid like I did."

"Mama, I'm thirsty," Jason said as he tugged on her shirt.

"Wait 'til we get home! Annie, what did you do? Uh, how'd you go about gettin' financial aid?"

"I went to the junior college and talked to a counselor. I know they'll be glad to help you."

"I'll do that," she said.

"Can we come in and play with Holly and Wiley?" Tina asked.

"They have to get ready," I said.

"No, Tiner honey. They have to go somewhere," Renee said.

"I need to go get ready now," I said.

"I want something to drink," Jason told me.

"No. Annie has to get ready now. Well, congratulations," she said with a sad smile.

"Thanks. Bye-bye," I said as I closed the door and locked it.

At four, I jumped into the bathtub, then got back into my nightgown. My makeup went on well, but my insides were mush. I fixed my hair with Gloria's hot rollers to give it some lift. I'd had it trimmed, though not as short as before. My graduation dress was pink with multicolored flowers—a typical spring dress. Mama dragged in, carrying her plastic cup.

Gloria came in griping. "My feet are killin' me," she said, dropping a tennis shoe on the floor.

"What time you gotta be there?" asked Mama.

She flicked an ash into an ashtray. Her tone told me that she really didn't want to go.

"Six thirty. I'll get my clothes on in a little while. Guess who came by to see you?"

"Oh, Lord!"

"Those kids were trying their best to get in here. I had to lock the door."

"Shit. Usually they walk on in without knockin'. I can't believe it."

"I told her everyone was going to my graduation tonight."

"She don't care. Stupid bitch."

Daddy came in with a bag of groceries, and Mama followed him into the kitchen.

"If you're going to go, you'd better start getting ready, Daddy," I said.

He didn't respond. Then the phone rang.

"I bet that's Mr. George," he said as he went to answer it. "Hello? Yeah, she sure is. Mama! It's for you. It's Renee," he said as he held up the phone.

Mama wheeled around with rage. Canned goods were flying out of the bag as she threw hominy and creamed corn onto the counter.

"That son of a bitch! I'll be on the phone three fuckin' hours!"

A bag of rice landed in the sink.

"Uh, she can't talk now," Daddy stuttered.

Glaring at the Reverend, Mama stomped to the bathroom and slammed the door.

"Okay, I'll tell her." He hung up.

Twenty minutes later, the phone rang again, and Gloria answered it.

"Hello? No. She can't talk. She's in the tub. No. No!" She hung it up. "I can't stand her and those damn kids of hers. Mama, she wanted to get you on the phone."

"I hope she don't come her ass over here and sit. I have to get ready."

"I'll get rid of her if she does, Mama," I said.

"Damn!" Gloria griped. Joey was peering through the screen door with big brown saucer eyes. "What do you want!"

"Can Holly come outside and play?"

"No! Go home," she screamed. He dawdled on the porch as if he hadn't heard a word she said. Gloria walked over and closed the door. "Little fucker."

"What a lovely way to spend graduation day," I said.

At ten 'til six I slipped into my dress. I looked great but felt destined to die tonight.

"Mama, come see my dress."

She walked out of the bathroom in her bra and panties, holding a bottle of makeup. She was in a hurry smearing it on.

"Oh, that's a pretty dress. Did the Prices buy you that?"

"We went in halves on it."

"I love that color. Too bad you have to wear an ugly robe over it."

"Where did Daddy go?"

"Over to Mr. George's place. Said he'd be back in a little while." She walked back into the bathroom.

"I need to go and get seated. I'll meet y'all down there. Don't get lost."

"It's at the stadium?"

"Yes. You'll see it. There'll be a lot of cars there."

"I hope we can find a place to sit. Ooh, I'm havin' dizzy spells, Annie."

"You're just nervous, Mama. I'm nervous, too."

"I hope people aren't dressed fancy there. My head is spinnin'."

She grabbed the sink and leaned into it.

"Just wear one of your dresses. People wear pants, too. I have to go."

"Be careful. Ooh, Lord."

I was wearing my necklace, and she hadn't even noticed it. My cap and gown were in my car.

Chapter Thirty Seven

Daylight would soon be darkness, and all would not be lost if my family didn't show up. I avoided driving by my former dorms. I had to park far and walk to an entrance in my heels. I waited for Marla, and we put on our caps and gowns in a bathroom with other excited graduates.

"I feel so sick," I said.

"Just take deep breaths," she said.

"Aren't you scared?"

"Nah," she shrugged. "I deserve that piece of paper, and so do you. My aunt is only thirty-five years old and has eleven kids. That's not going to happen to me. Or you."

Hysteria was knocking at my door.

"I don't know if I can do this, Marla."

"Yes, you can." She took my hand. "You're a queen. You smile when you walk across that stage. Your life is just beginning, and think of all the things you're going to get to do because you got a college degree." She checked out her face again. "And you worked for it. Let's go, girl."

I found my seat and sat quietly. The upper portion of the stadium was filled. A long-winded senator gave a speech on how hard he had to work to get his degree, and he sounded just like Henry. I didn't listen to half of it, because the thumping of my heart was beating out of my ears. At one point, I had to put my head between my legs, because I thought I was going to faint. The woman next to me asked if I was okay, and I told her I had dropped something.

I was able to relax a little when the degrees were being handed out. The school of business was the largest at UEM, so it took awhile for my name to be called.

"Thomas Michael Barnes!" the announcer said.

My heart sank as I watched Thomas walk across the stage. He seemed so confident, so much in control. He took his master of business administration degree and left the stage.

Then I panicked. I didn't want Thomas to see me when I had to go up, but I couldn't run away now. I tried to distract myself by thinking of the pictures of the Rocky Mountains I had seen in books at the junior college library. I thought of all the movies I had watched in my bedroom on Third Avenue.

"Annie Rochelle Lee!"

The stage lights were blinding, but I had my smile painted on. I walked back to my seat with my degree in my hands.

In the blink of an eye, I was standing among throngs of other graduates and their families. Reggie tapped me on the shoulder.

"Thanks for helping me. I mean it," I told him as we hugged. "Good luck at the tax firm."

Reggie disappeared into the crowds, looking for his folks. Then Denise and Christopher were hugging me before I realized they had found me. Denise handed over a small gift.

"What's this?"

She was bubbly, holding Christopher's arm the way Linda had.

"You'll have to open it and find out."

Leslie appeared next. She was there to watch Marla and me graduate.

"I just saw Reggie. He's a nice guy," she told me. "But I've decided he's not my type. I have two more years of school to go, and I need to get out of this place like you're doin'."

"Good for you," I said.

"Annie!"

Here came Clarie, along with Bill, Gloria, Jessie holding Holly's hand, Keith, and Wiley. Aunt Mooney, without Lonnie, was wearing her long black hairpiece and a new size-twenty dress. Tish's hair was bleached from root to end. Luckily, Pepper was working the evening shift at a chicken plant, so I didn't have to introduce him. Mama lagged behind them last, holding her purse and looking reluctant. This was the first time Denise and Leslie had met any of my family members, and they seemed impressed. Marla was pushing through people, and I ran to her.

"Annie, we did it. I watched you. You did fine. I want you to meet my folks. Where is she? Mom," she waved her over. "This is my mama Latisha and my dad Wallace Peters."

Latisha was a big woman. Wallace was tall, a basketball player in his younger days. He wore a mustache, and when he smiled, he flashed a few gold teeth.

"We've heard so much about you Annie," he said as he shook my hand.

Latisha was full of life, laughing and talking with everyone around her, giving each the same consideration. No wonder Marla carried herself so well.

I whispered to Mama, "Where's Daddy?"

"You know how he is. He said his stomach was botherin' him."

I knew where he was. Watching the television had been more important than my high school graduation, too.

"Annie."

I glanced around to the sound of the voice.

"Over here."

Thomas cautiously smiled and waved. What he was really doing was warning me of who loomed behind him. Mrs. Barnes pushed him aside and held out her arms.

"Annie!"

She grabbed and hugged me before I could move.

"You looked so beautiful when you walked across that stage and received your diploma!" she said.

"It's a college degree, Mom," said Thomas.

"Oh, of course," she laughed. "I'm sorry we didn't get here early enough to see you before the ceremony." She was looking at Mama and the rest of the family. "Dan and I were running late and—"

Thomas quickly interrupted, "I don't think they want to hear this."

"Annie, congratulations." Dan shook my hand.

"Thank you, Mr. Barnes. Uh, this is my mother, Penny Lee."

Maggie took her hand like they were old pals. "How are you, Penny? I was telling Thomas how much we love Annie. He certainly never brought her around us enough. Anyway, I knew Annie had a wonderful family, and I know you're proud of her."

"I sure am," Mama said, nodding her head and looking completely lost.

She was smiling, though. And about to die as she stared at this very made-up lady wearing enough diamonds to need a security guard.

"Mama, this is Thomas," I said.

"I knew Annie had a boyfriend," Clarie whispered.

"He's so fine," Jessie whispered. "Ain't he?"

"He sure is," Marla chimed in.

Kim began to tell me about her work and how she had been bugging Thomas to bring me back up for a visit. Maggie was gabbing so much that Dan took it upon himself to introduce himself to the guys.

Maggie continued, "This is my mother, Ida Jones. And here are Dan's parents, Daniel Senior and Stella Barnes."

I envied Thomas for having real grandparents, because the Prices were not there to meet this wonderful family. Mama was still bewildered as she nodded her head, saying hello to people she had no idea existed. Thomas was trying to keep me away from Maggie, but it was useless.

"Annie, these must be your lovely sisters."

"Yes."

"Beautiful, just beautiful," she gushed as I introduced each sister.

"This is my Aunt Mooney and my cousin Tish," I said.

"Oh, I was admiring your hair. It's so lovely," she said as she shook Mooney's hand.

"Thank you. It's not all mine. It's a hairpiece," said Mooney. "I wish I had this much hair."

Aunt Mooney was eyeing Maggie's diamonds, and I knew I had some explaining to do.

I was in a stupor as I moved from this mob of people. Thomas moved with me.

"How are you, Annie? Congratulations!"

"And congratulations to you! An MBA degree! I'm okay. And you?"

"Alive. Mom's been driving me crazy all day."

"I think she's great," I smiled.

"I wanted to get some pictures of Thomas and Annie before the ceremony, and wouldn't you know it. I forgot my camera, and we had to drive back and get it," she said.

Mama laughed as if they had known each other for years. For me, it was a sight to behold. One family so secure, one family so desperate.

"Annie's wonderful," said Maggie.

"I've never had to worry about her. She never gave me a moment's trouble," Mama told her. "Annie's always helped me around the house since she was a little bitty thing."

Thomas took my hand. "Can we get away from them and talk?"

"Oh, look at them!" said Maggie.

"Mmmm, mmm," said Marla.

"That's a nice-looking young man. Is that Annie's boyfriend?" Latisha asked.

"It sure is," Marla answered.

Thomas struggled for words.

"I don't want to leave here without saying goodbye to you."

My heart dropped. *Goodbye?*

"The truth is, I love you very much."

"I'm so mad at you," I cried. "I've been through hell this semester."

"It's my fault. I shouldn't have acted so childish."

"Oh, God, Thomas. I have so much to say to you. I've always wanted different things in my life. To see the mountains. To be able to touch the snow. My parents have no money. My father never made it to the seventh grade. Mama dropped out in the tenth. Daddy won't work. He's not even here tonight for my graduation."

"What? Why didn't you tell me?"

"I couldn't. I'm so ashamed. We live in a crummy roach-pit rent house!"

He paused, trying to sort out what I was saying.

"Do you think I care about that? You're more important to me than anything or anybody. I don't give a damn what kind of house you live in. All I know is the last few months have been horrible. I've wanted to talk, to tell you how much you mean to me, that I was wrong. . . . I thought I wanted to concentrate on my cycling. I thought I couldn't do it and love you."

"Gee, Thomas. I was working three jobs and trying my very best to see you and love you. I do love you."

"I know."

"You'll have to trust me. And I'll be more open with you, I promise."

"Denise told me that you'll be coming to Jackson this summer to see her, that you'll be looking for a job up there."

"I *have* a job up there," I confessed. "Dr. Fall, the professor I hated more than anybody, recommended me for an entry-level accounting position with the University Medical Center. I'll be in near Denise. I start in two weeks. I haven't told my parents, friends, nobody, until now. But I'm not staying there forever. As soon as I get some money saved, I'm moving to Colorado."

"Please tell me you'll see me when you move up. Or can I see you now? Starting right now. I'll come down to Soso and pick you up anytime you want."

"Look at those two," Maggie said to her mother.

"I don't know," Mama snapped in a whisper to Jessie. "I don't know who he is. Be quiet, so I can listen."

Mama needed a cigarette bad.

"Are you ready to be bombarded by my family for pictures?" Thomas asked.

"Honey? Thomas? Daddy and I want some pictures of you and Annie. Then we can take some group photos. And I want some family pictures. We'll just take pictures of everybody," she said. "Dan, get your camera ready."

Countless flashes later, I was walking toward the parking lot with my family. I said goodbye to my friends, though not for good. Most of us would be working in Jackson. Though Leslie would still be attending UEM, she'd be coming up to visit Denise and me.

Thomas would be coming by to get me at the Manor Sunday morning, so I could spend a few days with him while I looked for an apartment. I was in shock that I was letting him, but I'd have to get over that fear if I wanted him in my life, and I did.

"He's so fine, Annie," Jessie said.

"Did y'all see how polite he was?" Clarie asked.

"He sure was," Mama added.

"He's too skinny for me," Gloria said.

"You mean too young and ambitious?" said Mama.

"I can't get over how many diamonds his Mama was wearin'. Ooh, Lordy me, she had some rocks," Aunt Mooney said.

"I love that cluster diamond ring she was wearin'," Tish said.

"Mr. Barnes is so handsome with that gray hair," Mooney said. "I been tryin' to picture how they looked as a couple when they were younger."

"Probably like Thomas and his sister," I said.

"Yeah, I can picture that," she said. "His sister's a pretty girl."

"I didn't think she was that pretty," Gloria sneered.

"When's he comin' by to get you?" Mama was wearing that look of fear.

"At ten o'clock Sunday morning," I answered. "Don't worry, we got all day tomorrow to clean the mess."

"He'll get his eyes full," she said.

"He says he doesn't care about the house, Mama."

"People like that live in a nice home, I guarantee you," she said.

"I'll come over and help clean up," Clarie offered.

"Maybe you can help me find some decent curtains for the windows so I can take down those ugly sheets," I said.

"Well, Daddy can clean the yard," said Gloria.

"I'll make him haul off the toilets. Can we grow some grass by Sunday?" I asked.

"We gotta move again," Mama said to me.

"Well, I'm kind of glad, Mama."

Chapter Thirty Eight

Daddy was still in his clothes and asleep on the couch when we came in. Meaning he was scared to be by himself.

"Hey, baby!" He sat up. "How does it feel to be a college graduate?"

"It feels great, Daddy."

"You shoulda seen how many people were there," Mama said.

"That's a big college, Mama," he said.

"It sure is," she said. "My legs are so tired from walkin' up the stairs. We had to sit in the balcony, it was so crowded."

"Baby, come sit by your Daddy," he told me. I sat beside him and listened to his hard breathing. "Mama and I sure are proud of you. You're the first one of our girls to go to college."

"Thanks, Daddy."

"Now, you'll be makin' more money and can do anything."

"Show Daddy your certificate," Mama said.

I handed him my degree, and he grinned as he read it. He didn't understand half the words, but he was proud anyway.

"Bachelor of science . . ." he read aloud.

Mama nudged me while he was reading. "Tell Daddy about your boyfriend."

"I'll let you do it. I'm going to bed so I can get up early to clean and get ready for Sunday."

He handed it back to me. "Here, baby."

I walked into Mama's room to change into my nightgown. I heard Daddy saying, "Is that right!"

Mama thought for a moment. "I think he's the one she met in her accountin' classes that was worried about his grades."

She was so wrong, I thought.

"You better haul that junk off tomorrow."

"I sure will, Mama."

www.ingramcontent.com/pod-product-compliance
Lightning Source LLC
Chambersburg PA
CBHW030421310726
48979CB00009B/1553/J